The House of the Deer

Books by D. E. Stevenson

The House of the Deer
Gerald and Elizabeth
Sarah's Cottage
Sarah Morris Remembers
The House on the Cliff
The Marriage of Katherine
Katherine Wentworth
The Blue Sapphire
Fletchers End
Bel Lamington
The Musgraves
Still Glides the Stream
Anna and Her Daughters
The Tall Stranger
Summerhills
Amberwell
Blow the Wind Southerly
Five Windows
Mrs. Tim Flies Home
Shoulder the Sky
Music in the Hills
Vittoria Cottage
Young Mrs. Savage
Kate Hardy
Mrs. Tim Gets a Job
The Four Graces
Listening Valley
The Two Mrs. Abbotts
Celia's House
Spring Magic
Mrs. Tim Carries On
Rochester's Wife
Alister & Co.
The English Air
The Green Money
A World in Spell
The Story of
  Rosabelle Shaw
The Baker's Daughter
Smouldering Fire
Crooked Adam
The Young Clementina

Omnibus Volumes

Mrs. Tim of the Regiment
  and Golden Days
Miss Buncle *containing*
  Miss Buncle's Book *and*
  Miss Buncle Married

The House of the Deer

D. E. Stevenson

HOLT, RINEHART AND WINSTON
New York · Chicago · San Francisco

Library of Congress Catalog Card Number: 78-117278

First Edition

Designer: Marcia Erikson
SBN: 03-066560-4
Printed in the United States of America

In Memory of
D. W. M.
Who Killed the Hornless Stag

Contents

The House of the Deer

1

Which Introduces Sir Walter MacCallum and His Family

Gerald Burleigh-Brown had received an invitation to dine at Birkhill. He was *persona grata* at Birkhill, and dined there at least once a week, but this was "a special occasion," for it was Alastair MacCallum's ninth birthday and he was being allowed to sit up for dinner as a birthday treat.

As Gerald turned in at the gate and drove up to the front door, he remembered his first visit to Birkhill. It was almost a year ago now and he had approached the house with very different feelings, for, having arrived in Glasgow only that afternoon, he was a stranger in a strange land. It seemed a good deal more than a year ago—so much had happened in the interval—but all the same he remembered every detail clearly. At that time Sir Walter MacCallum was a widower; his mother lived with him and kept house for him and his small son.

They had dined well—Sir Walter appreciated good food—and when they had finished dinner, Gerald had been taken to Sir Walter's study to talk business. He had been informed that his host's "greatest ambition in life" was to become his brother-in-law and had been asked if he had any objections to offer.

Gerald had no objections: he liked Sir Walter immensely and felt sure he was the right man for Bess. He was older than Bess (but not more than forty); he was good-looking and friendly and kind. He was the owner of MacCallum's Ship-Building Yard, which was an exceedingly well run and efficient concern and, although he was a Great Man in his own line of business, there was no nonsense about him. Who could have objected to a brother-in-law so admirable in every way?

Unfortunately there was an obstacle to the marriage, which at the time had seemed insurmountable, but when this had been surmounted (chiefly by Gerald's efforts) Walter and Bess had been married; Gerald had been given a responsible post in MacCallum's Ship-Building Yard; old Lady MacCallum had moved to Bournemouth and Bess reigned in her stead.

Gerald parked his car in the drive and walked in; there was no need to ring the bell and disturb Frost, but Frost had heard the car and appeared from the back premises to welcome him and to take his hat.

"Hullo, Frost!" said Gerald. "It's a lovely evening, isn't it?"

Frost agreed and added that Sir Walter had been delayed, but would be ready in ten minutes. Then he opened the drawing-room door and Gerald went in and sat down in a comfortable chair.

The room looked different now, for old Lady MacCallum had taken her goods and chattels to Bournemouth in three enormous vans and Bess had brought her own furniture from her flat in London. It was a great improvement: the well-shaped room seemed larger without the clutter of small tables and uncomfortable little chairs. It was restful and spacious.

Gerald had been sitting in the drawing-room for not

more than two minutes when a gruff voice announced fiercely:

"Fee, fie, fo, fum,
I smell the blood of an Englishman!
Be he alive, or be he dead,
I'll gr-r-rind his bones to make my br-r-read."

"Help!" shouted Gerald, leaping from his chair and seizing the poker.

A small pink face rose up from behind a big sofa; it was grinning from ear to ear. "Were you frightened, Uncle Gerald?" demanded the imp.

"Terrified!"

"I thought you would be. You didn't know I was there, did you?"

"No. I thought you would be in bed. Why aren't you in bed?"

"Because it's my birthday, of course. You knew it was my birthday, didn't you? . . . And I expect that parcel is for me," declared Alastair, emerging from his hiding-place. He was followed by a smaller boy with bright red hair and bony knees, who stood and looked at Gerald somewhat sheepishly.

"That's Thom Two," said Alastair. "I've told you about him, haven't I, Uncle Gerald?" He gave his friend a push and added, "Go on, you ass! Say how d'you do."

Thom Two walked forward, and he and Gerald shook hands solemnly.

Alastair had now seized the parcel and was tearing the paper with small, strong hands. Thom Two knelt down on the floor beside him and whispered, "But, MacCallum, you haven't said thank you."

"I know," replied MacCallum. "I'm just waiting to see what it is. If it's a shunting engine for my electric train, it will need five times more thank yous than if it's a box of chocolates or—or anything else. . . . Come on, you can help me to open it."

Two small pairs of hands made short work of the brown paper wrappings . . . and as it happened to be a shunting engine for an electric train, suitable thanks were rendered to the donor:

"Thank you, thank you, thank you, thank you, thank you!" said Alastair, seizing his uncle's hand and shaking it enthusiastically. "It's absolutely super. I don't know how you guessed I wanted a shunting engine!"

There was no mystery about it—not really—for Gerald was a skilled electrical engineer and when anything went wrong with the electric-train system, he was called in to "sort it." He enjoyed this job, for he was very fond of Alastair and the electric trains were the best that money could buy; the rails were laid out all over the floor in one of the spare bedrooms with stations and bridges and level-crossings and tunnels and signal-boxes in the appropriate places . . . and, having discovered that Walter's present to his son was a goods station with extensive sidings, Gerald had "guessed" that a shunting engine would be required.

The shunting engine had been examined and admired and the boys were gathering up the torn paper from the drawing-room floor when the door opened and Bess came in, followed by Walter.

Bess rushed at the guest and hugged him. "Darling Flick! I haven't seen you for ages!" she exclaimed. "What have you been doing?"

"Working, of course," replied Gerald.

"You haven't seen him for four days—not since Tuesday evening," said Walter, laughing.

"Oh, it's all very well for you! You see him every day," retorted Bess, joining in the laughter. "You saw him this morning, I suppose. You're overworking Flick—that's what you're doing! The poor darling hasn't time to come and see his sister."

"Look, Dad!" cried Alastair, holding up his newly-acquired treasure. "Look what Uncle Gerald has given me! It's a shunting engine—exactly what I wanted. Isn't it absolutely super?"

The party was now complete, so the five members of it went into the dining-room and sat down to their meal. The two younger members ate in complete silence; their elders chatted.

"Have you seen an evening paper, Walter?" Gerald enquired. "I brought you one in case you hadn't. There's a good deal more about the robbery at Keble and Kidd's Yard. The police have caught two of the gang—the others got away."

"I'd like to see the paper afterwards," said Walter, nodding.

Alastair stopped eating and announced, "Everybody at school was talking about it this morning. Mr. Merryman said they stole all the men's wages for a whole week—it was thousands of pounds."

"How awful!" Bess exclaimed. "Don't they have men to guard the money? I mean, there have been so many robberies lately. They should have been more careful, shouldn't they, Walter?"

"Their security measures were inadequate," agreed Walter.

"Dad, how do we guard the money?" enquired his son.

"We take adequate precautions."

"What sort of precautions?"

"Our security measures are secret."

"Does Uncle Gerald know about them?"

"I, alone, am responsible for our security measures," replied Sir Walter firmly.

"But I want to know," explained Alastair. "Everybody at school wants to know, so I said I would ask you."

"You have asked me and I have given you my reply: the security measures at MacCallum's are secret."

"But, Dad, you always tell me things about the yard! I'll promise faithfully not to tell anybody if you like. I'll just say it's a secret, so I can't tell them about it."

"You will not," said Sir Walter sternly. "If anybody asks you about the security measures at MacCallum's, you will say that you know nothing about them. You will say that your father refused to answer your questions and that he, alone, is responsible for the safety of the yard."

Alastair gazed at him in silence.

"Do you hear what I say, Alastair?" shouted Sir Walter, thumping on the table with his fist.

Alastair nodded. He couldn't speak. His lips were trembling and his eyes were full of tears.

Gerald was amazed; he had never before known Walter speak and act intemperately. It was completely out of character. He was a gentle man—especially gentle in his dealings with his son. No wonder the boy was alarmed! The other boy was upset too, Gerald noticed.

Fortunately dinner was over, so the boys escaped. They ran upstairs to play with the trains and the adults went into the drawing-room for coffee.

"Walter, you frightened them!" exclaimed Bess.

"I meant to frighten them," replied Walter. He picked up the evening paper which Gerald had brought and sat down to read it.

It was such a lovely evening that Bess and Gerald opened the French windows and went out into the garden. The light was fading, but it was quite mild. They were happy to be together.

Bess put her hand through Gerald's arm. At last she said, "He's dreadfully upset, Flick. It's the robbery, of course. I suppose it might have happened at MacCallum's?"

"No, it couldn't."

"What do you mean?"

"Our security measures are adequate," replied Gerald, smiling down at her.

"Do you mean you know about them?"

"Yes."

"But he said you didn't!"

"He didn't say that. What he said was: 'I, alone, am responsible for our security measures'—and of course it's true. He's responsible for them; I'm merely the stooge who obeys his orders."

"I thought you were helping with the electrical equipment of the new German ship."

"I was."

"You're chatty tonight, aren't you?

Gerald smiled. "My job has been changed. Walter asked me to be his private secretary."

"Is it a rise?"

"I'm getting more money—if that's what you mean?" (It didn't matter telling her that much.)

"But you don't like it?"

"Some of it is very interesting indeed, but some of the work is—is rather unpleasant."

"The security measures?" asked Bess, who was no fool.

Gerald was silent.

"Oh, well, if you won't tell me, you won't tell me," said Bess. "But why did you agree to do it?"

"Because Walter asked me. When Walter gave me a job in MacCallum's Yard, I made up my mind that I would do anything for him (I made up my mind that I would be happy to clean his shoes) and my feelings haven't altered. I'm very fond of your husband, Bess."

"I know. That's what makes everything perfect."

"Are you happy?"

"Yes," she replied. "Walter and I love each other more and more. He's so considerate, so gentle! (I never saw him behave as he did tonight.) I should be a funny kind of person if I were not happy with Walter . . . and Alastair is a pet."

"You don't miss all the fun and excitement?"

"No."

"I just wondered," explained Gerald.

The fun and excitement to which he referred was Bess's success on the London stage. As Elizabeth Burleigh she had played the principal part in *The Girl from Venus;* she had been admired and fêted, idolised by her fans. Hundreds of people had stood for hours in the rain to see her. Her name had been blazoned in neon light over the portico of the theatre; her portrait had appeared in all the picture-papers. She had been showered with bouquets, half-buried in fan mail, pursued by men who were anxious to marry her—or to take her to Paris for a holiday!

Then, at the height of her fame, Bess had married Walter MacCallum and bowed herself out.

"It *was* fun," said Bess thoughtfully. "But I was beginning to get a bit tired of the fuss. I was beginning to feel I wasn't real. I was acting all the time. I'm glad I've done it (and made a success of it), but I'm not sorry it's over. I'm Walter's wife now and I think I'm making a success of my life as a real live woman."

"I'm sure you are. You're a success with Alastair too."

"I'm hoping to be a success with Margaret."

"Margaret?" asked Gerald.

"Margaret is coming. Oh, not for months, of course, but when she *does* arrive I want you to be her godfather. You will, won't you?"

"Of course I will!" agreed Gerald. He kissed Bess and added, "I'm so glad, darling! Glad about Margaret, I mean. Take care of yourself, won't you?"

"I'll take care of myself and Margaret," replied Bess, smiling happily.

(Gerald was not surprised that Bess had chosen the name. In all the wonderful stories Bess had told him when they were children the heroine had been "Margaret").

They walked on round the rose-garden and sat down together on a teak seat. It was quite dark now, but there was a silvery glow in the sky which heralded the rising moon.

"Supposing it isn't Margaret?" enquired Gerald, after a long silence.

"If it isn't Margaret, it will be Gerald. He will be just as dear and precious, of course. Gerald MacCallum sounds nice, doesn't it?"

Gerald didn't agree. He said tactfully, "It's very sweet of you, Bess, but I think it ought to be Donald or Malcolm or Iain, or, perhaps, Colin? Colin was Walter's father's name, wasn't it? What does Walter think about it? I expect Walter is tremendously pleased——"

"I haven't told Walter," interrupted Bess.

"You haven't told Walter? But Bess——"

"Oh, I shall, of course! But not until after his holiday. He has arranged to go and stay with some friends in the north of Scotland for the stalking. It will be good for him to have a complete break and he wouldn't go if I told him. See?"

"Stalking?" asked Gerald in surprise. It sounded an unlikely sort of holiday for Walter MacCallum.

"Yes. His friends have a deer-forest where they shoot stags."

"How can you shoot stags in a forest?"

Bess was chuckling. "Oh, Flick, how ignorant you are! There are no trees in a deer-forest. It consists of moors and rocks and burns and bogs and bens."

"Why do you call it a forest?"

"Because that's what it's called," replied Bess with irrefutable logic. She rose and added, "I must fly! I must send those children to bed. You had better have a chat with Walter before you go."

2

In Which Various Matters Are Discussed and Planned

Walter was in his study. He looked up from a letter he was writing and smiled. "Well, what have you and Bess been plotting? I saw you in the rose-garden talking very seriously indeed."

"Bess was telling me about your plans for a holiday. What have you been doing?"

"I've been busy," replied Walter, laying down his pen. "You'll be glad to hear I've made my peace with Alastair and the tom-tit. I was shown the shunting engine at work; it did its stuff in a satisfactory manner. Then I sent Alastair to have his bath and took the tom-tit home to its nest. I had a few words with its parent, who resembles his chick closely: small and boney with red hair and bright brown eyes. An intelligent bird! I returned home, tucked Alastair into bed and interviewed a detective who was waiting to see me, a man called Dawson, who is investigating the robbery at K. and K's."

"You *have* been busy," said Gerald. "I've just come to say goodnight."

"No. Sit down. I want to speak to you."

Walter began to fiddle with his paperweight. It was a trick

he had when he was arranging his thoughts, so his private secretary sat down and waited.

"Dawson was interesting. It's his opinion that the robbery was planned by the man who planned the train-robbery. He admits that he may be wrong, but he has cogent reasons."

"I thought those men had been caught and were under lock and key!"

"Some of the gang were caught, but we can't be certain that all of them were. Was the man with the brain apprehended? The man who planned the raid; the man who prepared the ground and made the preparations for it . . . and then watched the results from a safe hiding-place. Yesterday's affair was not on the same grand scale, but it was prepared and carried out with the same attention to every detail: the same timing, the same daring, the same method, and the same success."

"That puts rather a different complexion upon it!"

"Yes. The police are up against a ruthless devil—clever, cunning, patient—a genius in his own line of country!"

"Why did Dawson want to see you, Walter? Does he think MacCallum's will be the next objective?"

"He wanted to know what precautions we were taking."

"Did you tell him?"

"No," replied Walter. "I just said I considered our security measures adequate . . . and added that in my opinion the Planner's next objective will be something quite different. All the same we shall continue to practise our security measures; in fact I intend to tighten them up."

Gerald sighed. In his opinion the security measures at MacCallum's Yard were tight enough already. They were the bane of his life.

There was a short silence. Then Gerald said, "I don't understand why you thought it necessary to frighten the boys."

"Don't you?" asked Walter. "I've told you that the Planner of these raids is a ruthless devil. If by any chance he decided to raid MacCallum's, it would be convenient for him to know the details of our security measures; he would go to any lengths to obtain information about them. You and Bess were annoyed with me for frightening the boys, but wouldn't it be even more alarming if they were kidnapped and questioned?"

"Kidnapped?"

"Yes. If they went about saying that they knew, but had 'promised not to tell,' they might be believed. . . . Oh, I don't think it's likely, but I'm not taking any risks. I spoke to Mr. Thom about it (he was in America for three years as an agent for an oil company, so he wasn't surprised when he heard what I had to say). He wasn't incredulous, as you seem to be. In fact he took it very seriously. He suggested that the Planner might think we'd feel safe and so relax our precautions at MacCallum's—which would give the robbers a better chance of success. I saw what he meant, of course."

"But you don't agree? You think their next objective will be something quite different?"

Sir Walter nodded. "Yes. I think the Planner enjoys planning. I think it would bore him to do a repeat performance . . . and remember these raids are planned and prepared for months in advance. Suitable men must be found and briefed and inserted in key positions to be ready for the Day. You can't do that all of a sudden."

"You mean that was done at K. and K.'s?"

"Yes. Dawson said so. The man who drove the van was a member of the gang. He had come to K. and K.'s six months ago with unexceptionable references. They were faked. The man was a bad lot. He had been promised two thousand pounds for driving the van to a certain place where an ambush had been prepared. That was how it was done."

Gerald was amazed. He said, "Well, anyhow, it couldn't happen like that at MacCallum's."

"No, it couldn't. The Planner would have to think of a different scheme." Sir Walter sighed and added, "I wish I could see into that man's brain. It would be interesting—to say the least of it."

Gerald agreed that it would be interesting . . . but, as a matter of fact, he was more interested in what his brother-in-law intended to do to tighten up the security measures at MacCallum's Ship-Yard. He put the question as tactfully as he could.

"Don't worry," replied Sir Walter. "I intend to cable to Joseph Parker. You won't mind handing over the security measures to him, will you?"

"Joseph Parker?"

"Yes. The chap who tidied up that little muddle at Koolbokie."

(Gerald couldn't help smiling. "That little muddle at Koolbokie" seemed to him an understatement of the "tidying up" which Parker had accomplished.)

"You're pleased, aren't you?" added Sir Walter. "You don't like snooping? Parker doesn't mind. There's plenty for you to do without the security measures."

"Parker is welcome to them."

"Good! You had better wait until he comes and hand over the files. Then you can have your holiday."

"I thought you wanted me to wait until you had had your holiday? We can't both be away at the same time."

"My holiday must be put off until later."

"Why?"

"Various reasons. First and foremost I can't leave Bess. She is pregnant. . . . Oh, she hasn't told me yet. She hasn't told me because she knows I've arranged to go to Ardfalloch and stay with my friends the MacAslans, and she knows I wouldn't go if she told me. She'll wait and tell me her news when I come home. That's her idea."

Gerald knew this already (but he said nothing of course).

"Anyway I'm not going," Sir Walter continued. "Later on, when you come back, Bess and I can have a holiday together. We can go to the Riviera if she feels like it. Then there's this trouble at K. and K.'s I want to find out all the details . . . and I want to see Parker when he arrives and tell him what he's to do. He must examine the credentials of every man who has come to MacCallum's during the last year—examine them very carefully indeed."

"That includes me, of course," said Gerald.

"So it does!" exclaimed Sir Walter, raising his eyebrows in mock surprise. "Parker must start with your credentials, Gerald."

They looked at each other and smiled. They understood each other perfectly and were comfortably aware that this was the case.

"Where do you intend to go for your holiday?" Sir Walter asked.

"I don't know. I might go north for some fishing. Dickenson suggested Uist."

"You wouldn't consider going to Ardfalloch for the stalking? The MacAslans would be glad to have you."

"But I don't know anything about it! I don't know your friends—they wouldn't want me! I haven't got a rifle or anything!"

"Can you handle a rifle?"

"Oh, yes! I was in my college team. We shot at Bisley for the Ashburton Shield and didn't do badly . . . but you aren't serious, are you?"

"Perfectly serious," said Sir Walter, smiling. He took up a letter which was lying on his table and added, "I was just going to answer this. It's from young MacAslan. His name is Gregor, but he likes people to call him Mac. His father is MacAslan, the chief of his clan. He owns a large property in the Highlands."

"A deer-forest," said Gerald nodding.

"Yes, a deer-forest, grouse moors, a sea loch with an island in the middle of it, pine woods, hills with sheep, and a few stony fields of hay, oats, turnips and potatoes. Last but not least, a comfortable house on the shores of the loch."

"A wealthy landowner!"

"No, a poor landowner. You don't make money on that sort of property unless you can let it to a wealthy sportsman—and there aren't many of that kind going about nowadays. He *does* let occasionally, when he has to, but he loves Ardfalloch, so he hates letting it to strangers."

"That's natural, isn't it?"

"The property is a big responsibility," continued Sir Walter. "It has to be looked after if you don't want it to deteriorate. MacAslan can't afford a large staff of keepers and ghillies, so he and Mac do a lot themselves. I had promised to go up for ten days or a fortnight to help them to cull the deer. I thought perhaps you might like to go instead of me."

"How do you cull deer?"

"You shoot them."

"Shoot them?" echoed Gerald in horrified tones.

Sir Walter laughed. "A certain number of deer must be killed every year to prevent the herd from increasing."

"But why don't they want their herd to increase?" asked Gerald in bewilderment.

"Because there's only a limited supply of food for them. I don't know much about other forests, but Ardfalloch is high and wild. This means that they must keep their herd down to a certain number, otherwise the beasts would starve before the grass begins to grow."

"Can't they feed the creatures?"

"It wouldn't be easy," Sir Walter replied. "They feed the deer in the New Forest, but that's different. In Scotland the forests have no roads or tracks; there are mountains and moors and bogs. As a matter of fact, MacAslan said he was going to try feeding the stags this year, as an experiment, so I had a talk with the keeper and told him how to go about it."

"You told him how to go about it?"

Sir Walter nodded. "I've always been interested in the red deer. I've bought every book I could find on the subject; he's a noble animal, as wild and free as his native hills."

"It's all quite new to me," said Gerald hopelessly. "I'm sure your friends would rather have someone who knows the ropes."

"Mac wants a man who would be a congenial companion. . . . Here, you had better read his letter," replied Sir Walter. "You needn't read the first page—it's just thanking me for the present I sent him on his birthday—start at page two."

Mac's writing was large and clear so it was easy to read:

> Dad and I intended to do it ourselves with your help and the two stalkers. Malcolm is very good value—as you know—and we have got another man who is young and keen. Unfortunately Dad has had bronchitis. He is better now, but the doctor has forbidden him to do any stalking this year. So Phil has arranged for him to go to Edinburgh and stay with his friends the Maclarens, at Davidson's Mains. It will be much better for him not to be here. Also it will leave Phil free to come to Tigh na Feidh. She has asked Donny Eastwood to come. The two girls will keep each other company and help old Kirsty with the cooking. That is satisfactory—as far as it goes—but I must say I should like a congenial companion, so if you happen to know of anybody who would like to come, you might let me have his name. I will write and ask him. Needless to say I am terribly sorry you cannot come yourself, but I quite understand. We must hope for better luck next year.
>
> With love and again many thanks for the magnificent present,
>
> Yours ever,
>
> Mac.

"It's a very nice letter," said Gerald, handing it back. "But it doesn't tell me much."

"I'll tell you anything you want to know."

"But I don't know what to ask—that's the trouble," explained Gerald. "To begin with I thought the name of the place was Ardfalloch?"

"That's the big house. They go up to Tigh na Feidh for the stalking. It's a lodge high up on the edge of the forest. Tigh na Feidh means the House of the Deer—and that's just what it is! It's a queer old place, not what you might call luxurious, but I've always been very happy there. The view is marvellous and I enjoy the absolute peace and quiet."

"You've been there several times?"

"Often," replied Sir Walter. "In fact nearly every year, but not last year because MacAslan let the forest to a syndicate from Manchester. They paid him well and he wanted the money, but naturally enough they wanted trophies. They were out for heads with fine antlers so that they could have them mounted and could hang them up on their walls to show their friends what tremendous shikaris they were. See?"

"Not really," admitted Gerald apologetically.

"It isn't a good thing for a forest to have only the fine stags killed. MacAslan would have preferred a certain proportion of older beasts eliminated: stags that were past their prime and 'switches' with deformed antlers. The reason being that a stag in good condition with fine antlers is more likely to sire good calves."

Gerald understood this. "It's like race-horses," he said.

"Yes, but you know where you are with horses; you know their breeding. These creatures are wild and free; they roam over the hills for miles, so the only way to improve the herd is to eliminate those that don't come up to standard."

"Do they shoot the hinds too?"

"Not until later. You don't want to start killing hinds while they still have their calves running with them. I'll lend you a book about deer," added Sir Walter. He rose and found a small book with a brown leather cover and handed it to Gerald. "It's old and shabby, but you'll find quite a lot of useful information in it. As far as I know there are no modern books on the subject."

Gerald accepted the book and put it in his pocket. He said, "I'll read it, of course, but I doubt if it will help me very much. I mean I wouldn't know how to begin."

"You would go out with a stalker and do exactly as he tells you. It's difficult for me to explain to you because you haven't seen the place . . . but if you don't mind climbing rocks and scrambling about on steep hillsides, you'll get a lot of fun out of stalking without knowing a great deal about it. My guess is that you will find it so interesting that you will soon want to know more."

Sir Walter paused for a few moments and then added, "Now I had better tell you about the MacAslan family, hadn't I? We've known them for many years. My father used to go to Ardfalloch for the grouse-shooting, but I'm not keen on sitting in a butt and having coveys of birds driven over my head. Stalking is much more sporting. You would like the young MacAslans—I'm sure of that. Mac is a good deal younger than you are. He's twenty-three—and in some ways he's young for his age—but he's a friendly creature, interesting and intelligent, so you would get on with him all right. Phil is his sister; she's a year younger and full of beans. She's good fun. Her friend, Donny Eastwood, is a nice little thing—very quiet and gentle. She lives with her father at Larchester and keeps house for him. He's a professor of economics, but he has retired now. He writes books which are so clever that very few people want to read them. It's dull for the girl at home, so she enjoys coming up to Ardfalloch for a holiday now and then. She and Phil are fond of each other and have jokes together."

Gerald nodded. He was not interested in the girls; he had been interested in an American girl—a fair, fairy-like little creature—but she had gone home to America and had married a young man whom she had known all her life. Gerald still thought of Penelope sometimes, thought of her a little regretfully if the truth were told.

"Well, what about it?" asked Sir Walter, smiling. "What shall I say to Mac?"

"You really think I should go?"

"Yes, I do. I'm sure you'd enjoy it."

"All right, then. Tell him I'm on. I expect I can shoot a

deer if somebody leads me to it and puts a rifle into my hands. I'll do my best, anyhow."

"I'll tell him," said Sir Walter, laughing. "I'll lend you one of my rifles and I'll take you to a rifle-range tomorrow afternoon so that you can have a little practice with it before you go."

This seemed to end the matter, so Gerald thanked him and rose.

"Oh, half a minute, Gerald!" Sir Walter exclaimed. "You had better cable to Joseph Parker; he's at Wellington in New Zealand; you'll find the address in my files."

"What shall I say?" asked the private secretary, producing a notebook.

"Say 'Come earliest possible' and sign it 'Shipman.' Send it yourself, tomorrow morning."

The private secretary repeated his orders, said good-night and went home.

3

In Which an Inoffensive Gentleman Airs His Views

When Gerald arrived at the office on Wednesday morning, the doorkeeper greeted him as usual and informed him that a man had called to see him.

"Who is he, Ballantyne?" asked Gerald.

"He refused to give his name, just said he wanted to see Mr. Burleigh-Brown. I told him that he ought to have made an appointment, but he replied that he would wait."

Gerald hesitated. Now that he was Sir Walter's private secretary, he had a great many callers and he had found that some of them wasted his time.

"He's respectable-looking. Very inoffensive," said Ballantyne. "He's small and thin and neatly-dressed."

"Inoffensive?" asked Gerald. "Hasn't got a gun in his pocket? Well, if you're sure of that, you can send him up to my office in about twenty minutes."

"I'll frisk him," said Ballantyne, laughing.

Gerald had been given a small room as his private office; there was a big solid table in it and several wooden chairs. What with these and the filing cabinets, there was scarcely space to move . . . but it was his very own and he appreciated his privacy. As he hung up his hat on a peg behind the door, he remembered his first meeting with Ballantyne. He had been somewhat in awe of the man's imposing appearance and manner. It was different now for they were friends and could have little jokes. Most of the people in MacCallum's appreciated a joke and none of them presumed upon an informal approach. In this respect—as in many others—they were quite different from the men who had worked in the diamond mine in South Africa.

There was a pile of letters on Gerald's table, so he got down to work without delay. It saved time if he could get the morning mail opened and sorted before the arrival of Sir Walter—and time was important. Gerald was in a constant state of surprise at the amount of work his brother-in-law got through in a day. Walter's brain was crystal clear and extraordinarily retentive. It was seldom that he had to be reminded of a name or an engagement and he knew all the men in the ship-yard by headmark; he never cluttered up his mind with useless details, but grasped essentials and made decisions quickly. The more Gerald saw of the man the more he admired him.

Gerald was halfway through his morning task when there was a knock on his door and Ballantyne ushered in the visitor: "Gentleman to see you, Mr. Burleigh-Brown," said Ballantyne.

The visitor was a complete stranger, but he was exactly as Ballantyne had said: very respectable-looking, neat and tidy, small and thin and inoffensive. He waited until Ballantyne had gone and then put a paper on the table in front of Gerald and said,

"There's my calling-card, Mr. Burleigh-Brown."

The calling-card was the cable that Gerald had despatched on Saturday morning to Joseph Parker in Wellington.

Gerald sprang up and shook hands with his visitor. "Good heavens, you haven't wasted time!" he exclaimed.

"Earliest possible," quoted Parker.

"I know, but still . . ."

"And signed 'Shipman,' " Parker added, sitting down on the chair Gerald had drawn up to the table for him.

"It's a code-word, is it?"

"Not exactly. I'll tell you about it sometime. We had better get to business first, hadn't we? I've just arrived and came straight to the office."

"Sir Walter has gone to the Tail of the Bank this morning, so I had better put you in the picture. I'm his private secretary and I'm in charge of the security measures—but I'm to hand over to you. Have you had breakfast? Would you like a cup of coffee and a sandwich?"

Parker replied that he had had a cup of tea on the plane, but he could do with something more substantial, so Gerald rang his bell and ordered the food. (There were advantages in his position as secretary to a Great Man). A message boy was despatched to a nearby restaurant with the order; meanwhile the secret file was produced and opened.

"I guessed it was the Keble and Kidd robbery," said Parker. "I read about it, or course. The gang attacked the van on the way from the Bank to the Yard. That's right, isn't it?"

Gerald nodded. "I'll tell you what we're doing. Then you can study the files."

The coffee and sandwiches had arrived by this time, so Parker ate his meal and listened.

First of all there was "Operation Pie", which was Sir Walter's own invention: a bullet-proof van had been painted to resemble the fleet of vans which belonged to a large and flourishing Glasgow bakery, the chairman of which was a personal friend of Sir Walter's. (He had laughed inordinately when the scheme had been proposed to him and had suggested several improvements.) Once a week the van was driven to a garage which was next door to the Bank—ostensibly for servicing. All the vans were serviced at the same garage—MacBride's. (MacBride was the brother-in-law of Dickenson, a foreman at MacCallum's for fifteen years and completely trustworthy.)

The MacCallum van was serviced on a different day each week and at a different hour. The money for the men's wages was packed in cardboard cartons, labelled "Pies" or "cakes" or "sausages." These were carried out of a side door and packed into the van, which already contained trays of real pies and buns and chunks of fruitcake. The van was then driven to the ship-yard. On arrival it drove to the canteen to unload the food. The cardboard cartons were unloaded at the same time and carried down a flight of stone steps to a cellar which had been built below the canteen during the war as an air-raid shelter. They were stacked in a corner of the cellar until required.

"Here's the file about 'Operation Pie,'" added Gerald, passing it over: "It contains the names of the men who are in the know. They've all been at MacCallum's for at least six years. If you can suggest any alteration in the scheme, you can tell Sir Walter. I'm thankful to get rid of it."

"It's very ingenious," was Parker's comment.

The other security measures were more conventional and consisted of electric wires in certain places (they were hidden below the ground and set off alarm bells when they were trodden upon by an unwary foot) and detectives in overalls who patrolled the yard at night with watch-dogs. Gerald did not mind that. His chief objection was the "snooping." The credentials of new hands had to be thoroughly examined and men were kept under secret surveillance until it was established that they were neither troublemakers nor spies. He explained all this to Parker and added that he was going away for a holiday and Parker could work here, in his office, until he came back.

"What will you do when you come back?" Parker wanted to know.

"That's up to Sir Walter," replied Gerald. "There's plenty of work without the security measures. I'm quite willing to do anything he wants me to do, of course. You know what he did for me. If it hadn't been for Sir Walter, that horrible affair at Koolbokie Diamond Mine would never have been cleared up and I should still be going about with a stain on my name."

Parker knew. It was he who had unravelled the tangled skein at Koolbokie and caught the thief red-handed. He said, "Yes, but Sir Walter has done a lot more for me. He picked me up out of the gutter when I was eleven years old."

This was Joseph Parker's story. Gerald heard it that evening when the day's work was done and the two men were relaxing in Gerald's sitting-room in the comfortable little flat which Bess had found for him in a Glasgow suburb.

Joseph was born in a tenement in Maryhill. His father worked in a factory and earned reasonably good pay. His mother made a little extra by cleaning offices, so she too was out most of the day and the child was neglected. When Joseph was ten years old his mother died and his father—never very steady—got into bad company and was apprehended by the police for house-breaking. It was decided to send the boy to an institution where he would be looked after and taught a trade, but he had a horror of the word "institution", so he escaped and went off on his own. It was summer-time and for a while he enjoyed his freedom. He wandered about the country, sleeping in barns or under haystacks and by doing little jobs he made a few shillings, which he spent on food. It was a different matter when the weather worsened, for by that time his clothes were in rags. He drifted back to Glasgow, the only place he knew, but the tenement where he had lived had been pulled down to make room for a garage.

Joseph roved about the streets: cold and hungry and ragged and dirty. When darkness fell, he was so dazed and miserable that he staggered off the pavement in front of an approaching car. The car touched his arm and knocked him over.

Next moment a strong hand seized him by the collar of his jacket and dragged him out of the gutter and a voice said, "What d'you think you're doing?"

That was Joseph's introduction to Walter MacCallum.

(He was not Sir Walter then, for his father was still alive. He was a young man with a comfortable flat in Glasgow and was on his way home from an evening party.)

A crowd had gathered and a policeman appeared and offered to take the boy to the nearest hospital, but Mr. MacCallum replied that there was nothing much the matter with the boy. All he needed was a good meal. "I'll take him home with me and feed him," said Mr. MacCallum.

So Joseph went home with his rescuer. He was put into a hot bath and scrubbed from head to foot; he was wrapped up warmly and sat down at a table near the fire with a good meal before him.

All this time Joseph had not spoken a word (he was completely dumb), but when he had eaten some food, his brain began to work and his tongue was loosened. He looked up and said, "Are you God, mister?"

"No, just a ship-man," replied Walter MacCallum.

Joseph did not remember any more about that evening. He woke the next morning to find himself lying on the sofa in Mister Shipman's sitting-room wrapped in a big brown blanket.

"I stayed with 'Mister Shipman' for several days," continued Joseph. "He burnt my rags and bought me decent clothes. Then he arranged for me to go and live with Mrs. Frost, who had been his mother's cook. She was the mother of Mr. Frost who looked after his flat for him. (You know Mr. Frost, I expect?)"

"Yes, of course!" said Gerald.

"I was a heathen when I went to live with Mrs. Frost, but she was a true Christian, good and kind and motherly. She taught me her own simple faith; she taught me how to behave in a civilised manner. I lived with her for a year and loved her dearly. Then 'Mister Shipman' sent me to a boarding-school. I was backward at first, but I worked hard and soon made up for lost time. 'Mister Shipman' came and saw me quite often and took me out in his car. I knew by then that he was really

Mr. Walter MacCallum, a partner in his father's ship-building firm, but he was still 'Mister Shipman' to me. When I was old enough, I went to the Yard, first as a message-boy and later in a special sort of capacity. You see, I had had a different life from other boys. I had learnt to be independent; I had learnt to be quick. Sometimes Sir Walter wanted to find out the truth about a man's background—where he went and what sort of friends he had. I was good at that. I was so small and insignificant that nobody noticed me. . . .

"That's how it began," explained Parker. He smiled and continued, "Sir Walter told me that you don't like 'snooping.' Well, it isn't a pretty word, but I'm not ashamed of snooping. I don't think of it like that. I call it 'finding out the truth.' I find out the truth about people for Sir Walter. Do you ever read Browning's poems, Mr. Burleigh-Brown?"

"No."

"You should," said Parker. "There's a lot of meat in them. There's one called 'In a Balcony.' Parts of it are a bit obscure, but one thing is clear. It's this: 'Truth is the strong thing. Let man's life be true!' I like that. If a man's life be true, he doesn't need to be afraid of me—or anybody."

Gerald nodded thoughtfully.

"I'll tell you another thing," said Parker. "Nowadays there's too much sympathy for criminals and not enough for their victims. A hundred years ago a man could be hanged for stealing a purse, but now the pendulum has swung too far the other way and you can't hang a man for poisoning his grandmother."

"I'm not really in favour of hanging anybody," said Gerald in doubtful tones. "Criminals must be punished, of course, but——"

"Of course!" exclaimed Parker. "But people tell you that corporal punishment is unchristian. They'll tell you that if a man does wrong, you should reason with him gently; you should tell him to be good and not do it again. It's called 'binding him over to keep the peace.' I'd bind him over, of course, but first I'd give him a darn' good thrashing—just to help him to remember."

Gerald could not help smiling: there was something very funny about this inoffensive-looking little fellow and the ferocity of his views.

"Oh, you can smile," said Parker, "but I'm talking from experience. I'm thinking of cases in which I've been involved. I'm thinking of men who deserved thrashing (it would have done them a power of good). I'm thinking of their wrong-doing. I'm thinking of a little girl of seven years old who was waylaid when she was coming home from school. She was taken to a barn and assaulted. Her leg was fractured and she lay there all night in the dark. She didn't die. They took her to hospital and mended her leg, but they couldn't mend the damage to her brain. She'll never be the same healthy, happy, friendly little girl she was before. What about it, Mr. Burleigh-Brown? What punishment would you mete out to the brute who ruined little Nancy?

"Listen," said Parker, leaning forward in his chair and speaking very earnestly. "Two thousand years ago there was a Man who found something nasty going on. He found a lot of rogues cheating people in the Temple; they were over-charging and giving the wrong change and making a good thing out of it. Their victims were poor people who were too frightened to complain. I expect the Man stood and watched for a bit—just to make certain. When He had *found out the truth*, He took action. He made a whip and thrashed them and upset their tables and sent their ill-gotten gains rolling all over the floor."

Parker rose and added, "I'd better be going. I haven't been in bed for three nights, so I expect I've been talking too much. I don't often talk like this—in fact I don't remember ever having talked like this before. I'm sorry if I've bored you."

"You haven't bored me; you've given me a lot to think about. I shan't forget what you've said. Look here, would you like to stay here tonight? I've got a spare room—"

"No, thank you, Mr. Burleigh-Brown," interrupted Parker. "It's very kind of you, but it's better if we don't see too much of each other. I don't want people to know I've been talking to Sir Walter's private secretary. I want to keep myself in the background. I can do more that way. I've got your files—I'll study them carefully—and I'll give you my address so you can get in touch with me if necessary. I've taken a room in a Commercial Hotel. A Commercial Hotel is a good place if you want to be inconspicuous; there's a lot of coming and going, so nobody notices you."

Gerald went to the door with him and shook hands.

"By the way," said Parker. "You know why I was sent for in a hurry, don't you? He wants me to keep 'an unobtrusive eye' on his boy."

"Alastair? Does he really think Alastair is in danger?"

"Not really," Parker replied. "He just wants to take precautions about him and a friend of his. Apparently they go down to the Yard quite often and have the run of the place, so it's conceivable that they might know something which would be useful. They're both pretty smart."

"What do you think?" asked Gerald anxiously.

"I don't think the man who plans these robberies would bother about little boys. He would think they were 'just kids'—and beneath his notice. It wouldn't occur to him that they were smart. All the same I intend to be careful. Sir Walter has given me *carte blanche,* so I shall get hold of a couple of trustworthy chaps to help me. Those boys will be shadowed all the time—unobtrusively shadowed. See?"

Gerald saw. He said, "But Parker, what could you do if a man stopped the boys in the street? By the time you had called a policeman—"

"A policeman!" interrupted Parker. "I wouldn't call a policeman. What would be the good of that? If a man stops those boys in the street, I shall put a bullet through his heart without waiting to ask his intentions."

Parker tapped his pocket significantly, ran down the stairs and disappeared.

For at least ten minutes Gerald stood on the landing wondering what he should do—he weighed several courses of action and rejected them—finally he decided to do nothing and say nothing; the security measures at MacCallum's Ship-Yard were no longer his business.

4

Which Tells of a Rendez-vous at Ardfalloch Inn

It was a little after twelve o'clock on a fine September day when Gerald arrived in Ardfalloch village and pulled up at the inn. The village was small: just a double row of cottages, a post-office, a shop and an inn with MACTAGGART written over the doorway. A stout man with an apron tied round his middle was standing in the doorway and came forward with a welcoming smile.

"Can I leave my car here?" asked Gerald.

"You will be the gentleman who is going to Tigh na Feidh?"

"Yes. Young Mr. MacAslan told me to meet him here. Have you got room in your garage for my car?"

"It would be a strange thing if a guest of MacAslan could not be leaving his car at Ardfalloch Inn," replied Mr. MacTaggart.

This seemed satisfactory, so Gerald drove into the garage, the doors of which stood open.

The innkeeper followed him and leant against the side of the car. "This is a very small place," he said in deprecating tones. "It must seem very small indeed to a gentleman from Glasgow."

"It isn't very big," agreed Gerald.

"The inn belonged to my father, so I was born and reared in Ardfalloch," explained Mr. MacTaggart. "When I was a young man, I was not very fond of it, so I went to Glasgow and took service in a big hotel. I learnt to cook and to wait at table. It was my intention to own a big hotel someday and make a lot of money, but when my father died, I came home to Ardfalloch and found a wife."

"You gave up your ambition," suggested Gerald.

Mr. MacTaggart nodded. "But there are compensations," he said grandly. "In a big town I would be nobody, but in Ardfalloch I am Somebody. People come to me for advice. I am Captain of the Fire Brigade—we have smart uniforms and brass helmets. I am President of the Bowling Club. It is better to be a big fish in a wee pond than a very wee fish in a big pond. That is what I am thinking."

Gerald smiled. "What does your wife think about it?" he enquired.

"She likes to be a big fish. She is President of the Women's Rural . . . and, though the place is small, we manage none too badly. We have gentlemen for the shooting and the fishing. We are full up during the season. The gentlemen come back year after year and they tell their friends: 'You will get good food and a clean bed at MacTaggart's.' Och, we manage none too badly. You see there is no competition. There is no other inn—except the inn at Balnafin, which is not very clean nor very comfortable. Raddle is not particular about his clients (he will give house-room to anybody) and Mistress Raddle is a very poor cook. The Horseman's Inn would not be nice for a gentleman like you. Not nice at all."

Gerald was amused at Mr. MacTaggart's loquacity. Perhaps the man was a little too pleased with himself, but there was something rather nice about him.

"Two years ago," continued Mr. MacTaggart, "Mistress MacTaggart and I decided to launch out. We got a builder all the way from Inverness to make three new bedrooms and another bathroom. The bedrooms have fixed basins with hot and cold water so the gentlemen are willing to pay extra for them. Already we have got back our money and paid off the debt."

Gerald congratulated him.

"Yes, it was a good spec," said Mr. MacTaggart proudly. He added, "But you will not be wanting a bedroom. You will be staying at Tigh na Feidh?"

"Yes."

"Mac will be meeting you here in the Land Rover?"

"That's what he said in his letter."

"That is what he will do. He will be here for lunch and he will be taking you to Tigh na Feidh in the afternoon. How long will you be staying?"

"I'm not sure," replied Gerald doubtfully. He had received a very polite letter from his prospective host which began, "Dear Mr. Burleigh-Brown" and ended, "Yours sincerely, Gregor MacAslan", but he had sensed a lack of warmth in the letter and, despite Walter's assurances that the young MacAslans would be delighted to have him, he felt certain that they would rather have a guest who knew something about stalking. He had made up his mind that he would stay for a few days and if he found that he was not wanted, he would go on somewhere else."

"Och, you will be staying two weeks—or more," said Mr. MacTaggart. "Miss Phil has ordered plenty of food. It came in the van this morning and I have it ready for Mac when he comes with the Land Rover. Miss Phil is a very business-like young lady. She would not be ordering all that food if she was not expecting guests."

Gerald now perceived a pile of sacks and crates and boxes, which were stacked in a corner of the garage. "All that?" he asked in surprise.

"Stalking is hungry work," explained Mr. MacTaggart.

It was nearly half-past twelve by this time and Gerald had been told that his prospective host would meet him here at twelve, so he was beginning to wonder if there had been some mistake. Perhaps he should drive on to Tigh na Feidh in his car, taking some of the provisions with him.

Gerald was about to suggest this to Mr. MacTaggart when a Land Rover drove into the yard and out of it jumped a young man with fair hair. He was a very good-looking young man; his figure was slender and graceful; he was as lithe as an athlete in training.

"Hullo, MacTaggart!" he exclaimed. "Have you got the provisions? Phil said she had sent you a list of what she wanted."

"It is all here!" replied MacTaggart, hurrying out to meet him. "The flour and the oatmeal, two sacks of potatoes and two big crates from Inverness. The whisky is here, and the eggs and a side of bacon—everything Miss Phil wanted—and this is the gentleman from Glasgow that you were expecting."

"Oh, good!" said young MacAslan, coming forward and shaking hands. "I'm sorry I'm a bit late, Mr. Burleigh-Brown."

"Oh, it's quite all right. I was chatting to Mr. MacTaggart."

"These are the things, Mac," said MacTaggart, pointing to the pile. "Will I get the lad to pack them for you while you are having lunch?"

"I'll do it myself," replied young MacAslan. "Some of the stuff looks a bit too heavy for the lad. Then we can have lunch and go up to the house afterwards." He turned as he spoke and, seizing an enormous sack of potatoes, swung it onto his back and carried it over to the Land Rover as easily as if it were stuffed with feathers.

"Can I help you?" asked Gerald.

"Don't bother. It won't take ten minutes," said young MacAslan, seizing another, even larger, sack and dealing with it in the same way.

Gerald hesitated, wondering what he should do. His help had been refused, somewhat curtly. There were several other sacks, but they were all large and looked extremely heavy, so he was a little doubtful as to whether he would be able to carry them. He was strong and fit, but he was not used to carrying sacks—and probably there was a knack in this kind of work. It would be embarrassing if he tried to hoist the sack onto his back and found himself unable to do so. The crates looked even more unwieldy!

Another source of embarrassment was the fact that he did not know how to address young MacAslan. The boy (he was little more) had addressed him as "Mr. Burleigh-Brown". Should he call the boy "Mr. MacAslan"? It seemed silly (and probably it was the wrong thing to do). Gerald wished he had asked Walter, but he had taken it for granted that the boy would be friendly. The boy was polite, but he was not friendly; in fact his manner was distinctly chilly. It was going to be very difficult, thought Gerald unhappily.

Fortunately he was rescued from his state of indecision by Mr. MacTaggart who suggested that he might like to wash, adding that lunch was nearly ready and Mrs. MacTaggart would be "put about" if her guests were not prepared to eat it while it was hot.

"There is nice soup and fresh mackerel from the loch," said Mr. MacTaggart persuasively.

Gerald allowed himself to be persuaded.

At lunch they talked about the weather. Young MacAslan said it had been wet yesterday, but the glass had gone up, so he hoped it was going to be fine tomorrow. Gerald replied that it rained a good deal in Glasgow, but he was getting used to it and didn't mind. Young MacAslan said rain was rather a nuisance, but fog was worse. Gerald agreed that fog was a great deal worse.

When they had said all that they could think of about the weather, there was a short silence.

"I had better tell you," said young MacAslan at last. "There's another man coming. We've known him for years, so when he wrote and asked if we could have him, we couldn't refuse. He lives with his mother in Glasgow and goes about a good deal, so perhaps you know him. His name is Oliver Stoddart."

"I've never met him," Gerald replied. "As a matter of fact my job keeps me pretty busy, so I haven't got to know many people in Glasgow—but don't worry, it doesn't matter a bit."

"What do you mean?"

"I mean, if you haven't room for me, I can easily—"

"Oh, it isn't that! We've got plenty of room for you both. I just want to explain about Oliver. He's in some sort of business in Glasgow, but he doesn't seem to have to do much work. He lives with his mother (I told you that) and he has lots of money, so he goes about all over the place, staying with friends and shooting and fishing. Last year he went to New Zealand and the year before to Norway—there's very good fishing in Norway. He asked me to go with him, but I couldn't of course. I mean I couldn't ask Dad for the money and anyhow there's plenty to do here. . . ."

Gerald listened to all this and wondered what was coming.

"Oliver is a good shot. He has been here several times and enjoys stalking. He says in his letter that he wants some good heads and he's willing to pay for his sport. I asked my father about it and he said the money would be useful . . . so there you are."

"Where am I?" asked Gerald, smiling.

"Where are you? . . . Oh, I see what you mean! I'm not very good at explaining things. The fact is we didn't intend to shoot good stags this year and Sir Walter said you didn't mind."

"I don't mind in the least, but all the same I'm quite willing to pay the same as your friend."

"You can't do that."

"Why not?"

"It wouldn't be fair."

"Look here, let's get this straight. Sir Walter explained about what happened last year when you let the deer-forest to a syndicate and he told me that this year you wanted the less good animals shot. Well, that suits me. I'll shoot the ones you tell me to shoot—if I can. I want to learn about stalking. I want the fun of the sport and I'm quite prepared to pay—"

"You can't do that," repeated Mac. He added, "If you pay the same as Oliver, you must have the same sport. It wouldn't be right to take your money and not give you the chance of killing a good stag. It wouldn't be fair."

"But I don't want to kill a good stag! I'd rather not."

"You'd rather not?"

"I'd like to look at him," Gerald explained. "I'd like to see him standing on his own hills in all his glory—and let him go. I'd rather shoot a stag with crooked horns. That's what you want, isn't it?"

"That's what we intended to do this year. That's what we *would* have done if my father had been fit and Sir Walter hadn't been tied up in Glasgow.

"I've come instead of Sir Walter," Gerald pointed out.

"I know . . . and it sounded all right until Oliver wrote and said he wanted to come."

"It's perfectly all right. The fact that your friend is coming doesn't change the arrangement as far as I'm concerned."

"It does," objected Mac. "It wouldn't be fair to take your money—"

"You've said that before," Gerald interrupted. "I can only repeat that I've come instead of Sir Walter."

"We're going round in circles," said Mac. He thought for a few moments and then added, "All right, we'll compromise. You will shoot switches and beasts that are past their prime, but I won't take a penny from you. That's flat."

It was not a compromise, but Gerald saw that he was adamant and was obliged to agree. "There's just one more thing I want to say," declared Gerald. "I've come to help you, so if you find I'm useless, you'll tell me quite honestly—"

"Oh, you'll be useful! It's like this, you see. We can't afford a big staff of keepers and stalkers, so we do a lot ourselves. Phil is almost as good as a boy," added Phil's brother in patronising tones.

"How do you mean?" enquired the guest.

"She's a good shot with a gun and she doesn't mind killing foxes—they're very troublesome, of course—but stalking is a man's sport."

"I'm pretty fit," Gerald assured him. "My job at MacCallum's isn't strenuous physically, but it isn't sedentary either. There's a good deal of running about the yard—it's an enormous place, you know—and I take as much exercise as I can. I play squash in the evenings when I have time."

"What is your job—exactly?"

"I'm dog's-body to Sir Walter," replied Sir Walter's private secretary.

Mac looked at his guest critically and decided that he looked pretty fit, which was satisfactory.

"I've never done any stalking," Gerald added. "I expect you've realised that I know nothing about it."

Mac had. He said rather anxiously, "Sir Walter said you could shoot?"

"I've shot lions," admitted Gerald. "But that's different, of course."

Mac began to laugh . . . and couldn't stop. He laughed and laughed and laughed. It was the laughter of a boy and so infectious that Gerald laughed too.

"But I don't know why we're laughing," said Gerald at last.

"Don't you?" gasped the boy, wiping his streaming eyes. "Oh, lord! Just wait till I tell Phil!"

"I don't understand—"

"Well, quite honestly," gasped Mac, "quite honestly Phil and I—had a feeling—that you were a bit of a milksop. I don't know why, exactly—"

"It wasn't for sport," said Gerald, trying to explain. "I had to kill them because they were such a nuisance—"

"Oh, don't!" cried Mac in agonised tones. "Don't say another word or you'll start me off again . . . and I'm sore all over."

Obediently Gerald was silent and, after a few more

chuckles, Mac drank some water and calmed down.

The laughter had cleared the air, so things were more comfortable. Gerald felt the warmth in the atmosphere and responded to it by suggesting Christian names.

"I hoped you'd say that," agreed Mac, smiling cheerfully. "You're older than I am, of course, but you can't stalk all day with a man and not be friends."

"Mr. MacTaggart called you Mac."

"They all do; it's a compliment really—a sort of title. My father is MacAslan and I'm Mac. That reminds me, we had better fetch the letters at the post-office before setting out to the forest. I'm expecting one from my father. You could nip along and get them, couldn't you? I'll just see what sort of a hash MacTaggart's lad has made of packing the provisions. Mrs. MacTaggart wouldn't let me finish the job."

Gerald "nipped along" and asked for the letters—there was a sheaf of mail waiting—and a few minutes later he and Mac were on their way to Tigh na Feidh.

5

Tells of Gerald's Arrival at the House of the Deer

Gerald had wondered why he could not have driven to his destination in his own car. The reason became obvious: only a vehicle with a four-wheel drive could have ascended the rutty track. There was a gate leading off the road, then came a hump-backed bridge over a rocky stream; after that the track wound its way up the hill with hair-pin bends which necessitated backing. After that they came to a cut in the hills with towering cliffs on either side. Here the road narrowed and wound its way between huge boulders of igneous rock.

"This is called the Black Pass," said Mac. "It isn't really as perilous as it looks—and I'm used to it, of course." As a matter of fact he was quite pleased with his passenger for showing no signs of fear. Most people blenched and clutched the sides of the vehicle. Some had been known to scream. This passenger merely enquired, "What happens if you meet another car?"

"You don't often. If you do, one or other of you has to back till you get to a passing place . . . like that, for instance," replied Mac, pointing to a small quarry which looked to Gerald like a slimy bog.

"Phil said I had better warn you that there are no luxuries at Tigh na Feidh," he continued. "There's no electricity—just lamps—and no telephone. The roof leaks a bit here and there, but only in very heavy rain. We ought to have it seen to, of course, but we only use the house for the stalking, so it doesn't seem worthwhile. Malcolm lives here all the year round with his mother, but they don't mind."

"Who is Malcolm?"

"He's the head stalker. He's been with us for years and years—ever since I can remember. If you want to know anything about deer, you can ask Malcolm. He'll talk about deer for hours. My father is very knowledgeable too, but he's not here this year."

"He has been ill, hasn't he?"

"He had rather a bad go of bronchitis. He's better now, thank goodness! But the doctor said it would be madness for him to do any stalking. That's why Phil made him go to Edinburgh." Mac sighed and added, "It's awfully queer to be living at Tigh na Feidh without Dad."

By this time they had emerged from the pass into the sunlight. Mac drew up and said, "There it is, Gerald. That's the House of the Deer. It's a queer old place, isn't it? Long ago it was a Look-Out Tower (it has a wonderfully wide view in all directions), but it was neglected until it became almost ruinous. My great-great-grandfather renovated it and built onto it so that it could be used for stalking. He got the local builder and they built on rooms as and when they were needed for his family and his friends and made steps up to them and little passages—and added a few turrets just for fun—so Tigh na Feidh is a higgledy-piggledy mess. It's an architect's nightmare! All the same there's something rather attractive about it—at least Phil and I think so. We're fond of it," added Mac apologetically.

Gerald looked at the old house with interest. It was on the side of a hill near a burn and was build of rough grey stone. The windows were on different levels and were of different sizes and shapes: some were large and square, others were small and oblong. Those facing west were built into a kind of bow, like half a tower. Above that the half-tower became a whole tower with windows facing in three directions. The roof, which was made of slate, was steep and uneven; gables jutted out at all angles and twisted chimneys sprouted in unexpected places. The pepper-pot turrets, which had been added "just for fun", gave the place a rakish appearance.

"I've never seen anything like it before!" Gerald exclaimed.

"No, and you never will," declared Mac, smiling.

The House of the Deer was unique inside as well as outside. There was one large room which ran through the centre of the house on the ground floor and had windows facing east and west. It was used as a sitting-room at one end and as a dining-room at the other.

This was the old part of the house, as could be seen from the thickness of the walls. The windows were set in deep embrasures which were filled with cushioned window-seats. Halfway down one side of the room there was a huge stone fireplace with a wrought-iron grate for burning logs. The furniture consisted of large chairs upholstered in brown leather (which probably had been new in Victorian times) and large bookcases containing books about fishing and shooting and the habits of deer. There was a work-basket, bulging with grey woollen stockings, on one chair and a pile of papers on another.

Mac seized the work-basket and chucked it onto the floor. "Sit down, Gerald," he said hospitably. "This place isn't very tidy, I'm afraid, but we use it for everything. Old Kirsty does her best to keep it tidy, but Phil and I aren't tidy people so we don't mind . . . and, anyhow, it isn't a lady's drawing-room. It's just a place to relax when you come in from the hill, dirty and tired and cold."

He added, "We have a meal at six-thirty when we're here: fish and chips or sausages—or venison, of course—so there's plenty of time for a walk up the burn if you would like to stretch your legs. I must just look through these letters first in case there's anything important."

Gerald sat down and waited while his host skimmed through the letters. He was interested to see that although Mac had admitted to "untidiness", he was business-like with the letters. They were divided into several heaps and clipped together. Only one of them was pronounced "important".

"I shall have to see Malcolm about this," Mac explained. "It's from my father. He says you must be given the chance of killing at least one good stag. We shall probably find Malcolm in the gun-room."

"But I've told you I don't want—"

"You don't understand," declared Mac, smiling. "MacAslan says you're to be given the chance of killing at least one good stag. It's orders. MacAslan's word is Law. Come and talk to Malcolm."

"Wouldn't you rather talk to Malcolm yourself?"

"You'll be interested to see him; he's a curiosity like Tigh na Feidh. If he likes you, he'll show you his map. If he doesn't he won't—and it would be useful for you to see his map. Besides," added Mac frankly, "if you're there, he'll speak English."

"Speak English?" echoed Gerald in surprise.

"It wouldn't be polite not to," explained Mac. Then, seeing that his guest was still bewildered, he elucidated further: "Dad has the Gaelic and so has Phil, but I've been away so much that I've lost it more or less. First I was at school, then at Edinburgh University, and then for the last eighteen months I've been staying in Canada with my half-brother. He's in business—and would have given me a good post in his firm—but I'm needed here. . . . Come on, Gerald!"

The gun-room was a large square apartment on the ground floor. There were stands of guns and rifles and fishing rods; there were antlered heads on the walls; a huge stuffed salmon in a glass case hung over the fireplace. All was in perfect order.

In the middle of the room a man was seated at a table, cleaning a rifle. He was a short thick-set man with brown hair which was so tough and wiry that it stuck out from his head like an ill-trimmed bush. His face was reddish brown, tanned by the weather, and he wore a yellowish brown moustache, rather long and drooping, which gave him a somewhat lugubrious appearance.

"Hullo, Malcolm," said Mac. "We've come to talk to you. This is Mr. Burleigh-Brown, that I told you about. He's a brother-in-law of Sir Walter MacCallum's."

Malcolm rose and shook hands. Then they all three sat down at the table.

"This is a fine weapon," said Malcolm, pointing to the rifle he was cleaning. "It is Sir Walter MacCallum's 303 Express. I was cleaning it two years ago when he was here and I would know it anywhere."

"Yes, he lent it to me," Gerald explained.

"Is that so? Sir Walter must think highly of you to lend you this weapon, Mr. Burleigh-Brown," declared Malcolm, looking at Gerald with increased respect.

"He's very kind. He took me to a rifle-range near Glasgow so that I could have some target practice with it. I cleaned it afterwards very carefully"

"Och, it is nice and clean," Malcolm interrupted. "It is just that I am giving it a wee polish to make sure."

"Malcolm is never happier than when he's taking rifles to bits," said Mac, smiling. "No matter how carefully you clean your rifle he's never satisfied."

Malcolm smiled too, but did not reply.

"I've never shot deer," said Gerald. "I know nothing about stalking, but Sir Walter said you would be able to teach me. You'll find me very ignorant, I'm afraid."

"I will tell you all I can. I have been at Ard na Feidh all my life: first under my father and then as MacAslan's head-keeper—but there is still a lot about deer that I do not understand." Malcolm sighed and added, "Yes, there is a lot about deer that puzzles me."

"What about the feeding?" Mac asked. "MacAslan said you were going to try feeding them this year. Was it a success?"

"It was a good thing. The stags are in fine fettle. By the middle of August there was scarcely a stag in velvet to be seen on the hill. There are some pretty heads too. I was seeing an eleven-pointer up the glen on Saturday—and there is a fine Royal over towards Ben Ghaoth. Och, he is a fine beast."

"Tell me about the feeding."

"It was Sir Walter that suggested it," explained Malcolm. "He was telling MacAslan about it, so I did it the way he said. I asked Mackenzie for the loan of his tractor—I could not have managed without—and I was putting down the rock salt first. They soon found it! Then I was putting down the potatoes and the beans. I did the feeding early in the morning—like Sir Walter said. One morning when I was going up to the sanctuary, there was a score of stags waiting on me. Och, they liked it fine! It was quite tame they were, after a wee while (not minding me at all), but they are as wild as ever now."

"You really think it was a success?"

"It was indeed," Malcolm assured him. "I was not liking the idea of it—you know that, Mac. It seemed a queer thing to be feeding stags, like as if they were cattle, but the food was helping them a lot. I was hearing that they have lost a wheen of stags over at Glen Veigh with the late rut and the long hard winter."

Mac nodded. He said, "We shan't be able to do it every year. It costs a lot of money."

"There will be no need," Malcolm replied. "It was the long hard winter that was the trouble. The winters are not always long and hard." He paused and then added, "I have never seen so many stags at Ard na Feidh. I am thinking a good many must have come over the river from Glen Veigh. And will you tell me this, Mac: how could they be knowing about the feeding?"

Mac looked at him thoughtfully. "I wonder," he said. "Yes, it is a queer thing. So it is."

"It isn't what we intended——"

"Och, I know that fine," interrupted Malcolm. "But we need not be troubling ourselves. Glen Veigh is an ill-run forest. If Mr. Ross is wanting to keep his stags at home, he had better feed them (he can well afford it), but it is the grouse-moor he is keen on, not the deer. The young gentlemen are not caring about the forest either. Mackenzie takes them on the hill and they are shooting the first stag they see, whether he be a well-grown beast or not. The gentlemen will not content themselves to be stalking a switch. It is the good heads they are after. That is not the way to be improving a forest."

"MacAslan wants us to kill as many switches as possible this year," said Mac.

"I know that," agreed Malcolm. "and that is what we will do. It pleases me to see a switch killed, so it does."

"Malcolm," said Mac. "You remember I told you that Mr. Burleigh-Brown was quite content to kill switches? Well, I've just had a letter from MacAslan saying that Mr. Burleigh-Brown must be given the chance of killing at least one good stag, so——"

"MacAslan is always right," declared Malcolm. "I have not been happy about it, either. It is not right that a guest should come to Ard na Feidh and be given poor sport. A guest should be given the best a house can offer."

Gerald was about to object and to explain his views on the subject, but a look from Mac silenced him . . . and he remembered that MacAslan's word was law.

"Maybe you are wanting an easy day tomorrow," Malcolm was saying.

Mac looked at Gerald enquiringly.

"Just as you like," replied Gerald. "I'm perfectly fit for anything. If it's a fine day, it would be a pity to waste it."

"Good!" exclaimed Mac. "You can meet us in the usual place, can't you, Malcolm?"

The arrangements were made. Then Mac rose and explained that he must deal with the remainder of his letters. "You don't mind, do you, Gerald?" he said. "If we're going out early tomorrow, I had better get them off my chest. Perhaps Malcolm will tell you about the forest and show you his collection of horns."

"That is a good plan," declared Malcolm. "It would be as well for Mr. Burleigh-Brown to see the map of the forest before tomorrow morning. Are you interested in maps, Mr. Burleigh-Brown?"

Gerald was very interested in maps.

"This map is very rough," declared Malcolm in deprecating tones.

The map was produced from a locked drawer and was laid out carefully on the table.

"Och, it is not a proper map at all!" added Malcolm, looking at his handiwork with feigned disgust. "It is just a mess—not fit to be shown to a gentleman! I made it for myself, for the fun of it."

"It seems to be a very good map," Gerald assured him.

This was true. By looking at the map and following the stalker's explanations, Gerald was able to get quite a good idea of the lie of the land.

Ard na Feidh (the Forest of the Deer) was not a large forest. It was about eighteen thousand acres, but it was so well distributed that it was able to support more deer per acre than many larger ones. There was high ground and low ground, slopes of grass and heather and little corries where burns ran down to the river . . . and, by the river, was a sheltered holm (or meadow) where the hinds loved to feed. The high ground sloped up to Ben Ghaoth where there were heaps of boulders and screes of loose stones and where snow lay in deep drifts until well on in the spring.

Malcolm knew every yard of the forest; he knew it at all seasons of the year, so he was able to explain his map and to point out the details to his pupil. He also knew a great many of the stags by sight, for he had watched them grow year by year as he went about his work and he had tried to collect their horns and to mark their development. He opened a cupboard in the corner of the room and showed the horns to Gerald.

Fortunately Gerald was aware that stags cast their horns every year and grow new ones. "How do you find the horns?" he asked.

"It is not easy," replied Malcolm. "The hinds like to gnaw them—like a dog gnaws a bone—and I like to collect them when they are in good condition. Here is an interesting thing, Mr. Burleigh-Brown. Here are three sets of horns which were cast by the same stag three years running. See for yourself! The horns have improved, but the number of points remain the same. I am thinking he will improve yet, for he is only nine years old. . . . And here is a switch," he continued, taking up the deformed horn and handing it to Gerald. "It is an ugly thing, a switch. This beast has grown points this year, but they are not good points at all. If we are seeing him on the hill, they will not be saving his life. I do not like to be seeing switches at Ard na Feidh—nor hummels either."

"What is a hummel, Malcolm?"

"He is a beast without any horns at all—just hard bony knobs where his horns should be—but the queer thing is that he is usually big and heavy. Och, I do not like the look of him! I would have all my stags made in the right pattern."

"All fourteen-pointers," suggested Gerald, smiling.

"The twelve is best," replied Malcolm solemnly. "The Royal Stag, we call him. There is more grace in the pattern of a twelve-point horn . . . at least that is what I am thinking."

6

In Which a Young Man Is Dumbfounded

It was now six o'clock and Gerald had not yet seen his hostess. She had been out when he arrived at Tigh na Feidh, but Mac had said that the girls did most of the cooking, so probably by this time she would be in the kitchen.

The house was so strangely built—with so many queer little passages—that it was not an easy matter to find the kitchen. Gerald found it by hearing the sound of voices and laughter coming from a room at the end of a corridor. He opened the door and looked in. Yes, here were the two girls, cooking and enjoying a joke.

Gerald had heard quite a lot about Phil MacAslan (Sir Walter had said she was "full of beans and very good fun"; Mr. MacTaggart had said "Miss Phil is a very business-like young lady"; her brother had said she was "almost as good as a boy"). None of these descriptions had interested Gerald; in fact they had "put him off." He was struck dumb when he saw her.

She was beautiful—yes, beautiful! She was slender and graceful with dark curls and a smooth creamy complexion, slightly tanned by the sun; her eyes were greeny brown like a mountain burn, sparkling with life.

Phil was standing at the kitchen table, kneading a doughy sort of mess. She looked up and exclaimed, "Oh, there you are! I'm sorry I was out when you arrived. Donny and I went for a walk. I'm Phil, of course, and this is Donny Eastwood."

Gerald tried to say, "I'm Gerald," but he found that he couldn't. His lips were so dry that he couldn't utter a word. He stood and gazed at her.

"Mac said you were talking to Malcolm," said Phil. "But I expect he was doing most of the talking."

Gerald moistened his lips and said, "I'm Gerald, of course."

"Of course," said Phil, nodding.

Gerald came forward and held out his hand.

"Mine are all floury," said Phil. "I'm making oatcakes for tea, but you can shake hands with Donny. I hope you like oatcakes, Gerald."

"Yes, I like them very much," said Gerald.

"Good! We all like them—which means I must make a lot—but I'm so used to making them that I could do it with my eyes shut." She rolled out the oatcake, cut it into neat triangles and put them on the girdle.

"I'll watch them," said the other girl, who had not spoken before. "And I'll grill the trout (shall I?) while you show Mr. Burleigh-Brown his room. Or would you rather have them fried?"

"Grilled, I think . . . but you had better call him Gerald unless you want him to call you Miss Eastwood."

Phil rinsed her hands at the sink, took off her apron, flung it onto a chair and turned and smiled at him. "I'll show you," she said.

The smile finished Gerald. His heart bounded—and was lost. All in a moment he knew that his heart had gone forever! She was the most beautiful creature he had ever seen; she was dear and sweet and friendly; she was quite, quite perfect; there was nobody like her in all the world!

Gerald had met girls who attracted him; he had told Bess

that he was very fond of Penelope—and it was true. He had told Bess that if Penelope had been the daughter of a grocer (instead of the daughter of an American millionaire and used to every luxury that money could buy), he would have asked her to marry him . . . but he had never felt like this. He had never believed that he could feel like this about a girl.

So this was love! What was more it was love at first sight—a phenomenon which Gerald had always thought impossible! How could you love someone you had never seen before—someone you knew nothing about? Love at first sight was plain silly. It was something you read about in romances. It couldn't happen in real life—but it had happened to him. It had happened because he *did* know her, he knew exactly what she was like. I've been waiting for her all my life, thought Gerald as he followed her upstairs.

Phil led the way along a narrow stone passage, up three steps, round a bend, and down two steps to a little square landing with two doors opening off it. "That's Mac's room and this is yours," she explained. "The roof leaks—you can see the mark on the ceiling—but the bed is comfortable, which is the main thing—and the room is fairly warm because it's over the dining-room. The bells don't work, of course, but if you want anything you can hammer on Mac's door, can't you?"

"Yes," agreed Gerald.

"I wish we could put in fixed basins, but the walls are so thick and solid that we can't. There's only one bathroom, which is a frightful nuisance. You'll have to fight for your bath, Gerald."

"Fight for my bath?"

"Yes, you mustn't be polite about it," explained Phil. "When you hear the water running away, you must lurk in the passage and make a dash for it the moment the door opens. Fortunately we've got a marvellous stove, so there's always plenty of hot water. That's *absolutely* necessary of course." She added, "This room is in the old part of the house. Look how thick the walls are."

"It's like a fortress!" Gerald exclaimed.

"Perhaps it was—at one time," said Phil dreamily. "I wish we knew more about its history. In the old books it's just called 'the Look-Out Tower.' Daddy thinks that people lived here to keep watch for the approach of enemies and warned the surrounding country by lighting a bonfire . . . but nobody knows *really* because our great-great-grandfather rebuilt it and added on bits and pieces. The view is nice, isn't it?"

They stood at the window together and looked out.

The view was beautiful. There were mountains and rocks, heathery hills and green valleys and little sparkling burns . . . but, to tell the truth, Gerald was so conscious of Phil, standing beside him with her shoulder almost touching his arm, that he was unable to appreciate the view. He felt quite giddy. Then, when she looked up at him, surprised at his silence, he managed to control his feelings.

"It's a good site for a Look-Out Tower," he said at last.

"Yes, it is," agreed Phil. "Behind that door in the corner there's a sort of ladder which leads up to one of the funny little turrets. You can see for miles from there. If you've got a telescope, you can see deer on the hill. Sometimes, when Daddy and Mac are stalking, I bring a glass and climb the ladder and watch them. It's rather fun. I can see quite a lot of the sport—unless of course they go over the shoulder of Ben Ghaoth—but even then I know what's going on because if the wind is in the right direction I can hear the shot."

"Phil," said Gerald, "I don't want to shoot a stag."

"I thought you had come for the stalking," she said in surprise.

"I came because Sir Walter MacCallum said I would be useful. The idea was that I was to help to improve the herd by killing 'switches.' Malcolm showed me some of the ugly horns he had collected (and explained that the deformities are hereditary), so I wouldn't mind doing that. But now your father has written to Mac, saying that I'm to be given the chance of killing at least one good stag. What am I to do?"

"You must do it, of course," replied Phil with a little smile.

"But if I wrote to your father and explained——"

"It wouldn't be any good," Phil told him. "It isn't only that Daddy expects people to do as he tells them. It's partly because 'the Honour of the House' is involved. When a guest comes to Ardfalloch, he must be given of its best. That's the Gael's idea of hospitality."

"I suppose you think I'm crazy," said Gerald with a sigh.

"No, I don't," she replied. "You see I feel the same. I simply couldn't shoot a stag—nor a hind either—but it's illogical."

"I don't know what you mean!"

She sat down on the broad window-seat and looked up at him gravely. "I'll tell you," she said. "You've seen Malcolm's map, haven't you? The deer-forest looks enormous, but there are only certain places where there is food. So it can only support a certain number of deer. Daddy and Malcolm know the exact number of deer (stags and hinds) which can live in comfort at Ard na Feidh."

"Mac said you didn't mind shooting foxes," said Gerald.

"I suppose you think that's illogical too," Phil suggested. "It is—in a way—but foxes are cruel. Foxes kill deer-calves and young lambs and chickens. A fox got into my hen-run and killed eleven pullets . . . and then jumped out and left them lying. I wouldn't have minded if he had killed one and taken it with him to feed his cubs. Foxes are much worse now because there are no rabbits for them to feed on," added Phil with a sigh.

"You mean they all died of that rabbit disease? So the rabbit disease was a bad thing——"

"No, it was a good thing," interrupted Phil. "There's more good grass for the deer. It's awfully difficult to say what's good and what's bad. If you upset the balance by eliminating one pest, you find you've encouraged another. You find that something unforeseen has happened—something you never thought of—and you've got to do something about it. That's why I kill foxes."

"Do you shoot them with a gun?"

"No, with a small rifle—a .22—I have to because they're a frightful nuisance and Daddy and Mac haven't time."

There was a short silence. Then Gerald said, "Tell me more about deer. I want to learn all I can. You've been here all your life so——"

"Yes, I've lived here all my life," agreed Phil. "I've seen what happens when the winter is long and hard. Six years ago there was a very long hard winter. The snow lay deep in the corries . . . and the corries are the places where the grass grows, the places where the stags find their food. If the snow lies deep, it takes a long time to melt. That's the dangerous time. I went up with Daddy one morning and it was dreadful," declared Phil, her eyes widening at the recollection. "We found deer which had died of starvation. We found deer which were so weak that they couldn't get up and run away when they saw us. They were too weak to move when eagles attacked them. It was dreadful! And the worst of it was we couldn't do anything to help them. Daddy had to shoot them to put them out of their misery. It was the only thing to do. Daddy was so upset that he cried. His cheeks were wet with tears. I cried too. Oh, Gerald, it was so—so dreadful that I couldn't stop crying. I cried all night."

"You father shouldn't have taken you——"

"Yes, he should!" interrupted Phil. "It was right to take me and let me see it. We ought not to shut our eyes to things that happen, however dreadful they are. Before that I had been silly—I hated it when they killed deer—but after I had seen what happened (seen with my own eyes) I understood."

"Malcolm fed them this year."

She nodded. "Yes. He wasn't keen on it, but Sir Walter told him how to do it. I came up here one morning with Malcolm and saw them enjoying the food. It was rather nice watching them, you know, but feeding deer isn't natural; it isn't really the answer. (I mean, a deer-forest should stand on its own feet.) And anyhow you can only do it for a few weeks in the year until the snow has melted and the grass is growing. You couldn't go on feeding deer all the time. For one thing, it would be too expensive and; for another, there would be no stalking."

"No stalking?" echoed Gerald in surprise.

"They would become quite tame, of course, and instead of running away from the scent of man they would gather round, waiting to be fed. See?"

"Yes, of course! I never thought of that."

Phil continued, "I'll tell you another horrible thing that happens when a forest becomes overcrowded: the deer come down from the hills and eat the crops—and the farmers shoot them! You can't blame the farmers (the crops are their livelihood), but some of the farmers haven't got rifles, so they shoot the deer with shot-guns. That's awful because the deer are wounded and run away and die in agonies."

"But you've got high fences to keep the deer from straying, haven't you?"

"We try to do that," replied Phil. "But if they're very hungry they get through somehow. I've seen whole fields of crops—mostly root crops—which have been eaten and trampled on and destroyed by hungry deer. So you see, Gerald, they must be killed to keep the balance right. They must be shot by people who know how to shoot. A shot through the heart is an easy death compared with starvation."

"A deer-forest is a big responsibility," said Gerald thoughtfully.

"Yes, it is," agreed Phil. "If you own a deer-forest you've got to look after it properly. It doesn't pay, of course—in fact it costs quite a lot of money, one way and another. You can let it for the season, but it isn't very satisfactory because you never know what the people you let it to will do. Sometimes it's all right, and sometimes not. A deer-forest is like . . . well, it's like a hen-run," declared Phil, smiling at the ridiculous comparison. "If you keep too many hens in a confined space, they peck one another. If you keep too many in a barn, they eat each other's tails——"

"What!"

"They do, really, said Phil, nodding. She added, "Even a hedge has to be looked after properly. If you don't prune it every year, it straggles all over the place."

"A deer-forest has to be pruned," said Gerald thoughtfully. "That's what you mean, isn't it?"

"Yes."

"Sir Walter told me a bit—and lent me a book—but you've made it much clearer."

"I'm glad," said Phil. "You're going out tomorrow, and you're going to enjoy it."

"Well, perhaps."

"Listen, Gerald! You must shoot one good stag. Kill him with a shot through his heart. That will satisfy everybody. You need never kill another."

"You're making fun of me," said Gerald, smiling. "But that's what I shall do . . . if I can."

7

Which Concerns Itself with Four Good Companions

The day following Gerald's arrival at Tigh na Feidh was dull and rainy; the visibility was too poor for stalking, but the four young people arrayed themselves in rain-coats and walked up the path beside the burn.

Mac was disappointed—he had been looking forward to taking his new friend for a day's stalking—but Gerald did not mind.

There was something very pleasant about life at Tigh na Feidh. It was peaceful and easy-going and his companions were delightful. He was becoming more deeply in love with Phil every moment. Gerald was at the stage when it was a joy to watch her, to mark the graceful turn of her head, to listen to her voice. It was a pleasure to be of service to her, to fetch logs for the fire, or open a door for her, or to trim a lamp and to put it on the table by her side. Then she would look up and smile and thank him. (Later he would want more, but for the moment this was enough). He became fond of Mac too. In fact, Gerald decided that Mac was one of the best fellows he had ever known in all his life.

Mac and Phil were devoted to each other—that was easily

seen—sometimes they teased each other and occasionally, when they disagreed, they indulged in wordy warfare half in fun and half in earnest. Then suddenly one or other of them would begin to laugh . . . and it was all over in a moment.

He liked Donny Eastwood—nobody could help liking Donny—but she was so quiet and reserved that she remained a shadowy figure to Gerald.

The four had gone some way up the burn when they met Malcolm coming down and stopped to speak to him. He was carrying a string of small trout.

"I was just thinking these would be nice for your supper," he explained.

"Oh, lovely!" cried Phil.

"You didn't get those on a rod," declared Mac.

"That is so," Malcolm agreed. He smiled and added, "There are other ways of catching fish. You are knowing that, Mac. Or maybe you have forgotten what you used to be doing when you were a wee lad?"

"What about the weather?" enquired Mac anxiously.

"Och, it is not good," the man replied. "Tomorrow will be misty too, but it will clear when the wind changes. That is what I am thinking. Then we will be going out early and Mr. Burleigh-Brown will be killing his first stag."

"Sickening, isn't it?" Mac exclaimed as they walked on. "Last week we had splendid weather and now, when Gerald is here, down comes the mist. I'd like to take a huge broom and sweep it all away!"

There were two days of mist and rain, then on the Friday evening Malcolm came in to tell them that the wind had changed and tomorrow would be "a grand day on the hill" and to ask if they wanted to start early.

"Yes, of course!" cried Mac. "You're on, aren't you, Gerald? You don't mind getting up early?"

He did not wait for Gerald's reply, but followed Malcolm out of the room to make the necessary arrangements.

"Is Malcolm always right?" asked Gerald.

"Usually," replied Phil. She smiled and added, "If he

happens to be wrong once in a while, there's always a good reason for it. I mean, it doesn't affect his confidence in himself."

When Gerald awoke the next morning, he saw that it was still very misty and wondered whether this was one of the occasions when Malcolm was wrong. However, he heard Mac whistling cheerfully in his room across the landing, so he got up and dressed quickly, putting on the garments which Sir Walter had advised: old riding-breeches and khaki puttees and strong black boots with rubber soles. His brown leather jacket had weathered to a greenish tinge—he had worn it in Africa—so it was admirable for camouflage on a Scottish hillside. He went down to breakfast and found Mac already seated at the table wearing an old kilt, tattered and stained, a Harris jacket which had seen better days, thick grey stockings and nailed boots. Round his waist was a belt of khaki webbing in which he carried a telescope and a sheathed knife.

"What about the mist?" asked Gerald.

"It will clear," replied Mac. "Phil laughs at Malcolm, but he's lived here all his life and nine times out of ten he's right about the weather."

Old Kirsty had cooked breakfast—the girls had not come down—so the two young men ate quickly and, for a time, there was silence.

"Mac," said Gerald at last, "I'm rather scared about this business. As you know, I've never shot deer before. I'm quite a good shot at a target, but supposing I wound the creature? I'd really rather watch you shoot it."

"We've all got to start," Mac pointed out. "And Dad said in his letter that you were to have the chance of killing a good stag. I know how you feel; I felt the same about my first stag: butterflies in the tummy?"

"Yes," admitted Gerald.

"We may not see a stag—or have a chance to kill him. You realise that, don't you? But if we do, I'll be ready to finish him off. Does that make you feel better?"

"Yes, a whole lot better," said Gerald gratefully.

"All right then! But there's no need to say anything to Malcolm. See?"

Gerald nodded. The promise had taken a weight off his mind and he finished his breakfast with a better appetite.

The morning mist was still clinging to the hillside when the two set out together, but before they had gone far the sun was struggling through. It looked like a big golden ball in the sky. Mac had arranged to meet Malcolm and the boy with the pony at a certain rock. From here they could ford the burn by some stepping-stones and strike upwards to the shoulder of the hill.

The mist did not trouble Mac; he knew the path too well. Gerald, following him, could hear the tinkle of the burn and, far away, the cry of a curlew, very faint and wild. Gerald was excited now. He was not so "scared." He hoped that he would be able to do what was expected of him. He must do exactly as he was told. That was the important thing.

"It's a pity we can't go different ways," said Mac as he led the way to the rendez-vous. "But Malcolm wouldn't have it. Malcolm says Colin MacTaggart isn't experienced enough to stalk a stag—in fact, Malcolm doesn't think Colin will ever be any use. But I'm not worrying too much about that."

"Malcolm's standard is high," suggested Gerald, smiling.

"Yes, he expects too much. Colin is young and keen; he wants to do well, which is more than half the battle. I like him," continued Mac. "He's a good lad. He supports his mother (who is a widow) and two young brothers who are still at school. Dad has given the family a cottage to live in. It's a very small cottage near the bridge—not much of a place, but Mrs. MacTaggart has done what she can with it. She wants to make 'a nice home' for her boys."

"Any relation of the innkeeper?" asked Gerald.

"Yes, Colin's father was his nephew—and I rather think he helps them a bit—but all the same they're having a struggle to make ends meet. Colin's clothes are old and worn—

there's not much warmth in them—but, although they're darned and patched, they're always clean and tidy. I feel sorry for them, Gerald."

Gerald felt sorry for them too. He had seen Colin and liked him; the boy had pleasant manners. He was tall and good-looking with bright red hair, a clear complexion and a shy smile, which displayed excellent teeth. There was something very attractive about Colin MacTaggart. Gerald had decided that at the end of his visit to Tigh na Feidh, he would give Colin a substantial tip. (Gerald was getting a generous salary from Sir Walter, so he could afford to be generous.)

Malcolm was waiting for them at the stepping-stones with the boy and the pony, so they crossed the burn and set off up the hill.

"I thought you were bringing Colin," said Mac. "It would have been good experience for him."

"He is no use, that one," growled Malcolm.

"Give him time," said Mac.

Almost at once the mist began to evaporate; a breeze sprang up and blew the melting shreds away and the hills stood up in bold ridges and jagged crests against the pale blue sky.

Mac had been talking to Malcolm, but now he turned back to his guest. "We're going to try the shoulder of Ben Ghaoth," he said. "It's a stiff climb, but the stags are still on the high ground and we're pretty sure to find a good one up there."

Gerald nodded. "The air is marvellous; I could climb for hours without getting tired."

"Good," said Mac.

An hour's solid climbing brought them out of the heather onto the bare hillside. It was hot and shadeless, so Gerald was glad when they turned the shoulder of the hill and felt the wind in their faces; it was a cool west wind from the Atlantic.

They left the boy and the pony in the shade of a rock and went on up a scree of loose stones. Gerald, looking back, saw the country spread before him like a map: forest and heather, lochs and tarns sparkling in the morning sunshine. It was a glorious view. He was glad he had seen Malcolm's map of Ard na Feidh, for he was able to orient himself. He could see the green holms where the hinds found shelter; beyond that was the river and beyond the river was the road which divided Ard na Feidh from Glen Veigh. Just below the hill where he was standing there were heathery slopes and rough grassy hollows and screes of greyish black stones. He could see the funny little turrets peeping up from behind a rise in the ground and it struck him that perhaps Mac's great-great-grandfather had not added the turrets to Tigh na Feigh "just for fun;" a lantern, placed there on a dark night might guide a belated wanderer home. Perhaps, at this very minute, Phil was watching from the turret with a telescope. . . . Dear, sweet, beautiful Phil!

But this was not time to moon over Phil. His companions had gone on, so Gerald scrambled up the scree and found that they had reached the top of the slope and halted there. He saw now that this hill was not really the top but merely an excrescence on the shoulder of the mountain. The land dipped to a bog-filled dell and then rose, steeper and more rocky, to the mountain peak. Malcolm had taken out his telescope and was scanning the hills.

"Look you, Mac!" he was saying eagerly. "Look you over towards Ben Ghaoth! There is a staggie at the entrance of the corrie where we killed the fourteen-pointer two years ago."

Mac already had his telescope out and had rested it on a convenient rock, so Gerald took Sir Walter's field glasses out of their leather case and focussed them. For a few moments he could see nothing but the bare hillside, shimmering in the heat-haze that rose from the damp ground, but presently he caught sight of something brown, something that moved.

Mac had seen it too. "Yes, it's a stag," he said.

"It is a very big stag," declared Malcolm. "It is too far to see his points, but he is a good-sized beast—so he is!"

"There's your stag, Gerald," said Mac.

Between the stalkers and their quarry lay the boggy declivity and a steep hillside covered with boulders and loose stones—a difficult approach! If they were to dislodge a stone, they might start a small avalanche which would warn the stag. Malcolm explained this to Gerald, adding that one thing in their favour was the direction of the wind. It was blowing directly in their faces, so there was no chance of the beast getting their scent. Deer have such a keen sense of smell that they can scent man from an incredibly long distance and one whiff, borne by a vagrant breeze, will send them bounding away over the hills.

"They scent you before they can see you," explained Mac.

"Come," said Malcolm, shutting his telescope and starting off.

Gerald followed him and Mac brought up the rear. The boggy patch presented no difficulties, but when they had climbed up the other side, it was not so easy to walk quietly. The stones crunched beneath their feet and rattled down the slope, but fortunately the ground soon became more level and was knit together by tufts of coarse yellow grass. Gerald noticed that Malcolm was walking on these tufts and avoiding the bare patches, so he was careful to place his feet in the man's footprints.

By this time they had descended the hillock in an oblique direction and had lost sight of the stag. Its position was marked by a piled-up mass of black igneous rock. Malcolm stopped here and signed to his companions to wait while he reconnoitred. Then he swung himself up and disappeared.

Gerald and Mac waited without speaking. It was very still. Not a blade of grass moved, for they were sheltered from the wind; not a creature stirred. The sun beat down, warming their backs. The rocks were hot to the touch.

It seemed to Gerald that they waited a long time, but probably it was only a few minutes, then Malcolm reappeared and made a signal to them.

Gerald did not understand what he meant, but Mac had dropped onto his hands and knees and was creeping round the corner of the rocks, so Gerald followed his example . . . and presently they found themselves on a stony ridge looking down into a narrow valley. A small burn ran down the middle of the valley, zig-zagging its way between stones. There was no sign of the stag; he seemed to have vanished into thin air.

"He has moved into the upper part of the corrie," Malcolm whispered.

"Are you sure?" asked Mac.

Malcolm nodded. "I saw him go, but he moved slowly and quietly. He was not frightened at all. He will be there, feeding—that is what I am thinking."

Gerald looked up the little valley and saw that it narrowed to a cleft in the hills. From here the burn fell in a miniature waterfall over a flat rock. There was a passage between the burn and the cliff's edge, a narrow path masked by a huge black boulder.

"We could try the top part," Malcolm whispered. "It is a favourite place, for the burn rises there and the grass is sweet and good. The corrie widens out above the bend."

"Yes," agreed Mac. "The only thing is he might get our scent if we go up that way. Could we go back and come at him from the top?"

Malcolm considered this. At last he said, "I doubt if we could get near enough—and it is a difficult thing to be shooting a stag from above. I am thinking we will need to risk him getting our scent and follow him up the burn."

"We'll risk it," Mac agreed, nodding.

They went down to the burn as silently as possible, crossed it and climbed up the opposite bank. It took them several minutes to reach the little waterfall. Gerald could now see that the passage between the burn and the cliff was less narrow than he had thought, for the boulder stood in front of the opening, not flush with it.

Malcolm knelt down and examined the damp sod very carefully. "Yes, he has come this way," he whispered. "There are his slots . . . but I am a wee bit puzzled, Mac."

"Why? What's the matter?"

"It is just that he is a heavier beast than I thought."

"Well, it doesn't matter, does it?" said Mac impatiently. "Let's get on, Malcolm."

Malcolm nodded and rose. "We'll climb up the cliff. You will be getting a better chance at him that way."

The three of them scrambled up the side of the cliff. It was warm with the sun and its crevices were filled with tufts of grass and ferns and little pools of water. From the top of the cliff they could see into the top part of the corrie—a small valley filled with boulders which had fallen from the mountain. Between the boulders the grass was green and lush.

A stag was grazing quietly amongst the boulders, quite unaware of their approach.

8

Which Describes the Slaying of a Stag

Gerald could sense his companions' excitement. It was the excitement of the hunter when he sees his quarry within his grasp. Gerald's feeling was different: there, before his eyes, was the creature which he was obliged to kill. He was obliged to kill it—if he could. He had no option. There was no getting out of it now. If it had been a "switch," he would not have minded; there were good reasons for killing a switch, but this was no switch. This was a beautiful graceful creature, a stag in his prime with ten—yes, ten—points to his branching antlers.

All this had flashed through Gerald's head in a moment; meanwhile he had taken up his position; he had spread out his legs and settled his rifle on a jutting piece of rock. Mac lay down beside him, ready to keep his word.

The stag was about a hundred and twenty yards away—an easy shot—but he was grazing towards them, head on.

"Wait," breathed Mac.

Gerald waited. He realised that the stag might sense their presence and be off like an arrow from a bow, but there might be a few seconds when he would stand still with his head lifted, sniffing the air. That would be Gerald's chance.

I must do it, Gerald decided. If I do it properly, if I shoot him clean through the heart, I need never do it again. This will be my first stag—and my last. Having made this decision, he felt better; his heart, which had been thumping uncomfortably, slowed down and his breath came more easily.

The stag went on grazing. It was so still and sheltered in the corrie that Gerald could hear the click of the creature's hoof against a stone. He was coming nearer very slowly, seeking out the tender green grass between the boulders.

Suddenly the stag raised his head . . . and listened. His glistening brown body turned sideways, he sniffed the air. By this time he was a hundred yards away—not more.

Gerald aimed just behind the shoulder. The shot rang out, crisp and clear, startling the echoes, and the stag bounded into the air. Gerald thought he had missed—but he had not missed! After one bound towards the burn, the beast rolled over, his four feet beat the air for a few moments, then all was still.

"Oh, good work!" exclaimed Mac in delight. "Oh, well done, Gerald!"

He had scarcely spoken when a huge brown beast bounded up from behind a boulder and fled madly across the corrie.

"Shoot, man!" cried Malcolm excitedly. "Shoot, Mac—for Gaud's sake shoot!"

Mac hesitated with his finger on the trigger of his rifle. "But Malcolm, it's a hind!" he exclaimed.

By this time the beast had sprung across the burn with one enormous leap—an incredible leap—and was halfway up the other side of the corrie, its hooves clattering amongst the loose stones and sending small avalanches of stones down the steep slope. It was well out of range now, so Mac took his eyes off it and turned to look at Malcolm.

"Och, Mac, why did you not shoot?" lamented Malcolm. "Yon was no hind! It was a great big ugly hummel! Och, Mac, you should have shot when I was telling you!"

"Good heavens! Are you sure?"

"Am I sure? Have you ever seen a hind that size? The brute had buttocks like a horse! It was all of twenty stone—aye, it was more!"

"Oh, well, it's gone now," said Mac.

"Aye, it's gone," agreed Malcolm sorrowfully. "And dear knows when we will be seeing it again."

He rose as he spoke and leapt down from the rock to gralloch the kill.

Gerald followed. He was glad he had done it successfully.

Mac followed his companions more slowly. He was upset about the hummel and realised he had been a fool not to shoot when Malcolm had told him; he should have trusted Malcolm. The loss of the hummel had taken the edge off his pleasure at Gerald's success, but it was no use crying over spilt milk. Gerald had done well—he couldn't have done better—he must be given his due meed of praise.

Malcolm had taken out his tape measure and was measuring the stag's antlers.

"It is not a big head," Malcolm was saying, "but it is a very perfect one. You will not be seeing a more perfect ten-pointer for a long time, Mr. Burleigh-Brown. Look you, the tines are beautifully shaped above and below."

"Yes," agreed Mac, "it's a beautiful head. Your first stag, Gerald! You got him straight through the heart. It was a fine shot, wasn't it, Malcolm?"

"It was well judged," agreed Malcolm . . . and indeed he was satisfied. Mr. Burleigh-Brown had waited in patience until the right moment and then had shot without hesitation. It was a good performance for a novice.

Gerald said nothing. He had put his hand on the creature's neck, the fur was soft and warm to the touch. Ten minutes ago the creature had been alive. Now it was dead. ("I'm sorry, old chap," said Gerald inwardly. "I had to do it.") Aloud he said, "He's a beautiful creature. Can you tell how old he is, Malcolm?"

"He would be about eleven years old," replied Malcolm. "He is in his prime. When a stag is past fourteen, he will be going downhill, just as a man who is past forty. This head is worth mounting, Mr. Burleigh-Brown."

"Yes, that's right," agreed Mac. "We'll send it off to the taxidermist in Inverness tomorrow morning. I must write to Dad and tell him about it. He'll be pleased. Sir Walter will be pleased too." He added, "It's nearly three o'clock and I'm as hungry as a wolf. Let's sit down in the shade of the cliff and eat our sandwiches."

They sat down together and opened their packets of sandwiches.

"I was ready, but you didn't need any help," said Mac.

"It was a help," replied Gerald. "The knowledge that you were standing by steadied me."

"You were as cool as a cucumber!"

"Not really."

Gerald had not felt hungry, but now that he had begun to eat his sandwiches he discovered that he was . . . and he was beginning to feel a good deal better. "Hullo!" he added in surprise. "What is Malcolm doing?"

Mac looked up and saw that Malcolm had collected some sticks and dry grass.

"Is he going to cook the liver for his dinner?" asked Gerald.

"Good heavens, no!" exclaimed Mac, roaring with laughter. "Malcolm is much too civilised. He's going to send up a smoke signal for the boy to bring the pony, that's all."

Gerald laughed too. "How silly of me! I might have guessed that was what he was doing."

"It wasn't silly," said Mac quickly. "You couldn't possibly know what he was doing. It was just that I couldn't help laughing at the idea of Malcolm cooking the stag's liver—and eating it. Malcolm has no opinion of venison as food. Not even when his mother cooks it and hands it to him on a plate. Of course you're used to camping out (you've done it in Africa, haven't you?), so it was quite a natural mistake."

Gerald realised that Mac wanted to put him in the right—and he was rather touched. There was something very charming and boyish about Mac. He was intuitive and considerate; he was extraordinarily kind. I don't know when I've met any man I like so much, thought Gerald.

Malcolm had finished cleaning the stag and, having washed his hands in the burn, sat down a little way off to have his lunch.

"Tell me, Mac," said Gerald in a low voice. "I want to know more about that hummel. I suppose the reason Malcolm was so upset about losing the creature was the fact that calves sired by a hummel are unlikely to have horns."

"Very unlikely to have good horns, anyway," Mac replied. He smiled and added, "Malcolm will give us no peace until the beast is dead."

"It was strange seeing it."

"Yes, I was surprised. He must have been lying in the shade of that big boulder, sleeping or chewing the cud. Your shot scared him."

"He was a large brute."

"They often are. Some people think it's because they don't grow horns every year as other stags do, so all their strength goes into their bodies. Others say it's because they're so easily mistaken for hinds." Mac raised his voice and called to Malcolm: "Malcolm, have you ever seen that hummel before?"

"I have not," replied Malcolm promptly. "He would not be living now if I had been seeing him before. I would have put an end to him myself. We must see and kill him before the rut starts."

"Where can he have come from?"

"He will have come over the river from Glen Veigh."

Mac and Gerald smiled at each other: everything bad "came over the river from Glen Veigh"!

"Couldn't a hummel just be a freak?" asked Gerald.

"I suppose it might happen," Malcolm replied. "But, to my mind, it's unlikely. Besides yon hummel is not a young beast. I would have been seeing him before if he had grown from a calf in my forest. I am about the place at all seasons of the year—not like Mackenzie who sits by the fire on his backside for the most part of the winter," added Malcolm scornfully.

Soon after this the boy arrived with the pony; the carcase of the stag was lifted and strapped securely onto the pony's back.

"It looks too heavy for that small pony," Gerald remarked.

"These small Shetlands are very sturdy," Mac told him. "In fact they're ideal for the job. They're hardy and surefooted and very wise. One day we were right over the other side of Ben Ghaoth and a mist came down. It came suddenly and unexpectedly and it was so thick that you couldn't see a yard. Even Malcolm, who knows the forest like the palm of his hand, was doubtful about getting home. Not so Queenie! She set off quite confidently and brought us home over the hills by the shortest way. It's amazing what strong instincts these creatures have."

The little cavalcade started off. Malcolm and the boy and the pony in front, Mac and Gerald following . . . and talking.

"Did you enjoy your day?" Mac asked.

"I enjoyed the stalking; it was grand fun and very interesting indeed, but I didn't enjoy killing that lovely animal."

"You didn't enjoy it? But you did it splendidly!"

"I did it because I had to," Gerald explained. "I suppose I'm different from other men, but, quite honestly, I don't want to kill another."

"You don't want to kill another?"

"No."

"But, Gerald——"

"Oh, I'll shoot switches and I'm quite willing to shoot that hummel if we see it, but——"

"Didn't it give you a thrill? I remember my first stag: I was fifteen and I was out with Dad and Malcolm and Sir Walter MacCallum. It was a hot day (not a breath of wind) and we had done no good. The stags were restless. We had seen three and had toiled after them, uphill and downhill for hours. I was tired and bored and I had a blister on my heel, which was giving me hell. Then, quite unexpectedly, we came upon a nine-point stag grazing quietly in a little quarry. Malcolm gave the signal for us to lie down, so down we went behind a bank with heather on the top of it. Sir Walter was lying beside me—it had been decided that if we got within range of a good stag he was to kill it—but instead of shooting the beast he turned his head and smiled at me and put his rifle into my hands. I had shot with his rifle before, but only at a target, so I couldn't believe he meant me to kill the stag. I looked at him and he looked at me—and nodded. I was shaking all over with excitement and my hands were wet with perspiration, but somehow or other I pulled myself together and took careful aim and shot. The stag bounded for a few yards—I thought I had missed—then it rolled over and over down the slope and lay still. Sir Walter patted my back and said, 'Well done, laddie!' so then I knew it was all right.

"It was an easy shot, of course," explained Mac. "That was why Sir Walter had given it to me—but I had done it. I had killed my first stag! Oh, I was wild with delight! I could have sung and danced with joy. I felt like a king."

"I don't blame you," Gerald told him. "I just feel differently, that's all. My stag was a beautiful creature; he was alive and free; he was grazing happily; he had no idea that he had an enemy lurking behind a rock. Five minutes later he was a dead body, a carcase lying on the ground. I don't expect you to understand. We'll just have to agree that I'm a freak."

They looked at each other—and laughed—and went on down the hill in complete harmony.

9

Introduces Another Guest at the House of the Deer

When Gerald and Mac returned from the hill, Kirsty told them that Mr. Stoddart had arrived and was having tea with the two young ladies.

"Oh, good!" said Mac. "I told you about Oliver Stoddart, didn't I, Gerald? Come on in and meet him."

"I'll have a bath first—if you don't mind," replied Gerald (he had no wish to sit down at table dirty and dishevelled).

"Right-oh!" said Mac cheerfully. Then he arranged with Malcolm to send the stag's head to Inverness the following morning, and a haunch of venison to Sir Walter MacCallum, and went in to greet the new guest.

They all looked up when he went in, but it was Phil who spoke first. "Hullo!" she exclaimed. "You're back earlier than I expected. We didn't wait for you because Oliver was hungry."

"Hullo, Oliver! How are you?" said Mac. "I expect Phil has told you we've got a guest."

"Yes," replied Oliver.

"How did you get on?" asked Phil. "Did you have a good day?"

"Yes, splendid," replied Mac. "Couldn't have been better. Gerald did awfully well." He turned to Oliver and added, "Gerald Burleigh-Brown—he's a great chap—he has never done any stalking before, but he's got the idea all right. He killed his first stag today."

"Oh!" exclaimed Phil in delight. "Oh, I hope it was a good one?"

"A ten-pointer—a beautiful head! I'm having it mounted for him. He really did awfully well," repeated Mac, sitting down at the table. "Nobody could have guessed that it was his first day on the hill. He behaved like an old hand and was as cool as a cucumber; waited his chance and got the beast clean through the heart. Even Malcolm was pleased with his performance and said it was 'well judged.' "

Phil smiled. She was aware that this, from Malcolm, was the highest praise possible.

They went on talking about it. Oliver listened in silence, his face set in obstinate lines. He had been annoyed to discover that there was another guest at Tigh na Feidh, for he knew that the MacAslans could not afford more than one good stalker and it meant that he, himself, would not get so much sport. And, in addition to this, he was the kind of young man who prefers to be praised, rather than to hear of other young men's achievements. Last, but by no means least, it appeared to him that Phil was more interested in this new friend than she should be.

Oliver had known Phil for years of course; he had always looked upon her as a young sister; somebody who need not be considered very much. He enjoyed his bachelor life and the comforts provided for him by his doting mother.

Oliver was tall and good-looking with a pronounced wave in his fair hair. He shot well, danced well, and owned an exceedingly comfortable car, so he was able to amuse himself very pleasantly with the young women of his acquaintance . . . but just lately (for some reason or other) these simple pleasures had begun to pall and he had decided to get married. It was a big step to take and he debated it with himself, suggesting and rejecting various estimable young women who, he was assured, would accept him without hesitation. Finally he thought of Phil MacAslan.

There was no money there, of course (the MacAslans were as poor as church mice), but Oliver had enough money already. And there were advantages in an alliance with the family: not only would he be able to get good sport at Ardfalloch whenever he liked but, as MacAslan's son-in-law, he would be *persona grata* with other big landowners in the district.

Thus it was that when Oliver arrived at Tigh na Feidh, he looked at Phil with new eyes and saw at once how right he had been. She really was an attractive creature. Yes, thought Oliver, she was the very girl he wanted. So it was rather a blow to find a strange man in the house and to find that Phil seemed to be "interested" in him. It was rather a blow. . . . Well, perhaps not exactly a "blow," thought Oliver, because of course it would make no difference in the long run. Phil was a sensible girl and would realise her good fortune in having attracted such an eligible suitor as Oliver Stoddart.

Meanwhile Mac was feeling worried. Oliver seemed to be in one of his mulish moods. He had shown no enthusiasm over the story of this morning's sport. It would have been natural to say, "Oh, good show!" or something like that when Mac had explained about Gerald killing his first stag—any man would have said it! Mac was not used to dealing with difficult situations. His two guests were both older than himself and if they did not mix well, it would be ghastly. Mac wished—not for the first time—that his father were here.

Phil continued to chat . . . and she was so pleased at Gerald's success (which, quite rightly, she attributed to her talk with him) that she was unable to leave the subject alone. They had finished tea by this time, so they moved over to the big chairs by the fire.

"It *was* good, wasn't it?" said Phil, taking up a grey stocking which she had been darning.

"It was wonderful," agreed Donny enthusiastically.

"What was wonderful?" asked Oliver.

"I've just been telling you," said Mac. "Perhaps you weren't listening. This was Gerald's first day on the hill and he killed a ten-pointer—shot it clean through the heart."

Oliver hesitated. He had listened of course, but he had not been interested. He saw now that he should have shown a little enthusiasm for the exploit. His ill humour had done him no good, so perhaps it would be better to be civil about it.

"I wasn't really listening," he explained. "I've driven miles today and I was hungry. I think you said that this was your friend's first day at Ard na Feidh."

"It was his first day's stalking," said Mac (pleased that Oliver seemed to be emerging from his gloom). "It was his first day and his first stag. He has shot lions, of course."

Phil and Donny both looked up in astonishment.

"Lions?" asked Oliver incredulously.

Mac was smiling; he had just remembered this interesting fact. "Yes, when he was in Africa," said Mac.

"I don't believe it," declared Oliver.

"You don't believe it?"

"No, I don't," said Oliver, lying back in his chair and crossing his legs in a nonchalant manner. "You wouldn't believe it either if you knew the first thing about big-game shooting. My friend, Lucius Cottar, has done a lot of big-game shooting and he told me all about it."

"But, Oliver——"

"Big-game shooting in Africa isn't all that easy," declared Oliver, raising his voice and paying no attention to Mac's interruption. "You can't just take a rifle and go out and shoot a lion. You've got to get a permit; you've got to join a safari expedition and buy a lot of expensive equipment; you've got to hire boys to carry the stuff; you've got to——"

"I don't know anything about all that. I only know that Gerald has shot lions."

"How do you know?"

"He told me so himself."

"He was having you on, old boy," said Oliver, smiling in a supercilious manner.

"Do you mean he was lying?"

"You can put it like that if you like."

"How else can you put it?" asked Mac heatedly. "You say he's a liar. Well, he happens to be a friend of mine and I say he isn't."

"Oliver didn't mean that," put in Donny, trying to pour oil on the troubled waters.

"What did he mean?" asked Mac.

"If Gerald told Mac he had shot lions in Africa, he *did!*" cried Phil. "You can ask him of course——"

"I shall," said Oliver.

It was at this moment that the door opened and Gerald came in. He had had his bath and looked clean and cool and comfortable in grey flannel slacks and a blue pullover. He was a little surprised to find a somewhat strained atmosphere in the room . . . and dead silence.

10

In Which Donny Becomes Communicative

Phil was the first to recover. She jumped to her feet and introduced the guests to each other, adding hastily, "Go on, Mac. You can show Oliver his room; it's all ready for him. I'll make fresh tea for Gerald."

"Yes, of course!" agreed Mac. "Come on, Oliver. Where's your suitcase?"

The two men went off together, Phil fled to the kitchen and Donny came and sat down at the table beside Gerald.

"What was all that?" asked Gerald, smiling at her.

"Oh, nothing much! Oliver is rather a bore, that's all. Of course you don't know him yet, do you?"

Gerald agreed that he did not . . . though, as a matter of fact, he had sized up his fellow guest in one cool glance: rich and good-looking, rather spoilt and a bit too pleased with himself would have been his verdict on his fellow guest.

"Do you like it here?" asked Donny.

"Yes, it's a lovely place."

"It's like heaven," said Donny dreamily. "It's quite, quite perfect."

Gerald was a little surprised to find Donny Eastwood

communicative. He had liked her, of course, but so far she had spoken very seldom and had merely listened and smiled when the others were talking.

"Perhaps you think it's silly," continued Donny. "But really and truly Tigh na Feidh seems like heaven to me: the hills and the burns and the peacefulness and to be able to do what you like all the time; to talk or not talk; to be a little untidy; to go out for a walk and come in late—and make tea and have it when you want it—but principally to be with Phil and Mac. Phil is marvellous. You think so too, don't you?"

"Yes," said Gerald.

"They're so kind," continued Donny. "They're so good to me—and they don't think I'm silly."

"You aren't silly."

"Not here," she agreed. "I'm quite clever when I'm here. When people think you're silly, it makes you sillier."

Gerald agreed with this, for he had had much the same experience. He had been rather a fool. Then he had gone to stay with Bess in her London flat. She had cured him. She had made him feel clever. He explained this to Donny.

"That's very interesting," said Donny, looking at him with soft dove's eyes. "I thought perhaps I was the only person to feel like that—but you understand."

"Yes," said Gerald, nodding.

"Bess is your sister, isn't she? I read about her in the papers and saw her photographs. I wish I could have seen her on the stage, but of course I couldn't. I've often wondered whether she ever regrets leaving the stage and becoming an everyday sort of person."

"She doesn't," Gerald replied. "She's perfectly happy. She made a success on the stage and she's making a success of everyday life."

"Do you wish she were here, Gerald?"

Gerald hesitated. This was a very penetrating question. He was devoted to Bess; ever since he was a small boy he had loved Bess best in all the world. He still loved her dearly—not a bit less—but, somehow, he didn't wish she were here.

"Don't answer if you'd rather not," said Donny hastily. "I shouldn't have asked, of course. I just wondered, that was all." She sighed and added, "It won't be quite so nice now, you know."

There was no need to ask what she meant.

"We shall have to help them," Donny continued. "I mean help Mac and Phil. They aren't used to being patient and—and tactful. They're used to saying what they feel straight out."

"I like that," Gerald told her.

"Oh, so do I," agreed Donny. "People who have no fire in them are awfully stodgy. Phil and Mac often quarrel, you know. I mean they quarrel with each other. I used to be rather frightened, but then I realised that they were so fond of each other that it didn't matter. Now I sit on the fence and listen—and hold their coats. Then suddenly they begin to laugh and it's all over in a minute. Oliver Stoddart is quite different. If people don't agree with him, he gets angry and sulks."

There was a short silence.

At last Gerald said, "Perhaps he won't stay long."

"He'll stay as long as he gets 'good sport'—or until someone sends him an invitation that sounds more attractive," replied Donny. "And I think his friends are beginning to get rather tired of him. I don't know whether he's getting more didactic as he gets older or because the more you see of him the less you like him. I'm sorry for him," she added.

Gerald agreed that Mr. Stoddart was to be pitied. The reverse was true of Donny Eastwood. Gerald had begun by thinking she was a nice quiet girl—but rather dull—and now he found himself liking her very much indeed.

"Have you brothers or sisters?" he asked.

"Two brothers—Harold and Barney. They're both younger than I am and they escaped in time."

"Escaped?" asked Gerald.

She nodded. "Yes, they were rather stupid when they were little, but they got away in time and now they're quite clever. Barney is the lucky one. He fell down a cliff and broke his leg terribly badly, so he'll always be lame. I know it sounds queer, but it really was very lucky indeed because he has got exactly what he wanted, so he doesn't mind being lame. You can't have everything, can you?"

"What happened?" asked Gerald.

"We were staying at Targ with the MacRynnes (Tessa MacRynne was my best friend at school) and it was when we were there that the accident happened. It was nobody's fault, of course, but Colonel MacRynne took the responsibility for it and offered to have Barney trained to be his factor and to help him to look after his estate. Colonel MacRynne owns a great deal of property, so he really needs someone to help him—and Barney adores Colonel MacRynne, so he's terribly happy about it." Donny smiled and added, "You see what I meant when I said it was lucky that he broke his leg so badly."

Gerald saw. He said, "Well, that's Barney settled. What about Harold?"

"Harold is quite different," Donny replied. "He's much more serious than Barney. He's very good at figures, so he's going to be a Chartered Accountant. It's a very difficult exam, you know."

"I know," agreed Gerald.

"But he's working terribly hard, so I'm sure he'll pass . . . And I was just wondering if he could get a post in Sir Walter MacCallum's Ship-Yard?"

"I'll make a point of speaking to Sir Walter about him."

"Oh, that *would* be kind!"

"It wouldn't be kind," replied Gerald, smiling. "If Harold passes his exam, he'll be able to get a good post anywhere. Chartered Accountants don't grow on every bush."

"He's a good boy," said Donny earnestly. "He really is very good and conscientious and—and persevering, but I'm his sister, so naturally I think he's marvellous."

Harold's sister had become quite pink with excitement in talking about him and Gerald noticed that she was a great deal prettier than he had thought. In fact she was a very pretty girl (not beautiful like Phil, of course, but really very attractive). He soothed her down and assured her that Harold Eastwood sounded just the sort of chap that Sir Walter liked to get hold of. Young and keen and persevering. "Tell him to write to me," said Gerald. "I'll make an appointment for him. That's the best way."

As a matter of fact Gerald was rather intrigued by the story of Donny's brothers. She had said they had "escaped"; they had "got away in time." He wondered what they had escaped from and was about to enquire further into the matter when the door opened and Oliver Stoddart came in . . . and Donny shut up like a clam.

11

Which Concerns a Shopping Expedition

Early breakfast was the rule at the House of the Deer. Sometimes the girls had theirs later, but Mac was always early and so was Gerald . . . and today Oliver Stoddart was there too. He was sitting at the table demolishing a plateful of bacon and eggs when Gerald came downstairs.

"It's no good today," Mac was saying.

"No good? What do you mean?" asked Oliver. "You said I could have Malcolm today."

"So you could," agreed Mac. "But there's mist on the hill; the visibility is too bad for stalking."

"It's clearing," objected Oliver. "The mist is rising."

"Malcolm says it's coming down. Oh, it may clear in the afternoon, but that will be too late. I'm sorry, Oliver, but it really isn't any good when there's mist on Ben Ghaoth. You know that yourself."

Gerald changed the subject hastily by saying that he intended to walk down to Ardfalloch village this morning and asking if there were any commissions to be done.

"You can get a paper," said Mac. "And you can call for the letters at the post-office. I'd come with you if I could, but

I must write to Dad. I want his advice about several matters which can't be decided without him. I wish he were here," added Mac with a sigh.

"I want razor blades," said Oliver. "I can't use my electric razor here. You ought to install an engine and have the house wired. It would be much more convenient."

"Too expensive," said Mac crossly.

"It wouldn't cost much. My friend Lucius Cottar makes his own electricity. He has an engine that runs on oil. I could ask him about it."

"We couldn't afford it," declared Mac more crossly than before. Then he rose and stumped out of the room.

" 'Penny wise and pound foolish,' " muttered Oliver. "If this house were put in proper order, they could let the forest every season and get a lot of money for it."

"They wouldn't want to let it every season," Gerald pointed out. Then, before Oliver could reply, he too rose and went to get ready for his walk.

Tigh na Feidh was so cut off from the outside world that nearly everybody wanted something in the village, so Gerald was given a list of commissions. He was a little surprised at the variety of the things that were wanted and enquired somewhat anxiously if the shop (which adjoined the post-office) would be able to supply them.

"Oh, yes," said Phil. "Mrs. Grant has everything that anybody could possibly want. It may take her some time to find them, but you won't mind that, will you?"

Gerald replied that he did not mind at all. Phil's requirements included a shampoo powder to wash her hair—naturally this came first on the list! Gerald decided that if Mrs. Grant could not supply shampoo powder, he would take his car and scour the country for it.

Mac saw him off at the door and explained that there was a short cut to the village, a steep path down the hill, which led to a plantation of pine trees. "There's no bridge across the river," added Mac. "The nearest bridge is the hump-backed bridge—that's a mile farther downstream—but there are stepping-stones which will take you across dry-shod if the water isn't too high. We intend to put a light wooden bridge across the river one of these days, but there never seems to be enough money for the job."

"Don't worry. I'll get across somehow," said Gerald—and with that he strode off down the hill.

The thought of wet feet did not worry Gerald, nor did the gentle misty rain which had begun to fall. He had spent so long in Africa that he rather enjoyed the rain, and he had put on a khaki rain-coat, so he was equipped for any weather. The rain-coat was a peculiar garment (he had bought it in Johannesburg); it was old and faded and stained with red mud, but that was a mere detail. Nobody in Ardfalloch would care.

The object of Gerald's expedition this morning was to find out if there was a woman in the village who could knit him a pair of thick grey stockings like the ones Mac had been wearing. He, himself, had been wearing puttees for stalking, but they were hot and uncomfortable. At first he had put them on too tightly and then, when he had loosened them, they had flapped round his ankles. Stockings would be much easier.

At first the path was very steep and stony, but presently it took a turn round an outcrop of rock and broadened into a cart-track where there was a high wire fence. Beyond the fence was the plantation of pine trees. Gerald found the gate and shut it carefully behind him (he realised that the fence was there to protect the trees from the depredations of deer). The pines were about ten feet high; they stood in neat rows like a regiment of soldiers. No doubt they were a valuable crop and would be 'harvested' when they reached maturity, but you would have to wait a long time for your money!

The path went on down the hill for about half a mile. Then there was another fence and a gate which led to a clearing beside the river . . . and here, in this little sheltered corner, there was a group of oaks. They were old and gnarled with twisted branches, but in spite of their age they seemed healthy, for their foliage was green and thick. Perhaps this was because they were growing so close to the water.

These were the first hardwood trees that Gerald had seen in the vicinity, so he stopped to look at them. He wondered how they had come there and whether they were the survivors of a large forest. He must ask Mac their history—or perhaps he should ask Phil. She would be sure to know.

Just beyond the oaks Gerald found the stepping-stones (they were quite dry today), so he crossed the river and scrambled up the opposite bank onto the road. Ten minutes' brisk walk brought him to Ardfalloch village.

Mrs. Grant lived up to her reputation. She produced everything Gerald wanted, including the all-important shampoo powder, but these goods were so mixed up with a number of articles which Gerald did not want that he had quite a long time to wait for his parcel to be made up. Mrs. Grant had electric-light bulbs, brass door-knockers, postcards, fountain pens, headache powders, babies' rattles, seed potatoes, inkstands made of deers' horns, penwipers, artificial flowers, roller skates, sun-glasses, water pistols and boxes of fireworks all mixed up with knitted goods.

It was while Gerald was sitting upon the sack of seed potatoes—and marvelling at the diversity of Mrs. Grant's stock—that his eye fell upon a white Shetland shawl. It was a delicious garment, as light as a feather and as fine as lace—so he bought it for Margaret. He would have bought a postcard to send to Bess, but unfortunately the only ones left on the stand depicted Mont Blanc, the Statue of Liberty, the Eiffel Tower and the beach at Margate—all of which seemed unsuitable to despatch from Ardfalloch.

"How do you get all these things?" Gerald enquired.

"From my husband's second cousin's father-in-law," Mrs. Grant replied. "He has an emporium in Chicago and sends me a crate of articles he is not wanting. He sends it twice a year, so I am always well stocked. Would Miss Phil be interested in a mud-pack for her complexion? Mud-packs are all the go in Chicago."

"Miss Phil's complexion is perfect," replied her admirer.

"Well, maybe you are right," agreed Mrs. Grant.

Mrs. Grant tied up the parcel and Gerald stowed it away in the knapsack which he brought with him. Then he paid for the goods. He was surprised to find that his purchases were so cheap.

"Have you included the shawl?" he asked.

"Oh, I am not charging much for the shawl," replied Mrs. Grant, smiling. "It is just what I am doing to amuse myself in my spare time. I am very fond of babies."

This seemed a curious idea to Gerald. However, he could do nothing about it, so he thanked Mrs. Grant and said goodbye.

Then he called at MacTaggart's Inn.

12

In Which Gerald Makes New Friends

Mr. MacTaggart was in the bar, polishing glasses, but he was never too busy for a chat, so he greeted Gerald warmly and offered him one on the house.

"I am busy today," he said. "There is a meeting of the Ardfalloch Fire Brigade tonight, so we will be having drinks when it is over. Talking is dry work."

"You're the Captain, aren't you?" said Gerald, who had just remembered this interesting fact.

"That is so," agreed Mr. MacTaggart. He put down the glass which he had been polishing, leant his elbows on the counter and continued confidentially. "We are not exactly official, Mister Gerald. It was like this, you see. There was a fire in the stables at Glen Veigh and before the Brigade from Kincraig was arriving, the building was badly damaged, so one of the lads—it was Euan Dalgliesh—was saying it would be a good thing if we were having a Brigade of our own. The others were all for it. The only trouble was how to get the money. I was asking Mr. Ross and he was all for it too. He was giving us a cheque for a hundred pounds—he is a very fine gentleman, is Mr. Ross. So then we got together—me and some of the lads—and we bought a second-hand engine and brass helmets and such-like (just on our own, Mister Gerald). So far," said Mr. MacTaggart regretfully, "so far there has only been stacks and barns for us to be practising on, but we are always hoping for a real good blaze."

Gerald hid a smile. He said, "It was a good idea——"

"It was, indeed!" interrupted Mr. MacTaggart. "It was Euan's idea, but if it had not been for me, they would never have got much further. It is good to have ideas, but you need somebody like me to carry them out."

"You're the big fish," suggested Gerald.

"I am the big fish," agreed Mr. MacTaggart, smiling all over his plump face. "Everybody comes to me when they are wanting something done—or when they are wanting advice. They say, 'Ask Jamie MacTaggart; he is sure to know.' So they ask me why their hens are not laying and what time the bus goes to Kincraig and how they should vote at the General Election and where they can hire a trailer to take their lambs to the market and——"

"And you tell them," suggested Gerald.

"I tell them," agreed Mr. MacTaggart complacently.

Gerald smiled. "I've come to ask you something. I want a pair of thick grey stockings for stalking. Is there anyone in the village who could make them for me?"

"Katie will knit them for you," replied Mr. MacTaggart promptly. "Katie MacTaggart, Colin's mother, is a good knitter and she will be glad of the money. Will I tell her or will you be seeing her yourself?"

Gerald replied that he would see her himself. He had been interested in Mac's account of the family and the stockings would give him an opportunity of meeting the young woman who was so anxious to make "a nice home" for her boys.

"It is the wee cottage by the bridge," said Mr. MacTaggart. "At one time it was the lodge. That was when the road to Tigh na Feidh was in good repair and the house was used by MacAslan's great grandfather for his wild parties—Mad

MacAslan they were calling him. Och, he was a great chief if you can believe all the stories," added the innkeeper admiringly.

Gerald saw that Mr. MacTaggart was about to embark upon the stories and, although he felt sure that they would be very interesting, he had no time to spare. He thanked Mr. MacTaggart for his information and hastened away.

The cottage door was opened to him by a good-looking young woman with bright red hair—obviously Colin's mother.

There was no need for Gerald to introduce himself: she knew who he was, of course (everybody in Ardfalloch knew who he was). She greeted him politely and invited him into her kitchen for a cup of tea. It was half-past-eleven and Gerald had just drunk a glass of ale at Mr. MacTaggart's expense, so he did not really want tea, but he was aware that if he wanted a chat with Mrs. MacTaggart, he would have to sit down at her kitchen table and drink a cup of tea and probably eat a scone.

The kitchen was small but beautifully clean and there was an array of gleaming pots and pans on the shelf above the old-fashioned iron stove. Mrs. MacTaggart was genuinely pleased to see her visitor; Gerald got the impression that she was a little lonely and was ready for a chat. She spoke well, in a pleasant low voice without a trace of the local accent. He wondered who she was and where she had come from, but he did not need to "wonder" long, for she was quite willing to tell him.

Mrs. MacTaggart's father was the owner of a flourishing bakery in Inverness. She had intended to take her training as a nurse, but before she had finished her training, she had met Neil MacTaggart, who was a stalker in a big deer-forest. They were both very young and her father was anxious for her to finish her training, but she had not taken his advice. She married Neil and they went to live in a cottage on the hill. It was there that the three boys were born.

"We were very happy," said Mrs. MacTaggart with a

little sigh. "The boys grew up strong and healthy. They had freedom to go where they liked, so they ran about like wild things and often went out with Neil and learnt about deer. Then Neil died and Mr. Ferguson wanted the cottage for another stalker, so of course we had to move. The boys and I went back to Inverness, to my father's house. It was kind of him to have us, but it was not a success."

"It was so different from what you were used to," Gerald suggested.

"Quite different," she agreed. "The boys were not used to town life and they got into mischief. Colin was nineteen by that time—he is a good deal older than the others—and he could have got a post in Aberdeen, but that would have meant a break-up of the family, so I was glad when my husband's uncle found this post for him."

"You wanted to make a nice home for your boys."

"Yes, I wanted us to be together. It was what Neil would have wanted too, so I am hoping we can stay at Ardfalloch. Colin is a good boy and does his best, but Mr. MacGregor is difficult to please. That is the trouble, Mister Gerald."

Tea was ready now and as Mrs. MacTaggart set it out on the table, she went on talking. It was obvious that she was devoted to her boys. The two younger ones were at school in the village and were doing well . . . except that they preferred roaming over the hill to sitting in a class-room.

"Most boys do," put in Gerald, smiling.

"Yes, but Sandy and wee Neil sometimes 'play hookey,' " replied their mother. "Mr. Black came and spoke to me about it—but what can I do? Sandy is the wildest. Sandy is as wild as heather and where Sandy goes wee Neil follows. Their father would have taken a strap to them, but Colin just laughs and says it is good for them to be free. He says it is good to learn about deer when you are young. Sometimes they take a plaid and spend a night on the hill. At first I was worried, but they are strong and healthy and they know how to look after themselves, so it does them no harm. They are very much stronger than they were when they were playing in the streets at Inverness."

Gerald could well believe it.

"Are you enjoying the stalking?" asked Mrs. MacTaggart. "Colin was saying it is a very good forest with many fine stags. You killed a fine stag in the corrie on the shoulder of Ben Ghaoth."

"How on earth did you hear about that?"

Mrs. MacTaggart smiled. "Colin saw you. Colin was disappointed that Mr. MacGregor did not take him to see the sport, so he put his glass in his pocket and went up the hill and watched from a distance. He saw you kill the ten-point stag and he saw the hornless stag get up from behind the rock and gallop up the bank. It passed quite near where Colin was lying and fled in terror. It was a huge beast, not elegant like a proper stag, but coarse and ungainly. Colin says it ought to be killed before the rut."

"You know a lot about stalking!"

She nodded. "Neil used to talk to me—and now, Colin. I like to know what people are doing."

They had finished tea by this time, so Mrs. MacTaggart fetched her work-bag, took out a long grey stocking and began to knit.

"That's what I want!" Gerald exclaimed. "I want a pair of stockings just like that. Mr. MacTaggart said you might have time to make them for me."

"Indeed I will! Are you wanting them soon, Mister Gerald? I am making this pair for Colin and they are nearly finished. You can have them if you would like. Colin has several pairs, so there is no hurry for him."

Gerald did want them soon. In fact he wanted them to wear tomorrow if possible.

"You can have them today," Mrs. MacTaggart told him. "The first stocking is finished and I have just to finish the foot of the second. If you can wait for half an hour, you can take them with you. They will fit you nicely; you and Colin are just about the same size."

Gerald agreed to wait. He had a feeling that Mrs.

MacTaggart would be glad of the money and, as he wanted the stockings, both were pleased with the bargain. He was amused to discover that the MacTaggart family were calling him "Mister Gerald." The innkeeper had done so—and, now, young Mrs. MacTaggart. Perhaps they had meant to, or perhaps it had slipped out by mistake, but Gerald found it pleasant. He thought it showed that they had accepted him as a friend.

13

In Which Gerald Relates a True Story

The rain had stopped and the mist was clearing, so Gerald went out and, leaning upon the parapet of the hump-backed bridge, watched the water swirling beneath its high arches. It was a pleasant way of passing half an hour, but he had not been there for five minutes when he was joined by two boys. The bigger one had bright red hair, the smaller one was dark.

Gerald had had very little to do with children until he had met Alastair MacCallum and these two did not seem much older.

"Hullo, are you the MacTaggart boys?" he asked.

"Yes. I am Sandy and that is Neil," replied the bigger one.

"Dinner is late," said Neil with a sigh.

"So we were thinking we would talk to you," explained Sandy.

Gerald took the point: it was his fault that dinner was late, so it was up to him to do something about it. "What shall we talk about?" he asked, smiling at them.

"Neil is wanting to ask you something," said Sandy.

"It was about Africa," said Neil in a piping voice. "It was in school. There is a big river in Africa with hipper-potter-musses. There was a picture of them in my book. I would like fine to see a hipper-potter-muss," added Neil, looking up hopefully.

"I've seen them," Gerald told him. "They're ugly creatures—not like stags."

"Did you shoot them, Mister Gerald?" asked Sandy eagerly.

"No, never."

There was a short silence. It was obvious that the reply was disappointing.

"But I shot a lion," added Gerald, offering the lion as second best.

"A lion?" breathed Sandy in awed tones. "That's better than hipper-potter-musses. Lions are fierce."

"Did the lion try to tear you to bits and eat you?" enquired Neil with interest.

"No, he didn't get the chance."

"Tell us about it," said Sandy eagerly. "It's a story, isn't it? It's a true story. I like true stories best."

"Yes, it's a true story," said Gerald.

Two pairs of eyes were fixed upon him and he realised that he had let himself in for the story.

In Gerald's opinion the story was not very exciting, but perhaps it would entertain the boys until their dinner was ready.

While Gerald was in South Africa a lion and a lioness had suddenly appeared and had wandered round outside the high iron fence which surrounded the diamond mine. They never came very near the fence, but they disturbed everyone in the place with their roaring.

It was unusual to see lions at Koolbokie (nobody knew where they had come from), but it was reasonable to suppose that they had become too old to hunt and had wandered for miles looking for any sort of food that would stay the pangs of hunger. Lions in this condition are more dangerous than young active beasts as they are liable to become man-eaters if they can find no other food. The native "boys" who worked in the mine knew this only too well and sent a deputation to the manager, asking that the lions should be killed as soon as possible. Mr. Proudfoot was aware that something must be done—already some of the "boys" had fled in terror—so he borrowed a rifle from a friend in Johannesburg and asked Gerald to shoot them.

It was easy enough to say, but not so easy to do. There was no sense in taking unnecessary risks—indeed, it would have been foolish—for unless Gerald could be certain of killing the beasts outright, they would be more dangerous than before. To add to his difficulties, the borrowed rifle was an old weapon and a few practice shots with it proved it to be unreliable. This meant that he must get within easy reach of his prey.

Gerald remembered an old book, which had belonged to his father; it was *The Man-eaters of Tsavo* by Colonel J.H. Patterson. He had not read it for years, but it had fascinated him when he was a boy. Colonel Patterson had made traps for the lions, but Gerald could not do this as he had neither the materials nor the labour. He did not lack advice, of course. When it was learned by his colleagues that he had been deputed to kill the lions, Gerald received a great deal of advice as to how he should go about it, but none of it seemed very sensible, so he ignored it and made his own plans. He found a ruined hut on the hill above the mine and boarded up the windows, leaving an aperture from which to shoot. About thirty yards from the loophole he drove a strong stake into the ground and to this he tethered a goat. Then he took a thick rug, a flask of coffee and some sandwiches and settled himself in his hide-out.

The night was dark. There was no moon, and it was very quiet. Not a sound broke the silence. At first Gerald was all tensed up, straining his eyes and ears for signs of the lions, but towards morning he fell into an uneasy doze. He was awakened by a padding sound and realised that some beast was prowling stealthily round the hut. . . .

Gerald paused here for a few moments. His audience, which had been listening to every word in awed silence, could contain itself no longer.

"It was the lion," whispered Sandy.

"Yes, it was the lion. There was a space under the door. He stopped there and snuffled—and growled—I could hear him breathing heavily."

"He had scented you?"

"Yes."

"Were you frightened?"

"Yes," replied Gerald frankly. As a matter of fact he was terrified. He realised he had been foolish. The hut was a crazy structure, burnt dry by the African sun. The beast had scented him and if it chose to attack him, it could burst the door open with the greatest of ease. Gerald had seen lions before; he had seen them in menageries; he had seen them prowling about in Africa, but he had not realised they were so huge and fierce and strong. He had never been so close to a lion nor heard one snuffling nor smelt the sickening feral smell. He envisaged himself face to face with the monster, torn to pieces by a hungry lion with no hope of escape. Should he try to get out of the window? Would that give him more chance? Or should he aim his rifle at the door and hope to kill the beast with one bullet in a vital spot?"

"Go on," said Sandy breathlessly. "The lion couldn't get in, could he?"

"Fortunately he didn't try."

"Why didn't he?"

"The goat, which had been asleep, was wakened by the growling and tried to run away. Its chain rattled and it bleated. The lion heard it and was gone in a flash. It was still dark, but dawn was breaking. There was just light enough for me to see his great tawny body bounding down the slope."

"You shot him!" Sandy exclaimed.

"No, I waited. Dawn comes quickly when you're near the equator and I wanted to make sure of killing him. I waited until he had killed the goat and had begun to eat it. I waited until he turned sideways and then I shot him. I got him with both barrels, one after the other, just behind the shoulder. . . ."

"Bang, bang!" shouted Neil, jumping up and down with glee.

"Did you kill him?" asked Sandy.

"I wasn't sure. He rolled over and over several times. I reloaded quickly and let him have another. Then sun was rising and it was getting lighter every moment. Then, suddenly, about a dozen native boys appeared on the scene. They rushed down from a pile of rocks where they had been hiding and set about the beast's carcase, slashing it with knives and bashing it with crowbars and shouting like maniacs."

"Why did they?"

"They were pleased that it was dead . . . but I was furious with them. I was waiting for the lioness—I was sure she was somewhere about—and I wanted to bag her too. I thought the noise would frighten her away and I should have to spend another night waiting for her to come, but it didn't frighten her away. She came from the opposite direction, slinking along and taking cover where possible. She was long and lean and tawny—the same colour as the withered grass—so it wasn't easy to see her. I yelled to the boys to look out, but they were making such a racket that they didn't hear me and it wasn't until she was almost on them that the realised their danger and fled. They scattered and fled in all directions. It would have been funny if it hadn't been so dangerous."

"Did she go after them?"

"She hesitated. She couldn't make up her mind whether to go after them or not. She was about a hundred yards from the hut and if I had had a decent rifle, I could have got her quite easily, but I hadn't, so I couldn't be certain of killing her outright. If I had wounded her, she would have been even more dangerous."

Gerald paused again. He remembered that moment as if

it were yesterday . . . that moment and the awful decision he had been obliged to make!

"Go on, Mister Gerald!" urged Sandy.

"I had just made up my mind to risk it, and was taking careful aim when the beast saw the remains of the goat—or perhaps she smelt the blood. She let out a roar and, leaping up the slope, started on her meal. It was easy to see that the brute was ravenously hungry; she tore and crunched and snuffled and snorted. She was so hungry that she paid no attention to the carcase of her mate, which was lying only a few yards away. I waited until she was in a good position and then I killed her."

"With one shot?"

"I gave her two, just to make certain, but there was no need. She was a sitting target; I couldn't have missed her."

There was a short silence. Then the questions began: the questions were intelligent and searching—these boys knew a good deal about shooting—but Gerald had told his tale.

"Look!" he said. "There's your mother waving to you. Your dinner must be ready."

"Just one question!" cried Sandy, clinging to his arm. "Just one—please, Mister Gerald! Did you have the heads mounted like gentlemen do when they kill a stag?"

"No, I didn't," Gerald replied. "They were old beasts, lean and mangy, and by the time the native boys had bashed them about there wasn't much left of them . . . and anyhow I didn't want them. I didn't want to remember what I had done."

"Why?" asked Sandy in surprise. "Were you not proud?"

Gerald found it difficult to explain. He had not been proud of his achievement, nor had he been ashamed. It was just a job that he had had to do and he had done it. He had been very tired, so he had returned to his bungalow and had got into bed and gone to sleep. He had slept for hours (so deeply that the screams and yells of jubilation had not disturbed him) and by the time he wakened, the excitement was over. Some of his friends had tried to congratulate him, but he had accepted their congratulations ungraciously. He remembered saying, "For goodness' sake don't talk about it! It was horrible. If any more lions come to Koolbokie, someone else can kill them. I just want to forget about the brutes."

And the odd thing was that he had—almost—forgotten about the brutes. He had mentioned the lions to Mac, of course, but that was merely "by the way." It was not until he had started to tell his story to the MacTaggarts that it had come back into his head with all its grisly details.

Gerald was sorry now that he had told them, for he realised that his simple tale had made him a hero in their eyes and he had no desire to be a hero.

Sandy was still clinging to his arm. "Mister Gerald," he was saying. "Mister Gerald, listen. Lions are brave. If a lion is wounded, he comes for you, but a stag runs away."

"They're made differently. They have different instincts."

"A stag eats grass and a lion eats people."

"Not always, Sandy. It's only when lions are old and can't catch antelopes and zebras that they may become man-eaters."

"If a lion was coming to Ard na Feidh, he would kill a stag and eat it."

"A lion couldn't come here. Lions live in Africa so——"

"If he escaped from a circus, he could come here."

"There was a circus at Kincraig," put in Neil. "Sandy and me were creeping under the tent and we were seeing the lion in his cage. He was sleeping . . . but he woke up when the man came along with a bit of meat on the end of a stick and pushed it into his cage."

"It was bloody," said Sandy.

"There!" cried Neil, jumping up and down like a jack-in-the-box. "There! You said it! Mother said she would be putting soap in your mouth if you were saying it again."

"I was not saying it like a swear," replied Sandy in a dignified manner. "I was not, was I, Mister Gerald?"

Gerald was trying to disguise his chuckles by a fit of coughing, so he was unable to reply.

"Mister Gerald," said Neil. "If a lion was very hungry, would he be eating grass—like a stag?"

"No," replied Gerald. "His stomach isn't meant to digest grass any more than yours is. . . . Look, your mother is beckoning to you. We had better go back to the cottage."

He began to walk back to the cottage with the two boys (who were surprisingly heavy) clinging to his arms.

Mrs. MacTaggart saw them coming and rushed out. "Sandy! Neil!" she cried. "What a way to behave! What are you thinking of? Come here at once. Oh, Mister Gerald, I am sorry they have been bothering you. I had no idea——"

"They haven't been bothering me," replied Gerald, smiling. "They're very amusing and intelligent. We've been talking about lions."

"It *is* kind of you," declared Mrs. MacTaggart. She added, "They have no father, you see."

Gerald was very thoughtful as he walked back to Tigh na Feidh with the stockings in his pocket: there had been tears in Mrs. MacTaggart's eyes.

14

Which Describes a Picnic by the River

The weather was better that week, so Gerald and Oliver went out nearly every day with Malcolm. Gerald killed a switch—it was an old done beast and Malcolm was glad to see it killed.

Oliver killed two nice young stags with reasonably good heads and was pleased with his performance, but he had set his heart upon a "Royal." He confided to Gerald that he intended to have the head stuffed and mounted to give to his mother for Christmas. Needless to say Lucius Cottar had the finest Royal that Oliver had ever seen. It was in the hall of his house at Ascot and was much admired by all his sporting friends.

As a matter of fact Oliver Stoddart was surprisingly pleasant. He was the sort of young man who is pleasant and agreeable when he gets exactly what he wants—and Oliver was getting what he wanted. The weather was fine, he was getting good sport and haunches of venison to send to all his friends.

He disliked Gerald Burleigh-Brown and was jealous of the man's friendship with the MacAslans, but he was clever enough to realise that any display of animosity would do him no good. Oliver had a feeling that there was something mysterious about the man: he received very few letters; he rarely wrote letters and he had refused Mac's offer of venison to despatch to friends. In addition to these peculiarities he seldom spoke about himself. That was odd, thought Oliver, who was never happier than when he was holding forth about his own doings.

Oliver had written to two friends who had an orange farm in South Africa, asking them to find out anything they could about Gerald Burleigh-Brown and was awaiting their reply.

Mac was busy that week. He had received instructions from his father about Ardfalloch House. A new bathroom was being installed and the kitchen premises were being painted and redecorated—nothing had been done to them for years—so he went down to the Big House nearly every day to see that the work was being carried out satisfactorily. This meant that he was unable to stalk with his guests, but Mac was unselfish and as long as his guests were happy, and were getting good sport, he was content and cheerful.

Colin MacTaggart was not so cheerful. He had been out twice with "Mister MacGregor" and the two gentlemen, but "Mister MacGregor" gave him no chance to show his mettle, and he was beginning to wonder if he would be kept on at Ard na Feidh and, if not, what he should do. If he were dismissed, the family would have to move from the cottage to make room for another man. The responsibilities of his family weighed heavily upon his young shoulders.

A few days after this Mac received an invitation from Mr. Ross of Glen Veigh to go over for a grouse drive and bring a friend. The moors at Glen Veigh were exceedingly good, and famous for the size of their bag, so an invitation to shoot there was very much sought after.

"You must come, Gerald!" cried Mac, waving the letter in Gerald's face. "You said you had never shot grouse, so it will be a new experience for you."

Oliver was annoyed. The last time he had been here the invitation had come and he had gone with MacAslan—and had enjoyed his day immensely. This time he was to be left at home.

Gerald smiled. "No, Mac," he said. "You had better take Stoddart."

"Nonsense!" cried Mac. "Oliver won't mind. He's shot grouse hundreds of time. You don't mind, do you, Oliver?"

"No, of course not," replied Oliver in grudgling tones. "The only thing is Mr. Ross is keen on a good bag and if Burleigh-Brown hasn't had any experience of grouse-shooting——"

"That's right," agreed Gerald. "Stoddart will do you more credit. He's the man to take."

"But I want you to come," Mac expostulated. "I want you to meet Mr. Ross. You'd like him!"

Gerald shook his head. "I'm not much good with a gun. Honestly, Mac, you had better take Stoddart."

Mac was annoyed—and disappointed. It was Gerald he wanted to take. Possibly Gerald would not kill as many birds as Oliver, but he was a much more interesting personality. (Gerald was a friend to be proud of, whereas poor old Oliver was really becoming rather a bore.)

"Oh, all right," said Mac with manifest reluctance.

Mr. Ross had chosen a Saturday for his Big Shoot because he was able to recruit the schoolchildren to augment his staff of beaters. He would have got them anyway, whatever day he had chosen (not only did the children prefer a day on the moors to a day in the class-room, but the money they earned was useful to their parents), but Mr. Ross liked to keep on good terms with his neighbours and had no desire to fall foul of Mr. Black.

The Land Rover had been brought to Tigh na Feidh on Friday, so on Saturday morning Mac and Oliver started out immediately after breakfast, accompanied by Malcolm and Colin, to act as loaders. Gerald and the two girls watched them depart with their guns and cartridge bags and other impedimenta, including a large cumbersome shooting-stick which could be used as an umbrella. This belonged to Oliver, of course. It had been given to him by his friend, Lucius Cottar.

"You should have gone," said Phil, when the Land Rover had bumped off down the rutty road. "You would have enjoyed it, Gerald. Why should Oliver always get his own way?"

Gerald smiled. "Because it's so much more pleasant for everybody when he does."

"Yes," agreed Phil. "There's that, of course, but it's so terribly bad for him."

"Mac was disappointed," said Donny with a sigh.

There was a lot left unsaid in the short conversation, but there was no need to say more. The three were in complete accord.

"What shall we do?" asked Phil. "You're in for a dull day, Gerald. Would you like to take lunch and go for a picnic?"

"Yes, that's a marvellous idea?" Gerald exclaimed

The girls went to the kitchen to fill thermos flasks and make sandwiches and in a very short time the three friends were starting out for their picnic.

"I'm going to take you in the other direction today," said Phil. "We'll go up the valley towards Achnaluig."

"I don't mind where we go," replied Gerald. "This is one of the most beautiful places I've ever seen . . . and it's so peaceful! Time seems to stand still."

"I'm glad you're happy here," said Phil simply. "You'll come again next year, won't you?"

"If I can," said Gerald. "It all depends on when I get my holiday. You know that, of course." He hesitated and then added, "There's no other place in the world I would rather go to."

Donny said nothing. She walked along beside them like a little shadow. She seemed to be lost in dreams.

It was a glorious day: the sun shone with golden brilliance; the sky was pale blue; a few bright fleecy clouds hovered over the hills.

They had reached the river by this time: the place where

the little Ard na Feidh burn joined the river in a long silver cascade. Here the river ran through a wood of birch trees; it ran quickly, twisting this way and that way, prattling cheerfully in its stony bed. The birches had just begun to turn colour and amongst the green foliage a splash of gold showed where the frost had touched a branch and passed on. Away to the north the valley was spread before them, green and fertile; behind them the hills rose steeply, their rocky summits cutting a jagged line against the sky.

Phil loved this spot. It was the place she had chosen for their picnic lunch. She sank down, softly as a snowflake upon the mossy turf and looked up at Gerald with her lovely smile.

"Isn't this a beautiful place for a picnic?" said Phil.

If she had expected raptures she was disappointed.

Gerald sat down beside her. He said, "Oh, Phil, I want to talk to you."

"But you talk to me every day."

"Not alone. I never see you alone—not for a moment. I haven't seen you alone since that first afternoon when you showed me my room and told me about the forest. There's always someone there: Stoddart, writing letters, or Mac reading a book, or Donny sewing—or something."

"Where's Donny?" Phil exclaimed, looking round.

"She just wandered away."

"Perhaps she's lost."

"No," said Gerald. "I expect Donny knew I wanted to talk to you . . . and just . . . wandered away."

"We had better look for her."

"There's no need to look for her."

"But, Gerald, perhaps she has got lost——"

"Donny isn't silly."

"No, she isn't," agreed Phil, smiling. "Donny is quite clever in her own way. You like her, don't you?"

"Of course I like her. I'd like anyone you were fond of. But I don't want to talk about Donny, I want to talk about us. Oh, Phil, please listen——"

"We're friends, aren't we?" she interrupted breathlessly.

"We're friends, Gerald. Mac likes you awfully much. It's so good for Mac to have a friend like you. Mac is a bit wild sometimes—he's just a boy really—and some of his friends are—are rather queer. I mean they have queer ideas about things. For instance, Mac refuses to speak the Gaelic—he 'had the Gaelic' when he was little, so he could soon rub it up and it would be so useful to be able to speak to the people here in their very own language. They like it, you know. I wish you would persuade him, Gerald. Mac admires you so much that I'm sure he would listen to you."

"I'm sure he wouldn't! We were talking about it the other day and he told me what he thought about the Gaelic. His views were very definite and he isn't likely to change them . . . but Phil, need we talk about Mac and his views? I want to talk about us—about you and me. I want to tell you about my feelings. There's nobody like you, Phil. Nobody in the whole wide world. I thought that the first time I saw you—and I shall always feel the same. Please say you like me just a little——"

"Of course I like you," interrupted Phil. "I've just been telling you that I want you as a friend. I wouldn't want you as a friend if I didn't like you."

Gerald gave it up. He said, "I shall have to go back to Glasgow tomorrow."

"Oh, Gerald, why?"

"It's my work. There's a lot to do."

"But I thought you liked being here. I thought you were having your holiday. I know you don't get on very well with Oliver, but you mustn't mind what he says——"

"I don't mind what he says," muttered Gerald.

"—— and I expect he'll be going away soon," added Phil.

Gerald was silent. Another man might have made a more determined effort, but Gerald was too sensitive to press his case. It was obvious that Phil did not want to listen; she had put up a barrier and had retreated behind it.

"We had better have lunch," said Phil. She rose as she spoke and shouted for Donny to come.

Donny had walked up the hill by a little path which wound its way through the birchwood. She came down slowly, hoping to find two happy people sitting together on the riverbank. Perhaps they would be holding each other's hands. Perhaps they woud have something very interesting to tell her. But although they had had half-an-hour (which ought to have been enough), it was apparent that something had gone wrong. Gerald was too silent and Phil too talkative.

Donny was a gentle creature, so it was strange that she should have felt so angry with her friends—so angry that she would have liked to shake them! She could say nothing. She could do nothing. Later, perhaps, when she and Phil were alone (when they were wandering in and out of each other's rooms getting ready for bed) Phil might tell her about it . . . but she wouldn't ask, of course.

15

Is Conversational

Mac and Oliver returned from Glen Veigh in time for the evening meal. They were full of their day's sport: it had been a big party and they had made a record bag. The grouse-moors at Glen Veigh were well preserved and Mr. Ross chose his guns with discrimination, so it was considered an honour to be asked to shoot at Glen Veigh. Mac and Oliver were quite pleased with themselves, especially Oliver, who talked all through the meal about what he had done, and about his fellow guests and what they had said. According to Oliver they had all been very complimentary about the performance of Oliver Stoddart.

The new Chief Constable of the County of Northshire had been there: one Major Kane, a retired regular who had seen service in the Second War. Mac had talked to him at lunch and liked him immensely. Oliver thought him too lighthearted, too facetious. A Chief Constable ought to be dignified, complained Oliver. There was no dignity about the man.

"What nonsense!" cried Mac. "Look at his war record! He was all through the campaign in France and Germany. He was awarded the M.C. at the crossing of the Rhine. Mr. Ross said he ought to have got the V.C."

"That's easily said," declared Oliver. "Hundreds of men ought to have got the V.C. in their own estimation."

"It wasn't his 'own estimation,'" Mac retorted. "His Colonel put him up for it. Mr. Ross told me. Anyway I liked Major Kane. There's no red tape about him. He'll do what he thinks right—and if his superiors think he's done wrong, they can sack him. That's what he said."

"What an extraordinary thing to say!"

"It isn't extraordinary," Mac declared. "It's the right thing. He has been given a responsible position and he intends to exert his authority——"

"He intends to throw his weight about, I suppose?"

"That's right!" exclaimed Mac heatedly. "There are far too many yes-men in responsible positions. There are far too many men who are so strangled with red tape that they can't open their mouths. Major Kane isn't afraid of anybody. If I were in a hole, I'd go straight to Major Kane. . . ."

The argument continued, becoming more and more heated every minute, so the combatants were much too excited to notice that their three companions were unusually silent and abstracted.

Gerald had been happy at Tigh na Feidh. He had been almost sure that Phil was fond of him for, although he had had no opportunity of speaking to her in private, she had accepted his little attentions and smiled at him so sweetly. Perhaps it had been wishful thinking but—yes—he had been certain she was fond of him. He loved her so dearly that he could not believe his love was not returned. But today she had made it clear that she wanted him as a friend: a friend for herself and for Mac.

Phil was no "flirt." She was absolutely open and natural. She was as honest as the day. She had refused to listen; she had put up a barrier and he could not get near her any more. What should he do? Was it any good trying to break down the barrier? Wouldn't it be better to go back to Glasgow and settle down to work? There was plenty to do there. He could work until he was too tired to think.

They had finished the meal by this time, so they moved to the big chairs and the sofa which were grouped round the fire.

The movement broke up the argument and gave Gerald his chance. He said quietly, "Mac, I'm afraid I shall have to go back to Glasgow sooner than I intended."

"What!" cried Mac in dismay. "You've only been here ten days! I thought you had got three weeks' holiday. Gerald, you can't mean it. Have you had a letter from Sir Walter?"

"No, but there's a lot to do. I think I had better go tomorrow."

"You can't," declared Mac. "Tomorrow is Sunday. Please stay, Gerald. I know you've had a dull day, but we'll have a splendid day on Monday and another on Tuesday. The weather is clearing—Malcolm says so. Do stay for a few days longer . . . unless you're bored, of course."

"Of course I'm not bored. I've enjoyed myself immensely. It's just that I feel I ought to go back."

Mac did not understand it at all (how could he?) and he continued to press his friend to stay. He was so upset about it that Gerald felt obliged to agree.

"But I must go back on Wednesday," said Gerald firmly. That meant two more days at Tigh na Feidh—two more days of seeing Phil and not being able to get near her!—but Gerald comforted himself by the reflection that it would be easy enough to avoid seeing her except at mealtimes when the others would be there.

On Sunday, Mac and Phil and Donny went off to church and Oliver settled down to write letters. (Oliver received an immense number of letters and spent hours answering them.) So Gerald put a slice of bread and and cheese in his pocket and set off by himself for a walk. It was a dull cold day with an occasional shower, but he found walking pleasant. He strode along manfully over the hills. By this time he knew most of the forest quite well. The only parts he did not know were the northern slopes, which were avoided by the deer, so Gerald went that way and scrambled about amongst the rocks and the fading heather. There were bogs here and a few stunted trees: rowans with twisted branches. It was a bleak sort of place—Gerald was not really surprised that the deer avoided it—but he found a sheltered nook and sat down to have his bread and cheese. Then he drank some water from a neighbouring burn and walked home to Tigh na Feidh.

He felt better now. The exercise in the fresh air had cleared his head and he decided to have a talk with Mac. Mac was the only person in the house with whom he could have a private conversation without fear of interruption. He could knock on Mac's door whenever he felt inclined and go in and talk to him while he was dressing. (He could have done the same to Oliver Stoddart, of course, but as he never wanted a private conversation with Stoddart, the idea had never crossed his mind.)

16

Is Confidential

It was nearly time for supper when Gerald returned from his walk and as he went upstairs he heard Mac moving about in his room across the landing, so he tapped on the door and went in.

"Hullo, where have you been?" asked Mac.

Gerald told him.

"It's queer, isn't it?" said Mac. "Something a bit uncanny about it. As a matter of fact there's quite good feeding in places, but the deer avoid it."

"I don't wonder," said Gerald. He hesitated and then added, "I got rather a fright. I nearly got stuck in a bog . . . just realised in time that I was sinking and managed to back out."

"The bogs up there aren't really dangerous," Mac told him. "There's so much rock, you see. You wouldn't have sunk very far—just over your ankles. If the bogs were really dangerous, we should have to put fences round them. See?"

"Yes, I see."

There was a short silence. Mac was changing his socks.

"Look here, Mac," said Gerald. "I don't want you to

think I haven't enjoyed being here. It's a lovely place——"

"Well, why are you thinking of going away? Is it because of Oliver? He has become an awful bore, but he doesn't mean to be nasty and I think he has had an invitation from Lucius Cottar."

"Oh, has he?"

"And another thing," Mac continued. "I *do* want you to meet Dad. I don't know when he's coming, but he won't stay in Edinburgh much longer if I know anything about him. You'd like to meet him, wouldn't you?"

"Yes, of course," said Gerald. This was perfectly true. Gerald had heard so much about MacAslan that he would have liked to see him in the flesh.

"Do stay a bit longer," said Mac, looking up and smiling boyishly. "Please stay a bit longer, Gerald."

Gerald hesitated. He liked Mac so much that it was difficult to refuse.

"You will?" cried Mac. "That's lovely. You'll stay until the end of the week, won't you? By that time Oliver will have gone—and perhaps Dad will have come—and we shall all be much more comfortable."

"The only thing is——"

"Phil thinks he will come quite soon," Mac interrupted. "Phil thinks he's getting restive . . . and she knows a lot about Dad. There's a special sort of relationship between them. I mean they have scarcely ever been parted. Phil went to school for one term, but she absolutely refused to go back: they were both so miserable that they couldn't bear it. I don't know what will happen to Dad when Phil gets married," added Mac, frowning thoughtfully.

"Is she . . . thinking of getting married?" asked Gerald.

"She's sort of engaged."

"What do you mean by 'sort of'?"

"Well, it's been an understood thing since she and Simon were kids that someday, when they were older, they would marry each other. They weren't 'engaged' exactly. I mean as far as I know Simon didn't give her a ring . . . but they used to write to each other regularly. I don't know whether they still write to each other."

"I see," said Gerald.

"It's difficult," Mac continued. "Phil wouldn't leave Dad stranded, of course—and he would be absolutely stranded without her. She thought at one time that he might marry again. She had a plan that he might marry Miss Finlay of Cluan (they've been friends for years and years so Phil thought it would be nice for them), but the plan didn't come off. As a matter of fact I don't believe Dad wants to marry anybody. He's perfectly happy with Phil."

"I see," repeated Gerald.

"And another thing," continued Mac. "Another thing is that Phil loves Ardfalloch. I don't believe she really wants to leave Ardfalloch and go and live in the south of England. It's all rather vague."

"Who is Simon?" Gerald asked.

"Simon Wentworth. He's a baronet with a big estate and lots of money. He's at Cambridge just now. I don't know what he's supposed to be doing there—except playing cricket and acting in plays and having a jolly good time."

"I see," said Gerald. He added, "But, Mac, if they were in love with each other——"

"Oh, I know! If they were in love, they'd want to get married, I suppose. I mean if people are in love, they're sort of potty, aren't they? I've never been potty about a girl, but I've seen it happen to quite sensible chaps," added Mac.

"I'm 'potty' about a girl," admitted Gerald with a rueful smile. "I never thought it would happen to me—but it has."

"Well, why don't you marry her?"

"It's Phil."

"Phil?" echoed Phil's brother incredulously.

"That's why I asked you——"

"Good Lord! How amazing! You mean you want to marry Phil?"

"Yes."

"How amazing!" repeated Mac, gazing at his friend in

blank astonishment. He added hastily, "It would be very nice, of course."

"Not as 'nice' as a wealthy baronet with a big estate."

"It would be 'nicer,' " declared Mac. "I mean, you and I are pals, aren't we?"

"Yes."

"And, between you and me," said Mac thoughtfully. "In strict confidence, of course, I don't believe Phil would be happy at Limbourne."

"Why not?"

"It's too grand. Everything at Limbourne is terribly grand. If you want a cup of tea, you can't pop into the kitchen and make it for yourself. You ring for the butler and he brings it on a silver tray. You're almost afraid to sit down in a chair in case you crush the cushions."

Gerald was smiling now; he couldn't help it.

"It's true," declared Mac. "I stayed there once for the weekend, so I know. When I got up, the footman came in and beat up the cushions. I'm not very tidy. Phil isn't very tidy either. We're apt to leave things lying about, but you can't do that at Limbourne. The footman follows you and picks them up and puts them away. He comes into your bedroom and tidies it up. It made me feel an awful fool, really. The garden is terribly tidy. The paths have neatly cut edges, the rose bushes are pruned to within an inch of their lives, and there isn't a weed to be seen! You know the sort of thing, don't you?"

"Yes," said Gerald.

"The country is tame," continued Mac. "There are no hills . . . well, there *is* a hill, but it's tame."

"A tame hill?"

Mac nodded. "I suppose it must have been wild at one time, but they've brushed and combed it and tied a ribbon round its neck."

"Paths?" suggested Gerald.

"Yes, gravelled paths and neat steps with wooden banisters and seats where you can sit down and admire the view.

It's a pretty view," admitted Mac. "There are farms and green meadows with cows in them and there's a stream moving along slowly and sleepily . . . and on Sundays you can see men sitting on the banks watching a cork bobbing about in the water. If the cork disappears, they pull in their line and there's a fish on the hook. That's what they call fishing," added Mac, not so much scornfully as compassionately.

"And another thing," continued Mac very thoughtfully indeed. "Another thing is that if Phil married Simon, she would be absorbed into the Wentworth family and wouldn't belong to us any more. I can't explain properly, but I know what I mean."

Gerald thought he had explained the matter pretty well.

"I wouldn't want to absorb Phil," said Gerald gravely. "If Phil were to marry me, we should have to live in Glasgow because of my job, but Ardfalloch means a lot to her. I'd want her to come here often. I'd want here to have the best of both worlds, Mac."

"Yes," agreed Mac. "Yes, you understand Phil . . . but there's still Dad, of course. He's the real snag."

Gerald sighed. He saw that this was true: MacAslan was the real snag. He had not seen the man, of course, but you could not spend a week at Ardfalloch without realising that everybody in the place worshipped the ground he trod on—including his son and daughter. Mac was forever moaning and wishing his father were here, and, although Phil did not moan so much, her face when she spoke of him showed her feelings all too clearly—and when she received his letters, she seized them and gloated over them (as a mother might gloat over the letters of a beloved child).

So that was that, thought Gerald. He must just grin and bear it. He must "make do" with Phil's friendship and put the nearer and dearer relationship out of his head.

"I wish Dad were here," said Mac, breaking a short silence. "There's something special I want to ask him about. It's about the MacTaggarts. Malcolm was at me again today about Colin. He keeps on saying Colin will never be any good on the hill—but he hasn't really given the boy a chance."

"They're good people," declared Gerald, putting in a word for his friends.

"I know," Mac agreed. "The fact is everybody at Ardfalloch is getting old. We need young people here and it isn't easy to find young people who are willing to settle down in the country."

"The MacTaggarts would."

"Yes, the MacTaggarts would. Young Mrs. MacTaggart was in church this morning; she spoke to me afterwards and said they liked being here. She would be willing to come to Ardfalloch House and help Janet if we wanted her. That would be a god-send! Janet must be over eighty, so she really isn't fit for work. The MacTaggart boys would be useful too; they could be pony-boys when they're a bit older. What do you think about it, Gerald?

"I think they're all good value."

"Malcolm is the trouble," said Mac, frowning thoughtfully.

"Why?" asked Gerald. "Why has he got his knife into Colin?"

"Oh, because of his cousin. He wanted us to engage his cousin, Fergus MacGregor, but Fergus is an experienced stalker and we can't afford to have two experienced stalkers at Ard na Feidh. Besides, Fergus is as old as Malcolm. We want somebody young. We want a man who will settle down and learn all about the forest so that he can take over when Malcolm retires."

Gerald nodded. "It's jealousy, of course. What are you going to do about it?"

"I can't do much," replied Mac, with a sigh. "The only person who can cope with Malcolm is Dad."

"MacAslan is always right," murmured Gerald.

"What's that?"

"Malcolm said it," Gerald replied. "I'm just quoting, that's all. If you want my advice, you'll write to your father and explain the whole matter—just as you've explained it to me."

"Yes," agreed Mac. "Yes, that's what to do. You'll help me to write the letter, won't you? I'm not very good at explaining things, especially on paper. If only Dad were here, we could talk it over properly. That would be much easier, of course. Meantime I've arranged to take Colin tomorrow morning and go after the hummel. I want to see for myself what sort of stuff Colin is made of."

"I expect Colin is pleased," suggested Gerald.

"Yes, he seemed very pleased," replied Mac.

17

In Which Colin Lays His Plans

Colin had been very pleased indeed when he heard that he was to go out on Monday morning and stalk the hummel. He was determined to do his best and to show young MacAslan that he was worth his salt. To this end he requisitioned the services of his two young brothers and the three of them spent the whole of Sunday on the hills searching for the big hornless stag. By nightfall they had spotted the creature down near the river beyond the Black Pass. It was a favourite haunt of the hinds. There were hinds there now and the hummel was interested in them; he was moving about restlessly on the outskirts of the herd.

Colin knew that at any moment he might start chasing them . . . and a stag that is chasing hinds moves far and fast. This meant that Sandy and Neil must spend the night on the hill: the beast would not move far in the darkness and the boys would be here at dawn to see which way he went. Colin was not going to lose the beast now, after all the trouble they had had in finding him.

The boys were delighted; they had spent nights on the

hill before and had enjoyed the experience. It would be even better fun tonight, for Colin had given them a responsible task which made them feel important.

Colin left them his plaid and went home to tell his mother what had happened.

"I am hoping I will do well tomorrow," said Colin as he sat down to have his supper.

"You will do well, Colin," said Mrs. MacTaggart encouragingly. She was aware that Colin was to be on trial tomorrow and was anxious that he should do well. She gave him a good supper and sent him to bed early so that he should be strong and fresh for the day's sport.

Meanwhile the boys found a sheltered cranny between two boulders, wrapped themselves in Colin's plaid, curled up together like a couple of puppies and went to sleep.

The rising sun woke them and they saw the hinds moving up the valley towards Ben Ghaoth. The hornless beast was pursuing them. Sometimes he galloped after them and they fled like the wind; sometimes he dropped to a walk and the hinds stopped and turned their graceful heads to look back.

"They are not wanting that one," said Sandy slyly.

"He is ugly," Neil agreed.

The sun rose higher above the mountains; its beams crept down the hill into the valley. It was shining directly into the boys' eyes, so they shaded their eyes with their grubby little paws and watched patiently to see what would happen. After a little while a twelve-pointer stag came over the ridge at the upper end of the valley. He stood on the crest of the hill in the sunshine and stretched his neck as though he were about to roar . . . but no sound came.

The boys were high up on the hill, hidden in the deep heather, and the scene was spread before their eyes like a picture in a book.

"It is nice," said wee Neil. "Nicer than school, Sandy. Will he roar, do you think?"

"The Day of Roaring has not come," Sandy replied.

"But there are times when they will be roaring before the Day. Look, Sandy, he is trying again!"

The stag stretched his neck out three times and at last the roar came. It was a tentative sort of roar (by no means the full throated "Ha, ha!" that shakes the mountains when the rut is at its height), but, for all that, it was exciting.

"Will they be fighting, these two?" asked Neil.

"They will not," replied Sandy scornfully. "They will not be fighting. A stag would not be fighting with a hornless beast."

The hinds had stopped on beholding the twelve-pointer, but when he roared, they turned suddenly and with one accord set off up the hill. They passed within a hundred yards of the boys' hiding place, but the wind was in their nostrils, so they were unaware that anyone was watching. There were about twenty hinds, lithe and graceful, reddish-brown in colour, and about half that number of biggish calves. The whole party disappeared over the crest of the hill and was gone in a flash.

The two stags, horned and hornless, remained behind. They eyed each other for a few minutes. Then the twelve-pointer threw up his heels and went after the hinds. The hummel began to graze.

"That is fine," said Sandy with a sigh of relief. "Listen, Neil, you will go down to the cottage and tell Colin that he is still here."

18

Which Describes the Stalking of the Hummel

Gerald awoke to hear the stag roaring. He had not heard the sound before, but Mac had told him it was a prelude to "the rut." (As a matter of fact Gerald was a little disappointed; he had been told that the roaring of a stag was like that of a lion and this roar was feeble in comparison.)

A few moments later Mac tapped on his door and came in.

"Did you hear it?" he asked eagerly. "It wasn't a proper 'roar' of course; it was just a sort of rehearsal. You should hear them in October when the rut is in full swing—it's grand! I like when the rut starts. It makes stalking more difficult, but that's half the fun. You must get another stag today, Gerald."

"I don't want to kill another."

"What do you mean?" asked Mac. "You're going out with Malcolm and Oliver this morning. It's all arranged——"

"I told you," Gerald interrupted. "I told you I would kill one fine stag (if I could) because you and your father wanted me to do it, but I don't want to kill another. We agreed that I was a freak." He smiled and added, "Besides, I wouldn't get a chance, would I?"

"What do you mean? Malcolm has seen a Royal on the other side of Ben Ghaoth. It will be a pretty stiff climb, but you don't mind that, do you?"

"Stoddart will kill the Royal if we happen to see him."

"Oliver has killed lots of stags——"

"But he has set his heart on the Royal."

"Gerald, listen——"

"Don't worry," said Gerald, smiling. "Friend Oliver Stoddart is quite determined to have the Royal. 'He won't be happy till he gets it'! He intends to hang the head on the wall of his mother's dining-room in Glasgow. He told me so himself. I'd rather come with you, if you'll have me."

"Of course I'd love to have you, but you'd have better sport with the others," declared Mac. He added, "I'm taking Colin and going after the hummel."

"Yes, I know. I'd like to see you bag the hummel. He's so big and ugly, isn't he?"

They had seen the hummel twice since their first glimpse of him in the corrie, but so far he had managed to elude them. The beast seemed to have an uncanny knowledge of the approach of danger; he would graze quietly until his enemies were almost within shooting distance of him and then make off at a clumsy gallop, startling every stag in the neighbourhood.

"Yes, he's huge," agreed Mac with a sigh. He added, "Well, just do as you like, Gerald. If I'd known you were so keen to see the end of the hummel, I'd have taken Malcolm—we don't know what Colin can do—but we can't change it now. I arranged with him on Saturday that he was to meet me at the stepping-stones at the usual time."

It began to rain as Gerald and Mac started off to meet Colin, so Gerald stopped to put on his rainproof coat (there was no sense in getting wet if it could be avoided). Colin was waiting for them with the boy and the second pony. He greeted the two gentlemen politely and began to lead the way up the road to the Black Pass.

"Here, wait a moment, Colin!" said Mac. "We're not going that way." He had decided to cross the burn and climb the hill, for it was there that they had last seen the hummel and from there they could get a good view of the tops and might be able to pick out their quarry with a telescope.

"We will be going through the Black Pass," said Colin, smiling ingratiatingly.

"Through the Pass! But why? We shan't be able to see anything from there," objected Mac.

"It will be the best thing," Colin assured him. "We shall be seeing the hornless stag from the Pass."

"How do you know?"

Colin gazed at the hills for inspiration. "It is just an idea I am having," he declared.

"Have you seen him?"

"How would I be seeing him?" asked Colin in surprise.

Mac frowned thoughtfully: he had to make up his mind what to do. He knew that the stags preferred the high ground, but, on the hand, Colin might be right. Colin was obviously keen to do his best, so it was unlikely that he would insist on dragging them up to the Pass unless he had reason to believe that the hummel was in that direction. Why couldn't the man say definitely whether or not he had seen the beast? The answer was that these people never did answer questions definitely, thought Mac in exasperation. MacAslan could have spoken to the man in Gaelic and got it out of him—but Mac could not. Mac was obliged to grope in the dark.

Colin was thinking too. He was determined not to say that he knew where the hummel was. It seemed to him that there would be much more honour and glory about the affair if they were to come upon their quarry by accident—and Colin wanted the honour and glory! It was a poor sort of thing to go out and shoot a beast that was grazing peacefully in a meadow—a beast that was waiting for you to come. You might as well shoot a sheep, thought Colin contemptuously.

The third member of the little party had been watching his companions with interest and some amusement. He knew very little about the conditions of the forest, but he knew quite a lot about human beings and Colin's face was not difficult to read. Gerald felt pretty certain that Colin had seen the hummel—or at least Colin knew exactly where the beast was.

"Listen, Mac!" said Gerald. "What about trying Colin's way first? If the hummel isn't there, we can easily go up the hill afterwards, can't we?"

"That is the thing to do," said Colin eagerly. "The beast will be going after the hinds down by the river. Yes, indeed, that is what he will be doing. We must go after him; Mister Gerald is right."

Mac was still dubious about it, but he gave in, so they turned and worked their way across the shoulder of the hill, climbing amongst the rocks and scrambling down screes, and presently found themselves in the throat of the gulley leading from Tigh na Feidh to the river. The wind, which had been blowing steadily on their left cheeks, now swirled up behind them and whistled through the narrow cleft with a strange moaning sound.

Gerald had been here before, of course (Mac had brought him through the Black Pass in the Land Rover), but today he was on his two feet, so he was able to look about him and to see it better. As a matter of fact by dint of studying Malcolm's map and marking the salient features, he was beginning to get the lie of the land.

"This is a grim sort of place," he remarked.

"Yes, it's a bit eerie," agreed Mac. "It's worse at night, of course. None of the villagers will come through the Black Pass after dark, will they, Colin?"

"They would not like to come alone," agreed Colin. "They are saying it is haunted by a ghost that moans and groans, but I am thinking it is just the wind whistling amongst the rocks that is moaning and groaning."

This was probably true, thought Gerald, but all the same there was something horrible about the place. The high black cliffs were dripping with moisture and green slimy vegetation, the narrow road wound tortuously between boulders which had fallen from the heights.

Fortunately the Pass was little more than a hundred and fifty yards long, so they soon emerged from the gloom into bright sunshine. They left the boy and the pony and went down the hill towards the river. There was still no sign of the hummel. Mac, who had been annoyed before, began to feel angry. (If Colin had gulled them into coming all this way to no purpose—well—Colin should hear of it, thought Mac!)

But Colin was striding along as if he knew exactly where he was going and Gerald was following him, so after a moment's hesitation Mac fell into line.

It was warmer now, for they were sheltered from the wind by the barrier of rocks at their backs. Before them lay the river, winding along peacefully in the sunshine. On this side of the river lay an undulating meadow with small knolls crowned with bushes and scattered clumps of trees. It was here that the hinds loved to feed. (Mac wondered why there were no hinds feeding here this morning.) The river was the mark of the MacAslan property; beyond it the ground belonged to Glen Veigh.

The sheltered valley surprised Gerald. It was so different from the rest of Ard na Feidh and such a complete contrast to the rocky gorge. Here one could easily imagine oneself in an English meadow: the lush grass, the trees and bushes, the winding river were all in keeping with the idea. The diversity of the scenery in Scotland is part of its charm. Where else could one find the rugged majesty of crag and torrent and the smiling peace of watered pastures within a morning's walk?

Colin led the way downstream for about half a mile and left his two gentlemen to have their lunch in the shelter of a group of trees while he went on to reconnoitre. It was just here that the boys had seen the hummel, and it would never do to walk into him unprepared. The beast was probably resting in the lee of a knoll, chewing the cud and meditating upon the foolishness of his hunters.

Colin crawled along by the river's edge, taking cover beneath the overhanging bank; he was walking in the water most of the time—but what of that? The only thing that mattered was the hummel. So far Colin's plan had been successful (it had been a good plan).

Young MacAslan would be pleased with him and would keep him on at Ard na Feidh. Mother would be pleased too, thought Colin, smiling to himself. Presently he raised his head very cautiously and peeped over the river-bank and—oh, joy!—there was the hummel, grazing in the meadow. It was a huge creature—even bigger than Colin had thought—with massive shoulders and a thick ugly neck.

Colin grinned with delight. It was grand. He was so pleased that he almost forgot to look round and make up his mind where young MacAslan was to shoot from—almost, but not quite. The creature was a good bit farther down the meadow and not more than a hundred yards from the river-bank—a nice shot, thought Colin. He wetted his finger and held it up to test the wind. The wind had veered slightly, but not enough to matter; it was still coming off the hill toward the river, so that was all right too.

There was a small bluff covered with brambles on the bank of the river and therefore about a hundred yards from the beast. That obviously was the place. Colin looked at the hummel again: the beast was grazing quietly. Everything was fine!

Colin went back to the two gentlemen as quickly as he could and made his announcement: "The hornless beast is in the meadow. It is just as I was thinking," said Colin with justifiable pride.

Mac could scarcely believe his ears. "Are you sure?" he asked incredulously.

"I have seen him. He is grazing peacefully, but it will be better to go at once."

They rose, packed up the remains of their lunch, and Gerald took off his rain-coat.

"I'm coming to see the fun," Gerald explained.

"You take him, Gerald," said Mac generously.

"No, you. I want to see you kill him, that's all."

They argued amicably as they followed Colin down to the river. It was finally decided that Mac should have the honour of despatching the hornless stag to the Forests of Paradise.

"We must be keeping well down under the bank," Colin warned them. "I have the place marked. It is a little knoll with brambles on the top. When we get there, I will be holding up my hand."

Mac nodded. Colin had taken charge and if things were really as he said, he had taken charge to some purpose. Mac made sure that his rifle was ready and followed Colin into the river.

It was a wet passage. Sometimes the river curved into the bank and they were obliged to wade, waist deep in the water; sometimes the stream curved towards the opposite bank, leaving exposed a narrow strand of gravel; sometimes the bank was so low that they had to bend down and crawl along on their hands and feet.

At last Colin stopped and held up his hand. The bank was high and fairly steep at this point and was covered with brambles. Mac climbed up very carefully and found himself on the bluff. The brambles scratched his hands and knees and tore his kilt, but he was too excited to care. He edged himself along, lying on his face and pushing his rifle in front of him. As he neared the top, he felt the wind lift his hair; his forehead was damp with perspiration and the wind felt very cold. It was blowing straight down off the hills, so there was no chance of the hummel's scenting him.

Mac raised his head and peered through the screen of the brambles—and was transfixed with amazement at what he saw: the hummel was coming straight towards him at a gallop!

For a moment Mac believed that the beast meant to attack him; it was charging him. But no, how could it be charging? Mac was hidden from sight in the brambles and the wind was blowing directly in his face. The beast couldn't possibly have known he was there. Something must have frightened the creature and he was running away like all his tribe. There must be somebody on the hill. . . .

All this passed through Mac's brain in a flash.

The question was: what should he do?

Would a bullet penetrate that hard bony head? Would it?

Mac's finger was on the trigger. He hesitated. By this time the beast was almost on him; he could see the great coarse hornless head; the strange lumps where the horns should have been; he could see the whites of the frightened eyes.

Quick! said his brain. You must do something quickly. It was too late now: the hummel was too near to shoot. Mac raised himself onto his knees, the beast saw him—and stopped dead. They gazed at each other, face to face, for a second. Then, with a snort of terror the hummel swerved and galloped madly down the meadow. A sod of earth, thrown up by its hoof, struck Mac on the forehead.

Mac was too dazed to shoot . . . and anyhow, even if he managed to hit the flying flank, it would only have wounded the creature and Mac never shot a stag unless he could be sure of killing it; wounded stags sometimes run for miles before they can be followed up and despatched.

"Good lord!" exclaimed a voice at Mac's side. "I thought the beast was going to attack you."

"So did I," Mac admitted. "It gave me an awful fright. It seemed so uncanny, somehow. You don't expect a stag to attack you! For a moment I thought the brute couldn't be a stag at all. I didn't know whether to shoot or not," he added apologetically.

"You were right not to shoot," declared Gerald.

Colin was of a different opinion; he was bitterly disappointed at the hummel's escape. "Och, you should have shot him!" cried Colin. "You should have shot him when you had the chance."

"But he hadn't the chance," objected Gerald. "The creature was coming straight at him and it would have taken a very heavy bullet to penetrate that bony skull."

"I might have got his eye," Mac pointed out. He was annoyed with himself; perhaps he should have risked a shot. It was not as if the beast was a good stag. They wanted the hummel killed.

"It would have been a fluke if you had got his eye," Gerald declared. "You couldn't possibly have been certain of getting a vital spot in an animal that was coming at you full gallop."

"That's twice I've missed the chance of killing him," said Mac in mournful tones.

"Third time lucky," suggested Gerald consolingly.

"Maybe not," put in Colin. "I am thinking he will be away back over the river to Glen Veigh."

This was not improbable. The creature had been so terrified that he was unlikely to stop running until he had put as many miles as possible between himself and his hunters. Anyhow there was nothing more that could be done today.

"He wasn't really charging you, was he?" asked Gerald, as they walked back across the meadow to the clump of trees where they had left their coats.

"No, he wasn't," Mac replied. "He couldn't have known I was there . . . and in any case I've never head of a stag charging anybody. Something must have scared him. There must be somebody on the hill. Don't you think so, Colin?"

Colin agreed. He had been wondering if it could have been his brothers—but he could not believe the boys would be so foolish. They knew too much about the peculiarities of deer to allow the hummel to get wind of them. Yet, who else could it be? He unslung his glass and scanned the hillside for some movement which would betray the presence of a human being, but there was nothing to be seen.

By this time they had reached the place where they had left their coats and, almost at once, a huge cloud appeared over the hills and a thin misty drizzle began to fall.

"This is an extraordinary climate!" Gerald exclaimed, as he turned up the collar of his leather jacket. "At three o'clock there wasn't a cloud in the sky—I should have said there was no chance of rain for days—and look at it now!"

"I'm used to the sudden changes," Mac declared. He said it somewhat truculently and Gerald could not help smiling; he had noticed that Mac and Phil were both up in arms in a moment at the slightest aspersion upon their beloved Ard na Feidh.

"I wasn't complaining," Gerald said mildly. "As a matter of fact I find the sudden changes pleasant. In Africa I got bored to death with the weather. It continued for weeks on end without a change. I used to long for rain. Not heavy tropical rain, but a misty drizzle just like this."

"You will be wanting your coat," said Colin, picking it up off the ground.

"No, I don't want it," Gerald replied. "I'm wet already . . . and I've just told you I like the rain. Perhaps you'd like to put it on yourself, Colin. You look cold."

Colin was cold. He had not got his plaid (he had left it with the boys) and his clothes were old and worn, so there was not much warmth in them. "Well," he said doubtfully. "Well—if you would not be wanting it yourself, Mister Gerald . . ."

"Put it on; it will save you carrying it," said Gerald, smiling.

Colin put it on. He was too hot now, but he was so pleased with his appearance that he could not bear to take it off. He put on the cap as well. Perhaps someday he would be able to afford to buy a coat and cap like this, thought Colin, smiling to himself as he followed the two gentlemen up the hill. Today had been very disappointing, but he was not really worrying; he thought young MacAslan was too fair-minded to blame him for what was not his fault. It appeared that he was right.

When they reached the Black Pass the two gentlemen stopped.

"Come here, Colin," said Mac. "I want to speak to you. I don't know how you guessed that the hummel was there, but——"

"It was just an idea I was having."

"Well, it was a good idea," admitted Mac. "I'd have got him if he hadn't been scared by somebody on the hill. I'm very pleased with you, Colin. I shall tell MacAslan exactly what happened and he'll be pleased too."

"I was thinking," said Colin, a little diffidently. "I was thinking that if the hornless stag was away back to Glen Veigh, I would be seeing his slots on the edge of the river. He is a heavy beast and his slots would be big and easy to see. I was thinking that if he was not going back to Glen Veigh, we might be having another try at him."

Mac saw the point. "Yes, that's a good plan, Colin. If this mist clears tomorrow, you can walk along the edge of the river and see if you can find the place where he crossed over. If he hasn't crossed the river, he must be here."

"That is what I was thinking," agreed Colin eagerly. "If he is here we will be finding him on the hill."

They walked on together making plans. Gerald followed with the boy and the pony. Gerald was interested in the Shetland ponies and wanted to know more about them, but the boy was shy and appeared to have difficulty in understanding what Gerald said to him and even more difficulty in replying to the simplest question. It seemed strange to Gerald that a boy who had lived all his life in the British Isles could scarcely speak a word of English.

The mist, which at first had been gauzy and insubstantial, was now thickening and heavy clouds were massing behind the hills, so by the time they had reached the Black Pass it was difficult to see where they were going. The wind had fallen to a gentle breeze so that the mist swirled and eddied: at one moment you could see the cliffs towering grim and black at either side and the next moment they were blotted out.

Gerald had just decided to hurry on and overtake Mac and Colin when he heard the sound of heavy boots on the stony ground and saw two shadowy figures leap from behind the boulders. One of them had some sort of weapon in his hand and struck Colin on the head. Colin threw up his arms and went down like a log.

There was a scrimmage . . . somebody shouted . . . Gerald ran forward, but before he got to the scene of the attack the two shadowy figures had made off and disappeared in the mist. He found Mac kneeling beside Colin, trying to lift his head from the ground.

"What on earth happened?" asked Gerald.

"They've killed him!" cried Mac. "Gerald, they've killed him!"

"Who was it?"

"I don't know. I couldn't see them properly in this hellish mist. Ought we to go after them?"

"No, we must keep together. Let's see if Colin is badly injured."

"He's dead!"

"No, no! His heart is beating quite strongly."

"Thank God!" said Mac in trembling tones. "I tried to feel his heart—but I couldn't. I thought he was dead. Who could it have been? Who could have done it—and why? I knew nothing until I heard the rattle of stones and the two figures loomed out of the mist. One of them hit Colin on the head. The next moment Colin stumbled and fell. I tried to get hold of the chap, but he tore himself out of my grasp and ran away."

"They shouted," said Gerald.

"It was the other man who shouted, 'You fool, he's got red hair!' They they just—sort of vanished in the mist. Oh, Gerald, what are we to do? We can't leave Colin here and go for help."

"Call for the boy to bring the pony. You can do that, can't you? He doesn't seem to understand a word of English. We must take Colin up to the house. He's wet and cold, so the sooner we get him to bed the better. We can't take him home tonight."

Mac shouted to the boy. His voice was hoarse and echoed amongst the overhanging cliffs (the narrow defile was full of echoes). After a few minutes the boy appeared, leading the pony. The boy was as white as a sheet; he looked terrified.

Meanwhile Gerald had examined Colin. There had been

accidents at Koolbokie and Gerald had often helped the doctor so he knew a good deal about First Aid and he was relieved to discover that Colin's injury was not serious. The blow had fallen on the back of his head, but his hair was extremely thick and he had been wearing a cap so the skin was not broken. He had been stunned, that was all; already he had begun to recover his senses. He moaned and opened his eyes and clutched Gerald's arm.

"It's all right, Colin," said Gerald comfortingly. "You got a bash on the head. Just lie still for a minute or two. You'll soon feel better."

"It was Euan," muttered Colin, trying to struggle to his feet. "It was Euan, the dirty skunk!" Then his muttering changed from English to Gaelic and he uttered a string of what sounded like fearsome threats and imprecations.

"Wait," said Gerald, holding him down. "Stay where you are and rest for a few minutes."

"Where is Euan? Let me get at him!" Then came another burst of Gaelic which sounded even more fearsome than before.

"There doesn't seem to be much wrong with him," said Mac with a sigh of relief.

"He may have concussion," Gerald replied.

They lifted Colin onto the pony and set out for Tigh na Feidh; Mac walked on one side and Gerald on the other. The pony was so small that they were able to support Colin with their arms round his shoulders. Most of the time he was limp and quiet, but every now and then he struggled and tried to get off and raved in Gaelic.

Mac was thankful when they left the Black Pass behind them; his brain was busy in a dazed sort of way. . . . What ought he to do? He must tell the police as soon as possible—and he must tell Colin's mother. She would hear about the accident, of course. News of this kind got about quickly in Ardfalloch . . . and, like a snowball rolling downhill, it always gathered weight.

"Look here, Gerald," said Mac. "I shall have to send

somebody down to the village tonight. We must let Mrs. MacTaggart know what has happened and we must ring up the police. We ought to have gone after that fellow and found out who he was. Then we could have told the police——"

"We couldn't," interrupted Gerald. "We couldn't possibly have found anybody amongst the rocks in that mist. It would have been madness to try. We should have had to leave Colin alone and the thug might have returned and finished him off. The only sensible thing to do was to stay together. I agree that Colin's mother ought to be told, but who can you send?"

"I could send the two pony boys," replied Mac doubtfully.

"Wouldn't they get lost in the mist?"

"Not if they keep to the path. They're both local boys so they know their way about . . . but they couldn't ring up the police."

"I'll go if you like."

"No," said Mac firmly. "You'd just get lost. Besides you seem to know about First Aid. I don't know anything about it. Perhaps we should send for Doctor Wedderburn. Oh, gosh, I wish I knew what to do!" added Mac, in despair.

19

In Which Mac Boils Over

By this time Gerald and Mac—with Colin on the pony—had arrived at Tigh Na Feidh. Old Kirsty was there and received them with lamentations: "Och, what has happened? Och, the puir laddie! Has he been shot? He's as white as a ghost! Is he dying?"

"No, he isn't dying," replied Gerald. "There has been a slight accident, that's all. Fill some hot-water-bottles; boil a kettle and make tea. Be as quick as you can."

Gerald spoke with so much authority that the old woman was silenced and hurried off to the kitchen. Meanwhile Gerald and Mac attended to Colin. They carried him upstairs, took off his clothes, rubbed him with warm towels and put him into bed between blankets.

"You know what to do," said Mac with a sigh of relief.

"It's just common-sense," replied Gerald. "He's cold and wet. We don't want him to get pneumonia."

All this time there had been no sign of the girls, so when Kirsty came with the tea and the hot-water-bottles, Mac asked her where they were.

Kirsty replied with more lamentations: they had gone

out after lunch (she had told them not to go, but they would not heed her). They had got lost in the mist! They had fallen over a precipice and broken their legs; Malcolm and Mr. Stoddart had not come back either; she was sure something dreadful had happened.

"Och, it is a black day!" wailed Kirsty, wringing her hands. "It is a black day, so it is! I was dreaming of a black horse last night. A huge black horse came out of the river all dreeping wet with wotter. I was telling Malcolm, but he would not be listening to me. It is a sure sign of trouble to be dreaming of a black horse. . . ."

Mac was not worried about Malcolm and Oliver (Malcolm knew every yard of the forest and was unlikely to get lost), but he was extremely worried about Phil and Donny. He was worried about Colin too.

"Gerald, he looks dreadfully ill," said Mac in alarm. "Shouldn't we get the doctor?"

"How can we?" asked Gerald. "It would be difficult for him to get here . . . and he would only tell us to keep the patient warm and give him hot drinks. But you had better let Colin's mother know not to expect him home."

"What about the police?"

"I should wait, if I were you. We don't want a lot of fuss until we can make up our minds what really happened. Play it down, that's my advice. It will be time enough to ring up the police tomorrow morning."

"It was Euan," raved Colin. "I am not wanting the police. I will be after Euan myself with a big stick. . . ."

Mac went downstairs and wrote a short letter to Mrs. MacTaggart. He told her that Colin was staying at Tigh na Feidh for the night—that was all. It was no good frightening the woman unnecessarily.

Mac, himself, was upset and frightened. The whole day had been "queer": first there had been Colin's insistence that they would find the hummel in the meadow beyond the Black Pass (a most unlikely place); then the surprise of finding him there; then the hummel's extraordinary behaviour . . . and then, to cap all, the attack in the Black Pass!

Mac realised now that the men who had attacked Colin were probably the cause of the hummel's fright. Yes, thought Mac. That clears up *that* mystery. They must have been on the hill, watching for Colin, and the beast got a whiff of their scent. Then they must have worked their way along and waited for us in the Pass.

It was getting late now and still there was no sign of the wanderers. By this time Mac was nearly off his head with anxiety. He kept on opening the front door and peering into the mist . . . and listening. If he had had the slightest idea which way the girls had gone, he would have put on his coat and sallied forth to look for them; but he hadn't, of course, so there was nothing to be done. He had just made up his mind to go and consult Gerald when he heard footsteps on the gravel-drive and the whole party loomed out of the misty darkness.

Mac shouted and Malcolm replied. The next moment they walked in at the door: Malcolm and Phil and Donny and a somewhat bedraggled Oliver bringing up the rear.

"Good heavens! What happened?" exclaimed Mac. Now that they were all here—and safe—his anxiety changed to wrath.

"Nothing much," replied Phil. "You weren't worrying, were you?"

"Not in the least. Why should I worry? I just thought you were lost, that's all. Kirsty dreamt about a black horse 'all dreeping wet with wotter,' so she was certain you had fallen over a precipice and broken your legs. I suppose you know it's after eight o'clock!"

"I'm sorry, Mac," said Phil remorsefully. "I'm awfully sorry. My watch stopped, so I didn't realise it was so late. It was a lovely afternoon, so Donny and I went out for our usual walk and the mist came down so suddenly that we were taken by surprise. We wandered about for a bit and then we met the boy with the pony, so we waited for Oliver and Malcolm and all came home together." She added, "We're a bit wet so we'll go and change. If you're hungry, you can start supper without us."

Mac was not hungry, so he did not reply.

They ran upstairs to change . . . all except Malcolm, who lingered in the hall with a very glum expression upon his face. Mac turned to him and said, "What's wrong with you?"

"I am wanting to speak to you, Mac," the man replied. "There was a little disagreement between Mister Stoddart and me. He will be telling you his story and maybe it will be a wee bit different from my story. It was this way——"

"I'll hear your story later," interrupted Mac. "Meanwhile somebody must go down to the village with this letter. It's to tell Mrs. MacTaggart that Colin is staying here for the night."

"Colin is staying here?" asked Malcolm in amazement.

"Yes, he's not well."

"Och, what did I tell you? He is no good, that one! He would trip over his own feet!"

"He didn't 'trip over his own feet.' He did very well indeed. I was pleased with him—and told him so."

"Were you seeing the hummel at all?"

"Yes, and it wasn't Colin's fault that we didn't get him. There's no time to tell you about it now; I want this letter to go to Mrs. MacTaggart at once."

"Who is to take it?"

"You can send the two pony boys," replied Mac. "They can take Queenie; she'll find her way home all right."

"Och, there is no need for all that fuss," grumbled Malcolm. "I have had a long weary day and I am wanting my supper . . . and the boys will be rubbing down the ponies. They will not be best pleased if I am telling them that they must be going down to the village tonight. It will do well enough if they are taking the letter in the morning."

Mac boiled over. "Do as you're told and hurry up about it," he shouted. Then he turned, walked into the dining-room, and shut the door.

It was what his father would have done (if Malcolm had

dared to object to an order from MacAslan), but all the same Mac was a little worried, so he peeped out of the window from behind the curtain and was relieved to see Malcolm's thick-set figure hastening round the corner of the house towards the stables.

20

Is Concerned with a Serious Enquiry

Mac threw himself into a big chair near the fire and flung his legs over the arm. It was a favourite position of his when he was feeling tired. He was very tired indeed, so he was not pleased when Oliver appeared and began his tale of woe.

"Listen, Mac," said Oliver earnestly. "I want to speak to you before the others come down. That man is insufferable. He thinks he's indispensable and can do as he likes."

"Do you mean Malcolm?"

"Yes, of course! It's HIS forest and HIS deer. He thinks the whole place belongs to him. You ought to sack him."

"I ought to sack Malcolm? My dear chap, Malcolm was here before I was born!"

"That's just what I mean," urged Oliver. "He has been here far too long. Lucius Cottar always says that when a man begins to think he's indispensable——"

"Well, I can't sack him," interrupted Mac. "The only person who could sack Malcolm is MacAslan—and he wouldn't dream of doing any such thing. See?"

"Listen, Mac," repeated Oliver. "I want to tell you exactly what happened. We spotted the Royal quite early in the day and stalked him for hours. Then we lost him. I was fed up, I can tell you. He was a fine young beast with a beautiful head—just what I want! Lucius Cottar has a Royal, but his Royal is no finer."

"How nice!"

"It was four o'clock by that time," continued Oliver. "I wanted to have another look round, but there was a slight gauzy sort of cloud over Ben Ghaoth and Malcolm declared that it would spread and thicken, so I gave in and we started home. Then, quite by accident, we came across the stag. He was in a little valley near a burn, grazing peacefully. It was a narrow valley with rocks on either side; that was why we hadn't seen him before. He was well within range—an easy shot!—but, can you believe it? Malcolm refused to let me kill him."

"Malcolm refused——"

"Yes, refused, point-blank! He said the visibility was too poor. (There were only a few shreds of gauzy mist drifting up the valley!) He said it was difficult to shoot a stag from above. He said he 'was not wanting to spend all night on the hill searching for a wounded stag.' What do you think of that?"

"You must have riled him" said Mac, hiding a smile.

"Riled him!" exclaimed Oliver. "I was properly riled! I've never been so insulted in my life. I told him I wasn't in the habit of wounding stags, but he just turned his back and walked off. If I had had my rifle, I could have killed the stag quite easily."

"If you had had your rifle?" asked Mac.

"Malcolm was carrying it for me," Oliver explained.

Mac visualised the scene and began to shake with internal laughter. He was doing his best to stifle it when Kirsty came in with the supper, followed by Gerald and the girls. The situation was saved!

At supper the talk turned to the experiences of Mac and Gerald, the behaviour of the hummel and the attack in the

Pass. Mac had decided to walk down to the village the following morning and put the whole matter into the hands of the police. He knew Major Kane and liked him, so he would speak to him personally.

"What nonsense!" exclaimed Oliver. "Major Kane would laugh at you! It was the result of a fight in the village. You don't go running to the police every time there's a fight and one of the chaps get a black eye."

"But it wasn't a 'black eye,' " Mac pointed out. "It wasn't a fight either. It was a deliberate attack on an unsuspecting man. In fact it was an ambush."

"An 'ambush'!" said Oliver scornfully.

"Well, what else can you call it?" asked Phil. "Mac says the two men were lying in wait for Colin. That's an ambush, isn't it?"

"Mac doesn't know——" began Oliver.

"What do you mean?" interrupted Mac. "I was there and saw it happen."

"You couldn't see much in that fog. You said so yourself, didn't you?"

"But Gerald saw them too! Didn't you, Gerald?"

"Yes," said Gerald. "They were disappearing when I saw them. They were just two shadowy figures, but I heard their feet clattering on the stones."

"You'll have to have a better story than that if you want the police to take action," Oliver declared.

"A better story!" cried Mac. "How can we have 'a better story'? All we can tell the police is the true story of what happened."

"It's so vague," complained Oliver.

"It happened in a fog," Gerald pointed out.

The atmosphere was becoming extremely heated. Donny, who was always for peace, tried to change the subject by asking what Colin was to have for supper.

"Nothing solid," said Gerald. "He could have milk pudding, or something like that."

"There's a tin of milk pudding in the store-cupboard,"

said Phil. "I'll prepare it and give it to him. He had better have it now——"

"I'll do it!" suggested Donny.

"No, don't worry! I know where it is. It won't take long." Phil rose and went away to find it.

By this time the meal was finished, so the others moved over to the chairs near the fire; Kirsty came in to clear the table and as usual proceeded to collect the various garments and other impedimenta which were strewn about the room. When she had said "good night" and had gone away, Oliver remarked, "This room is always disgracefully untidy. I don't know how that woman can bear it."

"Oh, Kirsty doesn't mind; she's used to our ways," replied Mac.

"I like it," declared Donny. "It's so restful if you don't have to be tidy and punctual."

Gerald agreed with her (he, too, enjoyed the easy-going ways which obtained at Tigh na Feidh), but it was obvious from Oliver's expression that he disagreed profoundly.

"What about your friend, Lucius Cottar?" enquired Mac.

"His house is always in perfect order," replied Oliver, rising to the bait. "I think I told you that he has a house near Ascot with a couple to look after it. They have been with him for years. Crumbleworth is a well-trained butler and valet; Mrs. Crumbleworth is a marvellous cook and they are both so trustworthy that Lucius can leave them in charge of the place and go away for months with an easy mind. . . ."

"Like Bunter," murmured Donny dreamily.

"But Bunter wasn't married," whispered Gerald.

"He combined the perfections of Mrs. and Mrs. Crumbleworth in his own person," returned Donny in the same muted tones.

Oliver was still holding forth about the perfections of the Crumbleworths (and Mac had begun to regret his mischievous question) when Phil returned. She reported that Colin seemed much better; he had eaten his pudding and had settled down for the night.

"He still thinks it was Euan Dalgliesh who attacked him,"

added Phil. "But it couldn't have been, of course."

"Why not?" asked Mac. "Colin is sure it was Euan. They had a fight the other day and Euan got the worst of it, so——"

"There, I told you!" interrupted Oliver. "I told you it was the result of a fight in the village, didn't I? What fools you would have looked if you had gone to the police!"

"It wasn't Euan," said Phil.

"But Colin says——"

"It wasn't Euan," repeated Phil firmly. "Euan Dalgliesh is a nice lad. Oh, I daresay they had a fight: they're both red-headed and they're both rather keen on that girl who helps Mrs. MacTaggart in the kitchen. I can imagine them going for each other, hammer and tongs, but I can't imagine Euan hiding behind a rock and hitting Colin on the back of his head."

"No," said Mac thoughtfully. "No, you're right, Phil."

"Besides, there were two of them," Phil pointed out. "That makes it even nastier, doesn't it?"

"Let us talk it over thoroughly," suggested Oliver, leaning back in his chair and placing his fingers tip to tip. "We're all here—all five of us. Let us examine the possibilities in cold blood. That's the best way to get to the bottom of the affair. It isn't any good getting angry—like Mac—that doesn't help. We must all keep perfectly cool and calm. Phil says it wasn't Euan——"

"It wasn't Euan," interrupted Phil.

" 'What I tell you three times is true,' " quoted Mac under his breath.

Oliver took no notice of the interruption. He said, "Well, if it wasn't Euan, who was it? That's what we've got to decide. We want constructive ideas, so that we can discuss them frankly and come to some conclusion. Phil says it wasn't Euan—but she hasn't put forward any other solution to the problem," added Oliver, smiling superciliously.

"It might have been you," Phil suggested.

Oliver's smile vanished. He said coldly, "I have an alibi. I was with Malcolm all day."

"You and Malcolm were in cahoots. That's the solution, of course! Malcolm wants Colin's job for his cousin; he explains the matter to you and you agree to help him. You hide behind a boulder and hit Colin on the head while Malcolm stands guard—or perhaps Malcolm hits him on the head and you stand guard. What about that, Oliver? Or of course the ambush might have been planned and carried out by Donny and me; and we were wandering about in the mist for hours. We lurk in the Pass, I pick up a large stone and bash Colin on the head. Then we both run for our lives. I don't quite know why I wanted to bash Colin. Perhaps it was just a sudden fit of homicidal mania, or perhaps——"

"When you have quite finished talking nonsense, we'll get on with our enquiry," interrupted Oliver. He pursed his lips and waited.

There was a short silence.

"Go on," said Mac. "Go on, Oliver. What's your theory?"

"It could have been Burleigh-Brown. He's the most likely person."

"Me?" asked Gerald in astonishment.

"You had the best opportunity," Oliver pointed out. "You were walking behind Colin. You could have run forward and laid him out and dodged behind a rock, then you could have come out and asked Mac what had happened."

"But look here——" began Gerald.

"Oh, I'm not saying it *was* you. I'm just saying it might have been you," Oliver explained. "We agreed to examine all the possibilities in cold blood, didn't we? By the way Phil mentioned 'a large stone.' That's the first I've heard of any weapon being used in the attack."

"It was a blunt instrument," said Mac. "It's always a blunt instrument."

"Do you mean you saw the weapon, or are you just trying to be funny?"

"I'm just trying to think," replied Mac quite seriously. "I've got a sort of impression that the chap had something in his hand."

"It was a spanner," said Gerald.

"You mean you saw it?"

"Yes, that's exactly what I mean."

"That's important," Oliver declared. "We ought to find it. The spanner will have the man's finger-prints on it. The police can identify a man by his finger-prints."

"We all know that," said Mac. "I don't suppose there's a schoolchild over the age of ten who doesn't know that a man can be identified by his finger-prints."

"You may be interested to know that the spanner in question will have my finger-prints on it," said Gerald cheerfully.

"Your finger-prints?" asked Oliver.

"Yes. I found it lying on the ground when I was examining Colin, so I picked it up and brought it home with me and put it over there—on that chair."

"We ought to lock it up safely and keep it for the police," Oliver declared. He rose, looked at the chair, and added, "It isn't there now. Are you sure you put it there?"

"Perfectly certain."

"Oh, *that* was the spanner!" Phil exclaimed. "Kirsty showed me a dirty old spanner when I was in the kitchen preparing Colin's pudding. She said she had found it when she was tidying up the room. I told her to give it to Malcolm. I didn't know that there was anything important about it."

"We must get it from Malcolm and lock it up."

Mac began to chuckle. "Malcolm will have cleaned it thoroughly by this time—if I know anything about him. There's nothing Malcolm likes better than cleaning things. You can go and ask him if you like."

Oliver rose reluctantly (he was not very good friends with Malcolm at the moment). He paused at the door and announced, "If this were Lucius Cottar's house, he would ring for the man."

"Of course," agreed Mac. "He has electric bells in every room. He has only to press the button and Crumbleforth appears, like the genie in the story of Aladdin. I've often thought I should like to possess a wonderful lamp."

Oliver made no reply to this childish nonsense. He went out and shut the door behind him.

This seemed to Gerald a good opportunity of clearing up a point which had been exercising his mind. "Have any of you ever seen Lucius Cottar?" he enquired.

"None of us has ever seen him," replied Mac.

"But he's quite real—if that's what you mean," declared Phil. "I can 'see' Lucius Cottar if I shut my eyes: he's tall and thin, with sleek black hair receding from his forehead——"

"Sticking out teeth and no chin," put in Mac vindictively.

"His feet are so long and narrow that he has to have his shoes specially made for him," said Donny. She added, "That's true, you know. Oliver told me."

"He has his hands manicured once a fortnight," announced Phil.

"Except when he's shooting lions," Mac reminded her.

They had all been perfectly serious but now, with one accord, they burst into gales of laughter. Gerald laughed too, but all the same, Lucius Cottar had become "real" to him.

They were still laughing uproariously when Oliver returned. "Malcolm showed me the spanner," said Oliver. "He had cleaned it and oiled it and put it away. . . . I don't know why you're laughing. It's no laughing matter."

"It is to me," gasped Mac. "But I have a very keen sense—of humour."

"Your sense of humour is rather too keen," his sister told him.

"Oh, I know," agreed Mac. "My sense of humour gets me into awful trouble sometimes . . . but I can't help it. It's the way I'm made."

"Kirsty had no right to remove the spanner," declared Oliver. "She ought to have asked——"

"But, Oliver," interrupted Mac, "you're always saying that this room is 'disgracefully untidy' and now you're annoyed with poor old Kirsty for tidying up."

"Do you want to get on with this enquiry or not?" asked Oliver, raising his voice.

"Let's hear what he has to say," suggested Gerald. "I'd like to know why he picked on me as the villain of the piece."

Oliver resumed his position in the chair nearest to the fire. "Very well," he said. "I don't mind conducting the enquiry, but you must be sensible about it. I suggested Burleigh-Brown for several reasons. He has the best opportunity; he handled the spanner and admits that his finger-prints were on it (he didn't know Malcolm had cleaned it, so he had to make up some excuse); last but not least he had a very good motive."

"What was my motive?" asked Gerald in surprise.

"You wanted to silence him."

"Silence him?"

"Yes. Perhaps he knows too much about you."

"What on earth do you mean?" asked Mac.

"Ask him," replied Oliver, pointing at Gerald. "Ask him why he left Koolbokie Mine in a hurry. If he won't tell you, I will. He was sacked for stealing diamonds."

"What nonsense!" exclaimed Phil angrily. "I don't know where you can have heard such a ridiculous story——"

"It's true, Phil."

"I don't believe a word of it!"

"Oh, it's quite true," said Gerald. "I was sacked for stealing diamonds. The diamonds were discovered hidden in the lining of my jacket so, naturally enough, I was dismissed then and there. Stoddart's information is perfectly correct as far as it goes. It's a little out of date, that's all. He doesn't seem to have heard the end of the story: Sir Walter MacCallum believed I was innocent, so he sent his private detective to investigate the affair. The detective found out the truth; the thief was caught red-handed and was tried and sent to prison."

Gerald's companions had been listening with bated breath—and with very different feelings.

"There! What did I tell you?" exclaimed Phil. "I knew it wasn't true——"

"You've only got his word for it," Oliver pointed out.

"Are you calling me a liar, Stoddart?" demanded Gerald, half-rising from his chair.

"No, of course not," said Oliver hastily. "I just meant—I mean I heard about it from—from someone. I suppose you've got proofs? I mean——"

"I don't want 'proofs,' " Phil interrupted.

"Nor I," declared Mac.

"I have no proofs here," Gerald told them. "When I was packing my suitcase to come to Ard na Feidh, it never occurred to me to bring the letter, which I received from the manager of Koolbokie."

"Of course not!" cried Phil. "Why should you? Oliver is just being silly."

Gerald took no notice of the interruption. He turned to Oliver and added, "You can ring up Sir Walter MacCallum if you like."

"There's no telephone," said Oliver sulkily.

"No telephone!" exclaimed Mac. "If there were fifty telephones, I wouldn't ring up Sir Walter! Gerald's word is good enough for me. The whole thing is fantastic . . . and anyhow it has nothing whatever to do with the 'enquiry' we're supposed to be holding."

"How do you make that out?" enquired Oliver.

"Because it's senseless. To begin with how could Colin know anything about Gerald's private affairs? To go on with: if Gerald had wanted to 'silence' Colin, he certainly wouldn't have given the man a tap on the back of his head and then done all in his power to revive him. Furthermore I was there and saw what happened this afternoon. I've told you again and again that there were two men lurking behind boulders, one on each side of the track and that they sprang out and felled Colin and ran away. Gerald was behind us, walking with the pony boy. You had better ask the pony boy if you don't believe me."

There was a short silence.

Gerald had recovered his temper by this time (it was pleasant to be so hotly defended by Phil and Mac). He said,

"Well, let's leave that for the moment. Let's have another opinion on the subject. You've all said your say except Donny. Donny has been sitting there, listening, and saying nothing. What does Donny think about it?"

"Me?" exclaimed Donny, blushing to find herself in the lime-light. "I don't know, really. I was just—just thinking. I often read detective stories—and one of the most important things in a detective story is that you ought to take all the facts into consideration when you're trying to find the solution to a crime. You shouldn't just take some of the facts and leave out others because they don't fit your theory. That's what Poirot says . . . and Alleyn . . . and Miss Silver. They all say it."

"You mean we've left something out?" asked Mac.

"Yes," said Donny, nodding. "Yes, one man shouted. You said so, didn't you, Mac? You said the man shouted, 'You fool, he's got red hair!' So it couldn't have been Gerald, could it? It couldn't have been Euan Dalgliesh—or any of the local people—because they all know that Colin has red hair. It's the first thing you notice about Colin: he has the reddest hair I've ever seen in all my——"

"That isn't important," interrupted Oliver. "Besides it happened so suddenly and unexpectedly that Mac was taken by surprise. Mac might easily have been mistaken."

"No," said Mac thoughtfully. "No, I'm certain that was what he shouted. He shouted it in a surprised sort of way——"

"It couldn't have been that," interrupted Oliver. "It must have been something in Gaelic."

"No, it wasn't. I know it seems unlikely, but that was what he shouted: 'You fool, he's got red hair!' "

"Was it the man who attacked Colin or the other man?" asked Gerald.

"The other man," replied Mac without hesitation.

"That isn't important," repeated Oliver. "None of that has any bearing upon the case."

"In a detective story everything is important," said

Donny. "Every small detail has a bearing on the case."

Mac had been thinking it over. He said, "Donny is right, you know. It's very important indeed: it rules out everybody who knows Colin. The men who attacked Colin must have been strangers. Perhaps they were just a couple of tramps who wanted to pinch some money off us. MacTaggart said there were some queer types hanging about and making trouble in the village."

"It couldn't have been that either," said Phil.

"Why not?"

"Because, if they just wanted money, it wouldn't have mattered to them whether Colin's hair was red or black or yellow." She rose and added, "It has been a very long day. I'm dead tired and I'm going to bed. . . . Are you coming, Donny?"

They went away together and Gerald followed them; he was anxious to escape before his companions noticed that he had not put forward any solution to the problem. He had thought—and thought—but he could find none that satisfied him. It was a mystery. It simply did not make sense.

Gerald looked in to see if Colin had all he wanted and found him sleeping peacefully. Then he too went to bed.

21

In Which Mac Is Offered Advice

Mac and Oliver were left alone, sitting by the fire. No sooner had the door shut behind the others than Oliver leaned forward and burst out: "Mac, listen to me! There's something wrong about that fellow!"

"Something wrong? Do you mean he's not well?"

"No, I don't mean that at all. I mean there's something fishy about him. He isn't straight."

"What rot! He's the straightest chap I've ever met. I like him immensely and so does Phil. I can't think why you've taken such a dislike to Gerald."

"What do you know about him? You know nothing except what he has told you. Personally I don't believe a word of that story he told us tonight: about Sir Walter MacCallum sending the detective to Koolbokie."

"You're talking nonsense, Oliver."

"There you are! You just get angry when I try to talk to you."

"I'm not angry," declared Mac—not very truthfully. "I'd just like to know this: what on earth would be the use of telling us a story which could be so easily disproved? You have only to ring up Sir Walter——"

"We can't. There's no telephone. We can't go down to the post-office in this fog. Meanwhile——"

"Meanwhile I suppose Gerald walks off with the silver teaspoons in his pocket," suggested Mac.

"You won't listen," declared Oliver.

"I'm listening," said Mac, throwing his legs over the arm of his chair. "I'm listening, Oliver. Go ahead."

Oliver accepted the invitation. "Burleigh-Brown is very plausible, I admit. You and Phil have been taken in by the man . . . but I'm older than you are and more experienced, so you would do well to listen to what I have to say."

"I'm listening."

"It isn't the teaspoons he's after, it's Phil."

"Phil? What do you mean?"

"Burleigh-Brown is after Phil. I've been watching them: he's making up to her for all he's worth and she's infatuated with him. Oh, it's only a girlish infatuation—Phil is really quite sensible—but you ought to do something about it."

Mac hesitated for a moment and then said, "What do you propose I should do?"

"Well, to begin with, you could listen to my advice without getting in a rage. I'm only telling you for your own good."

There are few things more annoying that being told something "for your own good."

"Oh, how I wish Dad were here!" exclaimed Mac.

"If your father were here, he would send that man packing in double-quick time. That's what he would do." Oliver leaned forward and continued, "I'll tell you this—in confidence, of course—I asked Phil to marry me and she refused. I never was so surprised in my life."

Mac was surprised too . . . but not for the same reason. He said, "Good lord, I had no idea you were—er—particularly keen on Phil. I thought you were a confirmed bachelor."

"I was," admitted Oliver. "But just lately I decided to get

married. Phil is pretty and attractive and (as I said before) she's really quite sensible, so you can imagine how surprised I was when she refused to consider my offer. It's this silly girlish infatuation, of course. If you send that man away, she'll soon get over it and come to her senses. I'm quite willing to wait," added Oliver smugly.

Mac had been annoyed—he was still annoyed—but now, quite suddenly, his sense of humour got the upper hand and he was overcome by a fit of laughter. He tried to stifle it, but it was uncontrollable. He roared with laughter.

"I see nothing funny about it," declared Oliver. He rose in a dignified manner and left the room.

It was nearly midnight by this time and Mac was used to going to bed at ten. He was exhausted not only by the events of a long and tiring day but also by the various emotions which he had experienced. He had just risen and had put the guard on the fire when there was a tap on the door and Malcolm appeared.

"What on earth is the matter now?" groaned Mac.

"It is just that I was wanting to tell you my story," Malcolm explained. "You were saying you would hear my story later. So I was waiting."

Mac remembered that he had used those very words; he sighed and sat down on the arm of a chair. "All right, go on," he said.

"I could tell you better in the Gaelic, Mac."

"This was a 'pose,' of course: Malcolm could have told his story perfectly well in English. It was just that he thought MacAslan's son ought to "have the Gaelic." (MacAslan's son thought otherwise.)

"But I couldn't be understanding better," replied Mac with a little smile. "Listen, Malcolm! I'll tell you what happened and you can stop me if I go wrong: you and Mr. Stoddart stalked the Royal for hours; then he vanished. You had decided to come home when you discovered him grazing peacefully in a little valley with rocks all round. Mr. Stoddart wanted to shoot the beast, but you refused to let him. Then you turned——"

"It was a very deep corrie and it was full of mist," interrupted Malcolm. "There were wee puffs of air. At one moment you could be seeing the beast clearly and the next moment you could not be seeing him at all. We were above him on the side of the hill, so it would have been a difficult shot even in clear weather. You are knowing, yourself, that it is not easy to kill a stag from above. It is MacAslan's rule that you should not be shooting unless you are sure of killing your stag—it is your rule too. It is a good rule."

Mac nodded. "But Mr. Stoddart said it was an easy shot."

"Mister Stoddart is quite a good shot, but he is not as good as he thinks he is."

"He said you were rude to him, Malcolm."

"Maybe I was," admitted Malcolm. "I was a wee bit annoyed with Mister Stoddart. He is a very annoying gentleman."

Mac felt like saying he couldn't agree more (he had been "annoyed with Mister Stoddart" himself), but discipline had to be maintained, so after a moment's thought he said, "Well, it's a pity, but it can't be helped. I suppose you want me to write and tell MacAslan what happened?"

"That is what I am wanting," replied Malcolm, smiling in relief.

As Mac went up the stairs to bed, he decided that if anybody else wanted to talk to him tonight he would open his mouth and scream . . . but fortunately nobody did.

22

Is Concerned with the Arrival of a Letter

The mist, which had come down so suddenly, persisted for two days. Sometimes it lifted for a few hours, sometimes it thickened, but the visibility was too poor for stalking.

Colin was better. He had a lump on the back of his head, but he insisted on getting up and going home. Mac went with him to restore him to his mother and to tell her exactly what had happened. Mrs. MacTaggart had heard a garbled account of the accident, so she was delighted to see her son looking little the worse of his experience.

It was established that Colin's assailant could not have been Euan Dalgliesh as there had been a meeting of the Fire Brigade on Monday evening and Euan had been there. At least six lads of the village had seen him and spoken to him.

After his interview with Mrs. MacTaggart, Mac went to the inn and consulted Mr. MacTaggart as to what he should do . . . and, as usual, Mr. MacTaggart was delighted to offer advice.

"Och, I would wait for a bit," said The Big Fish. "It would be a pity to bother Major Kane. If you had seen the men, it would be a different matter."

"I wondered if it could have been those men you were telling me about," suggested Mac. "I mean the men who were staying at Raddles' Inn. You said you didn't like the look of them?"

"Neether I do."

"Are they still hanging about the village?"

"They are indeed. They are here now, in the Public Bar. Would you care to take a wee peep at them, Mac?"

This was by no means the first time that Mac had been invited to take a wee peep of the Public Bar, so without more ado he sprang onto a chair, slid back a piece of wood and placed his eye to a small round hole in the panelling. It was an old device—few people knew of it—but Mac found it fascinating, for from this vantage point you could see and not be seen. (It occurred to Mac that the old peep-hole was the reason why Jamie MacTaggart knew everything that went on in Ardfalloch).

The Public Bar was full of men, as it always was at this time of day, but they were all local men—except two—so it was easy for Mac to identify the strangers. He had expected to see a couple of villains, but these men looked harmless enough. In fact they looked quite peaceful and pleasant. They were standing at the bar-counter drinking beer and talking to each other. One was tall and thin with long legs and a sallow complexion; the other was shorter and stockily-built with a round red face and bushy eyebrows. Both were tidily dressed in shirts and slacks and cardigan jackets (the sort of garments one can buy "off the peg" in any shop which caters for men's requirements).

Mac gazed at them with interest, but it was quite impossible to decide whether or not these were the two shadowy figures he had seen in the fog. He replaced the small piece of wood and came down.

"Are they the ones?" asked MacTaggart eagerly.

"I don't know," said Mac. "They look quite harmless to me. Why are you worried about them?"

"They are different," MacTaggart explained. "In Ardfalloch we are used to gentlemen for the fishing, and shepherds and such-like, and chaps from the aluminium works, but these men are different. If you were seeing them in Glasgow—or any big town—you would not be surprised. It is just that I like to know who people are and what they are doing . . . and I would like to know where they get their money."

"Perhaps they're just having a holiday."

"Well, maybe," agreed MacTaggart in doubtful tones. "Maybe that's the way of it, but it seems to me that they are not the sort that would be taking their holidays in Ardfalloch."

"You said they were making trouble in the village. What are they doing?"

"They have a big shiny car and their pockets are full of money, so they are taking girls over to Kincraig to see the pictures. Maybe you will laugh, Mac, but it is not very funny."

In spite of his "keen sense of humour," Mac did not feel inclined to laugh. Obviously it was pretty sickening for the lads of the village to have their girl-friends snatched from beneath their noses and whirled away in a big shiny car to the cinemas in Kincraig.

"Maybe you are thinking I am a foolish old busybody," said MacTaggart. "But I am not liking it. No, I am not liking it at all—and Mistress MacTaggart feels the same as me. Time was when you could speak to a lassie for her own good, but nowadays they laugh at you. There's not one of them will take a telling."

"I don't think you're a busybody," replied Mac, patting his old friend on the shoulder. "I think you're a very useful man, but it's no good my ringing up Major Kane and telling him——"

"That is what I said," interrupted MacTaggart. "I told you it would be a pity to bother Major Kane. I will keep my eyes open and maybe in a day or two we will find something else to tell him."

It was on this somewhat mournful note that they parted.

Mac had hoped that Jamie MacTaggart would have been able to throw more light on the problem, so he was disappointed. He had a curiously strong inclination to ring up Major Kane and ask his advice . . . but what could he say? It was all too vague. He had been very upset at the time, but now the attack in the Pass was fading from his mind like a bad dream. It would have been quite different if Colin had been seriously injured.

Thus thinking, Mac got one or two things from Mrs. Grant, called at the post-office for the letters and went home.

There was a big sheaf of letters; most of them were for Oliver of course, but one of them was for Gerald from Sir Walter MacCallum. Gerald was pleased when he saw it; he had been expecting a letter for days. It was a large bulky envelope, so he took it up to his room to read in peace. He sat down on the window seat and opened it.

The first part of the letter was concerned with business matters: with news about the ship which had been built for a firm in Hamburg; her trials had been successfully completed and except for a few small adjustments, she was ready. (Gerald had helped with the electrical equipment of the ship when he first went to MacCallum's yard.)

Sir Walter went on to say that the security measures at the yard had been altered and instead of the wires below the surface, which set off the alarm bells, an entirely new system had been installed. It was more satisfactory in every way. Sir Walter seemed to think that the new system had been "invented" by Gerald and complimented him on his ingenuity.

Gerald smiled when he read this. He had not "invented" it of course, but had merely adapted it from a radar device which was used on main roads for testing the speed of cars. Gerald had shown his plan to Mr. Carr, the chief electrical engineer at MacCallum's, but Mr. Carr had refused to consider it. Apparently Mr. Carr had changed his mind! Sir Walter continued:

A funny thing happened last Sunday night. I went down to the Yard after dinner—as I often do—and I was prowling about in a leisurely way when suddenly all the alarm bells in the place went off with a frightful racket. Carr said I had broken the circuit—whatever that means! It was quite a good thing to happen as it gave the night-watchmen a fright and a chance to show their mettle. In less than five minutes the lights had been turned on and the whole place was full of men with guard-dogs. I don't mind telling you I felt rather ashamed of myself, but everybody seemed to think I had done it on purpose and we all congratulated each other on a successful rehearsal. Joseph Parker has been busy snooping, but has not found much wrong in MacCallum's. However he says I am to warn you about some men who were involved in the robbery at K. and K's. Parker is certain that they belonged to the gang, but they escaped capture. He says they have "gone north"—they were making for Inverness—but I don't think you need take the warning seriously. I fail to see how they could find you (you are well hidden at the House of the Deer). And why should they want to get in touch with you? It is much more likely that they are looking for jobs in the aluminium works.

Please thank Mac for the venison. It was excellent eating. I enclose a letter from Bess—her usual style!

We are all well and send our love and best wishes for good sport.

Yours ever,

Walter.

The letter from Bess in "her usual style" consisted of a brief message on a large sheet of paper, saying that she and

Margaret were flourishing and sent love and kisses.

When Gerald had read the letter, he went to find Mac and discovered him in the gun-room, sitting at the table doing nothing. He looked dejected.

"Hullo, what's the matter?" asked Gerald.

"I've been thinking," Mac replied. "Monday was awful, wasn't it? I behaved like a perfect fool. The fact is I was frightened—it's no good denying it. First I was scared stiff because I thought the hummel was charging me, and then I was scared by those thugs in the Pass. I had hold of that chap who attacked Colin and I let him go. I should have held on to him, but I thought Colin was dead. I lost my head completely. I don't know what would have happened if you hadn't been there. I don't think I'm a coward—not really. I mean, if it had been a battle, I'd have been prepared . . . but you don't expect things like that to happen on your own ground. It was all so uncanny. I expect you're absolutely fed up with me . . . and what Dad will think when he hears about it I simply don't know."

This moaning was so unlike the usually cheerful Mac that Gerald was quite alarmed. "Goodness, what nonsense!" he exclaimed. "I'm not in the least fed up with you."

"Well, I'm absolutely fed up with myself."

"If you want the truth, I thought you behaved extremely well in exceptionally difficult circumstances."

"Did you really?"

"Yes, really, and I'm quite prepared to tell your father so—if that's what's worrying you."

Apparently it was. Mac smiled wanly. "But I don't want you to hide the truth," he said. "As a matter of fact I've been trying to write to Dad and tell him about it. That's what got me down. It wasn't until I had written the whole story that I realised what a juggins I had been."

"You can't have written the true story," said Gerald consolingly.

It took some to time to comfort Mac . . . and, after that, it was a little difficult for Gerald to say what he had intended.

"Well, that's that," said Gerald. "We understand each other, don't we? Now I've got something to say to you—the mystery is solved."

"The mystery is solved?"

"Yes. Here you are! Just read this letter from Sir Walter and you'll see for yourself."

Mac took the letter and read it carefully. He said, "But Gerald, I don't know anything about radar, so——"

"It isn't that," interrupted Gerald. "It's the next bit, about those men. I don't want to involve you in trouble, so I had better make tracks. You understand, don't you?"

"I don't understand anything about it," Mac declared.

"It was those men who attacked Colin in the Pass. Colin was walking beside you; he was wearing my coat and cap so they mistook him for me. When the cap fell off and they saw his hair, they realised their mistake and fled for their lives. That explains everything, doesn't it?"

For a minute or two Mac was silent, thinking about it. Then he said, "Yes, I suppose it does, but what was their object? Why did they want to kill you?"

"They didn't want to kill me; it wasn't a killing blow. They just wanted to stun me and take me away and ask me a few questions."

"Questions about what?"

"About the security measures in MacCallum's Ship-Yard."

"I still don't understand," said Mac hopelessly.

Gerald saw that he would have to explain the matter more fully if he wanted Mac to understand . . . so he explained it from beginning to end.

"But all this has nothing to do with you," added Gerald. "The point is I don't want to involve you in my troubles. They're sure to have another try, so I had better leave here early tomorrow morning."

"No!" cried Mac. "No, that's rot! Why should you? To begin with I'm not sure you're right—it seems fantastic to me—and even if it *was* those men who attacked Colin, thinking it was you, and even if they *did* have another try to kidnap you (or whatever you think they're going to do)—well, we shall have something to say to that! There are three of us—four, counting Malcolm—so we'll give them a run for their money."

"Mac, listen, they may come here——"

"I hope they do! It will be fun!" cried Mac.

"It won't be fun," said Gerald gravely. "It might be very serious trouble. Those men will stick at nothing. They're dangerous."

"Dangerous?" echoed Mac incredulously. "The two men I saw at MacTaggart's didn't look dangerous."

"They may not look it, but they are," Gerald replied. "The chief of the gang is 'a ruthless devil.' That's what Sir Walter said about him . . . and the girls are here. We've got to think of the girls."

"Yes . . . well . . . what do you propose to do?"

"Nothing very heroic," replied Gerald, smiling. "I shall leave here early and go down to the village and ring up your friend, Major Kane. I can do it from MacTaggart's Inn."

"I'll come with you."

"No, you'll stay here and look after the girls."

"If it's still misty, you'll get lost."

"I shan't get lost. I know the place pretty well by this time. I shall go by the short cut and the stepping-stones. They may be watching the bridge."

Mac was frowning. He said, "I don't like it. Honestly, Gerald, it will be much better if I come with you——"

"No," said Gerald firmly. He had argued with Mac before—and had given in—but this time he stuck to his guns.

"Oh, all right," said Mac at last. "Have it your own way . . . but I shall get up early and see you off. I'll let you out by a little window in the cellar, in case they're watching the doors."

23

Describes a Man-Hunt Over the Hills

Gerald wakened early and saw that it was still misty. He dressed quickly in his stalking clothes and went into Mac's room. He, too, was up and dressed.

They went down to the kitchen together and Mac led the way to a trap-door with a ladder leading down to the cellar. It was a big old-fashioned cellar which stretched the full length of the house, low in the roof and vaulted like a crypt. The wine-bins were empty, but there was a pile of empty bottles in one corner. Gerald looked round the place with interest.

"By Jove, your ancestors did themselves well!" he exclaimed.

"Yes, there was a good deal of contraband trade with France in the old days. My great-great-grandfather used to have parties here. I expect he was mixed up with smugglers. We really ought to get these bottles cleared out——"

"Don't chuck them away," interrupted Gerald. "Most of these bottles are hand-made and quite valuable nowadays."

While they were talking, Mac had opened a small square window at the far end of the cellar. He had used the window when he was a boy as a secret entrance to Tigh na Feidh. He was surprised to find how small it was!

"Do you think you can get through?" he asked doubtfully.

Gerald thought he could. It was a tight fit, but by dint of pushing and squeezing he managed it and found himself in a thick shrubbery of rhododendron bushes.

"Be careful," said Mac anxiously.

"Oh, yes! I'll be all right."

"What are you going to do after you've phoned? You'll come straight back here, won't you?"

Gerald had not considered this point. He said, "I'll take Major Kane's advice. You said he was good value, didn't you?"

"Yes, I liked him immensely."

The two friends said goodbye; Mac shut the little window and Gerald started off. It was damp and cold and misty, but he was quite pleased about the mist: if those men were lurking about, it would be easier for him to avoid them.

Gerald ran down the steep path which led to the plantation of pine trees . . . and then stopped! Somebody had closed the gate with a loud click and there was a crunching sound of heavy boots coming up the path towards him. He hesitated, wondering if he should hide and let them pass, and then he decided on a better plan. It sprang into his mind all of a sudden. If he let them pass, they would go up to the house, thinking he was there. They might be dangerous (he had told Mac they were dangerous men). Gerald did not really believe they were dangerous—except perhaps to himself—but Phil and Donny were in the house and, at the very least, the men would be a nuisance. They might hang about all day at the house, waiting for him to come out.

All this passed through his mind in a flash and he saw what he would do. He would lead them away from the house and lose them on the hill. It would not be difficult, for he knew his way and the mist, though not very thick, was thick enough to hide him. Then, when he had thrown off his pursuers, he could drop down to the river and phone from MacTaggart's Inn as he had intended.

He shouted, "Hullo, who's there? What do you want?"

The footsteps stopped and for a few moments there was silence. Then a voice replied, "We want to speak to Mr. Burleigh-Brown."

"All right! Here I am!" shouted Gerald. He added, "Come and get me." Then he turned and ran.

The ruse succeeded. He heard them coming after him and made for the rock where he and Mac usually met Malcolm and the boy with the pony. He left the path, crossed the little burn by the stepping-stones and took to the heather.

He heard them crossing the burn, splashing in the water and cursing heartily, but instead of keeping on up the path, they came after him up the hill and he realised that he was leaving an easily defined track in the wet heather, so he turned left onto the bare hillside and increased his pace. He was not really afraid of being caught, for after ten days of stalking he was in good training and it was most unlikely that his pursuers could keep up the pace for long.

At first they kept on shouting to him to stop, assuring him that all they wanted was to talk to him for a few minutes, but when they saw that he had no intention of stopping, they ceased to shout and came on in grim silence. Probably they needed all their breath for climbing.

The mist became thinner as Gerald climbed upwards, for there was a stirring of air which lifted it and sent it whirling gently like smoke. He could now see all round him for about twenty steps; beyond that the mist was like a white wall. Gerald began to get a little worried, for if the mist became too thin, they would see him and it was just possible that they had a rifle with them! If so, would they shoot—or not?

It was then that Gerald saw a stunted rowan tree (he had noticed it when he had been for his solitary walk on Sunday and it had impressed him because of its strange shape) and he realised that he was approaching the "queer" part of Ard na Feidh, so he struck off his previous course at an angle and climbed on faster than before. He had hoped to shake off his pursuers, but it was impossible to climb fast without dislodging loose stones which rolled downhill and betrayed his whereabouts.

Gerald was in the "queer" part of the forest now with the rocks and bogs and stunted rowans. He came over a ridge and saw that at the bottom of the declivity there was a pool of slimy green water; it might have been the very same bog which had given him such a fright on Sunday or it might have been another. It looked the same. He ran round the edge of it as fast as he could and then stopped and looked back: two shadowy figures, one tall and lanky, the other shorter and thick-set, emerged from the surrounding mist.

"There he is!" shouted the tall one. With that they came towards him; next moment they were both stuck firmly in the mud.

Gerald left them there struggling and cursing and ran down the hill. He had lost his bearings by this time, but he found a burn and followed it—all the burns on this side of the forest drained into the river—and before long he found the wire fence and the creaky gate.

Once or twice during the mad chase Gerald had been a bit frightened. He was too imaginative not to realise that various things might happen: the mist might lift or he might fall and hurt himself; he might sprain his ankle; but now that he had eluded his pursuers and left them floundering in the bog, he had lost all fear of them.

All morning he had been too engrossed in avoiding capture to have had time to think about what he was going to say to Major Kane. He must tell him everything of course, but really there was not much to tell. He had not seen his pursuers except as two shadowy figures in the mist. How much better it would be if he could identify them!

He had got to this point in his reflections when he heard the click of the gate in the wire fence at the top of the plantation (it was a loud creak, a sort of grinding sound, so there was no mistaking it) and he realised that the two men must have managed to extricate themselves from the bog and were still in pursuit.

What should he do? There would be time to run on to the stepping-stones and cross the river to the road . . . but then, quite suddenly, he remembered a Red Indian trick (he had been an avid reader of Fenimore Cooper when he was a boy) and here was an ideal place to employ it . . . so he walked down to the river in the wet mud and then stepped backwards, putting his feet carefully in the same footprints. Then he swung himself up into the nearest oak, an ancient giant, and settled himself amongst its branches. That would give them something to think about, thought Gerald, smiling to himself.

A few minutes later the long lanky man came running down the path. He looked at the footprints, crossed the river by the stepping-stones and came back. Meanwhile the second man had come down the path. He was gasping like a fish. He threw himself on the ground.

"I'm done," he declared. "I'm not going a step farther—not till I have a rest. Besides you don't know that he's come this way——"

"Yes, I do," interrupted the tall lanky man. "Oh, it was luck, I grant you that. I had a hunch that he was on his way to get his car and bunk when we met him this morning, so I thought he would have another try. Then it was easy enough to pick up his spoor at the gate. The soles of his rubber boots are an unusual pattern. He's come this way all right."

"Oh, well, he's across the river and on the road by this time, so——"

"He didn't cross the river."

"What d'you mean? Those are his footprints, aren't they?"

"Yes, but there aren't any prints on the other side."

"Where is he, then?"

"In the river—unless he has wings, of course."

"How d'you mean, 'in the river'?"

"It's an old dodge. He's wading in the water."

"Has he gone up or down?"

"How do I know?"

"You're supposed to be tracking him."

"A man doesn't leave footprints in running water. We had better separate. You can go up the river and I'll go down."

"Nothing doing."

"What do you mean? He's only a few minutes ahead of us. Come on, Grooby. We'll get him if we hurry."

"I'm not going after him alone. That's flat."

"Spinner will be furious if we lose him again."

"Let him be furious. I'm just about sick of Spinner. Why does he want this fellow so badly?"

They were both sitting down now, just beneath the tree, but the foliage was so thick that Gerald could not see them properly. He could see their feet. He could smell the smoke from the cigarettes they had lighted and he could hear their voices quite clearly, but their voices were just like thousands of other voices. Neither of the men had any identifiable accent.

"Why does he want this fellow so badly?" repeated the man called Grooby in a lower tone.

"He doesn't tell me his secrets," was the reply. "As a matter of fact it's better to do as you're told and not ask questions. Spinner isn't a patient man."

"Have you ever seen Spinner?"

"I saw him this morning."

"Do you mean he's here?"

"Yes, at the Inn—but he's not liking it much. It's a foul hole, isn't it?"

"The new wing isn't so bad. I mean the new wing where we have our meals—but the old part of the house is full of dry rot and wood-worm. I know a bit about old houses (I was in the building trade at one time), so Raddle was talking to me about it, asking what he could do to the place. I told him the best thing he could do was to burn it."

There was a short silence, then Grooby rolled over onto

his stomach and groaned. "Oh, hell, I'm stiff and sore!" he complained. "I'm not used to climbing hills like you . . ."

Gerald could see him better now. He could see the greasy hair straggling over his collar.

"You'll be stiffer tomorrow," said his companion unfeelingly.

"It's not good enough," Grooby declared. "We do the work and take the risk—and what do we get out of it? What did you get out of the dockyard affair?"

"That's not your business."

"All right. Don't get shirty. You got the same as me, I suppose. I just meant, what does he get out of it? He takes good care of himself and rakes in the money."

"He's clever," objected the thin man. "You've got to have a planner to organise these affairs."

"It's not good enough," Grooby repeated. "I want to get out of the racket."

The thin man laughed. (It was not a pleasant sound.) He said, "Nobody gets out of this racket and stays alive."

"Rushton got out."

"Yes, Rushton got out—and what happened to him?"

"You mean, it wasn't an accident?"

"How do I know? All I say is: it was a lucky accident for Spinner . . . and I suppose you think it was an accident that Fison fell out of a top-floor window? And what about Harry Brown? Harry was on his way to Rome when his plane exploded in the air. Funny all these 'accidents,' don't you think?"

"I liked Harry," said Grooby reflectively. "He was a decent sort. If I thought Spinner had done for Harry, I'd put a bullet through him—that's what."

"You wouldn't dare."

"I would."

There was a short silence. Then Grooby spoke again. He said, "As a matter of fact, that might be the best way——"

"Well, don't tell me about it. I don't want to know your plans. See?"

"I've no plans," declared Grooby. "I just meant——"

"Be quiet!"

"Why? What's the trouble?"

"I heard something!"

The fat man sat up and looked round uneasily. "What did you hear?" he asked.

For a moment Gerald was alarmed; he had moved his foot slightly and one of the old dry twigs had snapped.

"Oh, nothing much, replied the thin man carelessly. "Must have been a rabbit or something." He rose and added, "Come on! You've had your rest. We'll have one more try—and then go back to the Horseman's Inn for a meal."

"What's the good? You said you didn't know which way he'd gone?"

"I've a hunch he's gone up the river."

"You and your hunches!"

"I was right last time, wasn't I?"

Grooby got up and straightened his back—and groaned.

"Come on," said his companion impatiently.

They set off together on their wild-goose chase.

Gerald saw them go. They were following the path up the river and talking as they went. It struck him that if they really expected to find him, it would have been more sensible for them to be silent . . . but that was their look-out.

Gerald was pleased with himself: he had led them up hill and down dale and finally he had outwitted them. He decided to give them five minutes to get well on their way, then he would climb down from his hiding-place and run as fast as he could in the opposite direction. He would make for the hump-backed bridge; from thence it would be easy to get to MacTaggart's and ring up the police.

Gerald waited for five minutes. Then he climbed down and jumped. He landed lightly on his feet and was about to set off on the last lap of his run when the two men sprang upon him and seized him. A sack was pulled over his head and tied tightly round his knees and he was flung to the ground. He struggled and tried to shout, but he was helpless. The next moment he felt a sharp stab in his thigh—like the sting of a wasp—and realised that he had been doped. As he drifted into unconsciousness, he heard his captors laughing. It was not a pleasant sound.

24

In Which Are Recorded Gerald's Adventures at the Horseman's Inn

When Gerald came to himself, he discovered that he was lying on a settee in a room that he had never seen before. His ankles were tied together and his arms were bound to his body so that he could not move hand nor foot. At first his brain was dazed, but gradually he recovered and remembered what had happened . . . and cursed himself for his folly! He had been too pleased with himself. He had underestimated his enemies and had been trapped like a silly rabbit!

The room was large and old and very dirty, with oak panelling on the walls and ragged curtains at the open window. Gerald could see the tops of trees: their leaves were moving gently in the evening breeze. He had just decided that this must be the old part of Raddles' Inn when the door opened and three men appeared. Two of them were the men who had captured Gerald (the tall thin individual and the short fat man). The third man was clean and well dressed in a brown tweed suit and was wearing large dark spectacles. He gave orders that the prisoner was to be lifted and placed in a wooden chair with arms, which stood beside a table in the middle of the room. His ankles were loosened and his feet were tied to the legs of the chair in a very uncomfortable position.

"Is that right, sir?" asked the thin man.

"He's still fuddled," was the reply. "Bring a large cup of coffee and loosen his arms. You must have given him too much dope."

"It was the only way we could get him. He was fighting mad."

"I don't want excuses. Do as you're told and hurry up about it, Lanky."

"Lanky" carried out the orders without another word.

So this was the Spinner, thought Gerald. This was the head of the gang! Gerald wished he could tear off the spectacles and see what the man looked like. (Walter had said he was a genius in his own line of country!)

Gerald's mouth was dry—his tongue felt like a piece of leather—so he was glad to see the cup of steaming coffee. He realised that there might be more dope in it, but he thought it unlikely. He thought the Spinner wanted to question him. He was right of course. His two captors were dismissed in a summary fashion; the Spinner locked the door and sat down opposite Gerald at the table.

"I want to talk to you," he said. "I'm sorry it had to be like this, but there was no other way. The dope they gave you is harmless; you'll feel better when you've had some coffee. Don't try any tricks. I've got a revolver in my pocket, but I have no intention of using it if you behave sensibly. All I want is information. If your information is useful, I'm willing to pay you a good price for it."

"What do you want?"

"I want a little information about the security measures in MacCallum's Ship-Yard. I know a good deal already: for instance, I know about the baker's van. It was quite a clever dodge, but not quite clever enough; a man at the garage tried to move it and found it unexpectedly heavy (it's bullet-proof, of course). I paid him handsomely for that information and gave him a passport and his fare to Australia. He's well on his way by this time. I'll do the same for you."

Gerald was silent. He was drinking the coffee (it was good, well-made coffee, hot and strong and sweet) and his brain was clearing.

"Come now," said the Spinner persuasively. "All I want from you is some information about the alarm signals. They are worked by electric wires which run beneath the surface of the ground. They start up the bells and turn on the lights. I want to know exactly where they are hidden. When you have given me the information you can walk out of here, a free man with a thousand pounds in your pocket—a thousand pounds, a passport and a ticket to any place in the world—or you can go back to your job at MacCallum's if you prefer it."

"What do you mean?"

"Nobody will know about our little arrangement except you and me. You will be the richer by a thousand pounds."

"Why ask me?"

"Because you're an electrician I expect you helped to lay the wires so you know all about them."

This was true: Gerald had helped to install the cables, so he knew exactly where they had been hidden. He also knew that quite recently they had been removed and replaced by radar device. The information that the Spinner wanted was worthless: it didn't matter whether he gave it or not.

Gerald thought about it seriously: Should he give this man the information? Meanwhile he played for time. "It's too little for such a big risk," he said sulkily.

"Two thousand, then?" suggested the Spinner. "I've got a chart of the Yard and a red pencil. All you have to do is to trace the course of the wires—it won't take you ten minutes. Then you can leave here, a free man. You can go abroad or you can go back to your job and forget all about our little piece of business. I shan't bother you any more."

"Supposing I refuse?"

"That would be foolish. It would mean I should have to send you to Mr. Spinner to deal with. He has ways and means of making people talk. Sometimes, if people refuse to carry out his orders, he's a little rough. You wouldn't like that, would you?"

"I thought you were the Spinner."

"Dear me, no! Mr. Spinner leaves all this sort of business to me. I wonder what gave you the idea that I was Mr. Spinner."

There was something in the man's demeanour which confirmed Gerald's conviction that this was the Spinner himself. He was certain of it. This was the man who planned the raids and the robberies and watched from a safe distance while his underlings carried out his orders. This was the "ruthless devil" who had eliminated Rushton and Fison and Harry Brown—and probably half a dozen others—when they ceased to be of any use to him. They knew too much, so he couldn't afford to let them go and he had taken steps to silence them forever. Gerald realised that he was in the same boat! He knew too much. Therefore it was better, for his own sake, to pretend that the information he possessed was valuable and to refuse to give it. Then, perhaps, the Spinner would keep him alive for a few days longer and he might have a chance to escape.

It was pretty hopeless; he saw that. The mere fact that the bribe was so large and had been doubled without the slightest hesitation showed that the Spinner had no intention of handing over the money. There would be another "regrettable accident" and this time Gerald Burleigh-Brown would be the victim.

Curiously enough Gerald wasn't frightened. He was surprised at this, himself. Perhaps it was because it was all so extraordinary that he couldn't believe it was real . . . or perhaps he was still slightly under the influence of the dope they had given him.

"Come on," said the Spinner impatiently. "Make up your mind. I can't wait here all night."

"Well, I don't know," replied Gerald in doubtful tones. "I've got a good, well-paid job and I shouldn't like to lose it.

Two thousand pounds is a lot of money, but it wouldn't last forever. I can't make up my mind in a hurry."

The Spinner hesitated for a moment and then took a large envelope from his pocket and produced a map. "Very well," he said. "You can have half an hour. Look, here's the map!"

Gerald watched while the Spinner spread the map on the table and smoothed out the creases . . . and was reminded of Malcolm who had done the same thing with his map of Ard na Feidh. But whereas Malcolm's map was a rough and ready sketch, this map was a professional chart, drawn to scale, and whereas Malcolm's hands were the hands of a worker—big and hard and brown—this man's hands were as smooth and white as the hands of a woman. There was something queer about these hands. Something that Gerald found rather disgusting.

"It's a good map, isn't it?" said the map-maker. "I see you find it interesting. Map-making is one of my hobbies."

Gerald found the map a little too "interesting." It was correct in every detail. He wondered how the Spinner had obtained all his information.

"You must have been there yourself!" exclaimed Gerald.

"Oh, yes! I have ways and means of getting into the place whenever I feel inclined. Bolts and bars and guard-dogs (and all the other silly devices) are useless to keep me out of any place when I make up my mind to get in." He laughed and added, "And the police know to their cost that bolts and bars are useless to keep me in if I want to get out."

He was mad, of course! The Spinner was a megalomaniac—like Napoleon and Hitler and all the other men who had wielded absolute power. For the first time Gerald was a little frightened.

"What do you want?" he asked.

"I've told you. I want you to study the map and draw the course of the wires with a red pencil."

"You want more than that."

"Well, perhaps," agreed the Spinner. "But we'll start with the wires. When you've done that—and done it correctly—I may ask you a few questions. Oh, nothing important, of course! You needn't be alarmed. I promise you faithfully that if you behave sensibly, you shall be a free man in half an hour."

"You must give me more time——"

"More time for what?" interrupted the Spinner. "Don't you realise your position? You're a helpless prisoner. I can do as I like with you. I can lock you up in the cellar and starve you, or I can give you some other unpleasant treatment. This wretched hovel is miles off the beaten track—that's why I chose it for my temporary headquarters—so you can shout and yell as loud as you like; nobody will hear you. I've got four of my own men here and the Raddles are in my pocket. That's your position, *Mister Burleigh-Brown.*"

Suddenly Gerald was angry—too angry to continue the farce!

"You can have your answer now," he declared . . . and, with that, he seized the map, tore it to bits and threw the pieces into a waste-paper basket which was standing under the table.

"How silly!" exclaimed the Spinner furiously. "You don't suppose that's my original map, do you? That was only a copy. You're a bit too uppish, *Mister Burleigh-Brown!* Perhaps you don't understand plain English! Perhaps you think I don't mean what I say? Perhaps a little psychological treatment is what you need; it may teach you better manners. . . ." He took a cord, tied Gerald's hands behind his back and then paused. "But I mustn't be too rough," he added softly.

The first blow landed upon the prisoner's right eye, the second on his left eyebrow. After that there was a succession of blows, first on one ear and then on the other. They were not very hard, but they sent his head swinging from side to side and made his ears buzz like a swarm of angry bees.

The brutal attack was so sudden and unexpected that,

Gerald almost fainted. It was not so much the pain (though that was bad enough), it was the absolute helplessness which was so unbearable. He had known that he was a helpless prisoner, but the treatment he was receiving brought it home to him; he couldn't raise a finger to defend himself; he couldn't even wipe away the blood which was running down his face from a cut in his eyebrow.

"There, that will do in the meantime," said the Spinner. "It's just a little foretaste of what you'll get if you're unreasonable. Not very pleasant, is it?"

The Spinner didn't wait for an answer. He turned and went away, locking the door behind him.

Gerald was too dazed to think. Then when his senses returned, he remembered reading about the treatment given to prisoners in Nazi Camps during the war—they had been tied up and battered. The treatment was given daily by men who had been trained in psychology and knew how to graduate the punishment. Each "treatment" had been a little more violent until at the end of a week the wretched prisoner's spirit was broken! Gerald saw that it could easily be true. For a while he remained inert, slumped in the chair, trying to regain some measure of courage. . . .

Then suddenly he sat up and gazed about him. There was a strange smell in the room! What was it? Where did it come from? Little spirals of smoke were rising from the cracks between the ill-fitting boards of the old oaken floor. They wavered in the still air and drifted, forming a thin cloud which rose to the ceiling.

Smoke! The place was on fire! Nothing could have revived the prisoner more quickly. He struggled to loosen the cords which bound his hands and feet, but the man who had bound him had known his job—the knots were secure; the cords too strong to break.

Somebody had said that the old part of The Horseman's Inn was full of wood-worm and dry rot and the best thing to do was to burn it. Who had said that? It was Grooby, of course! Perhaps Raddle had taken Grooby's advice—or (even more horrifying!) perhaps the Spinner himself had set fire to the place! It would be another "regrettable accident" like the explosion in the plane when Harry Brown was on his way to Rome.

"Fire!" shouted Gerald. "Fire! Help! Help! The house is on fire!"

It was useless to shout for help if Raddle or the Spinner had set fire to the place on purpose, but Gerald's instinct was to shout, so he kept on shouting until he was hoarse and the smoke caught the back of his throat and made him cough. He was still shouting and struggling and coughing—and his ears were still buzzing—when a hand was laid on his shoulder and a voice said, "Be quiet! It's a friend. It's Shipman's guttersnipe."

The cords which bound his feet and hands had been tied so firmly that even when they had been cut he couldn't move, but strong arms lifted him from the chair, carried him across the room and dropped him out of the window (strong arms which certainly didn't belong to "Shipman's guttersnipe"). He fell softly into a stretched-out blanket and was picked up and bundled into the back seat of a waiting car.

It was dark by this time—dark and misty and smoky—but there were people about: quite a crowd of men, moving hither and thither, talking in low voices. Some of them were carrying old-fashioned stable lanterns, others had electric torches. The lights were twinkling on brass helmets and on the shiny black peaks of policemen's hats. It was a weird scene; it was like a scene in a play; it was all the more strange because, although Gerald could hear the murmur of innumerable voices, he couldn't understand a word they were saying. Where had he got to? What was happening?

Then, suddenly, a hand was laid firmly on his knee and a well-known voice said clearly, "You are all right, Mister Gerald. There is no need for you to worry. I am here with the Ardfalloch Fire Brigade . . . and Major Kane is here with the policemen from Kincraig. Look, I will tuck this blanket round you and you can have a wee sleep. There, that is better. You are warm and comfortable now."

Gerald couldn't reply. His rescue had happened so suddenly and unexpectedly that he could scarcely believe it was real. Perhaps he was dreaming. Perhaps he would wake to find himself still a prisoner in a smoke-filled room, tied to a wooden chair!

"Oh, there you are, MacTaggart!" exclaimed another voice (the crisp, clear voice of a man, used to command). "I was looking for you. How many men have you got?"

"There are six of us, sir. Some of the lads are busy getting the engine started and laying the hose. It is not a very good engine, but Euan knows the way of it."

"Is Mr. Burleigh-Brown all right?"

"He is not bad at all, Major. I have him safe——"

"It was a neat job, MacTaggart!"

"Och, it was nothing," declared the Big Fish modestly. He added, "The lads are wanting to know if they can shoot. I was telling them we would need to get your permission——"

"Shoot?" exclaimed Major Kane. "Good heavens! Are they carring fire-arms?"

"Not fire-arms," said MacTaggart hastily. "Not firearms, Major. Some of them have wee pistols—just mementoes, Major. Just wee mementoes over from the war."

"And how do you suppose I can account for a body with a bullet in it?" enquired Major Kane. "No, MacTaggart, I can't give them permission to use revolvers. Tell them that, will you?" He had scarcely spoken when there was a loud report, followed almost immediately by two more.

"Good lord!" ejaculated Major Kane.

"It iss not uss, sir," declared a soft Highland voice. "It iss them, shooting each other. It iss a chentleman in a prown coat, sir."

"What do you mean, Dalgleish?"

"It wass one of his friends that hass shot him in the pack and kilt him—not uss, sir."

Major Kane accepted this somewhat surprising statement calmly and proceeded to give orders to his sergeant, who had joined the little group that was standing near the car. "We want them all, Sims," said Major Kane. "You had better station a man at every door and arrest them as they come out. The place is like a rabbit warren, so it won't be easy. I wish I had brought twice the number of men—but Mr. MacTaggart has six local lads who are willing to help."

"Only too willing," put in MacTaggart cheerfully. He added, "Once they have got the fire under control, I will tell them to report to you, Major."

"The fire is under control, sir," declared the sergeant. "They got it in time to prevent it spreading. It was an electric wire in a lumber room that set fire to a dirty greasy old carpet. Mister Parker is of the opeenion that it was set fire to on purpose, but there's no proof of that."

"Better not mention it, then."

"No, sir."

"It's funny that nobody noticed it before. There's a hell of a lot of smoke."

"That's true," agreed Sims. "But it's confined to the old part of the house. Everybody seems to be in the new part of the house having a meal. They've got enough whisky to float a battleship."

"How do you know?"

"It was Mister Parker. He climbed up a tree and looked in at the window and saw them. There are no flies on Mister Parker. He says it's raw whisky they're drinking—foul stuff! It's my belief Raddle makes it himself."

"Do you mean he has an illicit still?"

Sims nodded, "But there's no proof of that eether."

"We can keep it in mind and look for it later. You had better get going, Sims. Tell our men to be as quiet as possible—we want to take them by surprise—there's sure to be a mad rush for the doors when they see the smoke."

"Yes, sir, but it won't be all that difficult; most of them are half tight already."

"I want them all, Sims. Everybody in the house."

"Yes, sir."

"They're dangerous. Don't forget that."

"No, sir. We can—er—be a bit rough, I suppose?"

"As rough as you like," replied Major Kane cheerfully. He added, "Meanwhile somebody must take Mr. Burleigh-Brown to the nearest hospital."

"There is no need," declared MacTaggart. "He is sleeping now. I will take him to Katie."

"Katie?"

"Katie MacTaggart. It is the wee white cottage by the bridge. Katie will see to him all right."

25

In Which an Invalid Receives Visitors

Gerald did not waken until well on in the following day. He found himself in a small clean attic room with a deerskin rug on the floor. He was trying to remember what had happened to him when Katie MacTaggart came in with a bowl of soup.

"Oh, you are better!" she exclaimed. "You were unconscious when they carried you in last night and you looked so bad that I sent Colin for Doctor Wedderburn."

"I can't remember what happened to me," said Gerald, frowning.

"Don't try to remember," suggested his hostess. "Just take the broth and go to sleep. Doctor Wedderburn gave you an injection and put three stitches in your eyebrow, but he did it very neatly, so the scar will soon disappear. He left some sedative tablets to help you to sleep and said he would look in and see you tomorrow."

"I'm an awful nuisance," Gerald murmured unhappily.

"Oh, no!" replied Mrs. MacTaggart. "I am very pleased to look after you. I have had nursing experience, you know. I just wish I had a better room to give you; this is Sandy's room—and very small and bare. It is not what you have been used to at all. But Doctor Wedderburn wants you to keep quiet." She shook up his pillows, gave him the soup and the tablets and settled him comfortably for the night.

Gerald was young and healthy, so his cuts and bruises healed up quickly and the swelling went down, but it was not until the third day that he felt more like himself and began to remember things clearly. He explained this to the doctor.

"Don't worry," said Doctor Wedderburn. "It will take a few days for you to recover from the shock to your nervous system. The ear is a delicate piece of mechanism and closely connected with the brain . . . but it will soon come right. Just sleep as much as possible, that's the best treatment. Katie MacTaggart is a very good nurse; she'll look after you."

"I want to know what happened," Gerald told him.

"Well, you can see Mac if you like. He's here, asking for you, but I don't want you to get overtired."

Gerald wanted to see Mac (no other visitor would have been more welcome), so Mac came in.

"Poor old chap!" exclaimed Mac. "What a ghastly time you've had!"

"Oh, I'm better," Gerald declared. "Come and talk to me, Mac. I want to know what happened."

"I should think you know more than I do about it!"

"At first I couldn't remember anything at all—which was horribly frightening—but now I'm beginning to remember. In fact I feel all right except for a headache. I've been lying here kicking myself for being such a fool. I was caught in a bag like a silly rabbit and rescued like a sack of potatoes. What happened, Mac?"

"I wasn't there . . . and anyway I'm not much good at explaining things. If you really want to know, you had better see Major Kane. He's very anxious to talk to you when you feel well enough. Could you bear it?"

Gerald said he could bear it, so the second visitor was conducted up the steep little flight of stairs and ushered into the room. Mac was tall, but the second visitor was taller and a good deal broader, so the room seemed overcrowded. It was obvious that Mrs. MacTaggart didn't approve; she warned them not to overtire her patient and went away.

"I shan't stay long," said Major Kane. "I've got my prisoners safely locked up and Scotland Yard is sending guards to take them to London, but I shall have to write a report, so I'll be glad of any information you can give me. You've got very good friends, Mr. Burleigh-Brown, especially James MacTaggart. If it hadn't been for him, we wouldn't have been able to find you. It was he who rang me up and told me that you had been kidnapped by two men and were a prisoner at The Horseman's Inn."

"How did he know?"

"He didn't tell me—as a matter of fact I didn't ask—he was very upset about you. He was quite frantic. So I agreed to take some of my men and rescue you without delay. I didn't expect much trouble—certainly not a pitched battle—so I hadn't brought nearly enough police to deal with the situation. I was wondering what on earth to do when MacTaggart himself turned up with the Ardfalloch Fire Brigade."

Mac said thoughtfully, "I've sometimes wondered if a private Fire Brigade is legal."

"I don't know—and I don't want to know," replied the Chief Constable. "I can see snags, of course. It might cause jealousy and muddle if they interfered with an official fire-fighting force, but under the leadership of a man like MacTaggart I'm all for it. (I should hate to have to disband the Ardfalloch Fire Brigade, so we'll just keep dark about it, shall we?) Anyhow it arrived in the nick of time: five brawny Highlanders wearing brass helmets, like old-fashioned coal scuttles, and an insignificant little fellow in plain clothes. They looked like something out of the The Pirates of Penzance—but I can tell you I was pleased to see them (a band of angels straight from heaven couldn't have been more welcome) and the insignificant little fellow is worth his weight in gold."

"Joseph Parker," murmured Gerald.

"Yes, that's the chap. It was he who heard you shouting

and found a ladder in the stables . . . and he was first up the ladder, as nimbly as a monkey, with the blacksmith's son close behind. Meanwhile MacTaggart and Co. had organized a stretched blanket to catch you. The rescue was carried out smartly and efficiently. A professional brigade couldn't have done it better."

"Did they put out the fire?" Gerald wanted to know.

"It wasn't a serious fire—just a greasy old carpet. My fellows had found it and extinguished it before the Ardfalloch lads arrived." Major Kane smiled and added, "They were a bit disappointed; they had hoped for 'a real good blaze.' "

"There was a lot of smoke," said Gerald.

"Yes, I know. Your friend, Parker, thinks there was something fishy about it; he says the carpet was impregnated with a chemical which caused it to smoulder for hours—but I'm not a chemist so I don't know about that—and anyhow there are enough puzzles in this case without mentioning arson."

"Was anybody injured?" asked Mac.

"One of the prisoners is dead; somebody shot him through the heart."

There was a short silence.

Major Kane continued, "The police weren't armed, or course, but some of the local lads were armed. MacTaggart said they had wee pistols—'just mementoes over from the war.' None of the 'wee pistols' had been discharged, so I'm keeping quiet about it. If I were to mention that some of them had revolvers in their pockets, I should have to take measures against them for carrying fire-arms."

Gerald had been listening with interest; the pieces of the puzzle were taking shape. He said quietly, "I've no proof of course—so perhaps it isn't much use—but I shouldn't be surprised to hear that the Spinner was killed by one of his own gang."

"What!" exclaimed Major Kane. "Good heavens! Please tell me exactly what happened."

Gerald told him. The chase over the hills could be told in a few words but the conversation between "Lanky" and Grooby took longer and was more difficult to remember in detail. Finally he reported his conversation with the Spinner. Major Kane listened carefully and then said, "You heard Grooby threaten to put a bullet through Spinner? Sometimes people make threats and don't really mean to carry them out."

"Grooby meant it," replied Gerald with conviction. "Grooby wants to 'get out of the racket.' "

"So you really think he carried out his intention and that the man who questioned you was Spinner himself?"

"Yes, I'm almost certain he was the head of the gang. I couldn't swear to it, of course. He pretended he wasn't the Spinner, but he spoke as if he had complete authority and offered me two thousand pounds for the information he wanted."

"Two thousand!" echoed Mac in amazement.

"Oh, he didn't intend to give me the money! He just meant to get the information out of me. Then, when he had got what he wanted and I was of no further use to him, he would have put an end to me. There would have been another 'regrettable accident—' "

"But you would have been of use to him," interrupted the Major. "You underrate Spinner. He lays his plans with a view to the future. If you had accepted the bribe, you would have been in his power for the rest of your life. That's the way he gets hold of men for his gang. He begins by offering a man a bribe for a small misdemeanour, for something not quite straight (for something which appears simple and perfectly safe). Then he goes on to offer more for something definitely crooked . . . and the wretched victim daren't say no. Finally when the victim is thoroughly in his power, Spinner enlists him in his band of brigands. You say that the information he wanted was worthless, so it wouldn't have mattered whether you gave it to him or not, but it's quite possible that Spinner knew it was worthless and was just trying to tempt you to take the first step on the downward path."

Gerald considered this thoughtfully. It might be true. If so, it was diabolically clever. In his own mind he felt more than ever certain that the man who had beaten him up was the Spinner, but he saw that there had to be proof. He said slowly, "The man who questioned me and assaulted me was wearing big dark spectacles which hid his face, but you could identify him by his finger-prints, couldn't you? He wasn't wearing gloves."

"That's just what we can't do," replied Major Kane regretfully. "The room is old and exceedingly dirty. There are dozens of finger-prints all over the place. It looks as if it hasn't been cleaned for years."

"Probably it hasn't," said Mac, nodding. "Mrs. Raddle is dirty and lazy."

"There was one thing I noticed," Gerald said. "I was watching his hands when he was spreading out the map. His hands were unusual: they were small and white and the fingers were short and stubby—but I wouldn't like to identify him by that. It was a map of MacCallum's Ship-Yard. He had made it himself and was rather proud of it, so he was furious when I tore it to bits and chucked it into the waste-paper basket . . . The map!" cried Gerald, sitting up in bed in his excitement. "The map! Oh, what a fool I am! Why didn't I think of it before? He took it out of an envelope and spread it on the table . . . so of course it will have his finger-prints on it—his and mine."

"You tore it up and dropped it into the waste-paper basket?"

"Yes."

Major Kane didn't wait for more. He turned and ran out of the room and down the stairs. They heard him start his car and roar off up the road.

Gerald sighed and lay back on his pillow. "It's too late," he said wearily. "Mrs. Raddle has probably emptied the basket and burned the contents."

"Unlikely," Mac declared. "Mrs. Raddle is a lazy slut. Of

course if it had been Kirsty, she would have tidied up the room thoroughly."

There was a short silence.

"How is everybody?" asked Gerald at last.

"Everybody is fine," replied Mac cheerfully. "You will be sorry to hear that our dear friend Oliver took the huff at something I said and left us. He has gone to stay with Lucius Cottar, of course."

"Of course," agreed Gerald.

"Kirsty is in particularly good form. She was humming the MacGregors' Lament this morning—a sure sign that she's happy. Malcolm is happy too. He said to me that it was a pity Mister Stoddart did not kill the Royal—but he didn't mean it."

"Poor Stoddart!" said Gerald, smiling. "He isn't popular, is he?"

Mac hesitated and then said, "Gerald, listen! I've got to go to London next week. I don't want to go—I'm a country cousin—but Major Kane wants me. I saw two of those men in MacTaggart's Public Bar and had a good look at them, so I would know them again. All I shall have to do is to pick them out from a crowd of other men. See?"

Gerald nodded. He wondered what was coming.

"Then there's Donny," continued Mac. "Donny's father has written to say she's to come home. If she comes with me, I can drop her at Larchester; it's on my way, so it wouldn't be any bother and it would save her the expense of her railway fare. (They're rather badly off, you know.) Last, but not least, I can pick up a friend on the way back. He's a captain in the gunners and a good shot with a rifle, so he can help me to cull the hinds."

"You've got it all worked out," suggested Gerald.

"Yes, it fits in quite well . . . but it means that Phil will be alone in Tigh na Feidh. I don't like the idea at all. I wondered if you could come back and stay with her until——"

"I can't!" interrupted Gerald. "I've had my holiday. I must go back to Glasgow and do some work."

"You aren't fit——"

"I'll soon be better. Dr. Wedderburn says I can drive back if I stay a night on the way."

"Oh, I say! Couldn't you stay for a week? You won't be fit for stalking, but a quiet lazy time at Tigh na Feidh is just what you need. I'd feel much happier if you were there with Phil."

"Malcolm and Kirsty will be there, won't they?"

"Yes, of course—and they're very good value in their own line—but they aren't very bright if anything unexpected happens."

"What could happen?"

"Oh, I don't know," replied Mac, frowning. "Major Kane thinks he's got all those devils safely under lock and key, but they're as slippery as eels, aren't they?"

Gerald couldn't deny this. He rememberd what the Spinner had said about bolts and bars and guard-dogs.

"Do stay," urged Mac. "Sir Walter wouldn't mind, I'm sure."

No, thought Gerald, Walter wouldn't mind. Walter would be only too willing to extend his holiday. It was Gerald himself who "minded." He had decided that he must banish Phil from his heart (it would be terribly difficult of course, but she was not for him and the sooner he got over his madness the better). A week in her company at Tigh na Feidh wouldn't help his love-lorn condition.

"Do say you will," pleaded Mac. "You're so dependable, Gerald. I know you're fed up with Phil, but——"

"Fed up with Phil?" Gerald exclaimed. "Good heavens, No! Phil is marvellous! There's nobody like her in the Whole Wide World! I'm mad about her! I shall always love her as long as I live; but she doesn't love me. She made that perfectly clear. So I've just got to bear it. I've got to get over it as best I can. . . . but I don't know how I can ever get over it," added Gerald hopelessly.

"It's queer," said Mac, looking at his friend in surprise.

"What's queer," asked Gerald.

"I mean this 'love-business' seems a bit dotty. . . . Oh, well, it can't be helped."

Mac turned to go, but Gerald called him back. "I'll do it," said Gerald. "I'll go back to Tigh na Feidh and stay there for a week—if Phil wants me."

"Oh, it was Phil's idea," said Mac.

He was whistling cheerfully as he ran downstairs. Mac was always happy when he had got exactly what he wanted.

Gerald was tired now and his head was aching, so he snuggled down in bed and shut his eyes. He was almost asleep when a slight movement aroused him. He opened his eyes and found himself looking into a small face covered with brown freckles and topped by a bush of bright red hair. The owner of the bush was kneeling beside the bed so the face was very close—and the blue eyes which were gazing at him wore a somewhat anxious expression.

"Hullo, Sandy!" said Gerald sleepily.

"I did not waken you, Mister Gerald. Mother said I was not to waken you. I was just waiting for you to waken by yourself. I was as quiet as quiet."

Gerald wasn't sure whether or not Sandy had wakened him, but he said soothingly, "I wasn't really asleep. What's the matter, Sandy?"

"I was wanting to ask you something," Sandy explained. "It was on Wednesday. I was searching for you, and at last I saw you on the hill. I was meaning to speak to you when those men came along. They were shouting at you—and swearing at you—and the fat one had a rifle——"

"I know."

"I was frightened he would shoot you—and then I saw you had the legs of them, so I hid in the heather till they passed and then I stalked them. It was easy stalking them—they never looked behind—they were watching you all the time."

Gerald was interested in this recital. "What next?" he enquired.

"You led them into the bog, so I left them there and ran after you. I was wanting to ask you something. I followed you through the pine woods and down to the river and I saw you climbing the big tree. I thought you had jinked them, so I waited a bit. I was just going to call to you—I was wanting to ask you something—when I heard them coming. They sat down beneath the tree. The fat one was panting. His face was very red."

"Did you hear them talking, Sandy?"

Sandy nodded. "It was funny sort of talk, Mister Gerald. I could not be understanding what they said'—except about Raddle's Inn. Then away they went, up the river to find you! I was laughing to myself about it——"

"They came back and caught me in a sack like a rabbit," said Gerald bitterly.

"They were bad men," declared Sandy. "They put the sack over your head and threw you on the ground and kicked you. Then they carried you away. If I had a little rifle, like Miss Phil, I could have shot them—and I would too."

"What did you do?" asked Gerald.

"I waited for a wee while. Then I waded across the river and ran to Uncle Jamie and I told him. He was in a great way. He telephoned to Major Kane and he put out the signal for the Fire Brigade to come . . . and off they went in Uncle Jamie's car. There was six of them and there was no room for me, so I went home."

This seemed to be the end of the story. "It was the right thing to do," Gerald told him. "You couldn't have done anything better. Was that what you wanted to ask me?"

"It was not," replied Sandy promptly. "I was wanting to ask you about lions. Lions are brave. When lions are wounded they attack you—and kill you—and eat you. I was wondering about bools. Bools are not wanting to eat you. Bools eat grass—like stags—but they attack you just the same. Why do they, Mister Gerald?"

Gerald was tired now. His headache was getting worse (it was like a steam-hammer thumping in his head), but he owed this child so much that he felt obliged to answer the questions. I owe him my life, thought Gerald, looking with affection at the freckled face so near his own. (It occurred to Gerald quite suddenly that it would be very pleasant to have a little son of eleven years old. Not quite like Sandy, of course, because his own little son would have dark hair and hazel eyes . . . but that was madness!)

"Why do they, Mister Gerald?"

"Bulls are bad-tempered," suggested Gerald feebly.

Obviously this answer was not entirely satisfactory. "Why are they bad-tempered?" Sandy enquired.

"I don't know."

Sandy continued, "There was a bool attacked Mister Ross, but Mister Mackenzie took a pitchfork and went for it and drove it away. I would take a pitchfork and go for a bool that was attacking you, Mister Gerald."

"That would be very kind of you."

"But there were two big men," said Sandy regretfully.

For a moment Gerald was puzzled. . . . then he saw the point.

"It wouldn't have been any good," he said firmly. "You did the right thing, Sandy. You did the sensible things; you used your head."

"I was frightened," admitted Sandy with a sigh.

Gerald sighed too—the pain in his head was almost unbearable.

"Is your head sore?" asked Sandy sympathetically.

"Yes."

"Will it be better tomorrow?"

"I hope so."

"Could you tell me one more thing?"

"Tomorrow, Sandy."

"Just one more," said Sandy in wheedling tones.

"What is it?"

"Which is the bravest: bools or lions?"

This was much too difficult for Gerald in his present condition. He groaned feebly and shut his eyes.

"Are you wanting to sleep, Mister Gerald?" enquired his tormentor.

"Yes."

"Will you be telling me tomorrow?"

"Yes."

There was a slight sound. The door opened . . . then shut very quietly. Sandy had gone.

Peace—heavenly peace—descended upon the bare little room and Gerald slept.

26

Which Tells How Phil Carried Out Her Idea

It had been Phil's idea that Gerald should come to Tigh na Feidh for a week's convalescence. She wanted to look after him and coddle him until he had recovered from his horrible experience. She had decided to give him breakfast in bed, to feed him well, and to keep him warm and cheerful.

The weather had worsened. There was frost at night and the wind was from the north. The rut had begun; the stags came down from the hill-tops and roared in the early morning. There was ice on the Perilous Road.

Phil had never lived at Tigh na Feidh so late in the year, but the alterations at the Big House were not yet completed, so she stayed on with Malcolm and Kirsty and was comfortable enough . . . but now she began to look about her and to wonder whether it would be comfortable for an invalid. She consulted Kirsty and Kirsty entered into the spirit of the thing. She liked Mister Gerald. It was Kirsty who said that the Tower Room was cold and damp and suggested that the south bedroom (which was over the kitchen) would be warmer.

Malcolm agreed and pointed out that the south bedroom had the advantage of a chimney which didn't smoke (all the other bedroom chimneys were full of jackdaws' nests and had been completely blocked ever since Malcolm could remember).

He put a new cord in the window and oiled the lock of the door (these were jobs he had intended to perform for weeks). Then he brought several loads of wood and piled them beside the fire-place. Meantime Kirsty had given the room a thorough turn out.

Phil took the Land Rover and went down to the village . . . and the first person she saw, coming out of the post-office, was Dr. Wedderburn. She stopped to speak to him, to explain her idea and to ask his advice.

"That's good news," declared the doctor. "Oh, yes, I know I said he could go back to Glasgow, but a week or ten days at Tigh na Feidh will be very much better. His cuts and bruises have healed—he's a healthy young man—but the treatment he received has been a shock to his nervous system. Don't coddle him of course, but keep him warm and cosy."

"Yes, of course," agreed Phil. "What about food, Doctor?"

"Milk and eggs; fresh fruit and vegetables; chops and steaks, porridge and cream and wholemeal bread," replied Doctor Wedderburn. "A glass of burgundy would do him no harm. I've given him a sedative to help him to sleep—and a cup of warm milk at bedtime would be just the thing to send him off to dreamland." The doctor's eyes twinkled and he added, "If he gets bored talking to you, Malcolm can teach him to tie flies and he can read Jane Austen. Goodbye, Phil."

"Goodbye, Doctor," said Phil breathlessly.

She watched him drive off down the road—he was always in a hurry—but it didn't matter; she had got what she wanted.

Her next port of call was the Big House. Here she found a hearth-rug, an eiderdown quilt, a pair of red rep curtains and a bed table so she packed these invalid comforts into the Land Rover.

The doctor had said his patient was to read Jane Austen.

Phil approved of this; Jane was soothing. So Phil went into the library and looked at the shelf of Miss Austen's books. *Persuasion* was her own favourite; she was sure Gerald would like it . . . but then she remembered that Louisa had fallen down the steps at Lyme Regis and had injured her head, so perhaps it wasn't a good choice? Phil considered the matter and then took *Northanger Abbey*: Gerald had a sense of humour, so Catherine's behavior would amuse him.

Finally she took an electric torch and went down the stone steps to the cellar. Here she discovered ten bottles of burgundy. A dozen had been given to MacAslan by Sir Walter MacCallum as a Christmas present and it was produced only on Special Occasions. Phil herself didn't appreciate it, but obviously it must be "good." After a few moments' hesitation she took two bottles, put them into a wine-basket and carried them carefully upstairs. She had been well trained. It was a pity she had to take them to Tigh na Feidh over the Perilous Road, but she must just drive slowly and as smoothly as possible, so as not to upset her delicate passengers.

On the way home Phil called on Mr. MacTaggart and asked him to ring up the butcher at Kincraig and order chops and steaks and a piece of hough for broth. MacTaggart replied that he would be delighted to do so, and made several sensible suggestions. He produced two dozen eggs and a basket of fruit and offered to send the daily paper and the letters and three pints of milk to Tigh na Feidh every morning. It would be no trouble at all; the lad could take them. The lad was eating his head off and the walk would do him good. If there was anything else that Miss Phil wanted, she had only to make a list and give it to the lad. Mr. MacTaggart would see to it himself.

Having settled all this in a satisfactory manner, Phil sat down in the MacTaggarts' private parlour for a cup of tea and a cosy chat. As usual Mr. MacTaggart was full of information and only too willing to pass it on: four plain-clothes detectives had come from London and had made a thorough search of The Horseman's Inn.

"It was the chief of the gang that was killed?" suggested Phil.

"That is so," agreed Mr. MacTaggart, smiling cheerfully. "They call him the Spinner, for he was the one that planned all the raids and the robberies . . . and Major Kane is pleased about that, for the Spinner kept himself in the background so maybe it would have been difficult to be proving anything against him. There were three shots—I heard them myself—and the policemen from London found the weapon that had fired the bullets, but there is no telling who it belonged to. It had been wiped clean and kicked under the table. You see, Miss Phil, there is some way of knowing which pistol has fired the bullets—and all the bullets had been fired out of the same weapon. The sergeant from Kincraig was showing me the funny wee pistol. It was not like the Ardfalloch lads' pistols that they had over from the war—but maybe I should not be telling you that," added Mr. MacTaggart doubtfully.

Phil assured him that she wouldn't mention it to anybody. As a matter of fact, she had heard most of it from Mac, but some of it was news. Having listened with interest to Mr. MacTaggart's story, Phil was quite prepared to tell him about Mac's trip to London, but there was nothing she could tell him that he didn't know already. He knew that Mac had left Ardfalloch the day before yesterday, was breaking his journey at Larchester and then going on to London to meet Major Kane, and Mrs. MacTaggart had heard at a meeting of the Women's Rural Institute that Mister Stoddart had left Tigh na Feidh and had gone to stay with a friend at Ascot.

How did they know all that? wondered Phil, as she drove home slowly and carefully up the Perilous Road. It didn't matter, of course, because she had nothing to hide, but all the same it was a mystery and even the peep-hole into the Public Bar could not account for it.

27

Tells How Mac Solved All the Problems

Gerald had been reluctant to return to Tigh na Feidh; he had feared that his relationship with Phil might be awkward; but Phil had told him that she wanted him as her friend and it was as a friend that she received him. This was all the easier because she was his hostess and had inherited the true Highland tradition of hospitality to a guest. Last, but by no means least, Phil's guest was pale, beneath his suntan, and the scar on his eyebrow was still visible; it was obvious that he had had a bad time and required care.

Gerald had no idea of the elaborate arrangements which had been made for his benefit, but he *did* realise that he was extremely comfortable: the fire in his bedroom was a luxury he enjoyed. He still felt tired and lazy and a little giddy at times, so it was pleasant to be cosseted by Phil and Kirsty. Malcolm, also, was unusually kind. There was a conspiracy of kindness which created a very peaceful pleasant atmosphere in the house.

Doctor Wedderburn had said that the patient was not to be "coddled," so one fine morning Phil took him for a short walk. She took her .22 rifle, intending to shoot a fox which had been marauding Malcolm's hen-run, but her mind was not on the job, so wily old reynard eluded his huntress without difficulty.

The afternoons were cold and unpleasant, so Phil drew the curtains and she and Gerald had tea together beside the dining-room fire. It was extremely cosy. Sometimes they chatted and learnt a great deal about each other—they had had no opportunity of intimate talk before—and sometimes they sat together in silent companionship, Phil with her knitting and Gerald watching her flying fingers or reading *Northanger Abbey* and chuckling. (Gerald was an ardent admirer of Miss Austen and *Northanger Abbey* was the only one of her books which he had not read.)

Gerald was still desperately in love with Phil and now that he was beginning to know her better, he found himself loving her more tenderly than before and appreciating her goodness and kindness and unselfishness. A very sweet companionship grew up between them.

It was on the third day, when Mr. MacTaggart's lad had come with the milk and the mail (and was having tea in the kitchen with Kirsty) that Phil looked up from her letters and said, "There isn't one from Mac! You haven't got one either, have you, Gerald? He said he would write when he got to London. What can he be doing?"

"He may have changed his plans," suggested Gerald. "Mac isn't a great letter-writer, is he? I expect he's waiting till he gets home to tell us all the news."

"He will be in London now," said Phil, frowning.

Gerald agreed that he would be in London. It was strange to think of Mac in London. Mac was so much a part of Ardfalloch that it was difficult to imagine him elsewhere—especially difficult to image him amongst the crowds and the traffic and the noise of a big city! Mac, walking down Piccadilly, would be as out of place as a Royal Stag.

But nobody will know, thought Gerald, smiling to himself. Not one of the busy throng, rubbing shoulders with Mac, will realise that he is rubbing shoulders with a wild Highlander from the North. Mac, in his town clothes, looks just like other young men except that he is unusually good-looking.

Gerald explained this idea to Phil and discovered that she understood—and was interested—but did not agree. "I think I would know," she said thoughtfully.

"You would be too busy to notice," Gerald told her. "You would be too taken up with your own affairs to notice a stag. You would be thinking about Stocks and shares, bulls and bears, or hastening to a directors' meeting, or——"

"Oh, Gerald, you *are* silly," said Phil, laughing.

Gerald laughed too. He knew he was silly, but he had made Phil laugh and forget (for the moment) her anxiety about her brother.

Doctor Wedderburn had said "early to bed," and Phil was carrying out his orders to the letter, so at ten o'clock she rose and suggested that they should "make it a day."

Gerald had snibbed the windows and Phil was putting the guard on the fire when the door opened and Mac walked in.

"Mac!" exclaimed Phil and Gerald in amazement.

"Yes, it's me," agreed Mac, grinning.

"What has happened?" asked Phil in alarm.

"Nothing," replied Mac. "I mean an awful lot has happened. Oh, I know you weren't expecting me, but I had to come. I never went near London. I just came in a hurry because I wanted to see you and explain. Donny said, 'Ask Phil; she'll know what to do about it.' "

"About what?"

"About Donny's father. He'll be furious, of course. The point is—should we tell him or not?"

Gerald was waiting patiently for the point to be arrived at, but Phil was not so patient.

"Why will he be furious? What have you done? Tell us about it for goodness' sake!" she exclaimed.

"All right, keep your hair on," suggested her brother. "I'm telling you about it. I could tell you better if you didn't keep on interrupting me——"

"I'm not interrupting you——"

"Yes, you are. I've come all this way, driving like Jehu, to tell you that you can get married whenever you like. There's nothing to prevent you. See?"

"Mac, what on earth are you talking about?"

"About you and Gerald."

"You're crazy," Phil declared. "Who's going to look after Ardfalloch? Who's going to look after Daddy? Who's going to——"

"Donny and I, of course. We're going to be married."

"You're going to be married?" asked Phil incredulously.

"Why not? Dad is very fond of Donny—and Donny thinks the world of MacAslan—so that's all right. And Donny likes Ardfalloch. You know that, don't you? She thinks Ardfalloch is 'just like heaven.' You've heard her say it, haven't you?"

"But what about you?"

"What about me?" asked Mac in surprise.

"Do you love Donny?"

"Yes, of course!"

"You never said——"

"Oh, I know!" agreed Mac, sitting down and holding his head in his hands. "I know it sounds crazy, but it isn't, really. When Donny was here, two years ago, I liked her. I thought she was nice and she liked me. There was no silly nonsense about it—we just liked each other. This year I liked her even better. I thought she was sweet. She *is* sweet. She's sweet and kind and—and gentle. She's amusing, too, in her own quiet way. Then I took her home to Larchester and stayed there for a couple of days (you know that, of course). It was when I was there that I realised the truth. It was when I heard that foul old man being rude and sarcastic and saw Donny curling up like a sea-anemone! IT MADE ME SEE RED," declared Mac, seizing tufts of his hair as if he intended to pull it out by the roots. "I was so furious that I could have killed him. I wanted to kill him. I wanted to put my hands round his throat and strangle him. It was quite frightening, you know. I've never felt like that before."

Mac paused for a few moments; his hearers gazed at him in alarm.

Then he continued, "I wanted to strangle him—but I couldn't, of course. I mean I could have strangled him quite easily (his throat is thin and stringy, like a chicken), but he's Donny's father and he's old and frail. He's older than Dad, with a bald head and scrubby grey beard—and he's clever. He's much too clever for me. As a matter of fact, he was quite polite to me in a nasty sort of way, but he knows exactly how to make Donny squirm."

"Squirm!" echoed Phil in horrified tones.

"Yes. I had to sit there and watch her turning pale and squirming. She's terrified of him. Oh, he doesn't beat her with sticks; he just beats her with words."

"You're sorry for her——"

"No, I'm not! At least I am, of course, but it isn't because I'm sorry for her that I'm going to marry her. It's because I discovered that I love her—frightfully. It's because I want to—to pick her up in my arms and bring her home to Ardfalloch and make her happy forever and ever."

There was silence.

"Don't you understand?" asked Mac impatiently.

Of course they understood.

Gerald understood because he felt exactly the same about Phil: he loved her—frightfully. He wanted to pick her up in his arms and take her home and make her happy forever and ever. Phil understood because she knew Mac; she knew him inside out.

"Mac," said Phil, very seriously, "does Donny love you?"

"Yes, she does!" replied Mac triumphantly. "It's amazing, isn't it? Donny loves me. It makes me feel seven feet tall and as strong as an ox. It makes me feel like a stag with fourteen points. Donny loves me and she's going to marry me."

"What will her father do without her?"

"That's the snag," agreed Mac. "That's what I came to see you about. Should we tell him or not? He'll kick up a dust, of course—that goes without saying. Donny keeps house for him; she cooks and cleans and washes and mends his clothes. She's just an unpaid drudge—so naturally he won't want to lose her services. Nobody else would do all that—and do it for nothing. Nobody else would stand his beastly rudeness, but it doesn't matter."

"Doesn't matter?"

"Not a hoot," said Mac cheerfully. "If the horrid old man objects, we shall just have to wait until she's twenty-one—and she's going to be twenty-one next month. After that she's free to do what she wants and she wants to marry me. See what I mean?"

They saw.

"So you can go ahead and get married as soon as you like."

"But, Mac——"

"Dad will be all right," interrupted Mac. "Donny and I will live with him at Ardfalloch, of course. We'll look after him and keep him happy, and you can come up from Glasgow and stay with us as often as you want. That's right, isn't it, Gerald?"

"Yes, of course!"

"But, Mac——" began Phil.

"Don't keep on saying BUT," said Mac, somewhat unreasonably. "I've come here to solve all our problems (Major Kane will be annoyed with me if I'm not in London to meet him at the appointed time). I've come here at great inconvenience—and all you say is BUT! What are you butting about, Phil?"

"About Simon," replied Phil in a very small voice.

"Simon!" said Mac scornfully. "Goodness gracious, Phil! You're not worrying about Simon, are you? Simon doesn't love you—not like I love Donny. If Simon loved you—like I love Donny—he wouldn't be content to let things drift. He would want to marry you straight off—like I want to marry Donny. And what's more," said Mac firmly, "what's more, if you loved Simon—like Donny loves me—you wouldn't be content to drift either. I didn't realise this before, of course. It's only now that I see it clearly, it's only now that I understand."

"He's right, you know," said Gerald.

Of course he was right. Phil had seen already that Mac knew what he was talking about.

She said feebly, "But it seems unkind——"

"It would be unkind to marry Simon if you don't love him," declared Mac. "Of course, if you want to be Lady Wentworth and live at Limbourne——"

"I don't!"

"Well then, don't. Don't swither, Phil. Make up your mind. Here's Gerald, who loves you madly and wants to marry you straight off . . . and there's Simon who's having a rattling good time at Cambridge, dancing and playing cricket and speechifying at the Debating Society or whatever it's called. . . ."

Gerald was listening to all this. He had thought of intervening and then he had realised that it would be a mistake: Mac was fighting his battle for him and was making a much better job of it than he could have done. It was because Mac knew Phil so well. It was because he was her brother; they had grown up together; they had shared things; they had been in scrapes together; they had quarrelled and made it up and had become better friends than ever. For a moment Gerald felt a twinge of jealousy (however long he knew Phil, however dearly he loved her, he would never be able to understand her—like this) and then he smiled at his own folly. It's like Bess and me, thought Gerald. Walter worships the ground Bess treads on, but he will never be able to understand her as I do because he didn't know her as a child.

"You needn't marry either of them," Mac was saying. "You can marry Oliver if you like. He told me he had asked you and——"

"I wouldn't marry Oliver if he were the only man in the world!"

Mac nodded seriously. "I think you're right. If I had to

live with Oliver, he would drive me mad in a week."

"He would drive me mad in three days," Phil declared with mounting fury.

"Or you needn't marry any of them," Mac continued. "You can stay at Ardfalloch. Donny and I will be delighted; so will Dad. We all love you dearly—you know that, don't you?"

"How silly you are!" cried Phil. "Of course I want to marry Gerald. I love him just as much as you love Donny—probably more! All I want to know is: What am I to do about Simon? How am I to tell him? He has never asked me to marry him; it has just been an understood thing. How can you write and say you don't want to marry someone when he hasn't asked you?"

"You can write and say you're going to marry Gerald. That's the best way. That's the honest way, Phil."

Phil's eyes were bright with tears. She turned to Gerald and held out her hands. "Oh, Gerald, what am I to do?"

Gerald hesitated.

"Go on, kiss her!" hissed Mac—and fled. He paused at the door for a moment and saw that his advice was being taken with enthusiasm.

Lord Elgin's Lady

a novel by

Theodore Vrettos

Boston

Houghton Mifflin Company

1982

Library of Congress Cataloging in Publication Data

Vrettos, Theodore.
Lord Elgin's lady.

1. Elgin, Thomas Bruce, Earl of, 1766–1841 — Fiction.
2. Ferguson, Mary Nisbet, 1777–1855 — Fiction. I. Title.
PS3572.R38L6 813'.54 81-20059
ISBN 0-395-31333-3 AACR2

Printed in the United States of America

S 10 9 8 7 6 5 4 3 2 1

To John Updike
κοινὰ τὰ τῶν φίλων

Acknowledgments

I AM GRATEFUL to Mr. D. E. L. Haynes, Keeper of the Greek and Roman Antiquities at the British Museum, for his generous assistance. I am equally indebted to the Trustees of the National Library of Scotland and to the librarians there for helping me track down elusive documents and letters concerning the families of Lord and Lady Elgin, particularly the court records of the adultery trial against Robert Fergusson and Lady Elgin.

I should like to thank Mr. A. Anderson, Deputy Keeper of the Scottish Records Office in Edinburgh; also Mr. G. R. Barbour, Assistant to the Curator of Historical Records, and Ms. D. M. Hunter of the same office.

I was provided with additional help by the staffs at the Gennadios Library in Athens, the Library of the Archbishop of Canterbury at Lambeth Palace, and at the national museums at Athens and Olympia.

I am deeply grateful to my editor, Robie Macauley, who planted the seed for this book and nurtured it with his helpful suggestions; and especially to my wife, Vas, for living and working through every word.

— THEODORE VRETTOS

Lord Elgin's Lady

One

ABERLADY BAY.

The ship rounding the harbor and coming into full view of the cone-shaped hill of North Berwick Law, her mother and father waving to her from the shore, the cool fresh breeze of Archerfield on her face, peaceful Scottish woods, fields of autumn grass frolicking along the golden sand, endless ribbons of tern and gull zooming quietly over the sky. It was all so very real . . . little pup Boxer happily swishing his tail against her dress, scampering after her in the meadow, barking, one ear up, the other down . . . and in the purple distance, the kirk bells of Dirleton announcing Michaelmas.

But this was Palermo, not her beloved Aberlady Bay.

Strange sounds tore away her reverie — the clang of the anchor chain running out, the bare feet of the tars on deck, the faraway shouting of orders. Fully awake now and still qualmish, baking in the heat, she felt utterly helpless and distressed. Masterman magnified her misery, standing there alongside the bunk, wringing her hands and mumbling, "Your poor Ladyship. Your poor Ladyship!"

Once again the maid dabbed the vinegar-soaked cloth over her

wrists and forehead. Its obnoxious odor was intolerable. Before leaving the cabin, her husband had entreated her to remain in bed and take the glass of Portuguese brandy, but it lay untouched on the small table beside the bunk. She could not endure much more of this. Stricken by the sea, even as H.M.S. *Phaeton* began to pull away from Portsmouth harbor, she yearned for a merciful end that would close her eyes in peaceful sleep. Scotland seemed aeons away.

In despair, she rebelled and flung away the bedcovers. "Masterman, I'm getting up. Bring my blue frock."

"But my lady."

"Please do as I say."

"His Lordship left explicit orders."

"I can't bear another moment inside this horrible cabin. I'm going on deck."

"His Lordship will blame me."

"You needn't fear. He will understand."

"But my lady . . ."

"Bring my clothes. I want to hear no more about it."

Her clothes suffocated her even more, but as she emerged on the quarterdeck she was greeted by a soft breeze stirring over the water. Turning, she saw Elgin conferring with Captain Morris and stopping to look through a brass telescope at the Palermo shore. From the day of her marriage, this was the first time she had gone against his wishes. "Eggy, I simply had to come on deck. I was dying inside that dreadful cabin."

He was joyful to see her. "Did you take the brandy, Poll?"

She shook her head.

He gave her the telescope and asked her to look through it. She wished that she could share his enthusiasm, but the white arms of Palermo did not reach out to her, and she handed the telescope back to him. "Why is Duff taking so long? He has been gone all day. Any other courier would have found lodgings by this time."

He kissed her in front of Captain Morris. "Be patient, Poll.

Duff will find a suitable place for us. I'm certain of it."

She seized his hand. "Eggy, I can't endure this abominable ship another day. I must go ashore."

He stroked her hair and cheek.

"I wish we were back in Scotland."

"Nonsense. We've been gone only a few weeks."

"But we are nowhere near Constantinople."

"We shall get there eventually."

"You promised me the Mediterranean would be calm."

"It usually is this time of year. It was our misfortune to run into some foul weather, but Captain Morris just now confirmed that we have seen the worst of it."

"That is true, my lady." Morris nodded. "Once we reach the Aegean, the rest of the voyage will be very enjoyable."

"Ah, there!" exclaimed Elgin, holding the telescope. "I can see the cutter. Duff is returning."

She was greatly relieved when Duff showed his face on deck. Sensitive Duff, fearful of anything that moved, retreating from Captain Morris' harsh voice. "Well, what have you to report?"

"I never saw such a miserable place," the courier said, puffing. "There's not one bed available in Palermo."

She started feeling nauseated again. "But Duff, you should have searched more diligently."

The flushed face broke into a smile. "There was no need for it, my lady. I have wonderful news. We are all invited to stay at the house of Sir William Hamilton."

"What about Lord Nelson?" barked Captain Morris. "Did you locate him?"

"That I did, sir."

"Well, out with it. What did Nelson say to you?"

"Only that he awaits the pleasure of your company at Sir William's house."

"That was his full message? Not one word about what my orders will be after we reach Constantinople?"

Duff looked confused. "Sir William was highly pleased to learn

of our arrival. He insists that we abide at his house during our stay on Sicily Isle."

Captain Morris muttered under his breath. Before stamping away, he flashed a look toward Mary, his eycs wrinkled at the corners. She answered the smile. Underneath the loud voice, the constant haranguing of the crew, lurked deep veins of humor and merriment of heart, reminding her so much of her own father.

Elgin turned to Duff. "Are you certain about Sir William's invitation?"

"Aye, my lord."

Elated, Elgin said to her, "Just think, Poll, after these dreary weeks at sea, you will be treated in proper ambassadorial style. Indeed, you will meet the best Palermo society and feast your eyes on the notorious Emma Hamilton." He slapped Duff fondly on the shoulder and added, "Bring up the luggage from the holds."

"The trunks too, my lord?"

"Of course not; only the luggage containing our clothes. Ask Masterman to select what we shall need. After that, get a few of the lads to help you carry everything into the cutter."

She couldn't hold it inside her any longer. "Eggy, I absolutely refuse to go to that house."

He smiled. "But I thought you were eager to go ashore."

"Not if we are to stay under that woman's roof. I beseech you, please go back with Duff and find another place for us."

"But Sir William will be disappointed, and heaven knows, we could use the comforts of his house."

"We can visit with him later, after we get settled in our own place."

His eyes mellowed with sympathy. "Very well, but Duff is busy with the luggage. I'll take the cutter and go into Palermo with Captain Morris. There now, everything will turn out favorably. I'm confident of finding a suitable house, one that will please you and give you comfort."

She sank into his arms. "This voyage was to be our honeymoon."

"I know."

"I wish we were back in London. Two nights, that is all we had together from the moment we were married."

He kissed her on both cheeks, then, holding her at arm's length, began playing the comic, chiming in a high-pitched voice of singsong mimicry: "Hey, hey, damn this frigate with its one stateroom divided into six wee compartments by this horrible green curtain. See here, I pick my nose and the whole damned ship is aware of it. What is that you are saying, Mr. Hunt: 'My lord, how can I be expected to share this minuscule compartment with four other gentlemen? I beg you to take a closer look, my lord — it is but twelve feet long, six broad, and six high. My lord, I ask you to count the five beds, thirteen trunks, six basins, hats, dressing gowns, great coats and boat cloaks, five foul-clothes bags, four portmanteaux, brooms, blankets, quilts, an eighteen-pounder with carriage tackles, iron balls, grapeshot, a cabin boy brushing our shoes, servants preparing our shaving apparatus . . .' "

She burst into laughter.

Releasing her, he said, "If you want me to find another place, I must go ashore before it gets dark."

"Eggy, do you love me?"

"With all my heart."

She stood by the rail as he and Captain Morris made their way down the accommodation ladder into the cutter. He kept waving to her until the cutter was absorbed by the other ships in the harbor.

For the first time, she realized how beautiful Palermo was. Most of the haze that lay over the city throughout the day had now lifted, revealing the wide bay and purple mountains. The air was soaked with the tangy scent of oranges and pomegranates, the sweet aroma of jasmine and basil. Dazzling white pal-

aces with red-tiled roofs lay sprawled along the shore and on the sloping hills.

She walked to the captain's chair on the quarterdeck and sat, her mind still etched with the picture of Elgin waving to her from the cutter. Behind her, a dozen crewmen were busy on deck, fine-looking lads feverishly working with mops and soap, stopping every so often to glance at her.

She still found it difficult to believe that she was the wife of Thomas Bruce, seventh Earl of Elgin and eleventh of Kincardine — a noble gentleman educated at Harrow and Westminster, then at St. Andrews, before going to Paris and Berlin to study international law and military science; former Special Consul to the Emperor Leopold, Envoy at Brussels, Envoy Extraordinary at Berlin, and now Minister Plenipotentiary of His Britannic Majesty to the Sublime Porte of Selim the Third, Sultan of Turkey.

She would always remember that raw morning in March, only five months ago, when Elgin made his heralded appearance at Archerfield, armed with official documents and recommendations and a letter from King George the Third, attesting to his good name, his rank and title. There were countless young ladies on both sides of the firth, attractive and of sound family fortune, but he chose her — Mary Nisbet. They had met only recently at a ball given in Edinburgh to celebrate the King's recovery from illness, and almost immediately Elgin showered her with attention. In the beginning, she didn't take to him. He was two and thirty, and she only nineteen. So brash he was when he called at Archerfield a few weeks later in full uniform to make official request for her hand in marriage. The uniform indeed impressed her, although she momentarily nourished the thought that he was as daft as the King. Nevertheless, her parents, delighted to have their daughter marry into the nobility, gave quick approval, and she complied with their wishes.

From that moment on, she was no longer the sole pride and

possession of her father, no longer his treasure and joy. In the flash of a streaking meteor, she was miraculously transformed into a new being; given a new life, a new name: Lady Elgin.

A family of gulls was circling over the ship, shrieking and diving into the flotilla of garbage the messboy had just tossed overboard. The sight of it turned her stomach, and waves of nausea again assaulted her. She dashed down the narrow stairs to her cabin, flung open the medicine cabinet, sprinkled some vinegar into her handkerchief, then placed it over her face and breathed in the strong fumes.

She heard footsteps.

Through her smarting eyes, she saw Masterman hurrying toward her, rolling her head in pity. "Are you ill again, my lady?"

She nodded helplessly.

Masterman helped her into the bed, soothingly stroking her wrists. "A fine honeymoon this has been for Your Ladyship; a fine honeymoon indeed."

With the help of the British Consul, Charles Lock, Elgin succeeded in finding a spacious palazzo overlooking the bay. It was within walking distance of Sir William's Palazzo Palagonia. The enormous drawing room had a peaceful country scene painted on the ceiling — trees and rolling hills, wide meadows, birds soaring in a blue sky. Every ship in Palermo's harbor could be seen from the palazzo's balcony, and best of all, her *mal de mer* found instant cure. She offered no objection when Elgin informed her that Sir William Hamilton had invited everyone in the embassy for dinner that night. Arm in arm, she and Elgin led the party up the cobbled street, past top-heavy houses of white stucco leaning against one another. A sewage tunnel stretched along the two main streets, its powerful stench overpowering the aroma of jasmine and basil. Even so late in the evening, Palermo was teeming with schoolgirls, all of them rid-

ing in carriages. Some wore white uniforms; others, dark blue. "Sir William claims there are twenty-one nunneries in Palermo," Elgin remarked. "Every girl in the city must attend a nunnery until the age of fourteen."

"And after that?" she asked skeptically.

"She must get married."

The two large streets converged in the middle of the city, forming a great square. Elgin pointed to a magnificent church rising high above the rooftops. "Of course, Monreale!" he exclaimed. "This is one of the greatest cathedrals of Christendom. When we have time, we must explore it thoroughly. There are some marvelous mosaics inside, spectacular works of Byzantine and Arabic art."

"I didn't know that the Arabs were Christians."

He laughed. "What you see here is a fusion of diverse styles, the Norman talent of conciliating the native elements. William the Second, who started building this cathedral toward the end of the twelfth century, believed that religious freedom should be guaranteed not only to Greek Christians but also to Moslems and Jews. These feelings were transferred to architectural matters as well — and so Monreale is a living testament of William's philosophy."

"Eggy, how shall I make up to the Duke of Bronte?"

He was surprised. "Now how did you know about this?"

"Duff told me in the cutter. He said that King Ferdinand conferred the title upon Lord Nelson after he helped the King and Queen escape here from Naples. Duff also said that King Ferdinand gave Nelson a sword worth three thousand pounds. It's set with diamonds and once belonged to Charles the Third of Spain."

Elgin kept his eyes fastened on the cathedral.

"Eggy, where is Bronte?"

"It's a small town on the western side of Mount Etna, at the opposite end of the isle. We should be able to see Etna on a clear day. It's ten thousand feet high. Before we leave here, I would like to climb it."

"How old do you suppose Lady Hamilton is?"

"I would say about five and thirty. Why do you ask?"

"I'm just curious. What about Nelson?"

"He must be at least forty, perhaps older."

"I think the whole affair is shocking."

Elgin's attention was focused on another church, standing opposite the cathedral. After some contemplation, he muttered, "That must be the Royal Chapel."

Captain Morris overheard him and quickened his gait to join them. "It is indeed the Royal Chapel." He chuckled. "I dare say Sir William will be upset when he learns that we walked to his house."

"Why?" she asked.

"Only the meanest beggars walk the streets of Palermo. As you see, even the young schoolgirls ride in carriages."

"How many times have you come here?"

"At least a half-dozen."

"Then you must be very fond of the place?"

"Hardly. We stop here to take in food and water, nothing else. Napoleon is an elusive little runt, and he knows all the hiding places in the Mediterranean."

"Eggy, I wish you would take your eyes off that church."

He took hold of her hand again. "We must find the time to visit the Royal Chapel also. It looks quite interesting."

Captain Morris let out a raucous laugh. "I trust that we shall not be put to the same embarrassment I encountered when I called on Lord Nelson earlier."

"You did not tell me about this."

"Your Lordship was with the British Consul, looking for lodgings."

"Tell us about your encounter," Mary said.

"I was met at Sir William's front door by a little old woman in a white bedgown and black petticoat. 'What do you want, sir?' says she. 'Lord Nelson,' I reply. 'And what do you want with Lord Nelson?' again says she. I rebuked her on the spot and

warned that she should look after her own business, at which point a male servant appeared and escorted me into the great hall. 'You have an inquisitive housekeeper,' I remarked. He coughed politely and said, 'But she is not a housekeeper, sir. That is Lady Hamilton's mother.' "

Captain Morris left them and hurried to catch up with the rest of the party. Mary waited a moment and asked, "Eggy, what do you know about Sir William Hamilton?"

Elgin stopped walking. "It's a shame that the world sees him only as the aged and cuckolded husband of the notorious Emma. Indeed, Sir William has a well-deserved reputation as an authority on classical antiquities. While serving as Ambassador at Naples, he developed a fond passion for exquisite works of art and was the first to detect the true origin of Greek vases, which up until then were mistakenly called Etruscan simply because they were found in southern Italy. His treasures are numerous — hundreds of vases, priceless gems, and valuable coins."

"Where does he keep them?"

Elgin resumed walking, a faraway look in his eyes. "Passions that become obsessions often bring financial ruin. Unfortunately, Sir William fell into so much debt, he had to sell his entire collection."

Imitating Mr. Hunt's pompous voice, she quipped, "Lay not up for yourselves treasures upon earth, where moth and rust doth corrupt!"

He laughed.

Two male servants in longcoats were waiting for them outside the front door of Sir William's Palazzo Palagonia. A footman, well groomed in superb red livery, led them up the front steps. Elgin stepped aside and allowed her to enter the front hall first. A wide sweeping mural decorated the wall of the foyer: an ornate display of Italian flamboyance — pudgy little angels with pouting lips hovering around a bearded saint like a flock of pigeons, and high above sat God the Father on a puffy white cloud, granting His blessing.

They were met in the grand drawing room by Sir William and Lady Hamilton. A middle-aged naval officer in full dress stood rigidly by the bay window. Nelson came forward to greet them, offering his left hand. His right arm was severed above the elbow; a patch covered his right eye. He looked more like fifty than forty. His blue coat and white breeches hung worn and loose on his scarecrow figure.

Sir William, on the other hand, although quite old and fragile, still exuded a powerful sense of pride and elegance, all brocade and powdered hair — a courtly gentleman alongside Emma's wounded and wan admiral.

As for Emma, the basic coarseness of her peasant birth had already begun to reassert itself, and she was hardly the beauty who had enraptured the painter Romney when she was twenty. Mary had seen many of these portraits while visiting the galleries in London with her father. On one occasion, William Nisbet exuberantly remarked: "Now there's a fine woman for you. Good flesh and blood. A whapper!"

She wore a dress of white muslin, with a flounce embroidered in gold and colored silk defining a bold design of anchors and leaves alternating with medallions containing the words *Nelson* and *Bronte*. Nelson couldn't keep his eyes from her, and throughout Elgin's long and formal introductions, he kept exchanging glances of intimacy with her. Sir William took casual notice of it and didn't seem to mind.

Mary drew back to appraise her more closely, and, indeed, her features were well shaped, particularly her head. Her eyebrows and hair were uncommonly dark, and although somewhat irregular, her teeth were tolerably white. A noticeable brown spot in one of her deep violet eyes took nothing away from their magnetic sparkle. Between pauses in conversation and glances, she took on various attitudes, as though posing for an artist, assuming a succession of statuesque stances with amazing facility, swiftness, and grace.

When dinner was announced, Elgin accompanied Emma to

her place at the head of the table, and Sir William escorted Mary. Nelson entered with the rest of the staff and hurriedly seated himself beside Emma. Mary was awed by the size and luxuriousness of the dining hall and, even more, by the variety of dishes served — a colorful mixture of braised vegetables surrounded by steaming mounds of glistening rice, various assortments of meat and fish, an endive salad, a wide selection of cheeses, fruit, and wines. After her first glass of wine, her appetite surprisingly improved and she managed to finish most of each course that was served. Both Elgin and Sir William only nibbled at their food, and Emma devoted a great deal of her time to Nelson, tucking an apron under his chin, cutting his meat, and even pouring his wine. After this, she ate with passion and pleasure, ignoring all codes of good breeding and accepted social behavior.

Coffee and tea were served in the drawing room. Speaking in an unusually soft voice, Nelson started recounting one of his battles against Napoleon. "The man is a genius, a military genius. Under his command, the French had amassed a powerful army on the Channel coast, their intention to invade Britain, but in the final hour Bonaparte changed his mind and reported to his government that the plan was impossible, suggesting instead that these same forces, numbering fifty thousand men, be used in an invasion of Egypt. Meanwhile, I had all my ships scouring the Mediterranean and even the coast of France, but we were beset by bad weather and fog, and couldn't locate them."

"Where were they hiding?" asked Mary.

"At Toulon. I tell you, their armada blanketed the harbor. Try to envision all those soldiers cramped aboard each ship. Far worse, the sea was so choppy that almost to the man they were seasick . . ."

She wished he had not mentioned that word.

". . . but Napoleon's spirit had ignited them, and so this great convoy set sail from Toulon. It was a brilliant maneuver, an enormous risk for Napoleon to take."

"Was he successful?"

"Indeed he was. He knew the Egyptians would offer very little resistance. They had enough on their hands with the Mamelukes."

"Who are they?"

Elgin dispatched a perturbed look in her direction, but no one else caught it. Rubbing his good eye, Nelson went on, "The Mamelukes are a curious breed, I must say. They were first brought into Egypt in the thirteenth century by the Turkish sultans. They came from deep within the Caucasus, and after only a few years, took complete control of the Egyptian Government. They are fierce fighters and keep maintaining their numbers by continually purchasing young boys from the Caucasus and training them as soldiers. Yes, the pretense of Turkish authority has prevailed throughout all this time, but it is the Mamelukes who really rule Egypt."

"How strong are they, my Lord Admiral?" asked Elgin.

"Ten thousand."

"Is that all?"

"My dear Elgin, strength is not always found in large numbers."

Mary wanted to know more about the invasion, and Nelson was quick to oblige her. "Against the modern European firearms of Napoleon, the Mamelukes were no match. Indeed, it was a crushing victory, that Battle of the Pyramids."

"Which, by the way, was fought nowhere near the Pyramids," laughingly interjected Sir William. "Of course, out of a deep sense of humility, Lord Nelson neglected to tell us of his own great victory, that dazzling achievement of annihilating the entire French fleet. But surely, my dear Elgin, you must have been aware of all these events before assuming your post."

"I was indeed," said Elgin. "My instructions ran to six and twenty pages. Not only am I to keep watch over the interests of His Majesty, promote commerce, maintain British privileges,

persuade the Turks to open the Black Sea to English trade, establish a postal station at Suez — but above all, I'm to help in every way possible in keeping the Ottoman Empire on friendly terms with Great Britain."

Nelson's smile was sour. "And just how do you propose to accomplish that?"

"Frankly, my Lord Admiral, I don't know."

"Bully for you. At least you're honest."

Sir William again addressed himself to Elgin. "You do have certain points in your favor. Your embassy staff seems youthful and alert."

Elgin's face beamed. "With your permission, Sir William, I think a more detailed introduction is necessary at this point. That scholarly-looking man with spectacles sitting alone near the door is Professor Joseph Dacre Carlyle. He is nine and thirty, and has spent almost half of those years at Cambridge, where he holds the chair in Arabic. He has had several books published on this subject, and for diversion he likes to dabble in poetry. I suspect the chief reason he signed on with me is to fulfill a deep desire to convert the natives of Asia and Africa by distributing an Arabic version of the Bible, over which he has labored for several years. But I have no objection to this, just as long as he fortifies my embassy with his immense knowledge."

"We had a chaplain on our embassy at Naples," interjected Emma.

"And we have Mr. Hunt, my lady, there on the sofa. He looks a bit immature for the position, but he is eight and twenty and was formerly a clergyman under the patronage of Lord Upper Ossory before joining us. He has an excellent knowledge of architecture and sculpture, and can identify any temple or cathedral in Europe and Asia. Sitting on either side of him are my two secretaries, each of them two and twenty. Young Morier, that handsome blond devil on the right, already knows about the East, having been born in Smyrna, where his father was con-

sul. This is his first authorized post. And finally we come to William Richard Hamilton, slumped there in undiplomatic pose against the back of the sofa. He is a shy one, to say the least." Elgin smiled gently. "This is his first venture into the intricate world of government, as well. He studied both at Oxford and Cambridge, and when his sponsor recommended him to me, he did so with verve and hyperbole, boasting of Hamilton's good sense and great activity of mind."

"Have you no physician attached to the embassy?" asked Nelson.

"Certainly, my Lord Admiral. We have Dr. Hector McLean, an esteemed medical authority, but unfortunately he could not join us tonight, because of a slight indisposition."

Mary covered her amusement with a handkerchief, as she thought, "An esteemed medical authority, indeed. What has he done for my *mal de mer?* He sits in his compartment all day long, drinking whiskey and bemoaning his fate. A skinny old drunkard whom Elgin never should have assigned to the embassy staff."

Emma helped herself to more tea after pouring some for Nelson. There was a trickle of disdain in her voice when she said to Elgin, "My dear Lord Elgin, I can't comprehend what drove you to choose a post in Constantinople. There are far more interesting places than Turkey."

"Constantinople is a very ancient and beautiful city," Elgin responded.

"But the Turks, those barbarous Turks."

Nelson laughed.

"With their sinful harems and dens of hashish . . ."

Elgin shifted his gaze to Sir William. "I dreamed about this post from the time I was at Harrow. My chief interest is Greece, not just Constantinople. As you must know, Sir William, the best models of classical art are in Athens. This post will present an excellent opportunity to reveal the beauty of Greek sculpture

and architecture to Great Britain. This is the real purpose of my mission, but if I am to accomplish it, many things will be necessary — plaster casts of the actual works must be made, accurate measurements, sketches, and paintings. Before leaving England, I suggested my plan to Lord Grenville, the Foreign Secretary, and told him that I needed painters, artists, architects, *formatori*, and draughtsmen. After all, the job had to be done right."

"What did Grenville say to this?"

"At first he balked at the whole idea, but after a while he came around and advised me to present my plan to the Prime Minister. I called upon Pitt personally; however he refused to listen, stating that His Majesty's Government could not encourage such grandiose schemes. If I wanted to embark upon this venture, I should have to do so at my own expense" — Elgin winced — "but at my meager salary of six thousand, five hundred per annum, that was impossible. And yet I hated to abandon the idea."

Sir William leaned forward, eager to hear the rest.

"Even if it meant that I had to tap into my own resources, I was now determined to carry it through."

"But how?"

"I decided to invite England's foremost painters to Broomhall."

"Where is that?" asked Emma.

"My home in Dunfermline, on the Fife side of the firth. In the beginning, all of these painters were interested, but they fled when they heard I would pay them thirty pounds per annum. The narrow-minded fools; they should have offered to pay *me* for opening a new world to them."

"What did you do then?" asked Sir William.

"Turner was my last hope."

Sir William gasped. "J. M. W. Turner, that most remarkable painter whose landscapes surpass even the hand of God?"

"Exactly. I had no qualms about increasing my offer to two

hundred pounds, not for an artist like Turner. He seemed willing enough until I insisted that every drawing and sketch he was to make while in my employ would become my sole property. Nevertheless, I could see that the idea of going to Athens pleased him, and thus I increased the figure to four hundred pounds — but to no avail. The greatest painter in England slipped through my fingers like water into sand."

"You must persist, my dear Elgin."

Elgin laughed bitterly. "I'm more than halfway to Constantinople, and not one painter is with me. The only reason I requested this post, the only real reason."

"I repeat, you must persist."

"How?"

"The first essential," replied Sir William, "is to find a man who will supervise the entire project. He should be a capable artist and know how to handle the men who will work under him."

"Where will I find him in Sicily?"

"I think I know the ideal person."

"Who?" cried Elgin. "Tell me."

"His name is Giovanni Battista Lusieri. Everyone on the isle calls him Don Tita. He lives in Messina, but there may be one drawback."

"What do you mean?"

"Don Tita is engaged by the King of Naples as the court painter, but now that Ferdinand is in exile here at Palermo, I could prevail upon him to release Don Tita."

"But how much money would he demand?"

"Offer him two hundred. He will accept."

"What kind of work does he do?" asked Mary, her own interest heightening. On the other sofa, Nelson and Emma were exchanging glances once again.

"As far as I know," answered Sir William, "Don Tita devotes himself exclusively to large panoramas that sometimes reach eight feet in length. Friends of mine have observed him on several

occasions. He sketches every intricate detail in pencil before putting in his colors. My dear Elgin, I'm thoroughly convinced he is the man for you. If you wish, I can proceed with the necessary arrangements."

Elgin assented without any hesitation.

In a spurt of sudden vitality, Emma got up from the sofa and sharply clapped her hands. Four men appeared, dressed in formal attire. Three carried stringed instruments. They followed the other man to the far end of the room and waited until he had seated himself at the pianoforte before taking their own chairs. Emma went to the small marble table near the door and picked up two shawls of diaphanous silk, one red, the other blue. Then, moving a few steps forward, she began arranging them deftly until they resembled long Grecian folds. She next allowed them to glide over her body, twisting and coiling them together, twirling them around her head, and transforming them into a colorful Oriental turban. Smiling widely, she came closer to the musicians and stood beside them in a posture of absolute stillness. At last, she glanced toward them, nodded slightly, and waited for her cue. It was a lively French song rendered in a strong, vibrant voice — each note either soaring or falling in deep resonant tones, only once slipping almost imperceptibly away from the key.

Fascinated with every flamboyant move and gesture, Mary couldn't take her eyes away. Elgin led the applause when the song came to an end, and as Sir William and Nelson stepped forward to congratulate Emma, Elgin leaned toward Mary and whispered into her ear: "Look at that sick rooster. Any moment now, he will flip his one wing and start crowing."

"Hush," she warned.

"The drooling cock, the silly drooling cock."

"Eggy, please be quiet. Lord Nelson will hear you."

Recklessly, he put his hand on her thigh. "Do you realize that we haven't slept together in weeks?"

"I wish you wouldn't drink so much wine, Eggy."

"That damn frigate; not enough space in her to pass wind without getting it thrown back in your face. My beautiful Poll, how I longed to pull you out of that tight little bunk and carry you on deck; lie there with you on a blanket under the stars; feel your firm breasts against my chest, your velvet skin and soft thighs, the sea throwing its cool fingers over our naked bodies."

"Sir William is looking at you."

"Tonight, Poll. You can't complain about your *mal de mer* now. There's a small room on the second story of the palazzo, where the others can't hear us. It has a long couch and . . ."

"Eggy, I implore you."

"Tonight, Poll. Tonight. Cock-a-doodle-doo! Cock-a-doodle-doo!"

They were in the constant company of the Hamiltons throughout the following day — luncheon at Sir William's, then on to a rowing match, where they were introduced to the King and Queen of Naples. Standing beside the obese Ferdinand, Maria Carolina looked tiny and fragile. Even for the rowing match, she was exquisitely attired, her aquamarine silk dress adorned with jewels, a tiara of diamonds resting on her raven hair. They conversed in French, and immediately the Queen invited them to a grand *fête* to be held later that evening, the ninth birthday celebration for their son and heir to the abandoned throne. She was a captivating spark of a woman, and Mary took to her instantly, despite her inability to converse in English. Emma seemed strongly attached to her, and much affection was openly displayed between them.

Elgin pulled Mary away for a moment and whispered, "Poll, you're in the presence of Marie Antoinette's sister. Their mother is the Austrian Empress, Maria Theresa."

"She looks so delicate."

"Don't be fooled. Maria Carolina is a clever little thing, a real queen. Unfortunately, her reign didn't last long. When the French conquered Naples, she fled here to Palermo with that idiot of a husband. Look at him — he has the manners and appearance of a peasant."

Mary leaned closer to hear what Maria Carolina was saying. "Yes, my dear Sir William, the French divested us of everything. We are living under great deprivation, great deprivation." She flung her hands high in the air, the jeweled gold bracelets clattering loudly.

After the rowing match, Sir William suggested they all go for a carriage ride through Palermo. Nelson politely declined, complaining of a bilious attack. Emma too apologized. She wanted to rest before the Queen's ball.

Sir William was a fountain of knowledge. He kept directing his coachman to particular places, stopping frequently to explain certain buildings and land sites. In animated words, he described how Palermo was originally built on a tongue of land between two inlets, resulting in the creation of two excellent harbors and forming the beautiful bay that was spread out below them. He was greatly distressed over the incongruous dome of Monreale. "It's a pity that such a grand structure should be so monstrously disfigured."

They moved on, down the long winding street crowded with carriages, stopping again before a large white building. "Let's go inside," he said. "This museum was formerly a monastery. My dear Elgin, you will particularly enjoy the large collection of Greek vases and the extensive array of Sicilian majolica — all beautifully displayed in appropriate rooms — and I mustn't forget to show you the Etruscan sarcophagi."

Mary followed Elgin through the front door; then, waiting until Sir William was beyond range of her voice, she tugged at Elgin's sleeve. "What are sarcophagi?"

He smiled. "It's the Greek word for 'flesh-eater.' "

She didn't understand.

"What devours our flesh?" he said.

"I have no idea."

"Death, of course. A sarcophagus is a stone coffin."

She grimaced. "I don't care to look at them. I shall wait for you here in the hall."

He pulled her gently by the arm. "They're not at all what you think. Come, you'll never learn a thing if you bury your head in the sand like a silly ostrich."

They entered the room of Greek vases. Patiently and lovingly, Elgin explained their designs, their origins and varied styles. He lingered for a long time before a vase depicting young men chasing beautiful Greek maidens. "Look at the muscles," he marveled, "each figure so resplendent in motion."

In the street, Sir William was ebullient. "My dear Elgin, I can't tell you how pleased I am to find someone who shares my love for antiquities."

"I should like you to know," said Elgin, "that when I was at Harrow I read your book on vase engravings."

"Indeed?"

"In my opinion, Josiah Wedgwood was greatly influenced by your book, although he will never admit to it."

Sir William's voice trailed off. "I find it almost impossible to feel any fervor in my heart for the arts in this place of exile. Palermo is a poor substitution for Naples."

"Sir William, did you speak to the King about that painter?"

"Yes, just before the rowing match."

"Is he willing to release Lusieri?"

"At first he balked, but Maria Carolina convinced him it was only proper, now that they are in exile. The man's talents are being wasted in Messina."

"That's wonderful news, Sir William. Would you dispatch a letter to Lusieri, asking him to supervise my project in Athens?"

"I shall do so before we leave for the ball."

"I'm most grateful to you, Sir William."

"Think nothing of it, my dear Elgin. I'm glad to oblige."

The Hamiltons had yet to arrive when Mary and Elgin were escorted into the grounds of the Royal Palace. A large number of guests had already seated themselves at the tables on the lawn, and servants in Chinese dress moved busily about, serving champagne. The evening was stifling hot, and every woman's fan worked feverishly. No sooner had they settled into their chairs than everyone's attention focused on the rose-trellised archway at the far end of the garden.

"The *tria juncta in una* have arrived." Elgin chuckled.

Mary was stunned by the sight of Emma. Every voluptuous curve was now firmly restrained and sheathed in a gold gown of simple classic lines. Her hair was dressed in a severe style, exposing the full beauty of her face. She wore no jewelry. Her posture was both stately and graceful as she walked between Sir William and Nelson. Sir William was in full ambassadorial dress, and Nelson looked trim in his blue uniform with full decorations, the right sleeve folded neatly, the patch over his eye more an emblem than a bandage. Both men radiated pride as waves of applause greeted them. But the prize attraction was Emma. Every head was turned in her direction, every eye upon her.

Mary was equally amazed, watching Emma at the table. She handled her knife and fork daintily, lifting each tiny morsel of food to her perfectly poised mouth, chewing slowly, effortlessly maintaining every exquisite feature of her face. It was a notable feat throughout, and even Elgin was impressed. Several times during her conversation with the Queen, Emma's hand lingered on Maria Carolina's wrist, patting it again and again. Suddenly the Queen fell into tears, and as the King tried to comfort her, Emma turned to Mary and said, "The poor dear, she's thinking about Prince Albert who died on Christmas Day last year. He was only six years old and my favorite. We were all on board

the *Vanguard* after fleeing from Naples. A terrible day it was, what with a dropping barometer and every sign of threatening weather. But I was a good sailor, and when nearly all on board — with the exception of the regular ship's company — were prostrated with seasickness and fear, I kept up my spirit and my health, cheering, nursing, and waiting on everybody. Unfortunately, I could do nothing for the baby prince. He was taken with convulsions in the midst of the storm and, at seven in the evening of Christmas Day, expired in my arms."

In the very next breath, she added, "Did you know that Her Majesty has spent more than six thousand pounds for this affair? Heaven knows, I would do the same for my only son and heir to the throne."

A group of musicians had assembled on an elevated platform under a canvas canopy. Their leader, a violinist, nodded to Emma, and she left the table to join them. A hush fell over the crowd as she sang the national anthem, and to everyone's surprise, she rendered an additional verse of her own as embellishment:

Join we great Nelson's name,
First on the roll of fame,
Him let us sing.
Spread we his praise around,
Honor of British ground,
Who made Nile's shores resound —
God save the King.

There were wild cheers from the crowd, and when the excitement abated, the dancing began. Mary danced first with Elgin, a volte, which had been his favorite dance since he learned it when Envoy Extraordinary at Berlin. He had taught it to her on the day of their wedding, and with her deep love for dancing, she had taken to it immediately.

The next dance was a quadrille, and they were joined by a host of others, including Sir William and Emma. Nelson did not choose to participate.

After the dance, they were escorted back to their table by one

of the Chinese servants. Elgin tried to strike up a conversation with Nelson but got only a slight lift of Nelson's good eye.

"Is anything troubling you, my Lord Admiral?" Elgin asked.

Nelson exploded. "Here I am in Sicily, still nursing my wounds, and Lord Keith orders me to sail tomorrow for Malta as his second in command."

"Lord Keith *orders* you?" asked Mary.

"What can I say? He's Commander of the Mediterranean Fleet, a position that really should belong to me."

"I know Lord Keith very well," said Elgin. "We've been friends for at least a dozen years. But he should be retiring soon."

"I can't wait for the day," snapped Nelson.

"Will you return to Palermo?" Mary asked.

"God only knows." In his agitation, Nelson brushed his hand against her bare arm. There was something magnetic about his touch, and quickly looking up, she noticed that he was staring at her as though seeing her for the first time.

Two days after Sir William received a reply from Lusieri, she traveled with Elgin to Messina for a meeting with the artist. It was a dreadfully long journey over bad roads and perilous mountain passes, but fortunately Sir William had lent them his best and strongest carriage, a post chaise with oval windows, seats covered in shining black leather and studded with brass broadhead nails. The frames were painted bright red. Its roof rose in a dome with an iron railing around it, and a coachman and guard sat in a high seat in front of the railing. Attached to the rear was a large basket supported by iron bars.

She was fascinated by the immaculate little towns and hamlets that flitted past the window: Bagheria, Caccamo, Collesano. The two horses made good time, pulling into Cefalu just before nightfall. It seemed strange to see such a majestic cathedral in a little seacoast town like this, but, as always, Elgin had an answer

for Mary's puzzlement, recounting at great length and with melodramatic gestures how the mountainous waves battered a flimsy ship, threatening to capsize it, and the badly frightened king, vowing that should he by some miracle reach any part of the Sicilian coast alive, *there* would he build a cathedral for San Salvatore. And so it was at Cefalu that the ship at last found refuge, and true to his word, Roger II chose this obscure fishing village to erect his dazzling cathedral in the year 1129, sparing no expense, hiring the best Saracen and Norman architects, the finest Byzantine mosaicists.

They had time to investigate its interior. Above the altar, and nestled in the apse, an enormous mosaic of Christ Pantocrator stared down at them. In His left hand He held an open book, one side written in Greek, the other Latin. Elgin quickly translated it for her: "I am the light of the world. Whoever follows me shall not remain in darkness, but shall have light eternal."

The arches crowning the columns of the nave showed the influence of Arabic architecture, but the carved decorations on the capitals were unmistakably the work of Sicilian artists. Elgin was definite about this.

The next morning, Elgin wanted to spend more time at the cathedral, but Messina was still another full day's journey, and since the horses were well rested, he reluctantly decided that they should set off right away.

The views were even more striking after they left Cefalu — the Tyrrhenian Sea on their left hand, gigantic Mount Etna on their right. At noon, they stopped at Patti for a meal of meat and rice stuffed in tomatoes. The town was much smaller than Cefalu, and she was surprised to find no women in sight, only men and young boys — wild-looking Sicilians with flirtatious eyes. The boys danced around the post chaise, then ran after it, following it all the way to the outskirts of the town. She waved to them until they were lost from sight.

Swinging quickly around the northernmost tip of the isle, they

came to the broad road that led into Messina. It was almost dusk, and Elgin immediately sent the coachman into the center of the large square to make inquiries about Lusieri's residence. It didn't take long to learn that the artist lived close by, in a small stucco house less than fifty yards from the square. Mary remained in the post chaise while Elgin and the coachman walked to the door. Elgin knocked, and when he got no response he pounded on the door until it was finally opened. He spoke to a figure inside for a few moments and then beckoned to her. In the dimly lit room, she detected the man's strong features. He was Sicilian throughout — dark and mysterious, extremely handsome — and best of all, he spoke fluent English. With flustered hands, he cleared away the small kitchen table and asked them to sit. His long artistic fingers trembled when he brought out a bottle of red wine.

"I understand that Sir William Hamilton wrote to you," said Elgin.

"Yes."

"Did he explain what your duties will be?"

Lusieri crossed himself.

"What does that mean?"

"I cannot understand why you desire to take me to Turkey."

"But you're not coming to Turkey with me. You will work in Athens."

Lusieri's face brightened. "What exactly am I expected to do?"

Elgin became annoyed. "You are a painter, are you not?"

"I am the King's painter," Lusieri retorted, walking to a shelf to get some glasses.

Mary leaned over and spoke quietly to Elgin. "Don't be impatient; otherwise, you'll lose this man too."

Elgin immediately calmed himself. "My dear Don Tita, you are to supervise an artistic commission that will include an architect to take notes about buildings and temples, and several *formatori* to mold such sculptures and works of art deemed to be of classical importance. All drawings, pictures, sketches, and

moldings are to remain in my possession and will be my sole property. Is this clearly understood?"

"Yes, my lord."

Elgin was disarmed. She too had expected some resistance. "Tell me, Don Tita, what type of work do you like to do best?"

"I prefer to work on the large scale, my lady. When I was six and twenty, I worked on a drawing of Constantinople for two whole years — five huge sheets joined together. The view it embraced extended from the Seven Towers to the Bosphorus."

Elgin smiled. "I thought perhaps you disliked Turkey."

"Constantinople is not Turkey. She is a Greek city from cellar to rooftop."

"Signor Lusieri, you are an Italian, yet you seem to be enamored of Greece," she remarked.

"Yes, I am Sicilian, but in our hearts and souls we are Greek. This isle was founded by Greeks; most of her cities have Greek names."

"You didn't finish telling us about your drawing of Constantinople," Elgin reminded him.

"There is nothing further for me to say. Some insensitive fool left it in the chancellery of Pera, the dampest part of the cellar, and it was ruined."

Mary gave him a compassionate smile. "Perhaps His Lordship will allow you to return there someday so that you can draw it once again."

"Not if it takes him another two years." Elgin laughed. Lusieri laughed also.

"Did Sir William mention financial terms in his letter to you?"

"Yes, my lord."

"Do they meet with your approval?"

Lusieri nodded.

She stood up and gently said, "I do think this should be in writing."

"A contract?" said Elgin.

Lusieri cast a grateful look toward her. He brought paper, ink, and quill to Elgin and stood behind him until the document was finished. The last paragraph pleased Lusieri:

> In case Signor Lusieri wishes to make copies of some works during his employment for his own use, it is agreed that the choice will be made through the consideration of both parties. Signor Lusieri will also be at liberty to return to his country before the expiration of the term of his employment should unexpected circumstances oblige him.
>
> Made in Messina, Sicily,
> 9 August, 1799

Elgin affixed his signature on the lower right corner, just before Lusieri's, then passed the document to the painter. "I trust that we shall have an amicable relationship. Are you prepared to leave for Rome right away?"

"Rome, my lord?"

"I want you to go there with one of my secretaries."

"For what purpose?"

"To engage a full staff for your work in Athens. I shall give you complete instructions in the morning," said Elgin, rising to his feet. "Is there an inn where we can put up for the night?"

Lusieri crossed himself once again. "Forgive me, but my house is inadequate — just this kitchen and a small bedchamber."

"We should never think of imposing upon you, Signor Lusieri. I shall be grateful if you can recommend a clean place for us."

"Of course. The Hotel San Giovanni is in the square, only a few steps from here. I will show you the way."

"That's not necessary," said Elgin. "What about our coachman and his guard; where can they sleep?"

"Adjacent to the San Giovanni is a small inn. The rates are very reasonable."

Lusieri hurried to open the door for them. Bending forward, he took Mary's hand and kissed it. Elgin bade him good night. "We shall see you in the morning, Signor Lusieri."

"Good night, my lord."

In the street, she asked Elgin, "Which of your secretaries will you send to Rome with Lusieri?"

"Hamilton."

"But the poor lad is a cripple."

"Only in the foot, not the brain."

"I wish you would send Morier."

"Poll, I know what I'm doing. This is a very serious matter, one that will involve a great deal of money. Believe me, Hamilton is the better man."

The night air had turned cool. Edging close to him, she said, "Please ask Hamilton to bring back some musicians from Rome."

"Musicians?"

"He needn't pay too much for them. I feel certain they can be engaged at the second table of salary."

"Fifty pounds? That's out of the question, Poll."

"Lady Hamilton has musicians."

"So?"

"Eggy, this means very much to me. I beg you, ask Hamilton to bring back at least someone capable of playing the pianoforte. With that same fifty pounds, he should be able to obtain two or three additional musicians for accompaniment. We might even induce them to wear livery and act as servants occasionally."

Elgin squeezed her arm. "I'll tell Hamilton to look into the possibility — but I make no promises. Come, we must get to that hotel. We have a long day ahead of us."

The Mediterranean was chained to a season of storms. Captain Morris strongly advised against leaving Palermo at such a time, and as the weeks dragged on, Elgin became increasingly uneasy, Hamilton's long silence from Rome augmenting his discomfort.

On the evening of the Great Feast Day of the Archangels Michael and Gabriel, Mary tried to convince him that they should join in the festivities, and he finally consented. Palermo had been

lavishly prepared for the three-day festival. Lights flickered from large lamps interspersed among flowers covering the wooden arches at every street. The center of the main square contained garlands of flowers encircled by huge wreaths of laurel, and just behind it, the archbishop's palace was brightly decorated and illuminated. Carriages filled the streets, rattling through the jubilant crowds. There were horse races during the second morning of the festival, and later in the day a colossal conveyance, sparkling in gaudy colors, led the large parade through the city. The car was tall enough to reach the highest balcony and almost as wide as the broadest street. On its dome stood a ship, and above that were perched the two gigantic statues of the angels. Behind the conveyance marched scores of musicians, blaring away on their instruments.

That evening, they left the palazzo early to attend the services in the Cathedral of Monreale, and Mary was blinded by the brilliant light of a thousand tapers, the colorful robes of the archbishop and priests.

The long festival came to an end the following night with a deafening display of fireworks at the mouth of the bay. When they returned to the palazzo after midnight, a letter from Hamilton was resting on the marble table in the front hall. Masterman hurried to brew some tea, and Mary sat quietly in the drawing room until Elgin was ready to read it to her.

Rome
30 August, 1799

My dear Lord,

We encountered considerable difficulties here in Rome from the moment of our arrival. Many Italian artists have fled from the city because of Napoleon's armies, which are rapidly overrunning Italy. Those who have remained are not well known to Signor Lusieri. Nevertheless, after an extensive search, I am at last able to report to Your Lordship that all the necessary artists have now committed themselves to your employ.

The first to be engaged was a draughtsman for figures and sculpture. He was trained at Karlsruhe and is a native of Astrakhan, a Tartar. We have fixed his salary at one hundred pounds per annum.

Upon Signor Lusieri's strong insistence, I secured the services of two architects, one of whom is a hunchback. At first, I was wary about his inability to perform strenuous duties, and I did not favour this selection, but Signor Lusieri insisted, saying the man was quite capable.

The other architect has served as an apprentice to the aforementioned architect. We have fixed their total salary at five hundred Roman piastres, or one hundred and twenty-five pounds per annum.

We have recruited two men for making plaster moulds. Each is to receive one hundred pounds per annum. We were indeed fortunate to avail ourselves of their employ, since there are only six moulders in all of Rome, the others having abandoned the city under the threat of Napoleon's invasion.

Her Ladyship will be pleased to hear that I had the good fortune to procure a *maître de chapelle* with all the qualities Her Ladyship desired, except the inclination to appear occasionally as groom of the chamber. Since he is a very well-mannered young man, I did not think it proper to press it upon him, particularly as I learned from every quarter that persons of his profession would, with natural vanity, rather starve through want than stoop to such degradation.

He is bringing two musicians with him: one plays the clarionet, and the other, the violoncello. I believe it will be possible, though difficult, to prevail on them to wear livery, or at least a separate uniform, which would answer to Her Ladyship's request.

I trust that this message will reach Palermo before Your Lordship's departure for Constantinople.

Believe me to be,
Your most humble servant,
William Richard Hamilton

Mary was certain that Elgin would be pleased by the letter, but his reaction startled her. "Perhaps you were right after all. I should have sent Morier, not Hamilton. He must think that I manufacture money. A hundred pounds here, another hundred there. I gave him explicit orders; wrote down every word."

She tried to console him. "Eggy, the poor lad did his best under the circumstances. After all, these are critical times. As he said in the letter, most of the artists have fled Rome. We must do with what we have, and we must pay them accordingly."

"Of all people, he had to hire a hunchback."

"I see nothing wrong in that."

"Can you imagine what everyone in England will say: 'Indeed, things must be desperate for Elgin if he has to employ a hunchback!' "

Elgin's disposition remained sour through most of the next day, and after dinner he retired early. She wanted to converse with him in the bedchamber, but he turned the other way and buried his head under the pillow. Sighing, she took off her nightgown and slid into bed beside him. Just as she was about to fall asleep, she felt his hand on her thigh. It lingered there for a moment before creeping up to her breast.

To relieve Elgin's vexation Hunt and Carlyle persuaded him to accompany them on an exploration of the ruins at Taormina. They also hoped to climb Mount Etna, and to investigate the phenomenon of Scylla and Charybdis.

When the party of explorers returned the last week of September, Elgin looked rested and was buoyant in spirit. He spoke to her at length in the bedchamber, describing the breathtaking views from the summit of Etna.

"Did you visit Syracuse?" she asked.

"Indeed we did. It's a lovely city. It has a marvelously preserved Roman theater, but Hunt and I were drawn more to the

earlier Greek theater, which dates from the fifth century B.C., one of the largest and best-preserved theaters of antiquity. Even though hollowed out of the rocks, its seats are extraordinarily comfortable."

"Eggy, did you miss me?"

He took off his clothes and crawled into bed beside her. The stroke of his hand on her breast left her weak. "I must tell you what I did while you were gone," she said.

"Later."

He kissed her on the lips, then slid his mouth down to her breast. She felt her body quivering. Between gasps, she tried to tell him how she had occupied herself while he was gone — about the dinners and receptions, the opera — but his body had already captivated her.

In the morning, shortly after breakfast, Captain Morris came back from a visit to the harbor and announced that it was imperative for them to set sail for the Aegean as soon as possible. Except for her, everyone in the household was jubilant.

"Do you mean that we have to leave Palermo right now?" she complained.

"Wind and sea are at last favorable, my lady," Captain Morris replied. "We must not tarry here any longer."

Elgin was looking at her questioningly. "What's the problem, Poll?"

"It's such short notice, Eggy, leaving like this. Why can't we go in a day or two? Why must it be now?"

"Poll, I have work to do in Constantinople. We've wasted enough time here in Sicily."

Captain Morris cleared his throat. "We must set sail by noon, no later."

"You see?" said Elgin. "There's no point in discussing this any further. We're sailing today." He hurried into the hallway and yelled out to Morier and Duff: "Get everything packed into the ship. We shall be sailing in a few hours."

Hunt and Carlyle quickly attended to their own belongings; Dr. McLean worried about nothing but his whiskey. Masterman was beside herself with joy, and said excitedly, "My lady, I have grown tired of this life in Palermo. I cannot wait to settle in Constantinople — to rid myself of Lady Hamilton's endless parties and receptions, pressing all those dresses and gowns, those petticoats and skirts."

At eleven o'clock, after Elgin finished writing a lengthy letter to Rome ordering Hamilton to embark at once for Constantinople with Lusieri and the crew of artists, they called upon the Hamiltons for the last time. Both Sir William and Emma were sad to hear about their departure. Emma wept and waved from the front door until their carriage pulled away from the circular driveway.

Mary felt a deep sense of loss as they passed through Palermo for the last time. Captain Morris was standing on the deck of the *Phaeton,* waiting for them. She was the last to come aboard. Straightaway, the sails were hoisted, the anchor weighed, and the *Phaeton* started moving out of the harbor. Elgin and the others went directly to their cabins, but she chose to remain on deck, her eyes attached to Palermo's sinking horizon.

Soon the *Phaeton* was swinging around the Cape of San Vito, sailing rapidly under Sicily's belly, entering the wide Mediterranean. All this time, she was still at the rail, immersed in thought and peering down at the foamy sea.

Masterman appeared on deck and said in a concerned voice, "Is Your Ladyship feeling ill?"

She swayed from a sudden discomfort; then, leaning on her maid's thin arm, she struggled across the deck to the cabin stairs. The very thought of that horrible vinegar made her stomach churn.

Two

THE AEGEAN was indeed calm; days glistening under cloudless skies, each night giving birth to millions of stars. The *Phaeton* glided peacefully around the southernmost tip of Greece and came into sight of powerful Mount Taygetus. Even from a distance, Greece appeared to be even more sun-splashed than Sicily.

Elgin joined her at the rail and pointed beyond the rugged mountain range. "Just behind there lies the ancient city of Sparta."

She felt so much at ease — the smoothness of the sea, the scent of Greece — that she wished Elgin would ask Captain Morris to steer the *Phaeton* into the Piraeus and forget about Constantinople, but the ship kept ploughing toward the northeast, avoiding the harbor of Athens, catching the north winds off Mykonos Isle, and moving swiftly past the Isles of Chios and Lesbos. Here the sea became choppy, and she had to call upon the vinegar and Masterman's fretful nursing once again.

On the fifth day of October, the winds abated, and the *Phaeton* sailed smoothly into the tiny harbor of Tenedos Isle, which guarded the entrance to the Dardanelles. Before dropping anchor, they noticed a large Turkish vessel heading toward them.

It pulled up alongside the *Phaeton* and accorded them such a loud salute from its guns, Mary had to block her ears to keep from reeling.

Elgin was absorbing every moment. "I want you to retain this memory, Poll. It's our first official greeting from the Porte."

"How did they know we were here?"

"The Turks know everything, even the slightest movement in these waters." Swinging sharply around, Elgin ordered both his embassy staff and the crew to stand at attention and receive the Turks. The first to climb on board was a young officer in a red uniform and a white turban wound around his head. He had a pointed black beard and thick eyebrows. In slow but precise English, he introduced himself to Elgin and to Captain Morris as the Capitan Pasha, then took her hand and bowed. Four other officers followed, each greeting them in turn.

"My lord effendi," said the Capitan Pasha, walking with them along the deck. "We Turks shall be indebted to the English forever. Your glorious admiral, Lord Nelson, will be especially endeared by us for his magnificent victory. Yes, indeed, it is for this reason that Turkey has decided to enter into a treaty of alliance with your country."

Elgin's face changed color. "But who negotiated this treaty?"

"The joint ministers of England, my lord effendi."

"But that is impossible. I am His Britannic Majesty's duly appointed Minister to the Porte. I alone have the authority to negotiate such a treaty."

A nervous smile swept over the young Turk's face. "My lord effendi, the treaty was just signed by Sir Sydney Smith and his brother, Spencer Smith. Furthermore, provisions have been made to open the Black Sea to British shipping. This is the least we could do for our brothers-in-arms."

Elgin was now seething. "But this was to be my function, mine alone."

At first, Mary questioned the young Capitan Pasha's actions.

Each gesture, each word of flattery, seemed to unearth a mounting suspicion about his sincerity. But this soon disappeared when she realized that he indeed had a deep interest in their welfare. As for the four officers, they made her feel exceedingly uncomfortable, staring at her, undressing her with their sensual glances. Elgin was too disturbed to take notice, and when the Capitan Pasha invited them to dinner and an official inspection of his vessel, Elgin replied abstractedly, "Yes, yes, we shall come aboard in a few minutes."

Dr. McLean, who had remained surprisingly sober throughout most of the afternoon, took Elgin by the elbow and whispered, "My lord, I warned you about those treacherous Smith brothers. I repeat, they're not to be trusted."

Elgin paid no attention to him.

Hunt waited until the physician walked away. "Lord Grenville should have alerted Your Lordship to these matters before we left England. British nepotism; this is what I call it. It's a known fact that the brothers Smith are particular favorites of the Prime Minister. The whole business has a foul odor. Your Lordship must take severe measures with the Smiths as soon as we arrive in Constantinople."

"I intend to do so," said Elgin sharply. After calming himself, he ordered Duff to go below. "Bring out five gold watches from the trunk, the one marked *Constantinople.*"

Mary was bewildered. "Eggy, what's this all about?"

He shrugged. "This is the Levant. One can't greet a Turkish official without offering him a gift. There will be more important receptions when we reach Constantinople, many more gifts to dispense — English pistols, chandeliers, swords."

When they boarded the Turkish vessel, the officers and crew stood at rigid attention for Elgin's inspection. Morier distributed the gold watches, and one of the officers escorted them into a large cabin, where they were offered coffee, along with sweets coated with powdered sugar.

"You have a sturdy ship," said Elgin to the Capitan Pasha. "Where was she built?"

"In Constantinople, my lord effendi — by a Frenchman named Lebrun."

The Capitan Pasha pointed to one of his officers. "I want you to meet my great man, Isaac Bey."

"Your great man?" she asked, perplexed.

"Indeed, my lady. Isaac Bey is my emissary, my constant companion. He has traveled throughout the world and speaks many languages. He has a gift for you, my lady."

"Why should he offer me a gift?"

"In truth, it is my gift," admitted the Turk.

She flushed as Isaac Bey came before her and bowed. He was completely bald yet not unattractive. A thick black mustache stretched across his tanned face. He was exceptionally tall, and although the Capitan Pasha was by no means short of stature, Isaac Bey stood over him by more than six inches.

"Well," said the Capitan Pasha with a smile, "present the gift, Isaac."

The great man handed her a gold box, exquisitely engraved, lined with red satin and holding several bottles of beautifully etched glass. The Capitan Pasha pulled out one of the bottles. "My lady, the most exotic perfume of the East is contained here. Its scent is unmatched. I trust that my lord effendi will allow me to grant you this gift."

Elgin made no comment.

She accepted the box from Isaac Bey. "Thank you, Capitan Pasha. I shall treasure this."

"And now I leave you under Isaac's care until dinner. He will conduct you on a thorough tour of our vessel."

The Pasha's cabin held a large mahogany desk and a sofa with two matching chairs covered in blue and silver tapestry. Inside a glass cabinet were numerous pistols and guns richly engraved in silver and gold. Several swords, ornamented in Damascene work, hung on an adjoining wall. Elgin took one down and ran his

thumb over its edge, then quickly pulled it away. "In God's name, it's incredibly sharp — the best steel I've ever seen."

They followed Isaac Bey into a commodious drawing room — walls covered in white satin, a sofa of yellow silk embroidered in gold, finely carved mahogany chairs flanking a long oak table inlaid with ivory, crystal chandeliers, gleaming mirrors, tall silver candlesticks — and, at the extreme end of the room, large plump pillows of blue silk encircling a low round table.

The crewmen's quarters below were equally well furnished and impeccably clean.

Isaac Bey brought them back to the drawing room, where the Capitan Pasha stood waiting. He took Mary by the arm and led her into the dining room. The table was set with red linen cloth, knives and forks of gleaming silver, Dresden china, and crystal glasses. A team of attendants entered the room, carrying trays of food. One contained slices of meat smothered in onions; another, roasted breasts of chicken. A third tray had an assortment of vegetables cooked in a savory sauce of tomato. The wine, fragrantly sweet, was from the Isle of Samos.

Sweetmeats were served for dessert, along with preserved quince and pears, thick coffee in small fragile cups. The Capitan Pasha rose to his feet and asked them to follow him to the gallery in the stern, where an attendant stood, holding a tray of water pipes. The Pasha was hesitant about smoking in her presence, but she entreated him to do so. Elgin took only a few puffs from his pipe, and soon the gallery was saturated with the sickly sweet smell.

"What is inside each bottle?" she asked, brushing the smoke away from her eyes.

"Rose-scented water," answered the Pasha.

"Is that Turkish tobacco?"

The Pasha laughed. "We call it hashish. See here, it is placed in this special porcelain section at the top of the bottle and is burned by a piece of smoldering charcoal made from jasmine wood. Now, as I inhale deeply, the smoke passes through the

water into this long tube. When it reaches my lungs, it is moist and smooth and has the most divine flavor. But its greatest pleasure is the state of euphoria it brings."

She asked to be excused.

Going quickly on deck, she walked for a while, then stopped to lean against the rail, studying the wavering lights of Tenedos across the water and gulping in deep breaths of sea air. Her thoughts drifted to Palermo. She wondered what Emma was doing at this precise moment; what she was wearing. Was "the conquering hero" at her side?

Suddenly a soft voice trickled into her ear. It was Isaac Bey. "My lady, it is cool out here. Permit me to place this shawl over your shoulders."

The shawl was soft and weightless and exuded a pleasing scent of perfume. Her eyes moved once again toward the Tenedos shore. "How long have you been the Capitan Pasha's great man?"

"Three years."

"And prior to that?"

"I spent eighteen years traveling around the world."

"Are you happy with the Capitan Pasha?"

"Most happy — but I am not happy with Turkey."

"I don't understand."

Isaac Bey placed his hands on the rail. "At the present time, the Capitan Pasha is enjoying the highest favor of the Sultan, but this could change, and when that happens, we could all lose our heads."

"Why do you say this?"

"In the past, some Sultans have been excessively cruel."

"What about the present?"

"Selim the Third is a kind and merciful man. I hope that Allah endows him with a long life."

She moved away from the rail.

"My lady, do you want to know what the word *elgin* means in Arabic?"

"Yes, please tell me."

"Evil genius, the devil."

Jolted, she tried not to show her vexation.

"Forgive me, my lady. I meant no harm. I thought perhaps it would interest you to hear how the Turks reacted to the news of Lord Elgin's appointment as Ambassador to the Porte."

"And how did they react?"

"With great fear and foreboding. They could not understand why the King of England was sending the Lord Devil to Constantinople."

Elgin appeared on deck with the rest of their party. After they stepped into the cutter, the Capitan Pasha waved to them from the rail. "Long live England!" he shouted. "Long live our holy alliance!"

Elgin did not bother to respond.

At daybreak, she was awakened by Elgin and told to dress right away. "We are going on a picnic," he said, pulling the covers from her bunk.

She rubbed her eyes. "Where?"

"To Troy." He laughed.

"Eggy, be serious."

"I am serious. We're taking the cutter and crossing over to the opposite shore."

"But why?"

"I want to show you something."

"What?"

"I can't tell you now. I want to surprise you."

"Are we going alone?"

"No, the others are coming too."

She buried her face in the pillow. "Must we drag the whole embassy with us everywhere we go?"

He tickled her feet. "We shall have plenty of time alone, after we get to Constantinople."

She kept her face in the pillow. "It shall be far worse then — all the dinners and receptions."

"Come, now — get dressed. We mustn't keep the others waiting."

"What about Masterman?"

"She wants to join us too. She has already packed two baskets of food, fruit, and wine. Everyone is coming except Dr. McLean."

She sat up abruptly. "Eggy, I wish you would say something to that old man about his drinking. He will give the embassy a bad name."

"I don't want to think about that now. Hurry, put on your clothes, Poll."

"What should I wear?"

"Something comfortable." He leaned over the bunk and pecked her softly on the cheek. With a wild lunge, she threw her arms around him and tried to pull him down, but he slid away, laughing. "Later, Poll."

He was in high humor when they pulled away from the *Phaeton*. In the middle of the channel they were aided by a swift current that carried them to the Asia Minor coast within an hour, and the crewmen didn't have to lean on the oars except to beach the cutter.

Elgin told them to wait on shore until they returned. "There's a small hamlet farther down the coast. Captain Morris tells me it has a Greek taverna and some rather decent wine. Go there if you wish, but I want you back here on the beach when we return at dusk."

Hunt and Duff carried the baskets of food; Masterman and Morier brought the blankets and extra clothes in case the weather turned cool. Eager to prove the exact site of Troy to the doubting Hunt, Professor Carlyle headed the expedition, armed only with his text of Homer. They walked at a rapid pace and soon

reached a small village that was bleached by sand and sun. Speaking rapidly in Greek, Carlyle bargained for a guide and a half-dozen asses. Mary envied his facility with the language.

After a strenuous climb up a barren slope, they came to a desolate village and stopped beneath the shade of a large plane tree to rest and eat. Moving off again, they crossed a wide plateau, Carlyle zealously consulting Homer and once again getting embroiled in an argument with Hunt, who had his own theories about the actual site of Troy.

Carlyle walked away from him in disgust. Drawing up beside Mary, he pointed to a broad plain off toward the east. "There is no question in my mind that Troy lies over there, my lady." He had an enraptured look in his eyes. "On that ground, the greatest battle in history was fought. If we become perfectly still, we can hear the clanging swords, see the colossal wooden horse, reach out and touch Hector, so dear to Zeus, march with Achilles, Ajax, Agamemnon, Odysseus . . . listen to the mournful cries of Andromache and Hecuba."

Elgin came to her rescue. Pulling her away, he said, "We should be there soon."

"Where?" she asked.

"The place I most wanted you to see. It's called Yenishehr."

The asses labored up a steep hill, spurred by the guide's whip. At the summit they stopped to rest once more. Below them, sprawled over the desert like a crumpled white blanket, lay Yenishehr. The asses maneuvered their way down the perilous slope, and when at last they entered the village, the guide rewarded them with a long drink from the spring. She saw only a few inhabitants walking in the solitary street.

Elgin immediately headed for a tiny stone church, whose façade was cracked and pockmarked with age. "There!" he cried.

She was downcast. "Eggy, you brought us all the way out here just to look at a ruined old church?"

He took hold of her hand and rushed across the street so swiftly

that the others couldn't keep up with him. Stopping in front of the church, he panted in an excited voice, "Poll, aren't they beautiful?"

A marble seat sat on either side of the church's entrance. She wished that she could share his enthusiasm, but they were only old marble seats. To please him, she moved forward for a closer look, and discovered that they indeed were beautiful. The one on the left had a fine sculptured relief of mothers and children at work in a field under the protective scrutiny of a graceful female figure standing to the side. Hunt said it was the goddess Demeter. The other seat bore an ancient Greek inscription, but it was so faded with age that neither Hunt nor Carlyle could decipher it.

"I've known about these seats for many years," Elgin explained. "Thomas Harrison, the architect who renovated Broomhall for me, spoke of them in glowing terms. One day he supplied me with several drawings, and I was so instantly attracted to them, I did some reading on my own and learned that they were first discovered by Lady Montagu."

"Who is she?"

"Lady Mary Wortley Montagu was the wife of a former Ambassador to Constantinople and a widely known writer." He paused, perhaps noticing her withdrawal; then, peering at her for a moment, he continued in a soft patient voice, "She accompanied her husband throughout all of his travels and wrote extensively about them: long accounts of voyages, observations of Eastern life, vivid descriptions of places and people. And it was she who urged us in England to inoculate against smallpox. A crafty woman of letters, she once devastated Alexander Pope with a parody on his poem 'Epitaph on the Lovers Struck by Lightning.' " He laughed. "Men hated her for her outspoken manners. She indeed was a remarkably free-spirited woman."

Mary was still fascinated by the seats and couldn't take her eyes away from them.

"Lady Montagu could have had these seats for the price of a small bribe to the Turkish Pasha of this region, but the captain of her ship didn't have the proper tackle to remove them. The townspeople also objected vehemently because their regard for these seats centers on an ancient superstition."

"What do you mean?" she asked.

"If anyone in Yenishehr falls ill, a Greek Orthodox priest is summoned to exorcise him by reading long chapters from Scripture. If this fails, the priest then rolls the patient over one of these marble seats." He broke into laughter.

Hunt shifted his feet uneasily. "My lord, we should remember that much devastation has come to this land over the centuries, not only from her many conquerors, but especially from her cruelest adversaries: the rains and floods that inundate her in the winter. Inevitably, these bring on fevers and death. These people do not enjoy the luxury of medical science, so they must rely on their ancestral beliefs. Your Lordship calls them superstitions, but for the people these are accepted remedies."

"Eggy, you didn't finish telling us about Lady Montagu."

Elgin had his eyes fixed on the seats. "The poor woman contracted a hideous skin disease during one of her travels, and it became so acute, it drove her almost to madness. Her daughter, whose husband was then Prime Minister, implored her to return to England; she died a few days after she reached London."

Masterman was concerned about their not having eaten in hours. Elgin told her to take the basket of food and join Morier and Duff, who were resting by the water spring. "Get everything ready, and we shall come there shortly," he said.

Mary asked Masterman to carry a blanket too; then, turning toward Elgin, she saw him tracing his fingers over the sculptured design on one of the seats. She called out his name, and he spun around, his eyes frozen, touching hers for a moment and then fleeing off into space.

Behind her, Carlyle was saying, "It *is* a pity that these treasures are manacled to such primitive beliefs."

Elgin's eyes came alive. "They needn't be."

After they ate, they rested for a while before setting out once again. From the top of the slope, Elgin turned to gaze down at Yenishehr again with that distant look on his face.

They returned to the beach a few hours before dusk and discovered that the crewmen from the *Phaeton* had yet to arrive. A cool wind started rushing over the sea toward Troy. Morier and Duff lit a fire inside a deep cave on a rocky ledge high above the water's edge, and Hunt resumed his argument with Carlyle over Troy. With a mischievous grin, Elgin grasped her hand and brought her out of the cave.

"Where are you taking me?" she asked.

He didn't answer.

"But the crewmen will be here soon."

Elgin helped her down the ledge, then swerved away from the beach and headed up a steep embankment into the middle of a small meadow of sea grass. The wind was still howling as he knelt down and began patting the grass. "When I am old and feeble," he said, "I want to remember that I lay with you one afternoon on the plains of Troy."

She tossed away her shawl and dropped to her knees beside him. Slowly, his hands caressed her hips. She gasped when they crept under the hem of her dress and along her thighs. Squirming, she pulled free from her dress and petticoats; felt his lips on her breast. As they buried themselves in the grass to hide from the wind, his lips groped along her stomach to the hair of her womanhood. "Close your eyes," he said, panting. "Imagine that you're Helen and I'm Paris. There's no other face in all the world to match yours, no other breasts."

Almost before she realized it, he was inside her — large, moist, throbbing — and after her moment came, she clung to the ebbing strength of his embrace for what seemed an eternity. Spent and weak, she sighed. "Eggy, I must tell you something."

"What?" he asked languidly.

"I'm pregnant."

He laughed. "So soon?"

"Please don't joke with me, not at a time like this."

"Are you certain about this, Poll? Have you talked with Dr. McLean?"

"I don't have to talk with him. I know that I'm pregnant."

He lay back on the grass and closed his eyes.

"Are you unhappy about it, Eggy?"

"Of course not."

"But you're not saying anything."

"I'm thinking."

"About what?"

He leaped to his feet. "He will be Lord Bruce, and he will become the eighth Earl of Elgin and twelfth of Kincardine."

"But what if it's a girl?"

"Perish the thought."

"We shall call her Mary, Lady Mary Christopher."

"Lord Bruce," he retorted, sweeping her into his arms. He helped her into her dress, then picked up the shawl. The dress was so wrinkled, she tried to smooth it down with the palms of her hands, but it was futile. He laughed. "No one will notice. It will be dark by the time we get back to the cave."

The sailors were now at the beach, dragging the cutter to the water's edge. After the others got in and sat down, Elgin spoke to the crewmen. "You're on time, lads. Exactly on time!"

The next morning, she awoke and found a small note pinned to her pillow. She peered at it dreamily and smiled. Silly Elgin.

My dearest Helen:

I'm off to liberate Troy. I shall return to your bed before nightfall.

Paris

After a breakfast of tea and biscuits, she busied herself with Masterman, sorting out her clothes and jewelry, getting everything in readiness for their arrival in Constantinople. Hunt and Carlyle took the cutter to catch one last look at the plains of Troy. Grudgingly, Hunt now agreed with Carlyle about the actual site of the city.

Mary spent the rest of the afternoon strolling leisurely about the deck, tossing small chunks of bread to the gulls floating off the *Phaeton*'s bow, joyful over the new life being formed inside her.

Elgin returned to the *Phaeton* just before dark. Duff, Hunt, and Carlyle waited at the rail beside her to greet him. "Eggy, where did you go?" she asked.

Elgin told Duff to bring him a glass of wine. "I went to see the Capitan Pasha."

"For what reason?"

"A very urgent matter. I had to act quickly."

"I wish you would tell me what it was."

"I had to get the Pasha's permission."

"For what?"

"To take the two marble seats from Yenishehr."

There was a suffocating silence.

"It was easier than I imagined," Elgin went on, downing his glass of wine. "The Capitan Pasha gave it to me in writing. In another hour or so, the seats should be on board the *Phaeton*. Captain Morris' men are already transporting them to the shore by ox cart."

Duff filled the glass again. Before putting it to his lips, Elgin looked at her. "Do you want to come with me?"

"Where?"

"Ashore with the cutter. I don't trust those tars. I'd never forgive myself if they damaged my marble seats."

She was confused. "But why did you return to the *Phaeton*?"

"We shall need more hands, more ropes and tackle."

"My lord," said Hunt, "those seats are too heavy for the cutter."

"I'm well aware of that, Mr. Hunt. One of the Turkish officials at Yenishehr was kind enough to lend us his heavy barge and a winch. We should have no trouble hoisting the seats into the barge. After that, the *Phaeton*'s winch can complete the job, and into the holds they will go for their long journey back to England." Again he looked at her. "Well, are you coming with me?"

"Yes, if you want me."

"Of course I want you. In God's name, this is a grand moment — one that neither of us will forget. Do you realize how many people have tried to get their hands on those marble seats, the devious schemes and bribes? And now they're mine. But best of all, they didn't cost me a penny. Not one penny. The Capitan Pasha wrapped his arms around me and planted a kiss on my cheek. 'We are brothers, my lord effendi,' he said. 'If you had asked me for the Süleymaniye Mosque in Constantinople I would gladly have given it to you. May Allah be my witness!' "

Hunt and Carlyle joined them in the cutter. She sat up front with Elgin, her eyes toward the shore, not saying a word. Fortunately, the sea wasn't choppy.

"Are you ill again?" he asked.

"No."

"You're very quiet."

"Eggy, did you have to take those marble seats?"

"What kind of a question is that? Of course I had to take them."

"Why?"

"Because both the Greeks and the Turks at Yenishehr have no respect for them. They don't deserve such wonderful works of art."

"But they do respect them."

"As superstitions, nothing else."

"Eggy, those seats belong to the people of Yenishehr. You have no right to take them away. For my sake, please tell the sailors to take them back to Yenishehr when we reach shore."

"Poll, you're being ridiculous. Enough. I don't want to hear another word."

"This is the first time you've raised your voice to me."

"I'm sorry, but you provoked me."

"What do you intend to do with those seats?"

"Frankly, I do not know."

"Will you send them to Broomhall?"

"I cannot say at this time."

"Will you sell them?"

He was appalled. "Certainly not."

"For the last time, Eggy, I implore you."

He swung away from her. Leaning forward, he ordered the four sailors to pull harder on the oars. He couldn't sit still. For the third time since they boarded the cutter, he took out his telescope and peered at the approaching shore. "Captain Morris and the lads are waiting for us beside the barge!" he exclaimed. "Look, Poll."

Hordes of people were lined on the shore, their poignant threnody carrying across the water. In their midst stood an old Greek priest, his long black robes swept back by the wind, his tall stiff clerical hat tilted to the side of his gray head.

The cutter was about to be beached, when Captain Morris came splashing through the water to meet them. "My lord," he cried, "that rabble-rousing priest is creating a terrible stir. Listen to that wailing and shrieking."

"Did you inform him that we have the Capitan Pasha's permission to take the marble seats?"

"I did, my lord, but it made no impression on him."

The moaning cries unnerved her. The people of Yenishehr gathered around the priest, pointing to the marble seats on the

beach, weeping and flailing their arms. She dared not leave the cutter.

Stepping into the water, Elgin waded ashore and began issuing commands to the tars, ordering them to make certain the ropes were tied firmly around the crated seats, testing the strength of the tackle, the spin of the winch. With the extra hands from the *Phaeton,* they had no trouble hoisting the seats into the barge, but as they did, the priest and his flock came thrashing into the water up to their waists, shouting, pleading, invoking curses. Elgin paid no heed to them. Wading back to the cutter, he climbed in, spent but jubilant.

Mary didn't speak to him all the way back to the *Phaeton,* and even after she stepped on deck, the haunting lamentations of Yenishehr still pounded in her ears.

They left Tenedos Isle on a clear crisp October morning, a stiff breeze filling the *Phaeton*'s sails. In many places, the Dardanelles were so narrow that they could almost reach out and touch both sides of the shore. Fertile strips of brown earth ran in streaks along the northwest peninsula, and toward the east, snow-covered mountains climbed over Asia Minor. The passage through the straits extended more than a hundred miles, but with the help of strong winds they made remarkable time and entered the Sea of Marmara at dawn of October twelfth. Here the mighty current suddenly shifted, pulling fresh waters from the Black Sea and sending them over the silvery surface of Marmara. A more forceful current, moving in the opposite direction, carried a powerful surge of salt water to the Bosphorus. Many fishing vessels and caïques clogged the busy waterway, and the *Phaeton* had to make her way carefully through the maze, sailing around the treacherous currents and avoiding the shallow rocks at the entrance to the harbor of Erdek. The town's barren vineyards, the olive groves and fruit orchards, the dry leaves shivering in

the cold wind — everything looked withered and dying. Even Marmara's white mantle was embossed with the scar of winter.

They put into the small port of Erdek for food and supplies, and by midafternoon they were back once again on Marmara's bosom, heaving and tossing, fighting the fierce current. Without any warning, an armada of black clouds stormed across the sky, bringing a heavy rain, forcing the *Phaeton* to veer off its course and head into the squall. The demented motion of the ship plagued Mary. She hated to leave the deck. She felt some comfort there — the fresh air, the new sights and foreign sky. As long as the world unwound itself, even in a storm, there was no disquietude or malaise; but now in her cramped compartment she was instantly seized with torment, and Masterman came straightaway to her assistance, dabbing vinegar over her face and speaking soothingly to her misery.

Fortunately, the storm blew off within the hour, and after the *Phaeton* righted herself, Mary was able to go on deck once again. Elgin was just coming off the quarterdeck with Captain Morris. He took her by the hand and brought her close to the rail. Toward the west, the storm clouds were already breaking, and soon the sun appeared. He pointed to a narrow tongue of land that lay to the north, at the extreme end of Marmara, and said, "That's the Bosphorus. In God's name, Poll, we're heading into the very core of myth and history. Jason and the Argonauts sailed through there in search of the Golden Fleece, and on that far shore lived the monstrous Harpies, women with the bodies of vultures. Just beyond those narrows, King Darius spanned the straits with a chain of boats, then sat on a hillside throne to watch his great army attack the Scythians. His son, Xerxes, led another force thirty years later — two hundred thousand soldiers scuttling over that narrow strait on their way to Greece. And at last came Alexander the Great. First, he paid homage to the sea nymphs by pouring wine into the straits, and then he proceeded toward Persia. With one key, the Bosphorus opens the door to two

worlds, two mighty seas — and on both sides of it lies the most beautiful city in the universe, Constantinople."

She was feeling better now. Elgin's voice was a balm, and his eyes sparkled even more as he went on to tell her everything he knew about Constantinople — ancient rival of Rome, capital of the Eastern Empire, a city that divided Europe from Asia. Mary had trouble digesting all the names — Septimus Severus, Constantine, Theodosius, Justinian, Michael Cerularius — one Paleologus after another — and finally Hagia Sophia.

"Who was she?"

Elgin laughed. "She's a church, the most magnificent cathedral in Christendom at one time, but now she has been converted into a mosque. Nevertheless, she remains a work of superb art and true genius."

Hunt and Carlyle joined them at the rail, and with vigorous excitement Hunt spoke about the Mese — one of the greatest thoroughfares of the world, its marble porticoes forming an arcade of shops on the street level and a terraced promenade above, lined on both sides with statues of emperors, pagan divinities, and even popular actors and actresses.

Carlyle added, "During the reign of Justinian, the city basked in religious mysticism. Theology, not politics, was the chief topic of the day. Shopkeepers and tradesmen argued with their customers over the nature of God, the worship of icons, the function of the Trinity. Indeed, it was not uncommon for a man to sit in a barber's chair and exclaim to the proprietor that the Father is greater and the Son inferior."

"The cathedral's dome," Elgin broke in, "is the first thing that will meet our eye. It supplied the answer to the oldest architectural problem in the world."

More than ever, she was envious of Elgin's wide knowledge and was now determined to know all these things herself, to study art and architecture, new languages, even Turkish.

"The raising of a circular object over a rectangle," Elgin con-

tinued, "was accomplished by the use of curved triangles that converted the rectangle to the hemisphere. Thus, Hagia Sophia's architects were successful in creating a single roof to cover one of the largest enclosed spaces in the world. It has been said that when one sees it for the first time, he will swear that it does not rest on solid masonry, but is suspended from the roof of heaven."

As Hunt and Carlyle walked to the stern to catch a look toward the east, Mary tenderly squeezed his hand. "Eggy, I'm so proud of you. You know so many things."

He kissed her warmly on the lips.

"What do you know about me?" she murmured.

"I adore your sweet face, your firm breasts."

"What else?"

"The gasp of your innocent climax, the touch of your skin, your hair."

"What about the other things, those you can't see or touch?"

"I love them too."

"Tell me."

He pulled his arms free. "Poll, you're insatiable. How often must I repeat all this?"

"I like to hear it again and again."

His gaze shot toward the Bosphorus. "I can't wait to behold Hagia Sophia."

"You love her more than you do me." She pouted teasingly.

He swept her into his arms. They kissed, and when she opened her eyes, Hunt was standing at the rail, peering at the horizon.

"Mr. Hunt," Elgin called out to him, "I want you to conduct a service this evening, here on deck."

"Why, my lord?"

Elgin rushed forward and patted him fondly on the shoulder. "We're about to reach the end of our long journey, Mr. Hunt. It's appropriate that we thank God for His guidance and protection."

Three

UNDER THE thinning clouds of mist, Constantinople's hills and minarets slowly revealed themselves. Within a half-hour, they were sailing around Seraglio Point and entering the Golden Horn — a long channel of water clogged with docks and vessels, its marvelous harbor protected on the left by the old city of Constantinople and, on the right, by the Galata Tower, the imposing landmark of the district of Pera, with its sprawling gardens and rolling hills, its rich ambassadorial palaces.

Guarded by its four minarets, Hagia Sophia rose like a towering citadel, its glorious dome flashing under the waking sun, proudly withstanding the competitive presence of the domes and six minarets of the grand mosque of Sultan Ahmet I. Mary had trouble pronouncing the name and Elgin had to repeat it several times: "Ach-met'. Ach-met'."

Veiled in trees, and overlooking the waters of the Marmara, the Golden Horn, and the Bosphorus, lay the self-contained city of the sultans — the Seraglio. It emerged from the sea with a powerful thrust of light and majesty, its sloping fortifications crowned with towers and conical chimneys, moving in a jagged line along the shore. Within its walls hid stately pavilions, ele-

gant courtyards, gardens, arcades, secret gates and tunnels, and the veiled mysteries and intrigues of the mighty Ottoman Empire. Mary couldn't wait to explore it, though Elgin kept warning her that only a few foreigners ever penetrated beyond the second courtyard. And above all, not one woman.

Although it was early morning, throngs of people were walking along the docks and the tight little streets that crisscrossed around the harbor. Mary was surprised to see so many women. They were dressed in long, brightly colored costumes, the hems of their voluminous pantaloons almost touching the ground. Most of them had black scarves wrapped around their heads; white veils covered their faces. Others wore headdresses of white cotton that concealed everything but the eyes. She found delight in the brilliant robes of the men, their upturned slippers with red tassels on the toes, their enormous white turbans rolled many times around their heads. Pigeons were everywhere — soaring gracefully over the sky of the Golden Horn, flying so high above the domes and mosques that they looked like tiny gray butterflies.

The *Phaeton* trembled as its chain fell heavily into the water. At that same instant, a large Turkish vessel swung around Seraglio Point and headed toward them. Using Elgin's telescope, Mary made out its name: *Sultan Selim III.* Within a few moments, there was a deafening blast of cannons, and Captain Morris returned the salute. When the smoke cleared, the Turkish vessel pulled up alongside the *Phaeton.* Elgin assembled the entire staff and ordered them to line up on deck to await the Turks. A team of attendants was the first to climb aboard. They carried round silver trays laden with flowers and fruit. A young officer, representing the Grand Vizir, stepped forward. He placed a tiara of diamonds on Mary's head, and Elgin was given a handsome sword studded with rubies and diamonds. Speeches were made, and a band of musicians played "God Save the King." Morier and Duff then handed out pistols to all the Turkish officers; gold

watches and chandeliers to the dignitaries of the Porte. Even the attendants were included, each receiving a gold ring.

The ceremony lasted a full hour.

They were carried from the dock in golden chairs to several waiting carriages. The representative of the Grand Vizir rode with Mary and Elgin. He explained that they were to reside in the former house of the French Ambassador in Pera, just across the Golden Horn; but before going there, he suggested that they see the old city of Constantinople. The streets looked tight and dirty, and the carriage drivers had to whip their way through the throngs. Mary kept shifting from one window to the other, eager to catch everything. The young Turk was amused.

Elgin sat stiffly and properly, showing no emotion, glancing every so often from the corner of his eyes at the passing buildings. Suddenly, his face lit up. "There!" he cried, grasping her wrist. "Hagia Sophia!"

Behind the wooden dwellings that surrounded it, Hagia Sophia seemed to lift itself majestically into the sky. Guarded by its minarets, the massive temple was an awesome sight. Mary wanted to see more of it and resented the wooden dwellings that obscured the total view. But the Turk was impatient. "My lord effendi, there are other sights to behold in our city, many more sights, and particularly the grandest of all — the mosque of Suleiman the Magnificent, which was built by Turkey's greatest architect, Sinan, in the sixteenth century."

The carriage crossed the wide avenue of the ancient Mese and entered a narrow street that was dense with people. After a few minutes, the Turk commanded the driver to stop.

"This must be the site of the Hippodrome," said Elgin.

"How do you know?" asked Mary.

"The Egyptian obelisk, there, in the center."

They stepped down from the carriage and hurried toward the obelisk. "It is carved from a single piece of porphyry, with hieroglyphics engraved on all four sides," said the Turk. "The

sculptured relief on the base facing us represents the Emperor Theodosius sitting with his family in their royal box."

"But Theodosius was a Byzantine emperor," Elgin interrupted, "and that obelisk is Egyptian, built thousands of years before his time."

The young Turk nodded. "An acute observation, my lord effendi. Permit me to explain that after Theodosius brought the obelisk to Constantinople, he ordered his architects to build the base. Indeed, it required thousands of workers to lift the obelisk and place it on the base, as you see it now."

Two more columns stood in a row at the Hippodrome. One of them, made of bronze, assumed the shape of entwined sea serpents. Elgin told her that it had been brought to Byzantium from Delphi by the Emperor Constantine. The third column was a lofty pile of masonry, built in the form of an obelisk, that had once been covered with plates of gilded bronze.

It was hard to believe that on this very site there once had stood an immense stadium seating sixty thousand people, that chariots raced around these monuments to the applause and praises of emperors, that nothing remained of this glorious moment in history but these solitary columns, desolate and alone.

Night was about to fall on the city, and the young Turk commanded the drivers to turn around and head back toward the docks, where again they were lifted in golden chairs and transported to waiting caïques for the short crossing to Pera. Mary sat close to Elgin. "Eggy, it's been a long day, yet I don't feel a bit tired."

"Nor do I."

"I can't explain it, especially after that dreadfully long voyage."

He kissed her on the forehead. "This is what I meant about Constantinople. Don't look for explanations. Just be thankful that you are here."

Constantinople,
October 16th, 1799

My dearest mother:

We arrived here yesterday, and believe me, there is no other creature in the world more delighted in reaching this journey's end than I, for I most certainly agree with Elgin that Constantinople is indeed the world's most beautiful city. Standing on seven hills, wrapped in the Bosphorus, the Sea of Marmara, and the Golden Horn, she is a goddess of splendour. I especially adore her gently sloping forests of cypress trees, her still-remaining monuments of by-gone Byzantium — the Hippodrome, Forum, porticoes, and arches — but the most spectacular sight of all is the magnificent cathedral of Hagia Sophia.

Europeans and Christians are not allowed to inhabit the "City of the Faithful," and so we are assigned to a house in the quarter of Pera, across the Golden Horn. All ambassadors to the Porte reside here, as well as the *élite* of European society. Elgin says Pera is the dwelling place of the *beau-monde,* the St. James's of Constantinople. Here everything is *en magnifique* — the residences attached to the many embassies glory in the imposing emblems of their countries, and each morning the streets are clustered with diplomats and their staffs.

It is not difficult to ascertain the nationality of Constantinople's inhabitants. Within the city itself live the Turks in their brightly painted houses, and they alone have this exclusive privilege with colour, while the Greeks and Armenians have to content themselves with brown dwellings. Ours is a most excellent house. Thanks to the former occupant, the French Ambassador to the Porte, there is a grand pianoforte, which I have already tested and found much to my liking. I cannot wait for young Hamilton to come from Rome with his "Carro of Virtuosi." Only yesterday, after we arrived here, Elgin sat me down at the pianoforte and asked me to play his favourite song, "Battle of Prague." This opened the door to the others, and Masterman beseeched me to play a Scotch reel, which was followed by Mr. Hunt's request of "Rule Britannia." In time,

I pleased them all, even Duff, who tearfully entreated me to play a genuine French minuet. Dr. McLean was the only one in the staff to remain silent. Nevertheless, I could see from the wide grin on his old face that he enjoyed every minute of it.

I can readily determine the origin of every female that I encounter on the steep and narrow streets of Pera. The native Perotes wear the bonnet, the cloak, and the shawl. They have an indescribable taste for bright colours and are quite fussy about the adjustments of their *toilette.* The dark-eyed Greek women wear turbans of gauze or velvet, over which they fling a lace veil that falls low upon their backs and shoulders, leaving their faces entirely uncovered; and along with the Turkish women, they all dye their fingertips and palms with henna.

I was surprised to find that entrance into all the embassy buildings is an easy matter. Indeed, it is quite unusual to see not only the wives and families of ambassadors at the diplomatic *soirées* (which, by the way, are given almost every night), but even clerks and their fair partners, travellers, and total strangers. We dread the thought of entertaining and cooking for an army each day — and yet, we are warned to expect it. In such a close society, not a feather falls to the ground but in half an hour every person in Pera knows by whom it was plucked.

Please know that Captain Morris has been so obliging as to give me the cow that was on board the *Phaeton.* So now, my dear mother, I have cream for breakfast, as I did at your table at Archerfield. My dearest father shall be pleased to hear this, I'm sure.

Tomorrow, Elgin is off to the Seraglio for his official visit with the Grand Seigneur, Sultan Selim the Third. He is contriving with the Grand Vizir to have me accompany him, but Turkish custom strongly forbids the presence of women inside the Seraglio. Indeed, no European woman has ever beheld the countenance of the Sultan. Nevertheless, Elgin is doing his utmost to have me be the first to accomplish this impossible feat, constantly reminding the Grand Vizir that I am the wife of the British Ambassador, the greatest ally of the Turks.

Dearest mother, I pinch myself in wonder when I realize that all these exotic things are happening to,

Your Poll,
Ambassadress Extraordinary

Her sleep that night was interspersed with visions of grand Turks, vizirs and pashas. Elgin dropped off like a top, even though he had wrestled most of the evening with the long speech he was to make before the Sultan.

At five o'clock in the morning, she was awakened by Masterman. "My lady, I have wonderful news. The Grand Vizir has just sent word that you can accompany His Lordship to the Seraglio, but you must dress appropriately."

"What does that mean?"

"His Lordship suggests that Her Ladyship wear her riding habit and go as 'Lord Bruce, a young nobleman.' "

"That is absurd. I'm the wife of the British Ambassador. I shall go in my best gown."

Masterman bit her lip. "Furthermore, I am to accompany Your Ladyship. The Grand Vizir advised that I go as a dragoman, your interpreter."

"Where is my riding habit?" she muttered in exasperation.

"Here on the chair, Your Ladyship — in plain sight."

"I can't see a thing. Please light the small lamp on the table. Masterman, this is utterly ridiculous. I shall never be able to get into that riding habit."

"We must try, my lady. Please hurry."

She tugged and pulled at the clothes feverishly, but it wasn't until the last button was fastened that she realized with delight that they still fitted her. Quickly, she went to the mirror. Except for the slight strain at the waist, the greatcoat with gold epaulets still looked as trim as ever. Tucking as much hair as she could under the beaver hat, she patted the cockade, and swung around for Masterman's approval. Masterman squeezed her hands gleefully, then dashed into the other room to get dressed.

In the foyer, Elgin applauded when he saw Mary. "Lord Bruce, I believe. And who is that trailing behind you?"

Masterman strutted toward him. "Kind sir, my name is Masterman Bey. I am the exclusive interpreter of Lord Bruce."

"Did you come down from Oxford, Masterman Bey?"

"Yes, kind sir, and from Cambridge too. I am the master of eighteen tongues."

"Is this why they call you Masterman Bey?" Elgin grinned.

"Yes, kind sir."

"Where did you get that red cloak and expensive white turban?"

"It is a gift, kind sir, from the very hands of the Sultan's mother. You see, I am accorded the highest privileges of the Porte because of my noble ancestry. My father was the Prince of Wales, but he was stripped of his title."

"For what reason?"

"Incest, kind sir. Royal incest."

Everyone laughed, except Hunt, who was standing at the foot of the stairs, his hand clamped over his mouth. Mary had never seen Masterman so bold, playing the clown like this and doing it admirably. As soon as they stepped outside, they were lifted in chairs and taken down to the water's edge, and from there they climbed into a small caïque that transported them across the Golden Horn to the opposite shore. The Sultan's carriage awaited them on the dock. It was a short ride to the Seraglio, yet Elgin found the time to tell Mary about a secret world of golden domes and pointed minarets, of dark cypress groves hiding villas and kiosks of marble and exquisite mosaics, of artificial lakes and gardens, the air heavy with the scent of herbs, flowers, and fruit trees, the regal silence broken only by the gush of a hundred fountains. Both she and Masterman sat spellbound by Elgin's painting of the Seraglio:

"At a time when Europe was enjoying the golden age of the Renaissance, when Pope Leo the Tenth was cultivating Rome's

'intellectual garden,' and Henry the Eighth ruled England, the Ottoman Empire was at the zenith of its glory. The roots of this great dynasty were lodged inside the walls of the Seraglio. In its greatest moment, England never knew such splendor as this — a Moslem day of prayer, the streets lined with people waiting to catch a glimpse of the Sultan on his way to Hagia Sophia. First, the Master of the Wardrobe has to lay out all of the Sultan's clothes, scenting them with the best perfumes. It's a marvelous sight — the Sultan wearing a gown of white silk, and over it a sleeveless white robe trimmed with ermine. A huge oval turban with an aigrette of peacock feathers rests on his head. It's held in place by a clasp of diamonds. In the courtyard of the Grand Seraglio, the Sultan's white horse is ready, its rich leather saddle studded with rubies and diamonds."

"Please go on, kind sir," implored Masterman.

"Meanwhile, thousands of servants await that sublime moment when their Sultan will emerge and ride past them, past the low domes of the palace bakery, which bakes bread for thousands of people, past gigantic stores of wood that burn the fires of the harem, past the Tressed Halberdiers, whose headgear consists of thick wigs on either side of their faces to prevent them from stealing a glance at the Sultan's concubines. During all this time, envoys wait to bow before him and present him with gifts from their countries: desert horses, elephants, cargoes of priceless furs, egg-sized emeralds, fair-skinned Macedonian virgins. Moving proudly among them are the Janissaries, those privileged troops drawn from captured Christian families, swaggering in their ornate headdresses, loose jackets, and boots colored according to their rank: black, yellow, or red. Behind them stand the ambassadors, in red and gold, surrounded by their escorts."

"There you are, Eggy. I can see you. And who is that beside you? Why, it's Lord Bruce and his interpreter, Masterman Bey."

Elgin laughed. They were now in view of the sloping hills around the Seraglio. On their right hand climbed the gray shores

of Asia. "Before we enter the second court that leads to the Divan," he continued, "we see a medieval gate with towers and conical tops that look like giant candle snuffers." He shuddered theatrically. "A dungeon is concealed inside. From there, the severed heads of men with important rank are taken outside and shoved onto iron spikes to blacken in the sun. But now, heralds are announcing the arrival of the Grand Vizir. He is preceded by two officials in fur-trimmed robes who are striking the ground with silver staffs. Following closely behind are astronomers, dervishes, the Chief Cook, the Chief Armorer carrying the Sultan's saber in a velvet case, a host of other notables, all with flashing jewels on their turbans, with ostrich plumes, flowing robes, immense pantaloons, sable-lined pelisses, and finally, towering over all of them" — Elgin's voice deepened — "the Chief Black Eunuch, a man of great power and wealth, with his retinue of slaves."

"What is his position?" asked Mary. She was dying in that riding habit.

"He has complete control of the harem. Indeed, he is its only link with the outside world."

"What does he look like, kind sir?"

"He is that ugly, castrated man waiting by the Gate of Felicity. There, the one who is dressed in that ceremonial robe of flowered silk. But wait, here comes the Sultan. He is surrounded by his important officials — the Master of the Keys, Master of the Stirrup, Master of the Turbans, sword-bearers, attendants, and Janissaries. Led by the heralds, he rides under the Imperial Gate and into the streets of Constantinople, and when he reaches Saint Sophia, he changes his turban. The head of the Janissaries then removes the Sultan's boots and replaces them with a pair of velvet slippers, for even the Sultan must not defile the rugs of the mosque, which the faithful touch with their foreheads during prayer. After this, he climbs the flight of stairs to his private pew, which is perfumed with incense and adorned with flowers

and fruit. At the end of the service, he is escorted back to the Seraglio for a banquet consisting of fifty courses served by two hundred attendants in red silk and gold-embroidered hats who form a long line all the way to the kitchens."

The carriage moved through a deep avenue dense with cypress trees. Even though the sun's fingers were crawling over the Bosphorus, nightingales still sang.

"Kind sir, what does the Sultan do after his dinner?"

"He breathes a sigh of relief that the festivities of the day are ended, and after leaving the Selamlik, heads directly for the harem."

Masterman giggled.

Before passing through the gate leading into the first courtyard, they were stopped by Turkish soldiers, handsomely attired and quite austere. After inspecting the carriage, they permitted the party to enter.

"They are the Janissaries," said Elgin. "They were once the strongest body of guards in the Ottoman Empire, more than thirty thousand. They still wield a great deal of power. Many of them are admitted to the highest offices of the Porte, but with each succeeding Sultan, their strength has diminished."

The carriage was inspected again before they entered into the second courtyard of the Seraglio. On their left hand stood the Divan, the many-columned Parliament building of the Porte; on their right, the kitchens crowned with their circular domes. A wide central path led to the Gate of Felicity.

The Grand Vizir's attendant was waiting for them in front of the Gate of Felicity. Bowing his head, he beckoned them inside. Under the fierce scrutiny of the White Eunuchs, they kissed the gate's threshold and entered the small dark audience chamber, which lay peaceful and still under the many chestnut and plane trees, the silence broken only by the repeated chants of the muezzins from the lofty minarets of Constantinople's mosques.

The Imperial Throne Room stood opposite the gate, and as

they stepped inside, they beheld the Sultan sitting on the jewel-studded cushions of his gold throne. Everywhere Mary looked, she saw a blaze of gold and chrysolites. The halls along the eastern flank of the courtyard danced from the dazzling light: cases filled with jeweled knives and spoons, a sparkling gold cradle laden with pearls, rubies, giant emeralds, daggers and scimitars in gold sheaths crusted with diamonds.

The White Eunuchs stepped aside, and as they proceeded through a circle of attendants, they stopped before the seated Sultan. Mary was immediately struck by his pallid delicacy. He seemed more like a lonely and shy prince than a sultan of a great empire. The cushioned throne was twice his size; nevertheless, he sat with a graceful ease, gently nodding his head and never lifting his eyes as the Dragoman of the Porte spoke softly into his ear. His turban was adorned with a spray of diamonds shaped like a plume; and he wore a loose blue cloak over his thin shoulders, its collar bearing a mass of jewels. A brilliant diamond glittered on the third finger of his right hand.

Leaning forward, he whispered something to the Dragoman, who nodded several times, then spun around and quietly said to Mary, "His Highness wishes to know who you are."

"I am Lord Bruce," she replied, nearly stammering. "And this is my interpreter, Masterman Bey."

The Sultan exchanged more whispers with the Dragoman. In a bold moment, Mary stepped forward and bowed before the Sultan. *"Benim Büyük Sultanim,"* she said, her voice shaking. *"Sizinle tanismaktan seref duyurorum. Sizin sadik kulunuzum."*

The Sultan sat erect and, with his eyes still away from her, uttered some quiet words in Turkish. She smiled nervously and replied, *"Bendenim."*

She saw Elgin scrutinizing her as the Dragoman escorted them to a place a few yards from the Sultan's right hand. Her heart quivered when Elgin bowed before the Sultan prior to making his speech. Except for Mary, Masterman, the Dragoman, and

the Grand Vizir, no one else in the Throne Room appeared to understand a word he said, but he delivered the speech with such grand ceremony, she could tell that the Sultan was highly pleased.

Turning, Elgin presented his credentials to the Grand Vizir, who handed them quickly to the Sultan. The Turks in attendance let out a thunderous yell, and after it died down, the Dragoman explained. "That was our prayer for the Sultan. We all wished him a happy alliance with England."

"But the shouting is still going on," she said.

The Dragoman smiled. "They are now calling upon Allah to grant the Sultan a son."

"Of course," thought Mary, "this explains the gold cradle."

Throughout the commotion, Masterman kept casting terrified glances around the room. After the many gifts were exchanged, they were served coffee and sweetmeats by young attendants in bright long-flowing robes. Finally, they were all perfumed.

Before turning to leave, Mary saw the Sultan motioning to the Dragoman, and suddenly a tall attendant appeared, carrying an exquisite pelisse of sable in his arms. He stopped before Mary and placed it over her shoulders. She didn't know what to say. Looking toward the Sultan, who had his eyes on the floor, she bowed, then grasped hold of Elgin's arm and whispered, "Eggy, I think I'm going to faint. Please lead me out of here."

He made hasty apologies to the Grand Vizir.

"But His Highness will be offended if you do not remain," cried the Turk.

"Lord Bruce has been taken ill," said Elgin.

"His interpreter can take him home."

Elgin shook his head. "Lord Bruce suffers from a serious ailment. It's imperative that we leave right away. Please explain this to the Sultan. I'm certain he will understand."

She couldn't wait to get into the carriage. With frantic twists, she squirmed out of the pelisse, then unbuttoned her coat and blouse. She threw off her beaver hat, swept free her hair, which

was bunched under it, and slumped back against the seat, breathing heavily, her whole body soaked with perspiration.

Elgin had a twinkle in his eyes. "Well, what was that all about?"

"What?" She sighed.

"What did you say to the Sultan?"

She took in a deep breath.

"Poll, what did you say to him?"

"It was just a greeting."

"Tell me."

"I simply said, 'Your Most Exalted Highness, I am honored to meet you. I am your most humble servant.' "

"Where did you learn to speak Turkish?"

"I've been taking lessons from Professor Carlyle."

"Why didn't you tell me?"

"I wanted to surprise you."

He lowered his eyes.

"Eggy, I did it to please you."

"Yes, kind sir, you should be pleased," interjected Masterman.

Elgin let out a roaring laugh. Embracing Mary, he said, "Poll, if only you could have seen yourself, your eyes popping out, your face sweating . . . and Masterman trembling behind you."

"I do not consider that to be very funny, kind sir."

Suddenly the joy left Elgin's face. "Do you know how much all those gifts cost the British Government? *Seven thousand pounds.* Pitt refused to give me a penny for something that would improve the artistic tastes of an entire country, and there he was, throwing seven thousand pounds at the feet of that scrawny Turk!"

Early the next morning, Elgin leaned over her bed and asked how she felt.

"Much better," she replied, rubbing her eyes.

"Good! I've something wonderful to tell you. I obtained a special firman from the Grand Vizir, one that is never given to a woman. But because you are an ambassador's lady, you've been granted permission to enter Hagia Sophia."

She flung her arms around him. "Thank you, Eggy. Thank you!"

It was a damp day, and she shivered in the caïque as it crossed the Golden Horn. The carriage ride was swift, bringing them to Hagia Sophia almost before she realized it. After they had cut through a dust-filled street lined with wooden dwellings, she got her first unobstructed view and was dazzled.

To reach the entrance, they climbed out of the carriage and walked down a broad pathway bordered with sycamores. Moslem tombs were on both sides, their gilded stonework gleaming through the gratings.

They stopped before the entrance. One of the large bronze doors had the faded imprint of the Greek cross. An attendant was standing in front of it. He studied the firman carefully, asked them to exchange their shoes for slippers, then permitted them to pass through a large vestibule that was pierced with doors. The first thing that met Mary's eyes once she was inside the cathedral was the brilliant light. The interior walls basked under the bright streaks pouring down from the row of windows of the gigantic dome. Indeed, she felt as though the dome were suspended by an invisible hand. The vaulting burst with such brightness, it almost blinded her.

A mystical element prevailed here, glittering on the faded mosaics, dissolving every material substance, and transforming it into rich spiritual visions. It was a place of luster and incandescense — rows upon rows of lighted lamps suspended in festoons from the lofty ceiling, circles of colored light swarming over the immense space — everywhere a refulgence, even in the lattices and galleries, the deep recesses behind the giant pillars. As though

from a great distance, she heard Elgin say, "When its builder, the Emperor Justinian, entered this beautiful edifice for the first time, he exclaimed: 'O Solomon, I have surpassed thee!' "

Her eyes moved upward again. Nothing she had ever seen could equal this sight — columns with Corinthian capitals, sculptured animals, chimeras, and crosses, all enlaced among exquisitely carved designs. The balustrade, the capitals of the pillars, the doors and galleries, were of gilded bronze. A great chandelier was suspended from the main dome; others hung from the half-domes. "There are no pews, no icons or holy relics," murmured Elgin.

"What happened to them?" she asked.

His words resounded against the fathomless space. "The Turks took everything down." He paused. "And yet, something still remains here — a pure artistry, an acute awareness of perfect creation. I need not remind you that the Byzantines had a deep fascination with light. There were many more mosaics here, each tessera tilted just a fraction to pick up the shimmering brightness of a thousand tapers and lamps. Their illumination bore a marked relationship with the light from the forty windows, up there, circling the dome."

A veil of sadness crept over Elgin's face as he took hold of her hand and brought her to the eastern wall. "Try to envision the altar as a continuous slab of gold studded with priceless gems. A mammoth crimson curtain separated the clergy from the worshippers. It sparkled with a half-million pearls. Above the altar rose a canopy, and beyond that hung a gold globe crowned by a jewel-encrusted cross. On the day of the church's dedication, three hundred musicians, dressed in brilliant red robes, played harps and mandolins as a choir of women and eunuchs chanted praise to God."

It was difficult for her to imagine all this, seeing Hagia Sophia in her present state — a queen stripped of all her beauty and possessions.

"People are animals!" Elgin sourly exclaimed. "They have no appreciation of precious works of art like this."

The sky looked threatening when they came out; the air felt cold. Linking her arm with his, she impishly bumped into his hips, making him lose his stride. He laughed.

Suddenly she stopped and peered into his face. "Eggy, what's wrong with your nose?"

"Nothing."

"But it looks red and swollen."

"I believe it's from the catarrh I had last week."

"Has Dr. McLean looked at it?"

"Of course not. It's nothing serious."

They continued walking.

"Perhaps we should go to Belgrade for a few weeks. Many of the ambassadors go there with their families. They say the climate is ideal."

"Poll, we just got here. This is no time to take a holiday."

They entered the Avenue of the Mese and were immediately jostled by the crowds — Turks in elegant costumes, Janissaries with their upright white caps and broad flaps of red felt hanging down their backs, officers in flowing red robes and thick turbans of coarse white linen wrapped many times around their heads, merchants in baggy pantaloons, Turkish youths dressed in the same manner as their fathers, walking with a manly air that bordered on insolence. Mendicant dervishes were everywhere; wild-looking, half-naked, heads crowned with wreaths and flowers, they wound their way through the throng, shoving their tin cups before each passing face, beseeching everyone for a contribution in the name of Allah.

The gardens loomed before them. Turkish women were strolling along the wide paths, dressed in white scarves and long gray cloaks, their faces covered by a *mahramah* of fine silk, the lids of their eyes outlined in kohl, investing them with beauty. They moved about in a most charming way, greeting each other

with warm embraces and speaking in subdued voices. Many rode in tilted wagons drawn by a pair of oxen gaily decorated from head to hoof. Nowhere in Scotland had she seen such merriment among women, and, as if by magic, the same blissful spirit had already begun to flow through her own veins. "Eggy, I'm glad that you chose to come here. Constantinople is certainly the most beautiful city in the world."

This time, he bumped into her hip. "You dreaded the thought of coming here."

"I was terrified of leaving Scotland" — she paused for a moment — "but I was also afraid of something else."

"Tell me."

"The very idea of bearing a child, having it grow inside me, made me ill. I was certain that I could never go through with it."

"But you are doing so, and with little discomfort."

She hugged him. "Only because it's your baby, Eggy. Indeed, I'm no longer afraid. You've made me the happiest creature on earth."

Elgin's great anxiety over not hearing from Hamilton was relieved at long last by the secretary's letter posted from Palermo on October 4, 1799.

My Lord,

The pleasure I received from reading your long-awaited despatch from Constantinople was exceedingly lessened by the sad account of Your Lordship's health. The climate there at this time of year is particularly dangerous to Your Lordship's susceptibility for catching cold, and you must vigilantly guard against it.

The bad weather we have had here gives me little room to hope that it has been more favourable with you. I was greatly astonished at Your Lordship's saying that you had re-

ceived none of my letters written to you from Rome. I trust that this letter will be more fortunate. I am confident that you will attribute your not hearing from me rather to a failure of the post than to any neglect on my part.

From the time we arrived at Palermo, we have been continually prevented from proceeding on our journey to Constantinople by the most provoking circumstances. We have had to contend not only with the bad weather but also with dilatory merchants and captains who demand more money than I am willing to pay. Please be assured that I have kept a detailed account of all expenses and will present them to Your Lordship when I reach Constantinople.

In the meantime, I have found employment for our architects, *formatori,* and painters. Under Signor Lusieri's supervision, they have been busily at work amongst the temples and sarcophagi of Sicily.

In closing, let me assure Your Lordship that as soon as the weather permits, I shall embark immediately for Constantinople.

I am,
Your most humble servant,
William Richard Hamilton

While they were playing whist that night with Hunt and Morier, Mary noticed that Elgin's nose looked worse than ever. She didn't say anything to him until they were alone in the bedchamber. "Eggy, have you consulted Dr. McLean?"

"Yes."

"What did he say to you?"

"He prescribed a strong cathartic and two days of complete fasting."

"Does he expect this to cure the inflammation of the nose?"

"Of course."

Her hands trembled as she reached out for him. "Eggy, did Dr. McLean say whether it's contagious?"

"Decidedly not. It's a local infection. No one else in the

household is susceptible to it. McLean wants to apply a half-dozen leeches to the swelling tomorrow morning."

"Eggy, I'm so worried."

"You needn't be. I have implicit faith in McLean."

After breakfast the next morning, she went upstairs to her writing desk. Knowing how much her father loved to hear about government intrigues and military campaigns, she immersed herself in a long letter:

Constantinople,
February 20th, 1799

My very dear father,

The post goes off tomorrow, and I cannot seal up my packet today without including this letter, which is long overdue. Please tell my dear mother that our house here in Pera has been made quite comfortable. All the rooms are now entirely decorated, and each has its appropriate furniture. The wallpaper in the drawing room is in the French design, and so reminds me of Archerfield, I'm completely overcome and even take a fair greet out, but they are tears of pleasure. The cost of this renovation has already passed two thousand pounds, and there is still much more to do.

Please know that I'm sending you my grand pelisse to have it valued. It costs more than five hundred pounds here, but I'm sure the price is much higher in Edinburgh. It will be a great comfort on a cold Scottish night.

And now, the ambassadorial intrigues: from the day of our arrival here, the brothers Smith, even though they had been officially replaced by Elgin, persistently behaved as the recognized ambassadors to the Porte. Sir Spencer Smith was particularly annoyed by Elgin's presence in Constantinople, and during his short tenure as Ambassador, he refused to keep a file of official documents. Far worse, he was reluctant to give up his post and utterly ignored the fact that Elgin's appointment had come directly from King George the Third. Elgin's agitation was inflamed even more when he learned that Sir

Spencer continued to deal with the Turkish Government, boldly taking it upon himself to order all British representatives in the Levant to have no correspondence with Elgin.

Sir Sydney Smith has been equally vexatious. Soon after Bonaparte had captured Egypt, Sir Sydney invited him on board his yacht, *Tigre,* leading Bonaparte to believe that, as Minister Plenipotentiary to the Porte, he alone had the authority to negotiate a peace settlement between the Turks and the French. Alas, when the treaty fell through, Elgin suffered the full blame. Fortunately, he persuaded the British Government that he should not be held responsible, but Napoleon Bonaparte was convinced that it was Elgin who had destroyed the treaty and that its disavowal was an elaborate plot engineered by Elgin to deceive the French. Furthermore, Bonaparte strongly believed that Elgin sent information that eventually led to the destruction of the French fleet at the Battle of the Nile, an event that occurred fifteen months before we arrived at Constantinople! What does my dear father say to that? Did you ever think that your daughter's husband would be a prime enemy of Napoleon?

Elgin had yet another problem: a few weeks after assuming the post here, he insisted that General Koehler's Military Mission should be called back from repairing the Dardanelles forts and placed on more active service. Koehler is a complete bore who pompously introduces himself as "General Officer Commanding His Majesty's Land Forces in the Ottoman Empire."

Losing no time, Elgin submitted a full report of all these difficulties to Lord Grenville, demanding Koehler's immediate reassignment and the Smiths' removal from Constantinople. The Foreign Secretary replied with this curt note: "His Majesty's Government has no intention of offending such patriotic heroes as General Koehler and the brothers Smith." Can you fancy that, my dear father?

And now for the culminating incident: in the small Syrian town of El-Arish, Sir Sydney Smith again intervened and concluded the terms of another treaty, under which the French agreed to leave Egypt neither as victors nor losers, and even

be conveyed to France in British ships, providing they never again lifted up arms against Turkey. Here, Elgin displayed his own knowledge of intrigue and quickly despatched a message to Grenville, saying that he had infinite satisfaction in informing His Lordship that a capitulation was signed in the Grand Vizir's camp at El-Arish, in consequence of which the French were to evacuate Egypt within three months.

Elgin then wrote to his good friend Admiral Lord Keith, requesting him to provide ships for the evacuation of the French. With Morier's help, he embarked on the long and arduous task of issuing passports for the safe conduct of every French soldier from Egypt. But aside from that, and even up to this hour, Elgin has contributed money, supplies, horses, and arms to the Turkish forces in Egypt.

Lord Grenville responded within a fortnight, instructing Elgin that he should not accept any agreement from Bonaparte other than total surrender. Thus, the Treaty of El-Arish became null and void, and Elgin was put not only to the distasteful task of invalidating all the passports, but also of asking the Sultan to arrange a graceful withdrawal from the treaty. Selim the Third refused. In his opinion, Sir Sydney Smith had acted as Minister Plenipotentiary to the Porte, and this being so, the Treaty of El-Arish was still valid.

At the height of Elgin's humiliation, this additional word was received from Lord Grenville: "The British Government has been informed of the treaty at El-Arish, and although it is quite contrary to the policy laid down in our previous despatch, we have now decided to accept it."

Elgin fears that this is still one more reason for Bonaparte to hate him, but on the other hand, he has won the complete favour of the Turks, and they now regard him as their true champion. Needless to say, the brothers Smith have been dismissed permanently from Constantinople.

All this, in the short time we have been here. Now that Elgin has achieved his great diplomatic victory, I indeed look forward to a more relaxed life in Constantinople. With Madame Banou, the wife of the Turkish War Minister, I intend

to enjoy many teas and concerts, go on carriage rides through the gardens of Pera, and, weather permitting, take boat trips with Masterman and Duff around the Bosphorus.

Poor Elgin looks drained. I try to entertain him each evening by playing his favourite tunes on the pianoforte, and he does his best to respond. Aside from all these tensions, we have the further responsibilities of feeding a host of people each day and attending official receptions. There is no end.

Young Hamilton did not remain long with us. Elgin sent him to Athens to inspect the progress of Signor Lusieri and his artists, and since Morier has been bearing the full brunt of work, I suggested that we employ another ambassadorial assistant. I myself made the choice. He is a very pleasant young man named Alexander Stratton, who has recently come down from Oxford and is enjoying an extended stay in Constantinople with his parents. He is English to the core, and Hunt tells me that he is also a capital whist player.

Believe me,
Your truly affectionate daughter,
Mary Elgin

They were into April, and the signs of an early summer had a firm hold on Constantinople. The days were uncommonly mild and pleasant; and the earth in the gardens of Pera was abundant with beds of tulips. The catarrh that had plagued Elgin throughout the winter was now almost miraculously cleared, but despite Dr. McLean's weekly application of leeches, the affliction of his nose showed no sign of cure. In fact, it had deteriorated to such an alarming degree, Mary had to brace herself each morning before looking directly into his face. McLean tried to assure her that these were but temporary symptoms, brought about by the fierce bites of the leeches. "In my long experience as a physician, I have never encountered such violent bites, my lady. Nevertheless, we must continue with the treatment. It is my firm belief that this alone can cure the condition."

"But several months have passed," she said, at the point of tears. "His Lordship's disease seems to be getting worse, not better."

"My lady, I am doing my best." McLean raised his voice. "After all, this is Constantinople. My resources here are limited. We must do with what we have. Please be patient. I feel certain that in time a cure will be effected."

Elgin bore his disfiguration nobly, his only complaint during all this time being Hamilton's neglect in keeping him informed about the progress of the work in Athens.

At breakfast one morning, when Professor Carlyle commented that he had recently struck up an acquaintance with the Sultan's head gardener, a German named Mueller, a daring thought nudged Mary's brain. "Do you suppose this man could show us around the harem?"

Elgin was shocked. "Poll, that's the quickest way to lose one's head. No European has ever been inside the Sultan's harem."

"Indeed, the only men permitted in the harem are eunuchs," added Hunt, "and even they are submitted to thorough and periodic examinations."

"Why?" she asked.

"To make certain that they are eunuchs."

Carlyle began rubbing his hands. "Mueller told me that he has looked upon the women on several occasions. There is a house in the gardens, not too far from Mueller's cottage, where they go every day to rest and take naps."

"I should love to see them."

Hunt stiffened. "I'm rather surprised at Your Ladyship's desire to look upon a sinful harem."

She smiled. "It's curiosity, not desire, Mr. Hunt."

"Curiosity is the work of the Devil."

"I merely want to see how these women look, what they wear, how they conduct themselves."

"They conduct themselves in sin. The Sultan's palace is a den

of iniquity. We should not condone that despicable practice of using a woman's body for sinful pleasure."

Carlyle's eyes brightened. "My lord and lady, I already arranged to have Mueller escort us on a special tour tomorrow. Furthermore, Your Ladyship need not worry about a disguise. Mueller understands the situation."

Mary clapped her hands gleefully.

The next day they crossed the Golden Horn in a Turkish caïque, and before landing on the opposite shore, Elgin asked Carlyle, "What do you know about this man Mueller?"

"He holds a very powerful position in the Seraglio, my lord. Indeed, he is far more than a gardener. He controls half the palace administration, including the guards, the harbor police, the executioners, porters, bargemen, and a host of minor offices. He attends all official receptions at the Seraglio, and often acts as interpreter for the Sultan. Mueller has a great depth of knowledge and can speak many languages fluently."

"Is he married?" asked Mary.

"No."

"How old a man is he?"

"In his mid-thirties, I would say."

"Is he attractive?"

Elgin laughed. "He is uglier than sin, and loves fat, pregnant women."

A carriage took them to the gate of the Seraglio, where the German was waiting for them. The gardens blazed with roses and tulips in bloom. It was a glorious day, and Mary was glad to see Elgin enjoying himself. This was the first time he had come outdoors in over a week.

Mueller greeted them curtly, then asked them to follow him quickly into the court, past a nest of giant cypresses that protected a neglected sarcophagus. Fortunately, it was the season of Ramadan, and no one could be seen within the court. Hunt explained that the Turks imposed strict privations upon themselves

during this season, and even avoided the use of tobacco from sunrise to sunset; but at night they gorged themselves on food and wine, which induced heavy sleep throughout the day.

There was an immaculate silence in the court. When no one was looking, Elgin pointed to Mueller, then glanced at her tauntingly. The German was certainly forty, entirely bald, and no more than half Elgin's size. He wore a white shirt and tight-fitting breeches of purple velvet. Everything about him seemed fragile. He had kept his head down during the hasty introductions, and looked particularly ill at ease near Elgin, drawing away from him immediately after shaking his hand.

Mueller gathered them together and pointed to a deep passageway at the far end of the court that ran parallel to the high double walls of the Seraglio. "The women pass through there every day to take their air before the afternoon nap," he whispered. "A few meters from there stands a small shed where garden tools are kept. The eunuchs never search there. I sometimes hide and watch them, even though it is forbidden, under the penalty of death."

Quietly, they made their way to the shed. After closing the door, Mueller said, "There are two narrow slits on this wall through which we can behold the women."

Elgin immediately went to one of the slits. Mary took the other.

They waited several minutes; then Elgin warned, "They're coming. I can see them."

"Where?" she asked.

"Look closely, there by that small clearing."

First to appear before Mary's eyes were the Black Eunuchs. They examined every inch of ground, running before the women and shouting out warnings to earth and sky, wildly brandishing their scimitars. Some of the women had dark complexions and very long black hair. A few had flaxen hair and were quite fair. Their dress was rich beyond imagination: long spangled robes

with silk pantaloons embroidered in gold and silver and adorned with large pearls and precious stones so heavy that Mary was amazed they didn't impede the women's movements. Indeed, she was surprised to see how gracefully they walked. Their hair hung loose and in very thick tresses on both sides of the face, completely covering their shoulders and reaching down as far as the waist. Diamonds studded the tresses too, but in a haphazard manner, as though scattered at random. On top of their heads, they wore a small circular diadem. Their faces and necks, even their breasts, were quite exposed.

Mary and Elgin stepped away from the slits so that Carlyle and Mueller could take their places. Hunt preferred not to look. Standing behind Mueller, she asked, "Are all the women Turkish?"

Mueller kept looking through the slit. "Of course not. They are Christians, captured for the Sultan's pleasure and brought to him as gifts. Most of them are young Greek girls who were seized from their homes by the Janissaries."

"How do they spend their time?"

"Rarely with Selim the Third."

"I don't understand."

"He prefers the platonic relationship with the widow of the former Sultan, Abdul Hamid, who died several years ago. Her name is Aimée Dubucq de Rivery. She was captured by Algerian corsairs while returning from a convent in France. The pirates took her to the Bey of Algiers, who offered her as a present to the Sultan. She was a remarkably resilient young girl and was able to make a quick adjustment, forgetting the strict life of the convent, where she was made to wear a calico robe even when she took a bath. When the old Sultan died, she entered into this relationship with Selim. They were both in their early twenties and shared a mutual love for literature. Quite remarkably, their friendship still endures, even though they have not become lovers."

"Is she beautiful?"

"Extremely so. She has maintained through some incredible way the golden-haired innocent look of her convent days."

Carlyle started for the door. Mueller rushed after him and grabbed hold of his arm. "You cannot leave yet. We must wait until the women are asleep."

"What about the eunuchs?" asked Elgin, going back to the slit in the wall for one last look.

"They too will fall asleep soon."

Elgin came toward Mary with a glint in his eyes. "Well, what did you think of them?"

"They're quite beautiful," she said.

"I wish I were one of those eunuchs."

She laughed. "What could you do?"

"I most certainly would try."

"Eggy, if the Sultan has so many women at his disposal, how does he make his choice?"

"The Grand Vizir told me that the women are assembled each evening in the third courtyard. The Sultan then passes along the line and greets them courteously. If one in particular pleases him, he places a silk handkerchief on her shoulder and then slowly walks away with the Black Eunuch. After a short promenade through the gardens, where he observes the peacocks and gazelles, he dines with all the women in the harem. After this, he summons the Black Eunuch to his bedchamber and requests him to bring the girl who has his handkerchief. Meanwhile, the selected girl has been the center of much attention. The slave women of the harem have bathed her and massaged her with olive oil, removed all of her body hair, pomaded her skin with a reddish dye obtained from the leaves of the henna plant, which will prevent her from sweating, perfumed her hair, dyed her nails, darkened the edges of her eyelids with kohl. After the night's pleasure, the Sultan goes for his bath, leaving her to examine the pockets of his robes for money."

"What happens to the women when the Sultan dies?"

"They are taken away to a residence in the city, a place the Turks call the Palace of Tears, and here they must spend the rest of their lives. On certain occasions, they are permitted to visit a mosque or a church. Lady Montagu observed them in the public baths one day and found them to be still quite beautiful, with figures like Titian goddesses."

Mueller looked at his watch. "I think we can leave now. They must all be asleep."

He carefully locked the door of the shed behind them and led them around a winding wall of stone. Soon they were lost among the dense cypress trees. Mary wanted to stop and rest, but Mueller cautioned them to keep walking. "I think someone has seen us!" he cried. "Quick, down that slope."

She clutched Elgin's hand after she tripped and almost fell to the ground. When they reached the bottom of the slope, Mueller directed them toward a nest of scrub pines. She took only a few steps before slumping to her knees, gasping for breath, clouds of darkness swarming over her brain.

A familiar voice echoed in her ears. "Poll . . ."

She felt another sinking sensation.

"Poll, what is it? Tell me."

"Lord Bruce . . ."

Four

Constantinople
April 15th, 1801

My dearest mother,

Today, I must tell you of my sublime joy as I sit here on the sofa while little Lord Bruce is being rocked to sleep by Calitza, our Greek *paramana* and nurse. She is a handsome young woman, and a marvellous student of philosophy and Greek. She was highly recommended to us by the Dutch Ambassador's wife.

I find it hard to believe that I have been separated from you for over a year. Dearest mother, you shall adore Lord Bruce very much. Elgin claims that he has my dear father's features, especially the eyes, but I say he is a blend of Elgin and my dearest mother.

Mr. Hamilton and the artists have been busily at work in Athens. Our chief painter, Signor Lusieri, is quite taken to moods, and in his letters to us, Hamilton says that Lusieri prefers to keep to himself most of the day and even through the evening. Elgin is not perturbed by this, since he feels that all artists are a bit mad at times.

I am thoroughly enchanted with our musicians. The first violinist is especially gifted. Before coming to us, he con-

ducted the orchestra at the opera in Naples. Indeed, we are fortunate to have him with us. They play during all our receptions, and for us alone, as well. Our guests are quite pleased with them. Lord Bruce already adores music. He sits in the *paramana*'s lap and wiggles his feet happily throughout each performance.

And now for a bit of sad news — Dr. McLean is dead. He succumbed to the palsy a fortnight ago. Poor man; he earnestly tried to fit himself into the embassy, but as you know, he drank too much, and we all knew that the demon would soon destroy him. I shall miss him dearly.

The strange disease that attacked Elgin's nose still shows no sign of relenting. It looks more severe than ever after all this time, and I have the darkest of fears that it may be leprosy, despite Dr. McLean's repeated assurance. In fact, these were his last words: "His Lordship's ailment is nothing more than the result of an ague. I feel certain it will be cured in due time."

We expect Dr. McLean's replacement to arrive any day now. His name is Dr. Duncan Scott. Elgin claims he is a renowned medical authority, especially on the subject of plagues. Dear mother, I hope and pray that he will be able to find a cure for Elgin's disease.

By the way, you would be entertained to see Elgin at whist. Now that the Egyptian campaign is over, he plays nightly with us. He hates to lose, but unfortunately this happens quite often, and he becomes angry with our ambassadorial assistant, Mr. Stratton, who is quite skilled at the game.

Our expenses here are very great. Elgin complains constantly. It is not uncommon for us to have sixty people at dinner, week after week, independent of the embassy staff. Poor Masterman bears the burden nobly and has been of much assistance to our kitchen staff.

Abdullah, our chief cook, continues to give me lessons in Turkish. He says it is quite remarkable, the way I have mastered the language. I also intend to learn Greek — and for this, Calitza shall be my teacher. Furthermore, Mr. Hunt has

promised to instruct me in Greek art, philosophy, and literature. Dear mother, I shall be quite clever when I return to Scotland. As you very well know, philosophy is my dearest love, and I intend to immerse myself in it.

I think about you often, and for the past several weeks the Gainsborough portrait of you keeps flashing into my mind. Does it still hang in the same place over the mantel in the drawing room? Does my father stand before it each evening after dinner to admire it? I never told you this, but as a child, when I saw the painting for the first time, I wanted to announce "I have the most beautiful mother in the world: Mrs. William Nisbet of Dirleton."

I love you dearly,
Your own Poll

I include herein BULLETIN TWO for my dear father. It is a complete account of Elgin's endeavours in the Egyptian campaign.

As you know, dear father, from the very day Elgin assumed his post here in Constantinople, his labours were devoted entirely to the military situation in Egypt. The French had been in possession of Egypt for many months before our arrival here, and not one day passed when the Sultan did not plead with Elgin to solicit England's aid in evicting the French once and for all from Egyptian soil. Elgin made formal request to Grenville, but as the Foreign Secretary was slow in answering, Elgin decided to render assistance to the Turks at his own expense, securing vast quantities of stores, building special beachheads in the Levant, and sending grain ships to the Turkish army camped in Syria under the command of the Grand Vizir.

On the 31st of January, Elgin dispatched Morier and Professor Carlyle to the Grand Vizir's camp at El-Arish to establish a communication between himself and the Turkish ministry there; then, through his influence with Admiral Lord Keith, he transported several thousand horses to the Turkish forces in Cairo.

Carlyle's first message came from the monastery of Saint Saba in Jerusalem. In it, he included drawings of the Turkish campsites in Syria and Palestine, noting all points of geographical interest and identifying modern villages by their ancient names. He also took the liberty of examining many valuable manuscripts in the monastery. He requested and received permission to borrow six of what he judged to be the oldest manuscripts in the monastery library. These included two well-preserved copies of the Gospels of John and Mark, the Epistle of Paul to the Romans, two books of homilies and apostolic letters, and a copy of the sophist Libanius.

A month later, Elgin received the following communication from the Grand Vizir's headquarters in Jaffa:

My dear Lord Elgin,

I am pleased to inform you that your good friend General Abercromby landed at Aboukir Bay on 1st March, 1801. His army was vigourously opposed by French shore artillery and musket fire, but the fine training of the British troops enabled them to secure a beachhead, and before the day was over, the French were soundly defeated and had to escape to Alexandria.

During the French retreat, General Abercromby brought in more reinforcements by sea and sent them to assist our Turkish troops, which were drawn up on the outskirts of Cairo. His own forces then breached the ancient dykes around Alexandria, and as the sea poured into the city, we and the British surrounded the beleaguered French. On Turkey's other flank stood two thousand Mamelukes.

By this time, the French commander at Cairo had already surrendered, and when this news reached General Abercromby in Alexandria, he assailed the French forces there with new vigour, and in seven days General Menou too surrendered. Unfortunately, General Abercromby was mortally wounded in the battle.

It was a great victory for our alliance, but without Your

Lordship's generous help and assistance, it would never have been possible.

Believe me to be,
Bairactar,
Grand Vizir to Selim the Third

And so, dear father, my Eggy is a great hero. Constantinople has opened her arms to us, and Elgin stands in grand favour with the Sultan. On the first day of the victory celebrations, we stood by the drawing room window and watched Turkish men and women dancing in the hilly streets of Pera, their children waving Turkish and English flags while the muezzins chanted from their lofty minarets.

Elgin purchased a large vessel and had it decorated with roses and coloured ribbons, and even placed a gold star and crescent on the mast. It was to be lit with a lamp, but he was obliged to cancel this plan, because the Turks had bought all the lamps in the city and were displaying them everywhere. And then it started to rain. But this did not deter the Turks from proceeding with the festivities. At first, the fireworks did not go off well, and so the man in charge was replaced by another. Quite suddenly, the rain stopped and the Turkish sky adorned itself with a new moon and millions of bright stars, which the Turks took as a good omen from Allah. Both sides of the Bosphorus then erupted in the steady blasts of rockets, guns, and cannons, as Turks in masquerade danced wildly before our eyes, cheering, "Elgin! Elgin!" Before the night was over, Turkish warships gathered in the Golden Horn and re-enacted the naval battle of Aboukir Bay.

The next morning, the Sultan's carriage transported us from the docks to the Seraglio. We passed through the middle gate, into the second courtyard, and then were escorted to the Gate of Felicity, where Elgin was given the highest honours of the Porte: an aigrette from the Sultan's turban, the Order of the Crescent set in diamonds, a full-length pelisse, and a superbly caparisoned horse. I too was accorded an unprecedented honour. An escort of eunuchs carried me in a gold chair to the chambers of the Sultan's mother, the Valida. It was a grand

event. How I wish that my dear father were there to see me!

Elgin was waiting for me in the courtyard. As we followed the Sultan and his great dignitaries to the Green Kiosk of the Seraglio, every minaret tower proclaimed the Sultan's praise, and in one voice the Turkish dignitaries wished him a son.

And thus, dear father, your little Poll has made her mark in history. Did you ever imagine that such important things would happen to her? Quite frankly, both Elgin and I are glad that all the fuss is over. On Tuesday next, we plan to go to Belgrade, an elegant resort on the edge of the Black Sea. Elgin spent some time there last year, seeking relief from his chronic attacks of catarrh and rheumatism. The therapeutic springs lie in the middle of a forest, and there are many shaded walks, all within view of the Black Sea. The place is frequented mostly by the rich. They all meet in the center of town each night, sing and dance, and have a jolly time. Elgin was particularly struck by the beauty of the Russian women in Belgrade. He claims they bear a remarkable identity to the ancient Greek nymphs of Phidias. But then again, so does

Your own Poll,
Heroine of Constantinople

An attendant of the Sultan called one morning to invite them on a boat ride. Elgin had just returned from the Seraglio and a conference with the Grand Vizir. The day was bright and warm; Constantinople's reflection bounced upon the Golden Horn. When the caïque rounded Seraglio Point, Mary glanced toward the nearest hill and noticed the Sultan sitting in a chair under a canopy, peering at the caïque through a long telescope.

After dinner that night, Elgin took her aside and remarked that they were not the only ones to profit from the benevolent mood of the Turks. All British warships were now permitted to use any Turkish port, and would be granted free provisions and refitting privileges. Furthermore, every British officer who had taken part in the Egyptian campaign was to be given a gold medal by the Sultan.

"I also persuaded the Grand Vizir," Elgin added, "to release all French subjects imprisoned in any part of the Ottoman Empire, stressing that it was contrary to the laws of civilized nations to imprison civilians."

"Eggy, did you ask the Grand Vizir about a new embassy house for us?"

"I did. He graciously obliged and has already bestowed upon us a site not too distant from here. It has a remarkable view of the Bosphorus. An architect has already been commissioned."

"Will the house be completed before winter?" she asked.

"Yes, perhaps . . . but the final concession from the Grand Vizir was the most gratifying of all," said Elgin, in deep thought.

"What was that?"

"He agreed to release all the Maltese slaves, most of whom are kept in chains inside the prison at Bagnio." He sighed. "The Turks have subjugated the Maltese for centuries."

"Why?"

"The Knights of Saint John employed the Maltese to man their ships in their crusades against the Turks, and the Turks never forgave the Maltese for this."

"And you freed them?"

"They will have their freedom very soon. The Grand Vizir gave me his word."

"Eggy, I'm so very proud of you." She went to kiss him, but he drew back.

"Is something bothering you?" she asked.

"No."

"You pull away every time I come near you."

"I have other things on my mind right now."

"You have not slept with me in weeks."

"Poll, you know that I've been very busy. Throughout this Egyptian matter, I never went to bed before two or three o'clock in the morning. I didn't want to disturb you."

"But the war in Egypt ended weeks ago."

He became silent.

"Eggy, have you spoken to Dr. Scott about your nose?"

"Yes."

"What did he say?"

"He's certain that it's not contagious."

"What else?"

"Only that."

"Nothing about finding a way to cure it?"

"Before submitting me to any form of treatment, he wants to study it further. He has written to several medical authorities in Edinburgh and London. One thing is certain."

"What is that?"

"Scott says the leeches did immeasurable harm."

"That foolish old man . . ."

"It wasn't McLean's fault. Any other physician would have done the same."

She drew closer to him once again, but he swung his face away, and in a bleak voice mumbled, "Perhaps we should stay in Constantinople forever."

"Eggy, why are you talking like that?"

"How can I go back to Scotland looking like this? Everyone will laugh at me, call me a freak."

"Nonsense. We must be patient. Dr. Scott will find a cure. I feel certain he will."

Elgin kept his back to her. "I can't endure this any longer. Every morning I dread to look in the mirror. The Grand Vizir cringes in my company and keeps his head down throughout our conversation. Everyone runs away from me in the streets."

"You mustn't feel this way."

"I can't help it. Even the household treats me like a leper. They lower their eyes when I speak to them, especially Masterman."

"That poor thing is terrified of everything. She never looks directly into my face either."

Still with his back to her, he extended his hand. She took it and stroked it tenderly. "Eggy, I want you to sleep with me tonight."

"Stop patronizing me."

"I'm serious."

"You can't stand the sight of me either."

"That's not true."

"Admit it."

She tugged at his arm fiercely and pulled him toward the stairs. In the bedchamber, he wanted all the lamps put out, and he stood by the door as she undressed. She walked toward him and started taking off his clothes. He offered no resistance. In the beginning, she couldn't release the tightness in her body. His savage thrusts were relentless. She found redemption only after he had spent himself completely.

The next delivery of the post brought still another commendation for Elgin:

> His Majesty's Government is well pleased. All aims of your embassy have been achieved in a remarkably short time, and Britain is once again the dominant power in the East Mediterranean.

The message bore the signature of the new Foreign Secretary, Lord Hawksbury.

Elgin sat right down with Morier and dictated his response. Titling it "Memorial to the King," he recorded a complete account of his career to date, listing his accomplishments and stressing the enormous personal expense incurred during the Egyptian campaign. He closed with a straightforward request for a mark of royal favor, a knighthood or a United Kingdom peerage that would save him the trouble and expense of being elected to the House of Lords. After he finished, Morier read it aloud for final approval.

"Does this mean that we are leaving Constantinople?" Mary asked.

"We shall leave only after the work in Athens is completed. What I want with this request is a mark of favor. I deserve it, and Hawksbury should give it to me."

She waited until Morier left the room. "Eggy, I must tell you something."

"What?"

"I've grown tired of this life — being nice to people every hour of the day, listening to foolish gossip, feeding an army each night. I think we should go back to Scotland."

"That's out of the question."

"Why?"

"My real work hasn't even begun yet."

"What work?"

"Poll, how many times must I tell you this? My primary reason for accepting this post was to fulfill my deep desire to embellish the arts of Great Britain through a careful study of the treasures of ancient Greece. This is why I employed Lusieri and the artists. Now that the project has finally been launched in Athens, you want me to abandon it, give up?"

"I want my second child to be born in Scotland. I don't want to suffer the way I did with Bruce."

"Dr. Scott is a capable physician, not at all like McLean."

"But after all this time, what has he done for the disease of your nose, for Bruce's nightmares?"

"The man is doing his best under adverse conditions."

"We wouldn't have these conditions in Scotland."

Elgin charged out of the room.

She slept for a few hours in the afternoon, and when she awoke, Duff informed her that he was going on an errand to the Dutch Ambassador's house and would like to take Bruce with him. "Perhaps Your Ladyship will come along also?" he added.

She declined, but soon after they left, she felt a gnawing remorse. Bruce was just learning to walk, and he seemed to do

much better when she was watching and praising him.

After dinner that night, Professor Carlyle asked Elgin to request a firman so that he and Hunt could examine the Seraglio library.

"For what reason?" said Elgin.

"My lord, it has been the intense aim of scholars over the centuries to investigate the library. Many Greek and Latin manuscripts are housed there."

"As Your Lordship knows," chimed in Hunt, "no Europeans have ever been allowed inside it."

"What makes you think that I can get a firman?"

"My lord," said Carlyle, "the Turks are still in a most benevolent mood; but aside from this, Your Lordship must surely recall that my chief interest in joining this embassy was to search for ancient manuscripts."

"But how shall I profit from this?"

"Whatever manuscripts we find shall be known in history as 'The Elgin Scrolls.' "

Elgin squinted. "Perhaps the Grand Vizir could get me a firman, but he will have to convince the Chief Librarian of the Seraglio, who has the reputation of being very strict with Europeans."

"Nevertheless, it is worth a try," said Carlyle.

"Another thing," said Hunt; "it is known for certain that there are some rare manuscripts in the ancient monasteries of the Princes Isles. I think these too should be investigated."

Mary waited until they left the room; then, putting down the christening robe that she had started to embroider for her expected child, she said to Elgin, "If you do succeed in obtaining the firman, perhaps we can accompany Carlyle and Hunt to the monasteries on the Princes Isles."

"I have too much work to do."

"Would you object if I went with them?"

"Poll, you're a pregnant woman. In God's name, do you think

you can move about as you please? This is Turkey. Women keep to their place here."

"What place?"

He did not answer.

"Eggy, do you expect me to be like the Turkish women, hiding my face everywhere I go, burying my dreams under decaying customs? Is this what you want of me?"

"Of course not."

"Then I'm going with Carlyle and Hunt."

He started pacing around the room. "I can't understand what has come over you. You met Emma Hamilton and she twisted your brain with all those notions of freedom."

"Eggy, please calm yourself."

"You're a mother — a mother with one child and another on the way." He stopped to glare at her. "I can't permit you to do this."

"Eggy, just this once . . . please."

His voice softened. "You can visit the monasteries with me, after the child is born."

"But you're always busy. You never seem to find the time to do anything with me anymore."

"Poll, I'm very tired." He yawned, starting for the door.

"Do you have to get up early tomorrow?"

She caught a trace of warmth in his eyes. "The Grand Vizir is an early riser. You and the others will never get inside those monasteries without the proper firman."

She threw herself into his arms.

Carlyle and Hunt were disappointed with the Seraglio library. All of the books there were leather bound, arranged by titles, and kept inside padlocked cases. They found no ancient manuscripts. "The place had an aura of secrecy and mystery," explained Hunt. "Many of the library walls were lined in beautiful

mosaics; others had magnificent tapestries hanging from them."

"Perhaps you will be more fortunate on the Princes Isles," said Elgin. "Lady Elgin is to accompany you."

Hunt rose to his feet abruptly. "I can't understand why Her Ladyship would want to do this. Searching for old manuscripts in musty libraries is hardly exciting."

She refrained from answering.

After dinner, she sat at the pianoforte for about a half-hour, then devoted another hour to her Greek lessons with Calitza. Duff came into the drawing room to light the lamps before carrying Bruce to his bedchamber. Shortly after ten o'clock, she began to feel sleepy, and, closing her study book, she asked Calitza to put out all the lamps.

In the middle of the night, she was awakened by shrill cries coming from Bruce's room. She rushed there and found him on the floor, rolling to and fro, thrashing his arms about. He didn't recognize her. Masterman hurried to summon Dr. Scott, brushing against Duff at the door. Mary felt helpless. She bent over Bruce to try to calm him, but he shoved her away, his eyes frozen in fear.

Moments later, Dr. Scott ran into the room, panting and half-dressed. Elgin followed close behind him, his face drained of color. "What ails my son?" he cried.

Dr. Scott examined Bruce's eyes; placed his ear over the boy's heart while Duff held him still. "The lad is having a minor spasm," said Scott. "No doubt the result of another nightmare."

"It looks more serious than a nightmare," said Elgin.

Scott shook his head.

"He has never been this bad." Mary looked at Scott. "I'm frightened."

"My lady, we are all too familiar with the lad's active imagination. I'm certain it was only a nightmare."

She glanced wildly at Duff. "Did you spin any horrifying tales to him before he fell asleep?"

"I merely narrated the story of David and Goliath."

"Did you tell him how David slew Goliath?"

"Yes, my lady."

"How he put a rock into a sling and sent it crashing against Goliath's head, spilling out his blood and killing him?"

Duff bit his lip.

"Mr. Duff, if you ever do anything like this again, I shall see to it that you are sent back to England on the first ship. Do I make myself clear?"

"Yes, my lady."

At last the spasms stopped, and slowly the color returned to Bruce's face. Elgin picked him up from the floor and kissed him on both cheeks. "There now, laddie . . . your father is here beside you. Let me put you back into bed."

Masterman nervously straightened the covers and waited until Bruce lay back against the pillow before tucking him in. After everyone left the room, Mary knelt beside the bed and kissed her son on the lips. She wanted to whisper a few words of comfort but stopped when she realized that he had fallen instantly to sleep.

In the morning, she told Elgin that she had decided not to go to the Princes Isles with Carlyle and Hunt.

"Why not?" he asked.

"Eggy, I can't leave Bruce — not after last night."

"Nonsense. There's no reason for you to stay. Nothing is wrong with the lad. Besides, I had a difficult time getting that firman."

"But I shall feel terrible if anything happens to him while I am gone."

"If it makes you feel better, I'll stay with him. We can go on a boat ride along the Golden Horn."

"Eggy, will you?"

"Yes. Now get dressed. You mustn't keep the others waiting."

She kissed him. "I love you so much, Eggy."

"Will you sleep with me again tonight?"

"Yes," she whispered.

They crossed the choppy Bosphorus in an old Turkish caïque and headed for the port of Üsküdar. Marmara looked gray and threatening; only a few ships plied her wrinkled face. At Üsküdar, Carlyle negotiated for another caïque, much swifter and cleaner, and they set out immediately for the Princes Isles. The crossing required three full hours, but, strangely, she was not affected by the sea. Just before docking, Hunt said to her, "My lady, I'm very sorry about last night. I had no right to speak like that."

She smiled. "I was not offended, Mr. Hunt." She paused a moment. "Tell me, have you ever given thought to marriage?"

His face turned scarlet. "When I was only twenty, and under the patronage of Lord Upper Ossory, I decided then and there to dedicate my life to the pursuit of knowledge."

"Mr. Hunt, you never told us why you decided to leave Lord Upper Ossory."

"When I heard about Lord Elgin's appointment as Ambassador to the Porte, I consulted with Lord Upper Ossory, and he acknowledged that it would be most appropriate for me to seek the position of Embassy Chaplain."

"Appropriate for what reason?"

"The position has great advantages and should eventually bring an independent income."

"To whom?"

"Me, my lady."

She stared at him in bewilderment. "You expect to derive an independent income from your employment as Embassy Chaplain?"

"I do."

"But how? Has Lord Elgin promised you this?"

"He has indeed."

The caïque veered sharply toward port, and Hunt reached over to help her. "We are about to dock at Büyük Ada. It is the largest of the Princes Isles, and the oldest monasteries are here."

"Shall we visit the other isles also?"

"If time permits. There are six altogether. A very ancient convent still flourishes on one of them."

Carlyle was immersed in his notes, and when Hunt tapped him on the shoulder, his head shot up. "Are we here so soon?" he asked.

"Yes," said Hunt.

On the small dock, Hunt said to her, "Very few travelers come to the Princes Isles."

"Why is that?"

"Not too many people are driven by religious fervor, and the isles have nothing but monasteries to offer. Almost every priest in the Greek Orthodox Church has studied here. There is a grand tradition in these monasteries — of courage and faith, of scholarship, dedication, and sacrifice in the face of death."

They left the dock and climbed to the top of the grassy knoll overlooking the harbor. Mary followed closely behind Hunt until they worked their way down a long slope and came into the village of Büyük Ada. The bright colors of the houses vibrated in the spring sun. There was no turmoil here. Unlike Constantinople, it was a place of serene silence — no crowds jostling each other, no beggars in the streets, no travelers. A few horse-driven carriages passed leisurely through the cobbled street, and almost immediately her thoughts went to Archerfield.

The residents of Büyük Ada wore long bright swirling robes and huge white turbans, and they spoke Turkish, but their dialect was difficult for her to understand until she realized they left out the last syllable of each word.

The first monastery that came into view lay in ruins at a site called Kamares. Hunt explained that it had served as a place of refuge for emperors of the Byzantine era and that its chapel had

been built by the Empress Theodora, wife of Justinian. Close by stood the Convent of the Theotokos, its gray walls braced against the sturdy red rocks. In the center of the courtyard they came upon a tombstone that read, "Here lie the remains of the Honourable Edward Barton, Second English Ambassador to the Porte." It was a decrepit old stone, but somehow it made her heart swell with pride.

The convent's library was small and contained only religious books. The Lady Superior was emaciated with age and hard of hearing, and as Carlyle repeated his inquiries about classical manuscripts, she kept shaking her head absently and mumbling inaudible prayers.

At the far end of Büyük Ada loomed the Monastery of Saint George, a formidable fortress protected by high walls and cannons, its outer gate plated with heavy iron. They had to pass through two more gates before entering the quadrangle, where more cannons were mounted on carriages along the inner walls. A dozen monks were filing out of the refectory. One of them, a portly man, came forward to greet them. He introduced himself as Father Eusebios, abbot of the monastery. He was quite pleasant in his manner, and his ruddy face was framed by a bushy black beard. The customary black cylindrical hat rested on his head. When Hunt showed him the firman from the Grand Vizir, he smilingly shook his head. "My children, the Porte has no jurisdiction over our monastery. We take orders only from the Patriarch. But come, you must be hungry. We have some wonderful lentil stew in the refectory. Please follow me."

The stew was cooked in a sauce of tomatoes and olive oil, richly scented with herbs; the dark bread was freshly baked. When Mary finished, a young novice offered her more, and she thanked him, feeling proud about her knowledge of Greek.

Carlyle was fidgeting with his spoon. "Your Holiness, we have just come from the Seraglio library, where we had permission to inspect every volume."

The abbot's smile was captivating. "My child, I must tell you

again that the Seraglio has no jurisdiction over us, but since you have traveled this great distance, I shall permit you to visit our library — on one condition."

"Of course," said Carlyle.

"I shall have to remain close to your side at all times."

Carlyle nodded, then rose to his feet. After a hasty blessing, the abbot led them out of the refectory and through an iron door green with years. It brought them into a dank cellar. The abbot lighted a taper and held it high. The sputtering flame revealed many leather-bound books on tottering shelves and volumes of manuscripts lying on the floor in complete disorder and neglect.

Carlyle was shocked. "Is this your library?"

"Yes, my child."

"But these manuscripts are becoming ruined."

The abbot fingered his silver crucifix. "We keep asking the Patriarch to build us a proper library, but he does nothing about it."

"You have no other place to keep these books and manuscripts?"

"No, my child."

"Then perhaps you can let us have some of them."

"That is impossible."

"Would you consider selling them to us?" suggested Hunt.

The abbot scratched his beard. "You can purchase only those in the poorest condition. Is that agreed?"

"Yes," said Carlyle quickly.

"How many will you purchase?"

"That depends on the price."

"Five dinars for each."

Carlyle laughed. "That is preposterous."

The abbot played with his crucifix once again. "Two dinars."

Hunt stepped between them and said, "Your Holiness, in the name of His Excellency, Lord Elgin, I should like to make a gift of fifty dinars to the Monastery of Saint George."

Shifting the taper to his left hand, the abbot made the sign of

the cross, then blessed all three of them. "My children, you may take whatever manuscripts you deem worthy."

She stood to the side while Hunt and Carlyle began sorting the manuscripts. After a lengthy examination, they gathered the desirable manuscripts and took them outside. The sun was bleaching the quadrangle.

"We shall miss these old friends." The abbot sighed. "They have been lodged here for many centuries."

"We shall take good care of them," said Carlyle. Hunt helped him tie the manuscripts into two bundles.

"What do you plan to do with them?"

"First, we shall clean and dry them. After that, they will be collated and stored in a dry place until we find a suitable library where they can be studied by scholars."

"I have some oilskins in my study. Bring the two bundles there, and we can wrap them carefully so that the sea air will not harm them."

Mary waited in the quadrangle until Hunt and Carlyle returned. The bundles were neatly wrapped in oilskins.

"Did you pay the abbot?" she asked Hunt.

"Pay him, my lady?"

"You promised him fifty dinars, Mr. Hunt. You made an offer of a gift in Lord Elgin's name."

"No mention was made of it again."

"Mr. Hunt, I'm greatly disturbed by this. I want you to go back to the abbot and assure him in writing that Lord Elgin will pay him fifty dinars for the manuscripts."

"But how can I give such assurance?"

"With a promissory note. Professor Carlyle will co-sign it with you under my husband's name."

"I think we should not do this without His Lordship's permission."

"Then you must return the manuscripts to the abbot."

"But my lady."

"Mr. Hunt, I shall not leave this monastery until you do as I say."

Carlyle took off his spectacles and wiped them. "We must do exactly that, Mr. Hunt. There's no point in further debate. Come, I shall co-sign the document, and then we can take leave of this place. It's getting late. We don't want to miss the last caïque to Constantinople."

Elgin was exuberant over their success, and that same night he instructed Carlyle to join Hunt on a journey to Mount Athos, where twenty-four monasteries had survived the Turkish occupation. "I feel certain that you will find many valuable manuscripts there."

Hunt agreed. "My lord, that's an excellent idea."

"And before you leave for Greece, I think you should investigate the library of the Patriarchate here in Constantinople."

"Yes, my lord," said Carlyle.

"I want a full account, a detailed report of all your activities at Mount Athos, including military and political information about the mainland of Greece. After you complete your search at the monasteries, I want you to continue with the political and military survey. Go to Athens also, and assist young Hamilton with the artistic project there. Be especially watchful about the first signs of any rebellion or uprising. There's continued talk here of a Greek revolt against the Turks. I want to be informed about everything, even if it's a minor skirmish."

"When shall we leave?" asked Hunt.

"As soon as you investigate the libraries of the patriarchs. This shouldn't take more than a day or two."

"What about the passage?"

"I shall arrange it for this coming Monday. That will allow you five days to prepare yourselves."

On Monday morning, Mary accompanied Elgin on the car-

riage ride through Pera and stood on the dock at the edge of the Golden Horn, waving good-by to Hunt and Carlyle as they sailed off in the Turkish caïque. On the way back to the embassy, Elgin looked at her from the corner of his eyes. "I thought for certain that you would be eager to go with them."

She laughed. "I've had enough of monasteries for a while."

He patted her fondly on the belly. "I hope it's another boy."

"I wish it were over, Eggy. The thought of four more months is unbearable."

"You should keep yourself occupied."

"Doing what?"

"Start visiting the wives of the other ambassadors. They keep inviting you."

"They're such bores, all of them."

"What about Madame Banou? I thought you liked her."

"I do."

"Then call on her. After all, her husband is the Turkish War Minister."

"I know. You've told me this a dozen times."

"Do it, Poll. Call on her tomorrow."

"I shall."

She decided to take Bruce with her on the visit to Madame Banou. He loved the crossing in the caïque, and she enjoyed watching him, even though he frightened her to death when he tried to wriggle out of her arms and lean over the side to touch the water.

The War Minister's house lay in the heart of old Constantinople, in the very shadows of the Süleymaniye Mosque. When the carriage reached the crest of the high hill, she noticed that Bruce had his head turned and was staring across the Golden Horn, toward the Tower of Galata.

"Someday we shall climb it together," she said. "Think of it,

Bruce, you will be able to look down upon this glorious city as though you were God."

"Does God live in the tower?"

"He lives higher than that, much higher."

"I want to see Him. Where is He?"

"Be patient. We all shall see Him someday."

Madame Banou was overjoyed and could not keep her hands off Bruce, hugging him, fondling and squeezing his little arms. She was a beautiful woman, soft and kind, her raven hair parted in the center and pulled back in a plaited bun behind her head. They conversed in French.

"My little blond angel, you look tired, carrying all that unbecoming flesh."

She smiled. "Madame Banou, I'm five months with child."

"All the more reason for looking after your body. Yes, this is an appropriate time to pay a visit to one of our baths. I can recommend the best masseuse in Constantinople. Her name is Esmé. Believe me, she is quite competent. You will adore her."

"I thought the baths were reserved only for men."

"How ridiculous! The men have theirs and we have ours."

"Do the men use women attendants too?"

Madame Banou laughed. "Of course not. Why do you ask?"

"Lord Elgin visits the baths every week."

"My dear little hyacinth, you have no reason to be jealous. The baths are strictly segregated."

Bruce began squirming in her arms, struggling to get free. Mary coaxed him to sit beside her on the sofa. "We don't have baths for women in Scotland," she said to Madame Banou.

"But this is Constantinople."

"I'm not sure Lord Elgin would approve."

"He need not know."

"I have never hidden anything from him."

"But why should it upset you? He goes to his bath every week. You never question this."

"Yes, that's quite true," said Mary, feeling more relaxed.

They walked into the sun-splattered flower garden. Bruce scurried along the paths, touching the flowers gently, stopping now and then to nuzzle his nose in one.

"Madame Banou, I think I shall try it."

"Good. You should go as soon as possible. Tomorrow afternoon perhaps?"

She nodded.

"After we have tea, I shall write down the address. The *haman* is easy to find."

"What did you call it?"

"Haman, the Cagaloglu Haman. My servant can go to Esmé and inform her that you will be there at two o'clock. Does the time suit you?"

"Yes."

The haman was hidden in the deepest part of old Constantinople, overshadowed by a cluster of tall wooden houses, all of them infirm and tilting against each other. The streets were filthy, and frenzied tumult possessed the hordes of people that were crowded everywhere. Why did the Turks have to do everything in such perpetual intensity — pushing, shoving, arguing? Within this wild arena, vendors with two-wheeled carts sold their vegetables, fruits, and hot servings of rice and chickpeas.

She was reluctant to leave the carriage. Rubbish was strewn over the street, inviting cats and rodents, and from the doorways and windows old men cast lascivious glances. The driver offered no objection when she asked him to accompany her to the door of the haman. He remained there until the door opened, revealing a beautiful young woman with flashing brown eyes and auburn hair. Her skin was the color of autumn grass; her voice, silky and soft. "You must be Lady Elgin. I have been waiting for you."

"Am I late?"

"No, my lady. I wanted to be at the door when you arrived. Please come in."

"Are you Esmé?"

"Yes, my lady."

Inside, shafts of steamy sunlight pierced through slits of windows encircling a huge dome. The walls and floor were soaked with moisture. Following close behind Esmé, she passed through a long hallway and stopped before a gleaming white archway. Several women were disrobing and placing their clothes on a bench. They chatted with a flourish.

"Please take off your clothes, my lady. Put them on this chair."

"It's very warm in here," Mary said hesitantly.

"You will find it much warmer in the *hararet.*"

"I have never taken off my clothes in public . . ."

Esmé nudged her on the arm.

"Those women are staring at me."

"It's because you are so fair and beautiful. They mean no harm. Tell me, how did you learn to speak Turkish so well?"

"Professor Carlyle taught me; also our cook, Abdullah."

Esmé helped her with the dress and petticoats. She took off the shoes and stockings.

"Your hat, my lady. You forgot to take it off."

Mary felt awkward, standing naked in this strange room, all those Turkish eyes staring at her.

"My lady should visit the baths more regularly. Your skin is much too dry and a bit flabby."

"I am with child."

"Of course." Esmé smiled, her eyes twinkling. "When does my lady expect to give birth?"

"Sometime in early fall."

She followed Esmé to an opening on the opposite side of the room, and with each halting step she could feel the probing eyes of the women behind her.

"This is our *sogokluk.* You must remain here long enough to allow the warmth to penetrate into your pores and prepare you for the great heat of the hararet."

Esmé walked to a table, and from a small cabinet just above it she pulled out a glass jar and a flat rounded object that resembled the shell of a giant clam. "Before you enter the hararet, I must shave away all your body hairs."

"Why?" she cried.

"It is the tradition of the bath. Only after you are entirely free of these hairs can you fully enjoy the pleasure of the hararet. First, I shall apply a coat of this solution over the hairs, and then I shall scrape them off with the sharp edge of this mussel shell."

She wanted to stop her, especially when Esmé's hands began moving freely over her thighs and abdomen, but the girl continued until all the paste was applied. Taking the mussel shell, she guided it quickly over the hairs, cutting them away without causing her any pain. Esmé was lost in her work, lips straining, eyes riveted on the swift motion of her hand. Several times, she stopped to wipe the mussel shell with a clean towel. After this, she washed away the paste and hairs with soap and water. "You are now ready for the hararet," she said.

They walked toward another room. "Are you not coming in too?"

Esmé shook her head. "I will wait for you in the sogokluk. As soon as you return, I shall wash and massage you."

Mary advanced a few paces and peered into the thick vapors. "I can see other women in here."

"They will not bother you," said Esmé.

She felt very uncomfortable, standing naked and shaved like this. Esmé asked her to go in. "I want you to sit on that marble slab in the center of the hararet. We call it the navel stone."

"It is unbearably hot in here," she complained.

"But of course. You cannot see them, but underneath the stone floor are great tongues of flames. Intense heat is necessary, my

lady. It is the only way to expel all the poisons from your body. If you start feeling faint, douse your face with water from that marble bowl."

Slowly, she made her way through the hot mist to the round marble slab. High above, through the narrow windows of glass, slivers of light came streaking down on the navel stone. The floor, the columned side chambers, and the ceiling were of gray marble. In the dense shimmering moisture she could make out the vague shadowy forms of the women sitting on the other side of the marble slab. Their veiled whispers echoed darkly against the wet walls and ceiling.

The stone felt excessively warm. The moment she sat on it, torrents of perspiration began gushing from her body. Suddenly she felt weak and frightened. She tried to walk to the water bowl, but after two dizzy steps she dropped to her knees and had to call upon all her strength to crawl back to the navel stone. She rolled on her side, then lay back, helpless and terrified. It was so utterly foolish to have come here. What if she died in this place? What would Elgin think? What would happen to Bruce and her unborn child?

She felt something cool and moist — the refreshing sensation of smooth hands dabbing water on her hands and wrists. She struggled to open her eyes and saw an obscurely familiar face bending over her. She could not keep her eyes open. As the hands massaged her shoulders, easing away the tension and fear, she realized how tired she was, how spent and debilitated.

The supple hands kept moving over every inch of her body, stroking her breasts, caressing them . . . velvet fingers lightly brushing her nipples, gliding along her abdomen to her hips and thighs, lingering at her most secret place, immobilizing her and sending a frightful hunger over her loins.

Her hips began to thrust at the hunger, and in a frantic moment she threw her arms around the mysterious body, clinging

to it desperately until her last gasp reverberated against the throbbing walls of the hararet.

Hunt's letters arrived at the embassy with great regularity. His first message was dispatched from the Isle of Tenedos on the seventh of May, 1801:

> My Lord,
>
> After passing through the Dardanelles, we decided to stop on the Asia Minor coast for a last visit to the plain of Troy. With the help of the local Pasha, we obtained numerous marble slabs with inscriptions, and before leaving, we arranged to have them shipped to Your Lordship in Constantinople. Please know that we intend to persist in our search everywhere we go.
>
> Professor Carlyle has been working faithfully on his journal, and even composes poems at every site we visit. At Nicaea, where the great council of the early church formulated the Nicene Creed, he spent many hours on a poem of only three verses, whose criticism I reserve. He asks me to assure Your Lordship that he will be very diligent in his quest for manuscripts.
>
> We encountered another party of English travellers at Troy, under the supervision of Edward Daniel Clarke, a Cambridge don and mineralogist. They were making the grandest of grand tours, having already crossed Europe by way of Scandinavia, Russia, and the Crimea. Clarke is a most painstaking scholar and makes notes of everything he observes, including such bits of information as descriptions of scenery, modes of dress, current prices in the markets, species of plants and animals, weather patterns, and political systems of government. He has in his employ a professional painter who makes drawings of every ancient site, together with numerous sketches of statues and inscriptions. Clarke's ultimate goal is the confiscation of ancient statuary, manuscripts, and coins. For Your Lordship's information, he next plans to visit Greece, and we fear that he

intends to take away from that country all the antiquities upon which he can lay his hands.

It grieves me to report that Professor Carlyle became involved in a violent argument with Clarke — first, over their disagreement regarding the actual site of Troy, but more seriously, over Clarke's unscrupulous methods and demeanour. At one point, I greatly feared they would come to blows, and I had to pull Professor Carlyle away.

Another letter was sent from the village of Karyai on the Mount Athos peninsula, and dated 15th May, 1801:

After our perilous crossing of the Aegean, during which we nearly perished in a severe storm, we at last landed on the northern coast of the Athos peninsula and set out as soon as possible for the monasteries. The first to be visited was Vatopaidi, which is perched on a tall peak and surrounded by high walls and towers. In the embrasures were many cannons mounted on carriages and aimed directly at the slopes below. The monks here boasted to us that the Turks had tried many times to capture the monasteries on Mount Athos but had failed.

We found the monks quite war-like in their appearance. Nevertheless, they received us with great hospitality. At Vatopaidi, their number is close to three hundred. Twenty-seven churches are attached to this monastery alone. Most of the monks here are Albanians, Bulgarians, and Wallachians. There are very few Greeks.

Soon after we became accustomed to these strange surroundings, we requested permission to inspect the library, but the abbot was evasive. Professor Carlyle lost his patience and produced the letter from the Patriarch. The abbot apologised profusely and permitted us to enter the library. We found a substantial number of classical manuscripts, including the works of Homer and Aristotle. We tried our utmost to buy them, but the abbot refused, declaring he could not sell any church property without the express approval of the Patriarch. He

relented when Carlyle again produced the letter from the Patriarch, along with an offer of fifty dinars for the entire manuscript collection.

From Vatopaidi we travelled to all of the twenty-four monasteries on Mount Athos. Only a few are well organised and of sizable population. Each of the other monasteries has less than ten communicants. A small number of the monks seem educated, but on the whole they are poor, illiterate, and superstitious.

The libraries are quite neglected. We were appalled to find many manuscripts irresponsibly exposed to open air, and, as a result, a large number were in deplorable condition. Those that were unharmed we successfully obtained at a very reasonable price. They include valuable ancient copies of the New Testament, in addition to copies from the works of several classical authors. We were more fortunate in our negotiations with these monasteries, because we learnt to offer money in private to the abbot, rather than make payment to the monastery.

Tomorrow we set sail for the Piraeus.

Please be assured that my next communication will be despatched in haste from Athens . . .

Hunt's first message from Athens arrived one week later:

My Lord,

From the very moment that we docked at the Piraeus, we have been showered by the hospitality of Mr. Logothetis, the British Consul, with whose assistance we paid our respects (along with the customary gifts) to the Turkish authorities in Athens.

Your Lordship will be interested to know that Athens is a shabby and miserable town, inhabited by a mixed population from every part of the Ottoman Empire. Most of her dwellings are confined to the north side of the Acropolis Hill. Half her residents are Greeks, a quarter Turks, and the rest Albanians, Jews, and Negroes. Mr. Logothetis tells us there are no

more than thirteen hundred houses in all, many in deplorable condition. Around the city is a wall ten feet high, which was built ten years ago for two reasons: to keep roving bands of pirates away, and to make the taxes of the enclosed inhabitants easier to collect. Only a few of the houses are well-built or commodious, and the streets are dusty, narrow, and irregular.

The Turks of Athens are of more amiable disposition than those of Constantinople. Signor Lusieri attributes this to the more acceptable climate, which tames their ferocity. Of the Greeks, I give a less favourable report. Their character does not rank high amongst the rest of their countrymen on the mainland and in the islands of the Aegean. Indeed, a proverb circulates that best describes them: "As bad as the Turks of Negroponte and the Greeks of Athens."

Signor Lusieri is a figure to behold. His constant companion is an old black umbrella. His crew of artists taunt him daily in good humour. Nevertheless, he has firm control over them. I am quite impressed with the quality and quantity of their work.

As Your Lordship requested, I hereby submit in detail the following information about the system of government in Athens: since the middle of the seventeenth century, the most powerful man here has been the chief officer of the Sultan's Black Eunuchs, who is called the Voivode. His chief military aide is the Disdar, who commands from his citadel on the Acropolis Hill. He has a full complement of soldiers and the authority to regulate the access of strangers to the Acropolis.

Even with Your Lordship's letters of introduction and the additional help of Mr. Logothetis, we suffered humiliation at the hands of this Disdar. He forbade us to enter the Acropolis until payment of five guineas was made each day. Furthermore, we were subjected to constant insult, interruption, and extortion from his soldiers, and especially from his young son.

Early this morning, Mr. Logothetis summoned the Voivode to the Acropolis and heatedly demanded that all Englishmen be allowed to visit the Acropolis at any time without interference. The Voivode became incensed over the Disdar's behaviour and, pointing angrily to the Disdar's son, ordered him

into exile at once. He had compassion for the Disdar, as the man was ill and at the point of death.

Seizing this unusual opportunity, Mr. Logothetis interceded and obtained a pardon for the Disdar's son, but only on the condition that if another such complaint occurred, he would be sent to the galleys as a slave. The meeting ended with promises from the Voivode that the Acropolis would be open to all Englishmen from sunrise to dusk and that Your Lordship's artists would have access to all facilities without payment of any fee or bribe. Mr. Logothetis then presented the Voivode with a pair of brilliant cut-glass chandeliers and two English pistols with silver handles. The moment the Voivode's hands began to fondle the pistols, I took the opportunity to make still another request: an official firman that would seal the Turk's promise. Its text I now submit to Your Lordship:

FIRMAN

Under the penalty of death, no interruption shall be given His Excellency Lord Elgin, nor to his painters, who are now engaged in fixing scaffolds around the ancient Temple of the Idols . . . and that no one shall meddle with their scaffolding or implements, nor hinder them from taking away any pieces of stone with inscriptions or sculptures, nor from excavating when they find it necessary to discover inscriptions buried in the rubbish.

In the above-mentioned manner, see that ye demean and comport yourselves.

Signed with a signet,
Seged Abdullah Kaimmacam

Five

Constantinople,
September 15th, 1801

My dearest mother and father:

It shall bring joy to your hearts, knowing that Lord Bruce now has a sister: Lady Mary Christopher, born on the 31st day of August, at twelve past midnight. Unlike my first delivery, her birth was extraordinarily easy. She is a husky little lassie and constantly demands nourishment. You would adore her. Elgin worries about Bruce becoming envious of all the attention she gets, but thus far the lad has been quite unselfish. A true Scot.

Elgin and I have been continuously studying Greek with Calitza. Soula, our Turkish chambermaid, becomes exasperated with Elgin and often seeks to expand his knowledge of the Turkish language, but he is satisfied with the same everyday expressions he has been using for two years.

Although everybody says that Turkish is difficult to learn, it has presented little trouble for me. I speak it everywhere I go — the agora, teas, and socials. Everybody stares at me in disbelief, particularly my good friend Madame Banou. I tease Elgin, cautious of being boastful, and praise God, he never

sulks. Indeed, several times he has publicly commended my proficiency with the language.

Greek is another matter. Both Elgin and I are taken by it, largely because our Greek nurse is such an excellent teacher. I never realized how rich the language is, how but a few words require a whole paragraph in English. We have advanced to the study of Homer and Plato, and hope to be reading from the Greek playwrights soon. I suspect that Sophocles will be my favourite.

Elgin keeps complaining about his rheumatism and catarrh. The disease of his nose has shown no improvement, but Dr. Scott repeatedly assures me it is not serious.

Bruce grows apace, and right now, he has that gangling look, which I hope does not stay long with him.

There is a smart French *beau* just arrived here from Paris. His name is Count Horace Sebastiani, and he holds the title of Personal Agent to Napoleon Bonaparte. He called on us on several occasions, in company with another young Frenchman. They are both equipped *parfaitment à la mode,* and are very handsome indeed. I wish you could see the fuss everyone makes of them.

And how is my favourite pup, Boxer? I miss him so. How I yearn to frolic in the meadow with him, to hide and watch him flush out birds and rabbits.

I shall write to you again, my dear mother, and I sincerely pray that we shall all be together soon.

Your devoted Poll,
Mother Extraordinary

Much of the winter remained mild, and Elgin suffered less than usual from his rheumatism. Mary took advantage of the good weather and went walking in the gardens of Pera, taking Bruce with her while Masterman pushed little Mary in the carriage. Duff, whom Bruce loved dearly, was also a frequent companion.

Young Hamilton returned to Constantinople toward the end of February and stayed with them through the month of March. He wanted to remain longer, but Elgin dispatched him once again to Athens on the second day of April. He appeared thin to her, and she implored him to be more watchful over his eating habits, to sleep at least nine hours, and to avoid drafts and damp weather.

From the day Hamilton left, Elgin became restless and uneasy, that same troubled look in his eyes she had noticed first at Yenishehr. Every evening, he retired to the drawing room to read once more the firman from the Voivode of Athens. One night after dinner, he suddenly remarked, "We are going to Athens. We should have left with Hamilton."

"Eggy, are you serious?"

"I've had this persistent thought nudging me, haunting me, ever since Hunt sent me that firman."

"I don't understand you."

"It's been here all this time, obscured in these ambiguous words. Listen to them." He pulled the firman from his coat pocket and started reading: ". . . *and that no one shall meddle with their scaffolding or implements, nor hinder them from taking away any pieces of stone with inscriptions or sculptures, nor from excavating when they find it necessary to discover inscriptions buried in the rubbish.* Did you catch every word? There is a vast difference between permission to excavate and remove, and permission to remove and excavate."

"I still don't understand."

"You will. I have no time to explain it now. We must be ready to take the first ship available. Tell Masterman to start packing. I want everything ready."

"What about the children?"

"They'll come with us; Calitza and Duff, too."

"Eggy, you can't expect me to go off to Greece at a moment's notice. I need time to think, to prepare."

"There is nothing to consider. I've already decided. We're going to Greece."

"If you only knew how much I dread the thought of another sea voyage . . ."

"Poll, stop being childish. You have to realize that this means a great deal to me. I must go to Athens."

"May I take my cow?"

He flung up his hands. "In God's name, it's only for a few weeks. You can survive without cream for breakfast."

❦

She spent all afternoon of the next day with Calitza, reading and asking endless questions. She was fascinated with Calitza's knowledge of history and philosophy, her skill with language, especially English. "My family was very wealthy," the nurse explained. "My uncle stood in great favor with the Dragoman of the late Sultan, Abdul Hamid."

"Did you acquire your education through your uncle?"

"Yes, especially the study of Greek and English. I am also fluent in French and Turkish."

"Calitza, if your family was so wealthy, why did you decide to be a paramana?"

"My family lost most of its wealth, and since I love children very much, it is the most ideal occupation for me."

"Perhaps you should think about marriage."

Calitza fell silent.

"You would make an excellent mother."

"For someone else's children, not my own," replied Calitza, nervously walking to the window. She came back smiling. "My lady, I was reading from Hesiod the other day and discovered an interesting story."

"Tell me about it."

"Well, it pertains to Nemesis, the goddess of vengeance. She was also known by another name, Adrasteia, which means 'one from whom there is no escape.' "

"What else do you know about her?"

"She was identified by the apple bough she held in one hand, the wheel in the other."

"Why did she carry a wheel?"

"It represented man's destiny. It had golden spokes and symbolized the solar year. When the wheel turned half circle, it meant that a person had been raised to the summit of his fortune and was now about to die."

"What if it turned full circle?"

"Then that person's enemies would be hounded and avenged into eternity. Thus, Nemesis came to be known as the punisher of all evil deeds and crimes."

"She must have been a monster."

"No, my lady. It was said that she was as beautiful as Aphrodite."

"It's a strange myth."

"It's not a myth. Truth lies behind every word."

"Are you trying to say that Nemesis still exists?"

"Goddesses never die."

Mary rose from the chair. "I think we should get ready for dinner. Lord Elgin will be here soon."

"Yes, my lady."

"Calitza, I wish you would think seriously about what I said. You're a beautiful young woman and you should get married."

Throughout the first day, the sea was very calm, and Mary slowly began to feel a sense of marvelous tranquillity and freedom — no more receptions to worry about, no more dinners and gossip from idle tongues. The *Levantine* was a swift-moving brig with two towering masts and a wide aft mainsail.

At dawn of the next day, they came into sight of Lesbos Isle, and later, as the *Levantine* approached the Isle of Chios, she encountered a sudden storm of wind and rain, obliging the captain to steer her into the sheltered harbor of the isle.

They remained at Chios two whole days.

After the storm blew off, they proceeded on a rapid course as far as Patmos Isle, where another turbulence erupted, sweeping two crewmen overboard; but with the quick action of the tars on deck, they were rescued. The brig suffered much flooding, and for the first time since leaving Constantinople, Mary succumbed to nausea. She wanted to lie down in her bunk, but her cabin was immersed in water, and only after the brig had reached Mykonos Isle were the crewmen successful in bailing out all the cabins.

There was further delay when the storm refused to relent. In desperation, she requested the captain's permission to go ashore until she recovered from her malaise, but he was reluctant to grant it, warning that the surroundings might be unfriendly. Elgin mercifully intervened, and the captain consented.

Masterman's face had blanched instantly when the captain spoke about unfriendly surroundings, and she adamantly refused to leave the ship. Elgin agreed that she should remain on board with the children; then, along with two crewmen, Calitza, and Duff, they went ashore on the captain's barge.

After landing, the crewmen located a protected cave on a nearby cliff, and Duff helped them pitch two tents. Calitza prepared some beds with a few blankets. Soon a fire was lit, and the two crewmen perched themselves near the mouth of the cave to stand watch. The dampness of the place sent chills over her body, and Mary shivered under the wool cover until the fire brought warmth to the cave. Moments later, Calitza served some dark bread, cheese, and wine. Elgin was in no mood for conversation, and he quickly dozed off.

She waited until the men were fast asleep and then asked Calitza, "Please tell me everything you know about Athens."

"What do you want to hear, my lady?"

"Lord Elgin keeps talking about the Acropolis. Start there."

"It remained whole and perfect, exactly as it was built, for one

thousand years. Invading Romans and Byzantines stripped every building and temple in Athens, but they did not harm the Acropolis. Even Alaric the Goth displayed a deep reverence, warning his soldiers, on the penalty of death, not to take one stone away from the sacred Acropolis. The destruction began with the Christians. Does this surprise you, my lady? The first blow was struck when Constantine proclaimed Christianity the official religion of the Roman Empire. With fanatic zeal, Christian priests destroyed the entire east side of the Parthenon to make room for an apse and then knocked holes in the other sides for windows. The Erechtheum was next to suffer. These same priests tore out its interior and converted it into a church. But the devastation did not end here. To display their contempt for graven images, the priests defaced almost every metope and sculpture on the Acropolis."

"Lord Elgin never told me this. Please go on, Calitza."

"Another thousand years saw an endless line of conquerors. Franks, Catalans, Navarrese, Florentines, Venetians — all came and left, yet the buildings on Acropolis Hill somehow survived until finally poor Greece was overrun by the Ottoman Turks. They converted the Parthenon into a mosque and constructed a minaret on its crown. When war broke out with the Venetians, the Turks used the Propylaea as a gunpowder storage place. One day, it was struck by lightning and it exploded. Under the command of General Morosini, the Venetians launched an immediate attack against the Turkish positions on the Acropolis Hill, during which the Parthenon received a direct hit from one of the Venetian cannons. The roof was blown off and a huge gap was torn in both colonnades. Wounded and bleeding, the Parthenon did its best to remain standing, but word soon circulated around the world, and noble gentlemen flocked into Athens like vultures, picking through the fallen treasures, loading them into ships, and sending them to England and France to adorn their estates. Nothing was sacred to them. When the Turks realized that even

shattered pieces of marble brought high prices, they deliberately knocked off heads, arms, and legs, even noses, from the statues, and sold them to these traveling gentlemen. It was an endless plunder, my lady. The ravaged glory of Greece was carted off to Paris, Berlin, the Vatican, Karlsruhe . . ."

Calitza could not go on. Tears were choking her.

Mary took her into her arms. "There now, Calitza. Dry your tears. No matter what these cruel people do to her, Greece shall survive. Her glory shall live forever."

She had to brace herself at the top of the Propylaea steps when she beheld the Parthenon. The stately columns seemed to be praying to the sun, their arms sparkling in golden eternity.

Turkish soldiers were everywhere, their tents pitched close together and covering every corner of the Acropolis Hill. Tradesmen busily moved through the encampment, selling coffee, vegetables, roasted meat on sticks. Even the lowliest soldier had a servant, a groom, a water-carrier, and cook. The place was chaos and turmoil — the loud bargaining, the angry outbursts of impatient officers.

Elgin went to look for Lusieri and the others, but they were nowhere in sight. Holding Bruce on her lap, Mary sat on a large slab of marble and closed her eyes while Elgin went off again. Little Mary was whimpering in Calitza's arms, but she did not want to hear it. She did not want to hear anything except the immortal breath of Greece. Even against the loud clatter, it gushed through her ears, into her heart, clutching it fiercely, refusing to let go. She had never known a feeling like this.

"Poll, I'm speaking to you."

"What is it?"

"I found Lusieri on the northern side of the Acropolis, behind a row of Turkish tents. Hunt and Carlyle are with him. They were talking to a Turkish officer. Come, they are eager to see you."

"What about young Hamilton?"

"He is with Signor Logothetis, the British Consul. We shall see them tonight."

"Don't you think we should find lodgings first?"

"That won't be necessary. We are to stay with the British Consul as his guests. Lusieri and the artists are already staying there."

"How can his house accommodate such an army?"

"It's quite spacious, Lusieri told me, and it's not too far from here."

"Eggy, little Mary is very tired. The poor thing has been fretting most of the afternoon."

"She'll recover once we get settled in Logothetis' house. Come, everyone is waiting to see you and the children."

She had to suppress her amusement when she caught sight of Lusieri, his dark lanky figure stretched out on a chair. He looked so comical, sitting under a narrow blot of shade, holding a black umbrella over his head, issuing instructions to the artists. Suddenly Hunt and Carlyle came dashing toward her.

"Welcome to Athens, my lady!" exclaimed Hunt.

Lusieri put down his umbrella and stood up to kiss her hand. "Are these Your Ladyship's children?"

"Yes," she responded softly.

"Indeed, they are as beautiful as their mother."

Hunt led them to the south side of the Parthenon, where a high scaffold leaned against several columns. Behind them, the Turkish tents were close enough to touch.

Two men were working on the platform. One was a hunchback, but he seemed quite agile, moving over the planks freely and without the slightest fear. Several men were busy inside the sanctuary. Lusieri said, "My lady, it is too dusty here. Let us go back outside. Here, please sit on my chair."

In all the excitement, she hadn't realized how pale he looked. "Don Tita, how do you feel?"

"Quite well. Why do you ask?"

"You seem much thinner than when I last saw you."

Lusieri wiped his brow with a handkerchief. "We have been subjected to repeated agitation here."

"From whom?" said Elgin, rushing over.

"Even with the Voivode's powerful firman, we were refused permission to work on the Acropolis Hill."

"Why?"

"The old Disdar claimed the only reason we put up the scaffolds was to look down at the harem and spy upon the women."

"The Turks have a harem here, on the Acropolis?" she asked.

"Of course," said Elgin impatiently, his eyes attached to the workers on the scaffold. "The Turks bring their harems everywhere." He looked at Lusieri. "But your artists have resumed their work. How was this accomplished?"

"Signor Logothetis came to our rescue," answered Hunt.

"Yes," chimed in Carlyle, "he assured us that he would seek another firman from the Voivode, a more powerful firman than the first. In the meantime, we set the men to work on other buildings and temples in various parts of Athens, particularly the Theseion, but here too we were confronted with problems. There was not one piece of lumber to be found in Athens for scaffolding, nor even ropes to lift our materials. With the Consul's help, Mr. Hunt arranged for a caïque to set sail at once for the Isle of Hydra, where lumber is in abundance."

"Where did you get the ropes?"

"They belonged to Monsieur Fauvel."

"Who is he?"

"The antiquarian agent of the former French Ambassador here, the Comte de Choiseul-Gouffier. Fauvel had free access to everything in Athens when French relationships with Turkey were at their highest. Indeed, he collected a vast number of statues, vases, metopes, and jewelry."

"What did he do with them?"

"He sent them to France, to be stored in Napoleon's museum, the Louvre."

"Did he confiscate anything from the Parthenon?"

"At first, he was unsuccessful, but with unrelenting persistence he managed to bribe the old Disdar with an assortment of gifts and money, and eventually he obtained a most excellent frieze that was buried in ruins not far from this very spot. Later, he got his hands on a metope that had fallen from the Parthenon during a violent storm. He shipped these to France just at the time when his patron lost favor with the Revolutionaries. And so, Comte de Choiseul-Gouffier was replaced by another ambassador and then sent into exile somewhere in Russia."

"What happened to the metope and frieze?"

"I do not know. Fauvel remained in Athens with all his equipment, and when Turkey declared war on France after Napoleon's invasion of Egypt, he was taken prisoner. Mr. Hunt heard about his equipment and quickly made an offer to the Disdar. The Turk accepted and gave us everything you see here, even that large cart, which Fauvel used to transport the heavy materials."

Little Mary began crying again, and Calitza was unable to stop her.

"Eggy, I think we should leave now. The sun is dropping fast and the children are hungry."

"My lady," said Hunt, "Mr. Logothetis awaits the pleasure of everyone's company at his house. The rooms are already prepared."

"I do not see Your Ladyship's maid," said Carlyle.

"She is waiting for us with Duff, at the base of the Propylaea steps. Our luggage is there also. We took carriages from the Piraeus."

Masterman was blowing moist strands of hair away from her eyes when they reached the bottom of the Propylaea steps. Duff was sitting in one of the carriages.

The heat of the day still sizzled over Athens. Lusieri sat beside her in the carriage, and Calitza sat opposite with the children. Elgin went with the others.

"Don Tita," said Mary, "when I saw you for the first time in Messina, I detected much sadness in your eyes. I see that it's still there."

"Life has fed me many spoons of sorrow."

"Tell me. I should like to hear."

Lusieri glanced behind to make certain the other carriage was following. "Her name was Angelina. We were promised to each other from the day of our birth. It is a Sicilian custom. Her hair was the color of honey, her eyes deeper than the blue of the Aegean."

The carriage sped past a small kiosk that was raised up on four wooden poles and covered with a thatched roof. An old man stared at them from a tilting porch. He was smoking a water pipe.

A new neighborhood emerged at the end of the dusty street — buildings of granite, a tree-lined boulevard. Lusieri instructed the driver to halt before a magnificent stone dwelling. "My lady, this is Mr. Logothetis' house."

"You didn't finish telling me about Angelina."

"She died."

Mary didn't know what to say to him.

"A most dreadful death, a plague that spread over the entire Isle of Sicily."

Lusieri waited until Calitza stepped out of the carriage with the children; then, reaching into his trouser pocket, he withdrew a crumpled sheet of paper. "My lady, this is His Lordship's last message from Constantinople. It was delivered to me only a few days ago. I would like to read it to you."

"Please do."

"Signor Lusieri,

"I should wish to have of the Acropolis drawings in the

actual size of each architectural ornament, each cornice, frieze, fluted column, metope, and the like — also drawings of the decorated ceilings and the various architectural orders. Finally, I want you to embark at once upon a programme of assiduous and indefatigable excavation. History assures me that there are statues, treasures, and monuments of all description, and in such abundance that this excavation is deserving of any effort that can be made under your direction."

She fell silent.

"He wants me to dig in the ground, like an animal."

"Of course not, Don Tita. He is asking you to excavate, to be an archaeologist."

"I am a painter, the King's painter."

Elgin was waiting for them in the dusty street. The men carried the luggage to the front door, and she was surprised when Lusieri opened it without knocking. They were met in the hallway by a servant, and Lusieri requested him to summon the Consul. Mosaics, expertly created, lined the walls of the foyer, all of them describing scenes in resplendent colors and classical design.

She heard a commotion upstairs — excited voices, the heavy movement of feet. A man came bounding down the marble stairs toward them. He was of fair complexion and seemed quite youthful. Like those of most Greeks, every gesture was animated; he seized her hand and kissed it, then greeted them in a precisely intense manner. "It is an honor to have Your Lordship and Ladyship in my humble home."

More servants appeared and carried the luggage upstairs. Calitza asked one of them to direct her to the kitchen.

Logothetis was shocked. "But why?"

"The children are very hungry. I should like to prepare some food."

"That will not be necessary. We have cooks who can attend to this. Tell Fotis here what you need, and he will inform the cooks. Meanwhile, you are all hot and tired from your long

journey, and my servants are standing by to prepare baths for you. But first, please step into the drawing room. I must toast your arrival."

Fotis came back from the kitchen, carrying a silver tray with tiny crystal glasses and a long slender bottle. The drink was very sweet and had a lingering taste of licorice. Fotis filled their glasses once more.

"At times" — Logothetis sighed, settling deep into his chair — "I wonder if we are in the right profession, my lord. Diplomacy places far too many demands upon us."

"What do you mean?" asked Elgin.

"I am speaking about the situation here in Athens."

"Are the Turks very troublesome?"

"Not nearly as much as the Greeks."

"I don't understand."

"We Greeks have been subjugated too long, almost four hundred years. We cannot endure much longer."

"Do you expect a revolt to break out?"

Logothetis nodded. "Already there have been sporadic skirmishes in the Morea."

"But that's in the Peloponnesus. No real harm can come from there. Athens is the key area."

"But the Greeks of the Peloponnesus have a commander."

Calitza stared at him with disbelief. "Mr. Logothetis, no one commands a Greek."

"Of course, this is why we have been enslaved for four hundred years," replied Logothetis sardonically.

"Subjugated, yes," retorted Calitza, "but never enslaved."

"Ah, you must be Greek?"

"I am."

"Where did you learn to speak English?"

"My uncle taught me."

"And Calitza taught us Greek," said Mary.

Logothetis' voice became somber. "The Turks have inflicted

many cruelties upon us. We are forbidden to worship in public; our children have to conceal themselves in caves to learn their Greek letters; our daughters are taken at an early age and put into harems — but all this does not pain us the way something else does, something far more destructive."

"What is that?" asked Elgin.

"The devastating sight of our glorious temples being defiled by Turkish soldiers daily. Only yesterday, I saw one of them defecating in the inner chamber of the Parthenon."

They were interrupted by the noisy arrival of the artists. They came charging through the front door like workers from a field, their clothes soiled, faces sweating, hands caked with dirt. The hunchback was the first to speak. "Signor Lusieri, there was a scene on the Acropolis Hill only a few moments after you left."

"What kind of scene, Balestra?"

"The Disdar's son became involved in a heated argument with Feodor the Kalmuck. A blow was struck."

Lusieri glanced at one of the artists. "Were you hurt, Feodor?"

"It was I who struck the blow," answered the Kalmuck with pride. "It caused the Disdar's son's mouth to bleed."

"Why did you argue?"

"He tried to pull down the scaffolding after we refused to pay him more money. He shook it back and forth until I was forced to jump off."

"Did you get hurt?"

"I scraped my knee, Signor Lusieri, and then I struck him."

Calitza attended to the children while Mary took her bath. Before going downstairs for dinner, she closed the door of her chamber and nestled into bed to rest for a few minutes.

Merriment prevailed around the dinner table that night. The servants brought in one course after the other, together with a variety of wines. Feodor drank heavily. He seemed to tower over

everyone with his powerful shoulders and arms — a man with the strength of Heracles. In an effort to divert his attention from the wine, Mary started to converse with him. "Feodor, how much work have you done thus far on the Acropolis Hill?"

"The work of creativity cannot be measured in numbers," he roared, flinging his head back with the disdain of an artist.

Lusieri laughed. "The only way I can get Feodor to work at all is by the constant administration of wine."

"Raki is even more effective," bellowed the Kalmuck.

She found delight in his antics, but Elgin was paying no attention to him. Glaring at Lusieri, he snapped, "And what about you? Is this all you do every day, sit under that umbrella?"

Balestra slapped his thigh and laughed. "My lord, the talk around Athens is that Don Tita is such a slow worker, he often has to rub out part of a scene because in the interim the growth of trees and alterations to buildings have rendered the drawing out of date and inaccurate."

Everyone was amused but Elgin.

Hunt tapped his glass with a spoon and giddily rose to his feet. "My lord and lady, I think it is now appropriate for me to relate my travels with Professor Carlyle." He tossed an elfin grin toward Carlyle. "After visiting the monasteries of Mount Athos, we went to Thermopylae and Delphi, then at last to that ancient city of the Peloponnesus. But my tongue is poor and cannot convey the true splendor of Mycenae's glory — those massive walls, the two colossal lions in bas-relief, the panoramic view of the plain. Although storms of wind and rain had driven soil and mud over the mountain paths, we managed to reach Mycenae's acropolis and, indeed, were rewarded by a most commanding view."

Logothetis signaled to Fotis, who brought them a bottle of brandy and a tray of delicious pastry filled with crushed almonds and soaked in aromatic honey that still carried the scent of mountain blossoms. The brandy was of a subtle strength and did not burn Mary's throat.

Hunt rambled on, "We continued our inspection of the Morea, finding unmatched beauty in Arcadia. Olympia was beyond description, a place of serene grace and magnificence. Bearing in mind Your Lordship's instructions to record all military positions, we moved deeper into the mountains and discovered that conditions are indeed ripe for a large-scale revolt. Turkish morale has deteriorated to such an appalling degree, soldiers constantly disobey their officers and complain about the poor quarters and foul food."

"What about the firman?" Elgin interjected impatiently.

"The firman, my lord?"

"It was you who sent it to me, signed and sealed by the Voivode. What have you done about it?"

Hunt sank into his chair, a confused look on his face.

"For the first time in history, we have been granted permission to move about as we please, to investigate every important art treasure in Athens, to excavate and remove them . . . and you embark on this silly tour."

"We merely did as you instructed," responded Carlyle.

"I expected you to use your brains. Must I tell you everything?"

Carlyle cleared his throat. "My lord, there is something I must bring to your attention."

"Some other time."

"But it must be now. I have made arrangements to depart from the Piraeus tomorrow morning."

"What?"

"My sister has been alone for two years now and . . ."

"That spinster should have married long ago."

". . . and I wish very much to resume my work at Cambridge."

"Professor Carlyle, I cannot honor your request."

"It is not a request. I am giving you notice of my resignation from the embassy."

"For what reason?"

"Perhaps we should discuss this tomorrow after all."

"I want to talk about it now. Why do you want to leave?"

"Quite plainly, it is because I have not been paid one farthing since we left England."

Elgin started coughing.

Feeling very uncomfortable, Mary leaned forward and said to Logothetis, "Do you live in this large house by yourself?"

The Consul smiled. "But of course not. I have a wife and two children. Lilika is seventeen and Spyridon is twelve."

"It's hard to believe that you have such grown children."

"I am thirty-seven, my lady." He laughed. "I was married at nineteen. In Greece, if one does not marry before twenty-one, he is taken for an idiot or a freak."

Elgin could not stop coughing. She asked him if he wanted a glass of water, but he shook his head and rose quickly to his feet. Before leaving the dining room, he cast a menacing look toward Carlyle.

She was at a loss for words, and after a dense silence, she asked in Greek, "Where is your family now, Mr. Logothetis?"

"They went on a long visit to the Ionian isles and will not return for several weeks. My wife's sister lives on one of the isles."

"Oh, which one?"

"Ikaria, my lady."

She pushed back her chair and stood up.

"My lady," said Logothetis, "before you retire to your bedchamber, please permit me to say that your Greek is excellent. Superb. Only one thing, however . . ."

"What is that, Mr. Logothetis?"

"If you would only roll your *r*'s a little more, then one would surely take you for an Athenian."

She smiled, her thoughts flying instantly to her father, to the time when she was riding with him in the carriage to Edinburgh. She was only five, and when the buildings of the city came into view, William Nisbet shouted, "Ah, there's Auld

Reekie!" She tried to repeat the name but had great difficulty with the *r*. Laughing, he took her by the hand and, looking at her lips, said it once again, accentuating the *r-r-r-r* for almost a minute, but still she couldn't do it. Nevertheless, he was patient. "You will never be a true Scot, lassie, unless you learn to roll that *r*. Come now, try it once more, *Auld RRReekie!*"

She went with Elgin to the Acropolis Hill one morning, wandering past the Turkish tents, looking down at Athens, listening to him as he issued more instructions to Lusieri and the artists. Even to her, their work seemed very slow. Adding to Elgin's consternation, they stopped several times to complain about the lack of adequate supplies, the unbearably hot weather, the steady flow of insults from the Turkish soldiers. She could see that Carlyle's loss had greatly affected him. To make matters worse, that same morning young Hamilton left from the Piraeus, dispatched by Elgin to Alexandria for the purpose of keeping a close watch on an archaeological excavation under the supervision of Edward Daniel Clarke. Elgin didn't trust Clarke and felt that he should be scrutinized daily, knowing that the man had designs on every known art treasure he could find.

She was in no mood to hear the bothersome lamentations of the artists. Pulling away from them, she decided to study the genius of the Parthenon by herself. Grateful to Hunt, she was able to discern and identify quite a bit — Theseus victorious over a Centaur, then several figures grouped in various attitudes and representing a continuation of the battle between the Centaurs and Lapiths at the marriage feast of Pirithous. At one moment, the Lapiths seemed victorious; at another, the Centaurs. One Lapith, who was lying on the ground, looked so vividly real that she expected him to move at any moment.

For three days, Hunt had ushered her around the Acropolis Hill, pointing out everything, explaining what each sculptured figure represented. She could clearly hear him, "My lady, the

artist's chief function is to make the invisible understood by the visible. Phidias' great achievement on the Parthenon represents his definition of the gods and goddesses of Greece, the way he envisioned them. Like all gifted artists, he believed that pure thought cannot be perfectly portrayed, and yet, with the Parthenon a great achievement was realized — largely because he looked away from himself and contemplated the true essence of the gods. Indeed, Socrates felt the same way when he said, 'To find god is difficult. Having found him, it is impossible to describe him.' "

Above her, the sun was sailing in a golden sea — that same sun which had sailed in the golden bowl made by Hephaestus from the abode of the Hesperides. In one instant, the realities woven from the myths by Calitza night after night suddenly came to light . . . Heracles slaying the ever-watchful dragon that guarded the golden apples Earth gave to Hera on her marriage to Zeus . . . Heracles, the hero, bringing those same apples to Greece and presenting them to Athena — here, on this very site.

She found herself in the inner chamber of the Parthenon, standing before a section of the frieze that depicted a solemn procession during a festival. Some of the figures were on horseback; others, just about to mount. A herd of oxen led the procession, followed by a line of nymphs carrying sacred offerings in baskets and vases. Behind them came the priests and magistrates.

Stepping outside again, she lifted her gaze to the east pediment. Once completely adorned with sculptures, it depicted the birth of Athena from the brain of Zeus as he sat on a throne surrounded by the gods of Olympus. The goddess was portrayed in full costume, with the helmet and spear given her by the Spartans.

She walked around the columns, to the west pediment, grieving at the sight of the gaping spaces above her. Here once stood a group of sculptures representing the contest between Athena and Poseidon from which a name for the city would be chosen.

Athena gained the victory by proving that her gift of a peaceful olive tree was more worthy than the warlike offering of the god of oceans — a wild-looking horse whose rapacious eyes reflected every cruel deed inflicted upon mankind.

Still, there was a richness and majesty to the sculptures now remaining on the pediment — King Cecrops seated on a snake, his daughter Pandrosos kneeling beside him with her arm around his shoulders. They were surrounded by reclining female figures in robes so delicate and sheer, they actually seemed to move in the breeze. And yet, this was only a portion of what the Parthenon once contained — Phidias' statue of Athena standing in awesome golden and ivory splendor, a gigantic sculpture of forty feet that showed the goddess clad in a dress that reached to her feet, the head of Medusa wrought in ivory on her breast. In her right hand, she held a crowned Victory; and in the other, a spear. Her helmet was surmounted by a sphinx, with griffins in relief on each side. The Battle of the Centaurs and Lapiths was carved on her sandals, and at her feet lay a shield representing the Battle of the Amazons and the Athenians. The dress and other ornaments, all of solid gold, were so constructed that they could be temporarily removed, in case of national emergency, without injuring the statue.

It was still in its place until the fifth century, but now it was gone. What could have happened to it? A colossal statue like that disappearing without a trace? The words of Plutarch increased her sadness: "All the buildings and temples raised in Rome, from the founding of the city to the age of the Caesars, could not compare with the edifices and sculptures created during the brief administration of Pericles. Even after the plunders of Lysander, of Sulla and Nero, more than three thousand sculptures still remain on the Acropolis Hill."

Summer swarmed over Athens with unbearable blasts of heat from the parched lungs of Africa. Earth and sky burned. In the

midst of their discomfort, they were afforded some relief when they heard from young Hamilton in Alexandria:

26 July, 1802

My Lord,

While on a tour through Upper Egypt, I assisted in securing for the British Government a most famous archaeological treasure, the Rosetta Stone. This slab of black basalt contains an inscription dating to 186 B.C., and although the message of inscription is of little importance, it is repeated on the same slab in three languages: Greek, demotic Egyptian, and hieroglyphics. Its discovery now permits scholars to decipher the writings of ancient Egypt by comparing the three scripts.

With the assistance of a small detachment of British gunners stationed here at Alexandria, I rowed out to the harbour and managed to climb on board the unguarded, plague-infested French warship in whose holds the stone was hidden. At great personal danger, I succeeded in removing it from the ship, and now it is in the possession of the British Government . . .

On August 15, the Virgin's Day, Athens took on a new countenance — the olive leaves glistened, birds sang, faces beamed with purity and love. In the early hours of morning, they climbed, with Logothetis and his returned family, to the Byzantine chapel on the summit of Mount Lycabettus, and joined the throng of worshippers crammed inside the tiny church. During the long service, Elgin continually poked jabs at the superstitious Greeks, their bearded saints, their icons and interminable *Kyrie eleisons,* and she saw that Logothetis was becoming increasingly annoyed with him.

They dined later that afternoon. A whole roasted lamb was brought into the room and placed before Logothetis at the table. She couldn't take her eyes off Madame Logothetis, a very charming woman whose dark features contrasted dramatically to her husband's fair skin and hair. Young Spyridon was a Greek

spitfire, eyes never halting at one place, the boundless and free Athenian spirit exuding from every pore of his strong young body.

Except for her Macedonian hair, Lilika bore a strong resemblance to her mother and was far less talkative than Spyridon. And like her mother, she was a striking beauty. At her father's signal, she rose to her feet and recited the Lord's Prayer in Greek, after which Logothetis crossed himself, then toasted everyone's health with the red wine.

The annoyed look that she had detected in Logothetis' eyes during the church service had now melted away, and he was his former self again, laughing and joking, leaning to the side to kiss his wife over and over.

Mary slept deeply that night and did not arise until well past noon of the next day, stirring momentarily only when Elgin left for the Acropolis Hill at the crack of dawn. She had little appetite for food, but Madame Logothetis implored her to sit with her at the table and partake of a small portion of chicken livers and eggs. Between mouthfuls, she beleaguered Mary with questions about life in Constantinople, the important people who came to the embassy, the balls and receptions, the costumes that the women wore, the jewelry, the food.

It was almost three o'clock when Mary climbed the last step of the Propylaea. New scaffolds were propped up along one side of the Parthenon. Dozens of workmen labored with ropes and pulleys; several dozen more struggled with a windlass and long wooden beams. On the scaffolds, three groups of workers were pounding chisels into the metopes that ran between the triglyphs, and within seconds, one of the metopes was pulled free and hoisted into the air.

The scene terrified her.

Two figures were moving inside the shadows of the sanctuary. She sped forward and instantly recognized Hunt in his familiar black suit. Her legs crumpled at the sight of Elgin. She

kept telling herself this was only hallucination, a horrified mind playing games with her, taunting her — yet there he was, shouting wildly at the workers above him, flailing his hands and yelling. "Ease up on that rope, you bungling idiots. Now lower it . . . . slowly!"

Her first thought was to flee. It was all a nightmare. She did not know this man, this raging maniac who was staining the sky with his curses, his crazed look and demented commands. Hunt was trying to say something to her, but she could not hear him. Through clouds of dust, she saw Lusieri walking toward her, his face pale, hands trembling. "My lady, I will not be a party to this. In the name of the Virgin, it is sacrilege."

Elgin charged over and seized him by the arm. "You lazy Sicilian — you and that band of rogues you call artists — wasting my money on your silly sketches and childish drawings. Get back on that scaffold. I command you!"

Still in a daze, Mary said, "Eggy, please tell those men to stop. They are destroying the Parthenon!"

He did not listen to her.

"Eggy, I beg you . . . ."

All this time, Lusieri had not moved.

"We have a contract," said Elgin hoarsely.

He was interrupted by a commotion from above. Suddenly there were loud shouts. She saw men jumping off the scaffolds and fleeing from the sanctuary. One of them yelled, "The ropes have broken! Run!"

Lusieri thrust her to safety just as one of the metopes slipped out of the ropes and came thundering to the ground, shattering into pieces. She clamped her hands over her ears, but she could not block out the pounding throbs, the hollow echoes. Through her tears, she saw a figure rushing toward Elgin, his long-flowing red robe and white turban covered with dust. It was the old Disdar of Athens. *"Telos!"* he shouted into Elgin's face. "This is the end. I will not permit you to touch another stone of this temple."

Elgin's eyes were on fire. He reached into his coat pocket and pulled out a crumpled sheet of paper. "This is an official firman from the Voivode of Athens. It gives me permission to do whatever I wish."

"But it does not grant you the right to destroy."

"I'm not destroying. I'm saving. It is you and your soldiers who were ruining these temples of art. I'm taking them away before they die in oblivion."

Elgin moved away from the old Turk, more possessed than ever. He ran in and out of the sanctuary, shouting commands to everyone, hurling curses everywhere. Hunt was still speechless. Mary searched frantically for Lusieri and saw that he had heeded Elgin's threat and was now back on the scaffolding, his dark silhouette pinned against the dying sun.

Again she tried to reach Elgin. "You must stop. Please, you have no right to do this."

His wild eyes defied her. "I have every right."

"But you're destroying a sacred temple."

"You silly woman," he retorted hysterically, "I'm preserving genius and beauty, saving it forever from the barbarous Turks and unappreciative Greeks."

Logothetis' house was a mausoleum that night. She wanted to hide somewhere, flee to a place where Elgin's frenzied voice could not find her. Throughout dinner, he boasted repeatedly about his great victory over Napoleon, telling everyone at the table that he would be remembered into eternity for redeeming the glory of Greece. Only Hunt responded, nodding his head several times, but his eyes remained cold throughout. Logothetis hardly touched his food. Hands rigid, mouth twitching, he sat there in deep silence, staring at his plate.

She had never seen Calitza so melancholic, so inattentive to the children. Every movement, every glance, was stiff and mechanical.

Bruce fondly patted the paramana's hand and said, "Calitza, are you sick?"

"I have a headache."

"I hope it goes away."

Calitza gave him a sorrowful look. "This pain can never go away."

"Why not?"

"Because it comes from the heart."

"Dr. Scott can make it go away."

Calitza shook her head. "No medicine can reach the heart."

"But how did the pain get in?"

"It knows the secret tunnel to the heart."

Bruce wanted to go on, but Mary patted him on the back and said, "Enough. You look very tired. It is time for bed."

"Yes, Mother."

Little Mary was already asleep in Calitza's arms. After Bruce's kiss, she followed them as far as the stairs, then asked Calitza to wait.

"What is it, my lady?"

"I'm curious about what you just said in the dining room."

"About pain, my lady?"

"You made it sound as though pain alone knows the way to the heart."

"That is true."

"But what about love?"

Calitza did not reply.

"Surely love must know the secret tunnel to the heart."

"Perhaps."

"You're not certain?"

"It's hard for me to say."

"What do you mean?"

"I think it's because I find it difficult to discern the difference between pain and love."

Mary wanted to continue, but Calitza had already started up

the stairs, Bruce tugging at her dress. Mary was tempted to go with them, to escape into her bedchamber, but Elgin's eyes were pulling at her, ordering her back.

When she returned to the dining room, she saw Fotis ushering Hamilton to a chair. Logothetis asked Fotis to bring him some food. The Consul poured him a glass of wine, but Hamilton didn't touch it. He seemed eager to bring something to Elgin's attention. "Your Lordship should know about an archaeological treasure that was recently discovered by Edward Daniel Clarke . . ."

"Please, Mr. Hamilton, not now," she begged him.

Elgin threw her a vicious look. "Go on, Hamilton — where did Clarke make this discovery?"

"In Athens. Just before Your Lordship's arrival here, Clarke found a small marble relief at the foot of the Acropolis Hill and pronounced it to be the certain work of Phidias, but it was at Eleusis where Clarke acquired something that will prove to be of lasting benefit to the arts of Great Britain. My lord, I am referring to that enormous statue of a woman with a basket on her head."

"Are you speaking about Demeter?" Elgin asked sharply.

"Yes. The Eleusinians have been paying her homage all these centuries, and indeed they still believe that the fertility of their land depends on that statue. Many foreigners tried to take it away, but they changed their minds after they were warned that the arm of any person who dared touch it would fall off."

Logothetis, still with that blank expression on his face, was oblivious of what Hamilton was saying. Mary wanted to shake him, tell him to speak out once and for all against these boastful plunderers, but Hamilton had turned to Elgin again and was saying, "My lord, Clarke came to me one night at Eleusis and announced that he had found the goddess Demeter, and that she was buried up to her ears in a dunghill. I concluded immediately that he had decided to take her away, and, indeed, when he at-

tempted to do so the very next day, the Eleusinians began wailing and gnashing their teeth. 'What will become of our corn?' they cried. 'We shall perish if you take the old lady and her basket away from us!' "

Mary felt ill. Why did she have to listen to all this?

"Well, get on with it," said Elgin.

"Clarke refused to be dissuaded. Before the day was over, he made a hurried application to the local Pasha, aiding his request by letting an English telescope glide over the Turk's hands. And thus, the business was done. But there were more obstacles to overcome. Clarke needed ropes and pulleys, and the jetty at Eleusis had to be repaired. Still, Clarke persisted. On the night before he was to remove the statue, I was awakened by strange noises coming from the street. An ox had broken from its yoke and was butting violently at the ground with its horns. Bleeding and frothing, it then ran amuck over the plains of Eleusis, bellowing far into the night. At dawn, the townspeople stormed to the Pasha's house and demanded that he rescind Clarke's firman. He refused. A riot was averted just in time by the sudden appearance of the village priest, who, after calmly leading everyone to the statue, put on his full vestments and began chanting one prayer after the other while swinging his censer over the kneeling populace. Clarke, not to be put off by any of this, brazenly stepped forward and placed both hands on the old lady. Needless to say, his arms did not fall off. After this, the workmen reluctantly began clearing away the rubbish from the statue, and a crew of several hundred men hauled it all the way to the shore, from where it was finally hoisted into Clarke's waiting ship."

Logothetis excused himself and walked abruptly out of the dining room, followed by his wife and Lilika. Spyridon was yawning but made no move to get up until he heard his father's curt voice from the stairs.

Before long, Mary was alone with Elgin, wrestling with her

thoughts, not knowing how to begin. "Eggy, this has gone much too far. You're alienating yourself from everyone. I can't understand this sudden change in you. You must not continue with it. The Parthenon belongs to the Greek people. It's wrong for you to despoil it."

He banged his fist on the table. "The Greek people don't deserve works of art like the Parthenon. They have no respect for it."

"How can you say this? It was the Greeks who created it."

"The ancient Greeks, yes, but the Greeks of today regard it as nothing more than a rubble of worthless stones."

"Can't you see what this is doing to you? You've become a total stranger, someone I don't know. It frightens me."

Some of the wildness left his eyes. "Poll, my aims are honorable, entirely honorable. Believe me, my only concern is to preserve these wonderful works of antiquity."

"But what do you intend to do with them?"

"I shall decide that when the time comes, but for the present, it is imperative that I get them out of Greece before they are completely ruined."

"You plan to take down everything from the Parthenon?"

"Yes, and from all the other structures on the Acropolis Hill."

"But Eggy . . ."

"If I don't, someone else will — and you know very well who that is. Napoleon."

She turned her face away. "I wish we had never come here. I wish we were back in Scotland, where we belong."

She was startled by his reaction. "*Belong*. Aye, lass, that's it. This is what I must do with them — put them where they belong, inside a museum where they can be preserved and admired forever!"

His heavy snores awoke her in the middle of the night, and when she tried to fall asleep again, it was impossible. Her brain throbbing, she eased herself out of bed, took off her nightgown,

and walked quietly to the closet. She groped in the darkness for her clothes, then took them into the dimly lit hallway and hurriedly put them on.

She found herself in a dark street, walking blindly, now running . . . a powerful magnet drawing her toward the bulging shadow of the Acropolis Hill, to the Propylaea steps. The Turkish tents lay in darkness. Nothing moved. She groped her way to the Parthenon, then trembling, she reached out and touched one of the columns. She wanted to speak, say something, but a gnawing terror prevented her. She couldn't identify it, yet it was there — she was certain of it — an overpowering disquietude, a mysterious and awesome power from which she would never escape.

Elgin's obsession did not let up, and now, more than ever, he was determined to take away not only the treasures on the Acropolis Hill, but everything in Greece. At night, as she lay frozen beside him, she listened to his demented hallucinations, his sharp commands to Lusieri, his suspicion and distrust of Napoleon. Even in his waking moments, he was consumed with this madness, and she did not want to be near him.

Late one afternoon, he returned from the Acropolis Hill in a rage. At first, she thought it was the manifestation of still another nightmare, the way he kept pacing around the drawing room and cursing.

"Eggy, what is it?"

"A French physician was attempting to cut off the water supply to the Acropolis Hill this morning. I apprehended him in the very act."

"But why would he want to do this?"

"Napoleon put him up to it. Without water, it's impossible to wash down the marbles and get them ready for crating. I blame Lusieri for all this."

"Lusieri?"

"I don't trust that Sicilian. He's a deceitful conniver. Hunt saw him talking with this French physician several times in the past few days. On one occasion, he overheard the physician negotiating with Lusieri, asking him to conceal his drawings from me and sell them instead to Napoleon."

"I can't believe this."

"Nevertheless, it's true. I confronted Lusieri before I left the Acropolis Hill. I warned him that if I ever caught him consorting with the French or with anyone else, I'd send him to prison."

On the last day of the month, Elgin announced that he had successfully warded off all devious attempts by Napoleon to sabotage the work on the Acropolis Hill. The most important metopes and sculptures were now crated and under guard on the Piraeus docks, awaiting shipment to England on one of Admiral Lord Keith's warships. As the days wore on, he continually lashed at Lusieri and the artists, instructing them to scour all of Athens for further acquisitions, cajoling them one moment, then threatening and insulting them the next. Even the Voivode of Athens felt his wrath. Elgin never allowed the Turk to forget the firman, and constantly reminded him of Turkey's alliance with England and the treachery of the French.

One evening after dinner, he told her that he was now ready to extend his hand beyond Attica. Accompanied by Hunt and Lusieri and a crew of workmen, he sailed from the Piraeus two days later on an extensive search of the classical sites in the Peloponnesus. From Mycenae, he sent her a detailed account of the treasures he had confiscated there, adding that he seriously contemplated taking away the colossal lion gate. His visit to Tripoli comprised three whole pages.

Having received the most pressing and repeated invitations from the Pasha of the Morea, we set off in the company of the Dragoman, and six Albanian guards in the dress of the

ancient Macedonians. In the evening, we halted at a small village called Aklatho-Cambo, whose houses were but mud huts covering the side of a perpendicular mountain interspersed with evergreens and wild pines. After a hard climb, our party was given lodgings in a poor Albanian hut. At the bottom of the mountain slope runs a narrow rivulet, which was dried up, but I was told that the winter rains come down from it in wild streams.

The lassies in this village are uncommonly beautiful. One in particular took immediate liking to me and remained in my presence throughout most of the day. The next morning, the inhabitants of the village, preceded by their priest and elders, came and entreated me to have the Pasha repair their little church, which lay in shambles from an earthquake two years ago.

I was then placed inside a covered litter carried between two mules and guided by six officers of the Pasha. You would have been amused to see how I got into this *tartavan*. A man was summoned whom the Turks called "the Step." He lay himself down on the ground and I stepped on his back and got into the conveyance.

That afternoon, we were treated to the sport of the *dgerit,* a game played by the Pasha's guards. They used a ball and a straight white stick somewhat thinner than that of an umbrella, and quite crooked at the head. It is a sport not entirely without risk, as a blow on the temple might prove fatal. The Dragoman informed me that the Pasha once cut off the head of a guard who had carelessly struck him on the shoulder while playing the game.

The next morning, as we prepared to enter Tripoli, the Dragoman hinted that it would be more appropriate that I ride on horseback. A parade horse was quickly sent for, and I mounted it. Soon I was surrounded by all the officers of the Pasha's court, on chargers richly caparisoned, and followed by pages and guards. I doubt that Tripoli will ever see another procession like it — first, the Pasha, his officers, myself, and my party, the horses with the most brilliant furnishings, the Lieu-

tenant-Governor and the First Chamberlain riding just behind me.

The city's population had lined the avenues to the gate, all in their native costumes. The cannons from every fort around the walls of the city sounded off, and the First Chamberlain — from out of an embroidered box — tossed coins to the screaming children at his feet.

In the evening, we alighted at the house of the Dragoman, and here we were waited upon by the officers of the Pasha, who celebrated our arrival by a lavish dinner of forty dishes in the grandest Turkish style.

His appearance in Athens, two weeks later, horrified her. He not only looked wan and emaciated, but a white cloth was wrapped around his face, completely covering his nose. She wanted to know why he had bandaged it this way, but he swung his face to the side.

"Eggy, please let me look at it."

"No."

He ate very sparingly that night, speaking to no one, casting wild glances first at Lusieri, then at her. Later, in the bedchamber, she was afraid to go near him. She had wanted to tell him that she was pregnant again, that she had missed him, but he discouraged her with his behavior.

He kept everyone waiting at the breakfast table the next morning, and when he finally appeared, he was wearing a fresh white cloth around his face. She decided to walk with him as far as the Propylaea steps. In the dust-filled street, she stopped and said to him, "Eggy, you must let me look at you."

Surprisingly, he made no effort to prevent her, and with a trembling hand she lifted up the bandage.

His eyes reached out for her.

"Oh, dear God! My poor Eggy . . . my poor, poor Eggy!"

He seized her by the arms. "Why are you turning your face? You wanted to see. Here, look."

She braced herself before bringing her head around. Most of his nose had been eaten away, leaving only a raw cavity oozing with pus and streaked with blotches of dead skin. She started to weep. She wanted to hide in his arms, feel his strength once again, but she could not move. "Eggy," she moaned, "I . . . I am with child again . . ."

He made no reply.

". . . I want to leave this horrible place. I want to go home to Scotland. Please take me home, Eggy. Please!"

Six

Constantinople,
11th November, 1802

My dearest mother:

I open my heart to you and say that Lady Matilda Harriet Bruce was baptised yesterday morning by Mr. Hunt, after which a small reception was given here at our embassy house. The baby is an adorable little thing and is thriving most wonderfully. I would give anything in the world to have all three of the children at your side in Archerfield. Mary will be your favourite, I'm still certain of it — she is so uncommonly pretty. But please assure my dear father that Bruce is still king of the clan.

Will you say God bless them, my dear mother and father?

It saddens me to say that Elgin persists with his tormented desire to possess every work of antiquity in Greece. The Parthenon is now entirely stripped, and not one inch of ground on the Acropolis Hill has been spared from excavation. I beg him repeatedly to put an end to this madness, but he pays me no heed. Already, it has cost him thousands of pounds out of his own pocket, yet there is no end in sight, nor any promise from the British Government that he will ever be reimbursed.

The illness of his nose continues to disturb me. He keeps it

bandaged all the time, and permits no one to look at it, even Dr. Scott.

As you must surely know, I'm not easily given to idle superstitions. Nevertheless, I cannot free myself from the haunting notion that Elgin's disease was brought about by some ancient Greek spell or vengeance, especially since it became most severe the moment he started taking down the Parthenon marbles.

Even as I write to you, more crates of antiquities are piled about the Acropolis Hill and at the quay in the Piraeus where they await shipment to England. Lord Keith has obliged Elgin many times, sending one warship after the other to pick up these crates, all of which has brought great indignation from Lord Nelson, who argues that these ships are needed for fighting the war, not for Elgin's personal ventures.

At one time, the antiquities had piled up so rapidly on the Piraeus docks, Elgin put himself into greater debt by purchasing his own ship, a brig named *Mentor.* After every crate was brought on board, young Hamilton was told to accompany the brig to England.

The *Mentor* sailed out of the Piraeus two fortnights ago, but within two days she ran into a violent storm, struck rocks at the entrance to the harbour of Cythera Isle, and sank. By good fortune, Hamilton and the crew were able to save themselves, and the exact place of the sinking was marked carefully.

The next morning, Hamilton employed expert sponge divers from a nearby isle, and when they discovered that the *Mentor* rested in only twelve fathoms of water, Hamilton instructed them to cut holes in the *Mentor*'s decks and haul out every crate. The ship was beyond salvage, and this operation had to be done in deep secrecy, lest the French hear of it and send a force of men to steal the marbles away.

Elgin once again sought Lord Keith's assistance, but no warship was available at this time, and, in desperation, Elgin instructed Hamilton to rent another ship. Meanwhile, all the marbles had to be buried in the rocky beach and covered with seaweed and stones.

At last a ship was rented and the marbles were put on board. Thus, every magnificent sculpture that once basked under the clear sky of Athens is now on its way to England with Hamilton. Elgin, of course, is beside himself with joy, and boasts daily of his great victory over the indifferent Greeks, the treacherous Turks, and the envious Napoleon.

Snow has fallen in Constantinople, clogging the streets and making passage difficult. I cannot wait to set foot once again on Scottish soil; to catch that first glimpse of Aberlady Bay, of Archerfield.

Bruce's nightmares are less frequent now. The thought of another winter in Constantinople sends cold arrows into my heart. I worry constantly over Elgin's health. He eats very little and sleeps hardly at all. Many times I am shaken from my sleep by his nightmarish commands to Lusieri and his rage with the government.

My days are hollow and without happiness. Were it not for the children, I could never survive.

Pray for us, dear mother and father.

Your heartsick daughter,
Poll

Warm sultry winds converged upon Constantinople, days unusually mild for January, birds and flowers bursting in premature beauty.

One humid morning, Mary learned that the wife of the German Ambassador, whose residence was nearby, had died suddenly of swollen glands and high fever. Before nightfall, dozens of similar cases were reported throughout the city, sending waves of alarm over the populace. Stricken households were marked with a black crescent and star on the door, above which were painted the words "Allah have mercy."

Dr. Scott was reluctant to diagnose it as the plague, although Mary already suspected it, having seen its black hand in Scotland when she was twelve years old — the vomiting, giddiness, intolerance to light, the numbing pain of limbs, delirium, and

merciful death. Scores of tenants in her father's estates had been scourged by it.

She fretted about the children, but she was even more concerned about Elgin. Traces of redness were showing around his eyes, and his speech became thick and confused. Her anxiety was heightened one day when he stumbled and fell as he was preparing to leave the house. He retired early that evening, and she remained in the dining room to talk to Dr. Scott.

"My lady," he said, in his calm didactic manner, "I must stress once again that His Lordship has not been afflicted by the plague. Yes, he has been suffering from additional complaints of late, particularly with constipation, but I have already prescribed a strong cathartic, and I am certain that this will remedy the problem. The redness around His Lordship's eyes is a result of insomnia, and as for the thick speech and uncertainty of gait, these too will be cured."

"What about the children?" she said. "The contagion is spreading into every corner of the city."

Dr. Scott asked her to sit at the table for a moment. "My lady, I want to explain something to you." He took a chair and sat down beside her. Thin and studious, his eyesight poor, he wore powerful spectacles, whose gold rims flashed every time he turned his head in the direction of the small lamp on the wall.

"It is of the utmost importance that we not submit to panic during this crisis. The only thing that will save us is knowledge, precise scientific knowledge. Thus far, the plague has been victorious in the long span of history because the medical profession has focused its attention only on the symptoms, not the cause. Recent medical studies confirm that a great mortality among rats exists during epidemics of plague. However, a comparison between rat-infested and rat-free districts in Glasgow has shown a much higher incidence of plague in areas that were free of rats. Now what does this tell us?"

She wanted to pay attention to him, but her mind kept flitting

to Elgin and her children. What good were medical studies now? The plague was already running rampant.

"After many prolonged studies, the conclusion has been reached that the plague is not caused by rats but by rat fleas. In twenty-one experiments out of thirty-eight, it was discovered that more than half the healthy rats living in flea-proof cages contracted the disease after being subjected to fleas taken from rats that had died from the plague. But let us go one step further, my lady: the plague can be transmitted even through the feces of a flea. Thus, we must all be particularly careful about clothing and linen, because they can be carriers of the disease. A complete smoking system must be established in the household. I want you to write everything down. The moment His Lordship returns from any business outdoors, he must be thoroughly smoked from head to toe. After this, he should change into fresh clothing, making certain that he has first washed himself in a vinegar and lye solution. Finally, I must admonish you about the strolls you have been in the habit of taking each afternoon through the gardens of Pera with the children and Duff. These must stop, because the air is heavy with infection."

She hated to lose those marvelous moments with the children in Pera. They were her chief source of joy.

"Do I make myself clear, my lady?"

"Yes."

Dr. Scott stood up. "I have to alert the rest of the household." He looked at her with squinting eyes, magnified alarmingly by the powerful spectacles. "My lady, it is imperative that we all adhere to these strict rules."

"I shall make certain that they are enforced," she promised.

The captain of the brig *La Diane* joined them for dinner the next evening. His name was Maling, and during the dessert he nervously referred to the rumors circulating in the Levant that eighteen sailors on board his ship had died of the plague. "There is no truth to them," he barked. "Not one man on my ship is ill."

Elgin adjusted the bandage on his nose. "What about the two Russian ships that just arrived here from Egypt? I have heard that the disease is most prevalent on them."

Captain Maling grunted in assent.

She could not hold back any longer. "Eggy, I think we should leave Constantinople as soon as possible. We can stay in Belgrade until it is safe to return."

A flicker of a smile brushed across his eyes. "We shall leave Constantinople, but not for Belgrade."

"Where then?"

"Scotland. Yes, we shall be sailing with Captain Maling on *La Diane.*"

"Eggy . . ."

"I have already written to Lord Hawksbury, asking him to grant me permission to close down the embassy." He paused. "But before we leave, I have one important matter that needs attention. It concerns the Maltese slaves. All this time, the Sultan has held off on his promise to release them. This morning, I reminded him once again that Malta is now a British possession, that the Maltese are British subjects. To commemorate their release, I arranged to have the slaves present for the laying of the foundation stone at the new British Embassy site. The ceremonies will start next Friday. I want everyone present, the children too."

"What about the contagion?" asked Dr. Scott.

"They can wear cloth masks over their faces," Elgin snapped.

Elgin was the first to arise on Friday morning. When Mary came downstairs with the children, he was already dressed in his white uniform and red sash. After breakfast, Dr. Scott asked Duff to help him tie the cloth masks around the children's faces, but little Mary took it for sport, and Duff had all he could do to keep her from darting about while he tied the mask.

A heavy rain was falling, and the entire party had to be carried in canopied chairs to the waiting carriages. When they reached the new embassy site, Mary saw two lines of men in shabby clothes shivering in the rain under the watchful eyes of the Janissary guards. Suddenly the men broke away and started running toward the carriages, cheering and shouting Elgin's name. One of them opened the door of their carriage, knelt, and kissed Elgin's foot.

She wept.

The ceremony at the foundation stone was brief, and although tents had been pitched and a dinner prepared, the bad weather drove the Turks into a frenzy. Speeches were hastily delivered and gifts handed out. Each of the liberated slaves received new clothes and twenty-four piastres from the Sultan, and during the brief reception, many Turkish officials came forward and congratulated Elgin. He seemed relieved when the festivities came to an end.

Calitza put the children to bed as soon as they returned home. Elgin asked Masterman to bring him a bottle of brandy and a glass. At midnight he was still drinking. Mary begged him to stop but he didn't bother to answer her.

"Eggy, it's very late. Please go to bed."

"Will you sleep with me?" he murmured.

"If that is what you want."

"I do."

She helped him upstairs. He tried to kiss her as she unbuttoned his uniform, but she drew away from him and started pulling off his boots. He giggled like a child when she put his nightshirt on him and walked with him to the bed. He wanted the lamp on while she undressed, but she blew it out.

"I asked you to keep it lit," he said.

"Eggy, I always undress in the dark."

"Light the lamp!"

She cringed and couldn't move.

He leaped from the bed and touched the wall lamp with the flame from the small taper burning dimly on the bronze stand near the door. He clamped his eyes on her as she undressed. Every nerve in her body became taut when she walked toward him. Trembling, she slid into bed and accepted his hungry arms. She closed her eyes tight before kissing him again. His tongue probed her mouth. Suddenly, he was inside her, hard and thrusting. In a flush of desperation, she wanted to free herself, push his drunken weight off her body — but in that same instant his moment came, and he slumped heavily over her, imprisoning her.

On the cold damp morning of March 27, Elgin left the house at ten o'clock to make his final call on the Sultan. For three days the embassy had been closed down while all official records were put on board *La Diane,* along with the trunks of clothing, books, gifts, and furniture. Mary kept repeating to herself that indeed it was true — they were going back to Scotland, really going back. Throughout the morning, she was so excited and nervous, she hardly touched a bite of food. She didn't want to think about the long sea voyage.

Elgin returned from the Seraglio in time for the noon meal, then went from room to room, making certain that nothing was left behind. She was the last to leave the house. Eyes fastened on the cold Constantinople sky, she closed the front door and walked down the steps, never once looking back. As the two carriages moved slowly toward the docks, the minarets of the city stood rigid and silent. Hagia Sophia's dome remained dauntless and sublime.

A small crowd had assembled on the dock. Turkish children waving English flags circled around both carriages, shouting, "Elgin! Elgin!" Behind their white veils, the women bade goodby with their eyes as the men bowed in silence.

There was a final reception on board *La Diane*. Gifts were exchanged with the Grand Vizir, music was played, guns sounded, and at last they were escorted out of the harbor by the Sultan's flagship, *Selim III*. Elgin seemed happy over all the attention, but as he waved from the rail to the Grand Vizir, she heard him grumble, "This is a fine time to pay me proper respect."

Calitza immediately went below with little Matilda. Duff remained on deck, holding Bruce and little Mary in each arm, and when Bruce noticed the tears in his sister's eyes, he too began weeping and waving good-by to Constantinople.

Alongside *La Diane* sailed an English brig, a precaution that Elgin had insisted upon as a defense against attacks from pirates. A Ragusan vessel trailed behind, carrying the Maltese slaves back to their isle. *La Diane* was large enough to carry the entire embassy staff, including Calitza, who had requested to travel with them to Scotland and to stay with the children until they were fully grown. Elgin thought this an unnecessary expense, but Mary was thrilled, and prevailed upon him to consent.

After a slow passage through the Dardanelles, they anchored off Tenedos Isle for the night. Although the sea was calm, she was determined to spend the night on shore. The children were left on the ship with Calitza and Dr. Scott, and Mary climbed into the small boat with the others. A sudden wind began to howl, but they managed to reach shore within an hour. Duff pitched a tent, went after some dry wood, and soon they were all huddled around the fire, listening to Hunt's long account of his travels with Carlyle on the Mount Athos peninsula.

The wind was still blowing in the morning, and they had to fight gigantic waves to get back to the ship. The children were overjoyed to see her, particularly little Matilda, who wiggled her feet so gleefully, Calitza could hardly contain her. Mary wanted to sweep her into her arms and hug her, but she was feeling ill again and had to rush below for the vinegar.

The winds persisted for three days, but Captain Maling's seamanship brought them successfully within sight of Tinos Isle. Elgin wanted him to continue toward the Piraeus, but Calitza begged his permission to go ashore.

"Why?" asked Elgin gruffly.

"I have something very important to do."

"What? Why are you so secretive?"

Calitza glanced nervously toward her. "I want to visit the grave of my husband."

"Your husband?" cried Mary.

"Yes, my lady. Shortly after we were married, we made a pilgrimage here."

"For what reason?" said Elgin, staring at her in bewilderment.

"Demetrios was very ill, and we wanted to offer a prayer to the Virgin."

"You could have done that anywhere in Greece."

"No, it had to be offered in the Virgin's cathedral, here on Tinos Isle. This is where most of her cures are wrought. As was the custom, we placed pure olive oil inside two walnut shells and brought them before the Virgin's icon . . ."

"Go on."

". . . but it did not cure Demetrios. He died two days later."

Mary embraced her. "Calitza, do you want me to come with you to the grave?"

"No, my lady. With your permission, I should like to go by myself."

"Of course. We understand."

"I shall not be long."

"I'll ask Captain Maling to get the small boat launched," said Elgin. "Take as long as you wish, Calitza. We shall wait for you."

"Thank you, my lord. Thank you, my lady."

After the small boat had pushed away from *La Diane,* Mary stood by the rail, peering at the stark white houses of Tinos. The

cathedral crowned the isle, and she could make out hundreds of steps leading up to it from the street. They too were sparkling white.

She still hadn't recovered from what Calitza had said. All this time, living with someone, knowing each movement of the hand, each step, each flicker of the eye — yet never really knowing. But she could say this of Elgin also. What did she really know about him? And what did he know about her? She too gave only a part of herself to everyone, to her parents, even to her children. She too lived in a closet of secrecy, revealing only what she wanted others to see, closing her heart to everything else. Pieces of a puzzle, that's what life was, broken chunks of thoughts and hidden feelings, a mirror cracked in a million sections, each of them caked with shame and desire, wanting to be touched, to be loved, but afraid.

Two days later, *La Diane* dropped anchor off the Cape of Sunium. The sight of Greece was a balm for her — radiant Greece, resplendent in light, Poseidon's strong arms arched toward the healing sun, the tall grasses around his temple spiked with wild cyclamen, his fields aflame with poppies.

By sea, it was a short journey from Sunium to Athens, but she was grateful when Elgin decided that they should go ashore and travel it by land. That way, they could visit a few villages and come into contact with the real Greece and her people.

Hunt procured horses and donkeys and a half-dozen asses from a stable in the nearby village of Anavyssos. After Elgin instructed Captain Maling to proceed on a direct course to the Piraeus, they prepared to set off. Two of the asses conveyed the luggage for their necessary clothing. She had difficulty mounting her donkey, but after a while she managed to do it. Calitza rode on another donkey, carrying little Matilda in her arms. Bruce went with his father on a horse, and young Mary rode with Masterman.

After two hours of tedious riding, they arrived at a small vil-

lage nestled between two sloping hills. They were rapidly losing the day's light, and Duff was told to search the village for lodgings, but all he could find was a shepherd's hut of one large room. A crude fireplace hugged the wall near the door. Masterman attended to the beds while Hunt arranged for food to be brought in. It was a simple peasant's meal of rice, stewed vegetables, black olives, and white cheese. No one was in the mood for conversation, and immediately after the meal, they all fell into their beds, exhausted.

After a breakfast of goat's milk, dark bread, and cheese, they were ready to move off. Duff contrived a way to put a straw basket on the back of an ass, and after testing it, he placed Bruce and Mary in it, then, as an added precaution, tied the basket securely with heavy twine. Calitza refused to part with little Matilda.

Just before noon, they circled around a cluster of small hills and entered a wide valley choking with scrub pines. The horses and mules made their way through the trees and rocks, braying loudly. Suddenly, it began to rain. Duff placed a blanket over the children in the basket, then helped the muleteer tether the animals under one of the trees.

Within an hour, the sky cleared.

Before setting off again, Duff playfully tousled Bruce's hair. The lad proved to be quite a Spartan, and didn't complain at all during the storm. They followed the muleteer out of the drenched valley and headed toward another cluster of hills. At the top of a high ridge, they stopped to rest. The children wanted to get out of the basket, but Duff forbade them, making comical gestures and uttering dire warnings. They all burst into laughter.

Elgin slid off his horse and took hold of Mary's hand.

"Where are we going?" she asked.

He took her to the highest point of the ridge. The cloth around his face had become soiled; his hat was crumpled and still damp from the rain. Clutching his hand, she moved to the very edge of the jagged rocks and looked down. Through the racing

clouds of fog and mist, she beheld Athens, gray and sorrowful, kneeling at the feet of the Acropolis Hill.

Logothetis' greeting was cool, but he eventually became warm and hospitable, instructing his servants to bring food and wine, gifts for the children.

After the children were fed and taken upstairs, Elgin immediately began peppering Lusieri with questions about more acquisitions. Lusieri's answer was strained. "My lord, all the cases of marbles taken down thus far are now safely on their way to England."

"Did Lord Keith send that last ship?"

"No, but it was our good fortune that Captain Clarke of H.M.S. *Braakel* happened to be in Athens at the time. He ordered his crew to load all the crates into his ship, but when she prepared to sail out of the Piraeus, she ran aground and was in serious danger of sinking. Losing no time, I hastened to the Voivode's house and beseeched him to free the ship, and, in time, the wind caught her sails and sent her out into the open sea."

"I can't understand how Clarke allowed this to happen." Elgin frowned. "Every captain in the navy knows these waters. Was the weather unfavorable?"

"No."

"What about the wind?"

"Off the land."

"Who had the watch?"

"Captain Clarke himself."

"The man must be an idiot."

"My lord, his ship was burdened by the excessive weight of the marbles. Indeed, Your Lordship should be grateful. Captain Clarke risked his life and the lives of his crew, not to mention the loss of his ship."

Elgin cleared his throat. "What else have you done? Any further acquisitions?"

Logothetis kept picking up his napkin and dabbing his lips with it nervously. All this time, Madame Logothetis had remained silent. Mary inquired about her health, and she responded in a formal way, "I am quite well, my lady." It was apparent that the conversation had been bothering both of them. They sat stiffly in their chairs, heads down, lips taut. During one silent moment, Mary saw Madame Logothetis reach under the table for her husband's hand.

"Yes, my lord," continued Lusieri. "Just this morning, after digging near the Parthenon, we discovered several colossal sections of the pediment."

"Could you identify them?"

"Mr. Hunt recognized them as the torsos of Zeus, Nike, and Hermes. Two days ago, we excavated on the south side of the Acropolis Hill and uncovered a number of fallen metopes and other large sections of the frieze."

"What did you do with them?"

"They were so enormous, we had to send out for saws."

"Why?"

"They had to be cut into transportable parts. It was the only way we could haul them to the Piraeus."

"Are they there now?"

"Yes, my lord, they are well guarded. The Kalmuck stands watch over them every day."

"What about the night?"

"I make periodic visits. Believe me, they are much too heavy for anyone to steal."

"What else have you done?" said Elgin, pacing around the table.

Logothetis rose to his feet, his voice shaking. "My lord, in all the excitement of your arrival, I neglected to tell you our good news."

"What good news?"

Madame Logothetis suddenly perked up. "My lord and lady, you arrived in Athens at the most appropriate moment. There is to be a wedding this Sunday."

"Lilika's wedding?" guessed Mary, smiling.

"Yes."

"But she is so young."

"She is seventeen. If we wait any longer, everyone will take her for a spinster." Madame Logothetis forced a laugh.

"Who is the groom?"

"His name is Basil," replied Logothetis. "He is the private secretary to the Greek Liaison Officer in Athens."

"And he is very good-looking," added Madame Logothetis.

"Where is Lilika now?"

"She went to Basil's house with Spyridon. As Your Ladyship knows, there are many last-minute details before a wedding, especially a Greek wedding."

Mary could see that Elgin was annoyed with the interruption; that he was chafing to get back to Lusieri. "Madame Logothetis," she said, "what a great stroke of fortune that we arrived in Athens at this time. Indeed, we shall come to the wedding on Sunday."

"That's impossible," asserted Elgin. "Captain Maling is waiting for us in the Piraeus. We have to leave on Friday."

Madame Logothetis smiled, and in her most gracious manner said, "But Your Lordship must prevail upon the captain to stay a few more days. It would be the greatest honor for us if Your Lordship and Ladyship were to attend the wedding."

Elgin straightened his shoulders. "I suppose Captain Maling can wait a few more days, but we shall have to leave the Piraeus at dawn on Monday."

As Mary went to embrace him, he chided her with a harsh whisper, "Where are your manners?"

Logothetis offered a toast to them before going upstairs, arm in arm, with his wife. Elgin looked fretful again, as though he could not wait to pounce upon Lusieri once more. "You are to

remain in my employ for an indefinite period," he commanded.

"But my lord . . ."

"Furthermore, I want you to continue the search for more acquisitions in other parts of Greece. Go everywhere. Allow no one to stop you or prevent you from taking anything that you deem to be of value."

Lusieri slumped into his chair.

Shifting his attention to the artists, Elgin went on, "Your contract with me is now concluded. You are free to return to your countries."

After breakfast, Duff and Masterman went to the Piraeus to bring back appropriate clothes for the wedding, and Elgin left early for the Acropolis Hill with Lusieri. Mary returned to her bedchamber to write a letter to her mother. At noon, Madame Logothetis sent a message with one of the servants, inviting her on a visit to the seamstress, but she politely refused, saying that she preferred to stay and rest a while.

Just when she was about to doze off, Bruce and Mary came dashing into the room and threw themselves on the bed, imploring her to read from Aesop in Greek. Sighing, she took the book from Bruce, settled back against the pillows, and began to read. Bruce comprehended most of the words, and Mary, desiring so much to emulate him, cuddled into her arms, eyes wide open, lips moving with each syllable. Halfway through the fable, Calitza entered the bedchamber, carrying Matilda in one arm. At this point, Bruce lost interest in the fable and slid off the bed, saying he wanted to walk with Fotis in the garden. Little Mary went scampering after him.

Calitza handed Matilda to her, then walked to the other side of the room for a chair. She brought it back and placed it beside the bed. "My lady, what kind of place is Scotland?"

"Well, Scotland is quite different from Greece, Calitza, but it does have mountains and a marvelous coast."

"Is it warm there?"

"Only during the summer; the rest of the time it's quite cool."

"Where is Archerfield?"

"That's the name of my parents' estate. It's in the small town of Dirleton, about ten miles east of Edinburgh."

"Is Your Ladyship's mother as beautiful as you?"

She smiled. "I would say so. As a young woman, she was painted by the artist Gainsborough, who admired her beauty very much. But why are you asking all these questions?"

"Since I have decided to go there, I want to know everything about it."

"Are you sure you want to come with us, Calitza?"

"Of course."

"It's not too late to change your mind. Athens is not that far from Constantinople."

"I have already decided, my lady."

"Perhaps you should think about it more seriously. If there is no reason for you to ever return to Constantinople, you could stay here in Athens, find yourself a husband, and raise your own children."

Calitza reached over and took Matilda away from her, showering her with hugs and kisses.

Mary touched her on the hand. "Calitza, I shall not give up. You are too young and too lovely to remain a widow. I'm more determined than ever to find you a husband." She laughed. "And who knows, he may even be a Scot."

Toward the end of the afternoon, Duff and Masterman returned from the Piraeus with two valises. Bruce ran to Duff, then began pulling at one of the valises to carry it upstairs, but the courier smiled and said it was much too heavy for him. Masterman tugged at her gloves, yanking each finger one at a time, her eyes wild and agitated.

"Masterman, what is it?" asked Mary.

The maid blew away some strands of hair that had escaped from under her hat. "My lady, I just want to say that I can't wait for the day of my wedding."

"Your wedding?"

"I have already given notice to His Lordship. I am betrothed."

"To whom?"

"Josiah Nichols. He is a greengrocer in Edinburgh."

"Masterman, why didn't you tell me about this?"

"I was afraid of your reaction."

"What do you mean?"

"Mr. Nichols is one and forty, and I am only three and twenty."

"Lord Elgin is thirteen years older than I. Age doesn't really matter, Masterman. The important thing is to love one another."

"But I have never seen Mr. Nichols."

"What?"

"The marriage was arranged by my father when I was fifteen. I was to marry Mr. Nichols at one and twenty, but I was in Constantinople."

"When is the wedding to take place?"

"As soon as I return to Scotland."

"Then stop fretting. Everything will work out well. When we get back to bonnie Scotland, you will marry Mr. Nichols, live happily together, and have a house filled with children."

Masterman bowed before her, cheeks streaked with tears.

"Now then, I must go out for a while. You can help Calitza with the children. What about the dresses? Did you find a suitable one for the wedding?"

"I did."

"Which did you select?"

"Your Ladyship will be quite pleased, I'm sure."

"Tell me."

Masterman shook her head teasingly. "Am I permitted to say something further?"

"Of course."

"It's nothing serious, but I think Your Ladyship is bestowing

an inordinate amount of interest and affection on the Greek nurse."

"I have the same affection for you, Masterman."

"I don't feel that Your Ladyship does."

"Nonsense."

"Your Ladyship spends much more time with her than with me."

"But that's because of the children. I don't do it intentionally."

"It seems that way."

"Masterman, you're jealous!"

"Perhaps I am."

Mary smiled. "Is this why you can't wait for your wedding day?"

Masterman's eyes filled with tears again. "In truth, it frightens me to think about it, not knowing what Mr. Nichols looks like, and his being so much older. I'm just horrified that everyone will take him to be my father."

She was pleased with Masterman's choice of the blue silk dress with the lace ruffles, and Madame Logothetis joyfully embraced her when she volunteered to attend the bride in the Byzantine Church of Saint George on the crest of Mount Lycabettus. The ceremony was unbearably long, and the clouds of incense almost choked her. Toward the end of the service, the aged bishop took the bride and groom by the arm and led them thrice around the altar table, with the floral wreaths joined by a ribbon perched on their heads, while they carried lighted tapers in their hands.

Lilika seemed very nervous throughout the ceremony, whereas the bridegroom bustled with confidence and energy. He was exactly Lilika's height, with a thick crop of black hair and flashing black eyes. Indeed, Madame Logothetis was right — Basil was a very attractive young man.

The reception was held at Logothetis' house. Greek and Turkish dignitaries attended, as well as relatives and friends. Mary smiled when money was pinned to Lilika's wedding gown by some of the guests as she and Basil greeted them at the head of the receiving line. In the drawing room, a group of musicians had already begun to play lively Greek folk tunes.

There were two long dinner tables bearing a dazzling display of tantalizing dishes: taramo-salata, dolmades in a rich egg-lemon sauce, roasted young lambs, veal braised with artichoke hearts, grilled lamb cutlets — tender and full of flavor — morsels of rabbit in tarragon sauce, platters of smoked fish, quail with rice, casseroles of steaming eggplant and ground meat covered with a fluffy custard. There was no end. Bruce and little Mary had a grand time, skirting the tables, tasting everything, but eating very little.

Later, Mary sampled several of the desserts, taking two pieces of a crisp filo pastry that was filled with cream and heavily laced with brandy. Feeling satiated, she withdrew into the drawing room with Elgin, then sat on a sofa and watched a line of dancers, led by Basil, weaving around the room. There were no women in the circle.

She was so carried away by the music, the intricate steps, the uninhibited spirit of the dance, she turned to Elgin and said, "Eggy, let's join them."

He was shocked.

"It's not difficult. Look, they're just holding hands and following everything Basil does."

"They look utterly foolish."

"You do not care to dance?"

"Of course not."

She got up from the sofa.

"Where are you going?" he demanded.

"I feel like dancing. I want to join them."

His voice cut into her. "Sit down. Only men dance in Greece."

She bristled; then, moving quickly away from him, she hur-

ried across the floor toward the dancers. She could feel everyone's eyes fastened on her, but she was unyielding and did not intend to go back. Basil widened his eyes, then offered his hand. Another man took hold of her other hand, and soon she was gliding around the room, following Basil's graceful movements, tossing her head back, absorbing every note, every step.

Logothetis came forward to join her, taking her by the hand and forming his own circle. He was even more agile than Basil, and kept tossing his head to the side, spurring her on, shouting, *"Opa! Opa!"* She responded with an exalted sense of freedom, weaving around the gaping faces, spinning and twisting, losing herself entirely to the alluring rhythm. Suddenly, there was a burst of applause.

The musicians refused to stop. With wide grins of approval, they moved into another tune, and although the beat was different, she managed to follow Logothetis until she captured it. She heard more applause. Against the music and hand-clapping, a commotion erupted in the rear of the drawing room — loud shouting and waving of hands. She laughed nervously and, dropping Logothetis' hand, walked back toward the sofa. Elgin was not there. She made her way through the crowd, seeking him, and at the far corner of the room she saw him surrounded by a group of men in noisy discussion. One of them, white-haired and bent with age, heatedly addressed Elgin. "Sir, who gave you the right to despoil our ancient shrines?"

"I was granted this authority by Seged Abdullah Kaimmacam, Voivode of Athens."

"But he is not the rightful owner of these antiquities. The Greek people are."

Elgin shifted his gaze to the others in the group.

Not to be deterred, the old man continued, "Why did you seek this authority from the Voivode?"

"I was motivated by a sincere desire to preserve these antiquities."

"Preserve them from what?"

"From the destructive hands of the Turks and from the apathy and languor of the Greeks."

A wave of questioning looks passed from one man in the group to the other. Several guests standing nearby moved in closer, encircling Elgin completely.

"Sir, that is an insult to the Greek people," retorted the old man. "Pericles and Phidias adorned Athena with exquisite beauty, but you . . . you have raped her!"

Enraged, Elgin cried out, "You dare call yourselves Greeks? You have the audacity to identify yourselves with the glorious heroes of ancient Greece? In God's name, you have absolutely nothing in common with them. For centuries you have permitted the Turks to subjugate you. Far worse, you have treated these great works of art with ingratitude, coldness, and neglect. You do not deserve them!"

She tapped the wrist of a man standing beside her. "Who is that old man?" she asked.

"Ioannes Venizelos. He is the Master of the Venetian School here in Athens. His name is greatly respected."

The old schoolmaster was shaken by Elgin's words. His voice trembled. "Sir, I want you to know that I have just completed the last pages of a history of Athens under Turkish rule. They refer specifically to that terrible scene when you and your artists removed the best Caryatid from the Erechtheum. The loud lamentations from the remaining Caryatids resounded through every corner of Athens, and later, as your workmen were hauling our treasures to the Piraeus, they dropped everything to the ground and swore they heard the doleful moans of Athena in each vein of marble."

Elgin tried to move away.

"These are not senseless stones that you stole, sir. They are the gods of Greece."

A hush fell over the group.

"You have spat upon our people, defiled Athena by destroy-

ing her sacred temple and carrying off her gods of marble. But hear this, sir . . . hear it well . . . we shall come to your cold shores one day and redeem them. We shall redeem every last one!"

On Wednesday morning, *La Diane* called at Cythera Isle on the southernmost tip of the Peloponnesus. Mary remained on deck with the children and Masterman while Elgin and Hunt went ashore to inspect the broken remains of the *Mentor,* and when they returned at noon, Elgin mournfully reported that any hope of ever raising the ship had to be abandoned. The raging storms of the Aegean had rendered her beyond salvage.

He kept away from everyone that afternoon, and at dinner, after several glasses of wine, he sputtered out his wrath, reminding them that the whole affair had cost him six thousand pounds, in addition to the loss of the *Mentor.*

She hated to hear all this again.

In the morning a strong wind filled the sails, and they were able to put into the harbor of Candia on the Isle of Crete. They went ashore in the small boat and landed on a sandy beach. The touch of solid earth under her feet, the cloudless sky, the warmth of the day, brought comfort to her disturbed thoughts. After walking along the shore for a few hundred yards, they encountered a group of people squatting in the sand. They were shabbily dressed and looked destitute.

"They are lepers," warned Hunt.

Everyone in the party swerved from the shore to avoid them, but Elgin veered suddenly around and headed toward them.

"Eggy, where are you going?" she called out to him.

He didn't turn around.

She was appalled when he moved into their midst, making no effort to elude their clutching hands. They beseeched him for alms, and he obligingly emptied his pockets and purse. One of

them, a skeleton of a lad, clung to his trousers as he turned to walk away. She gasped when Elgin tenderly picked him up and carried him to the water's edge. After dousing the scarred face with sea water, he dried it with the tails of his shirt, then carried the boy back to his family.

Dr. Scott was livid. "My lord, what on earth induced you to do such a thing?"

Elgin gave no answer.

"Eggy, that was utterly unwise." She went to grab him by the arm, but Dr. Scott pulled her away. "I forbid you to touch him, my lady." In a grave voice he said to Elgin, "My lord, I want you to go back to the ship immediately."

"Why?"

"You must take off all your clothes before you step into the small boat, and as soon as you climb on board *La Diane* ask one of the sailors to prepare a bath. Tell him to put one cup of lye and three cups of vinegar in the tub. Do I make myself clear?"

"Nonsense," Elgin retorted.

"Eggy, you must do exactly as Dr. Scott says."

Angrily, Elgin swung around and told the four crewmen to row him back to the ship. Dr. Scott instantly forbade them.

"I can't row that blasted boat by myself," argued Elgin.

"You must, my lord, but before you step into it, please take off all your clothes."

Elgin threw him a menacing look. "You're carrying this too far. Will you be satisfied if I go down to the water's edge and scrub my face and hands with sand?"

"That will not suffice. You must do as I said. Otherwise, all of us will be endangered, including Your Lordship's children."

Elgin petulantly kicked at the sand. Waiting until Masterman and Calitza had turned their backs, he pulled off his clothes, flung them on the beach, and scrambled into the small boat. With the first tug, the oars did not grasp the water sufficiently, and he fell back, almost losing them. His curses bounced over the water,

but in time, he acquired a rhythmic stroke and was able to pull up alongside *La Diane*.

A full hour passed before Mary saw him step down the accommodation ladder and get back into the small boat. He was wearing a fresh linen shirt and his white breeches. After he beached the boat, he looked exhausted.

Dr. Scott was the first to speak to him. "Did Your Lordship bathe in the solution of lye and vinegar?"

"I did."

She stretched forth her hand. He took it, and they walked together behind Hunt and Dr. Scott. Bruce broke away from Duff and started skipping around Elgin, shouting, "We saw you, Father . . . we saw you without your clothes!"

Duff hurried ahead of them and stopped on a grassy knoll near the shore. The crewmen pitched two tents, and Duff proceeded to light a fire. Looking sullen, Masterman did not volunteer to help Calitza with the cooking, but she ate two full bowls of the hearty soup abundant with beans and a variety of diced vegetables.

Mary was awakened early in the morning by the sound of wild voices and scuffling feet. Peering out of the tent, she saw some fierce-looking men dressed in long white pantaloons and black leather boots. They were grouped around Elgin and carried long scimitars. One of them addressed him in Greek. "I am Nouri Bey, Governor of Crete."

Elgin started to introduce himself, but Nouri Bey put up his palms and stopped him. "I already know who you are. In the name of Allah, why did you do this?"

"What?"

"Shun my hospitality. This is unforgivable, sleeping on the sand like lepers. I invite you and your party to come immediately to my palace. We shall transport you."

"I am grateful to you, Nouri Bey, but we cannot accept your kind offer. Our ship is waiting for us in the bay. We must continue on our voyage."

Nouri Bey refused to listen. He clapped his hands loudly, and several attendants standing nearby brought chairs and placed them near the tents. Before anyone could understand what was happening, they were lifted into the chairs and carried along the shore for almost a half mile. Nouri Bey's palace lay on the outer rim of a wide plateau overlooking the sea. It was a huge mansion with Doric columns of marble protecting its façade. Nouri Bey claimed that they once belonged to the Temple of Aphrodite at Canae.

Mary quickly realized that, underneath the harsh voice and layers of excessive flesh, Nouri Bey was a kind-hearted and sensitive man. Even with his obesity, he was very light of foot and had a regal posture. He spoke excellent Greek, boasting that he had been instructed by the best tutors of Athens and Constantinople.

By midafternoon, the palace was filled with people — Greek and Turkish dignitaries of the isle, friends and relatives, privileged officers. After the toasts were made, the Governor's harem arrived, carried across the yard to the front door in canopied baskets slung over the mules like Gypsy panniers. Sheer scarves of white silk were wrapped around their faces, leaving only the eyes exposed. They looked quite young, and they twittered when they saw Mary, pointing first to her dress, then to her hair. The eunuchs stuck close to their side, helping them descend from the baskets, walking guardedly with them toward Mary. One of the women knelt before her and presented her with gifts of perfume; another came timidly forward and touched her hair, the hem of her skirt. From the corner of her eye, she saw Masterman shaking with fright throughout the whole proceeding.

Before dinner, Nouri Bey took them on a carriage ride through the narrow streets of Canae. It was a town of stately buildings

and clean houses. The people looked warm and friendly.

Elgin appeared sullen at dinner. Nouri Bey did his utmost to please him, calling in dancers and dervishes, but to no avail. Concerned that the Governor would regard Elgin's behavior as an affront, Mary turned to him during a moment of noisy conversation and remarked that Elgin's health had been impaired in Constantinople. Nouri Bey's only response was a nervous look toward Elgin's bandaged nose.

They were carried in chairs to the beach the next morning. Captain Maling was waiting on the deck, agitated by their long absence. Duff stuttered an explanation, but Maling swung sharply around and started barking out commands. Quickly, the sails were lifted, the anchor hoisted, and *La Diane* moved at a rapid speed out of the harbor, passing under the lee of Crete into the open sea toward Malta.

La Diane dropped anchor at Malta two days later, but the authorities there placed everyone on board under twenty days' quarantine as a precaution against a contagion that was spreading in that part of the Mediterranean. However, they were permitted to walk about the isle as long as they did not come into direct contact with the inhabitants. This infuriated Elgin, and when he learned that a large segment of the British fleet was anchored in the harbor, he accompanied Captain Maling to Pratique House for a talk with the commanders. He returned late in the afternoon, flushed with victory. Not only was the quarantine lifted, but they were assigned to excellent lodgings inside Boghi Palace, a magnificent villa overlooking the harbor, complete with servants in livery and chambermaids. Best of all, Elgin's good friend Admiral Lord Keith was expected at Malta the next morning.

Dr. Scott insisted that the children remain on board *La Diane*, especially since little Matilda was suffering from a troublesome cough, which she had caught the night they slept in the tent.

"My lady, Malta is the steppingstone of the Mediterranean, and I need not remind you that the isle has a long reputation for contagious diseases. The children must remain on board."

Elgin's black mood increased at Malta, and he became more withdrawn than ever, spending long hours by the sitting room window of the palace, looking off at the ships in the harbor. He spoke only when she asked something repeatedly and loudly.

The next evening, they were accorded a formal reception as guests of the commanders, and Elgin's eyes immediately lit up when he saw Lord Keith seated at the dinner table. He had aged considerably since they last met at Portsmouth. He was overjoyed to see them, and patted Mary's wrist affectionately while asking about her parents and the children.

There were only a few women in attendance: the wife of the Governor, their daughter of nineteen, the wife of the British Consul, and the matronly widow of an Italian banker who was a native of Malta and had come back to the isle to live out the rest of her life. An excessive talker, she was unpleasant in her manner and demanded total attention from everyone.

During the dessert, one of the commanders made reference to Lord Nelson, causing Lord Keith to pound his fist on the table. "I don't want to hear about that scoundrel!"

The commander sat back in his chair, open-mouthed. "Your Lordship is rather censorious. After all, Lord Nelson is a national hero . . ."

"A hero who cuts the most absurd figure," Lord Keith said, scowling, "so cocky and vain. Indeed, he's more a prince of the opera than an admiral."

Another commander piped up. "My dear Lord Keith, when I last talked with Nelson, he was enraged at not being elevated to First in Command of the Mediterranean fleet. He feels insulted remaining Second in Command under Your Lordship all this time."

"He can blame the Admiralty for that, not me."

"He claimed it is Your Lordship who keeps denying him the promotion."

"Let him claim what he wants. I can't stand the thought of the man. He makes me ill, he and his Emma."

The Governor of Malta lifted his glass of brandy and offered a toast to Elgin, thanking him for his successful efforts in freeing the slaves. Lord Keith then rose to his feet and extended a second toast: "To Lady Elgin, a woman of virtue and beauty, a true daughter of Scotland."

Elgin reverted to his morbid demeanor as soon as they returned to their rooms. He didn't go immediately to bed. Instead, he slumped on the sofa, peering blankly at the wall, ignoring all attempts she made at conversation.

On Friday morning, *La Diane* lifted her sails and headed north, rounding the eastern shore of Sicily Isle, and passing through the swirling currents of the Straits of Messina into the Tyrrhenian Sea. The water was perfectly calm, the sky cloudless. On their left hand, a chain of isles loomed before them — Vulcano, Liperi, Stromboli, Capri — most of them volcanic and desolate.

Just before the ship docked at Naples, they dined with Captain Maling and the officers of *La Diane*. Elgin sat at the extreme end of the table and spoke to no one. Mary felt very uneasy watching him, troubled by every move he made, every gesture of his hand, the abstracted look in his eyes, the feeble lift of his fork. Not once did he raise his head. The bandage over his nose was still horrifying to her.

Dr. Scott whispered softly, "My lady, I have something important to discuss with you."

"What is it?"

"Not here. Let us go on deck."

The sun had already plunged into the sea, leaving a purple blanket on the horizon. The sounds of Naples drifted to her ears.

"My lady, I am deeply concerned over Lord Elgin's health. His symptoms of depression and melancholia have progressed

alarmingly from the day we left Constantinople. If they continue at this rate, I am afraid they could bring catastrophic results."

"What do you mean?"

"I am referring to His Lordship's sanity. Certainly Your Ladyship has been cognizant of his unusual behavior."

"I have, but what can we do to help him?"

Scott looked at her intently. "Forgive me, but I must ask you this . . ."

"What?"

"When did you last sleep with His Lordship?"

"How dare you!"

"If I am to be of any help, it is important that I know the answer to that question."

"My private life need not concern you, Dr. Scott."

"But I am not trying to pry into Your Ladyship's intimate life. As embassy physician, my only concern is everyone's health, physical as well as mental."

She gripped the rail with both hands. "Dr. Scott, you came to us as a highly qualified physician. You should be able to seek a cure for His Lordship's condition."

"Where does Your Ladyship expect me to seek a cure?"

"Anywhere you please, Dr. Scott. Consult your medical books, your knowledge. One thing is certain — you won't find it in my bedchamber!"

Seven

THE PORT AUTHORITIES at Naples handed them a packet of letters as soon as they stepped on the docks. One was a brief dispatch from Lusieri, notifying Elgin that he was about to pursue the search for further treasures at Olympia and at Delphi, adding that he intended to excavate wherever possible. There was also a long letter from Elgin's mother, the dowager Countess of Elgin.

London,
15th April, 1803

My dear Thomas:

Please be advised that H.M.S. *Braakel* docked in Portsmouth this week and unloaded fifty cases of marbles, which I arranged to have stored for a time at the house of the Duchess of Portland in Westminster. After a few days, however, she had a change of mind and begged me to move them elsewhere, because they were cluttering up her garden and lawn. Fortunately, the Duke of Richmond came to our rescue and agreed to have them transported to his estate. Alas, he too showed his vexation when he realized that all those marbles were strewn over his grounds, and therefore I was left with

no other choice but to rent a large house at the corner of Piccadilly and Park Lane, which has an ample garden and a sizable shed about fifty feet square.

As soon as the workmen unpacked the marbles, I had them arranged in the best manner possible, considering their great weight. I found it impossible to lay out the collection in a systematic way. This must await your arrival. Meanwhile, the sculptures, inscriptions, metopes and friezes, and all the architectural works are now safely housed inside this shed. In the center stands the Caryatid from the Erechtheum. The rest of the marbles are placed around her, according to size and shape. The torso of Hermes is perched a-top an inscribed column and is splendidly balanced on the other side of the room by the horse's head from the Parthenon.

I need not remind you that there are many more cases of marbles at the docks in Portsmouth. Smaller lots arrive at steady intervals. But do not fret, Thomas. I have employed two agents to stand guard at the Customs House until all these antiquities are brought to the shed at Park Lane.

One thing troubles me, however. Do you intend to restore these marbles? Many have battered noses, broken arms and legs, missing heads. There is a man here named John Flaxman. He is called "the English Phidias." He is of the opinion that the restoration should be done immediately, because this would increase the financial worth of the collection. He estimates the cost to be in the vicinity of twenty thousand pounds. Please inform me as soon as possible whether you wish him to start.

I trust that this letter finds you and the children in good health. Please convey my love to Mary.

Your ever-affectionate mother

While Hunt went to summon a carriage, Elgin wrote a hasty reply to his mother and warned her not to spend another penny. He handed the letter to the Italian authorities and asked them to dispatch it to London with the first ship. Walking down the dock, he ranted, "Twenty thousand pounds! That English Phidias must think that I manufacture money."

She saw a worried look on Captain Maling's face. "My lady, I think it would be unwise to allow the children ashore."

"Why?"

"The Italian authorities just now informed me of their concern over a contagion that could spread into Italy."

She glanced at Dr. Scott, and he nodded his head in agreement. "May I make a suggestion, my lady?"

"What is it?"

"I see no point in risking the health of the children. I think we should all return to the ship immediately."

"But we have been anticipating this trip for weeks," said Elgin, looking sadly toward her. "We planned to proceed overland through Italy; visit Florence and view the works of Michelangelo, Raphael, Botticelli, Giotto, Donatello . . ."

Mary remained silent.

Rubbing his chin, Dr. Scott added, "In that case, perhaps Your Lordship and Ladyship should do so, but not with the children. Mr. Duff and the Greek nurse can remain on board and attend to them."

"What about risking our own health to the contagion?" asked Elgin.

"Adults are apt to be immune, my lord. Children are more susceptible to contagion. Besides, this is a precaution. No one can foretell where or when a contagion may strike, but one thing is certain: the children will be safe on board *La Diane*. Indeed, I suggest that Your Lordship and Ladyship carry out your plans. Mr. Duff and the Greek nurse will assist me in caring for the children. We shan't need Mr. Hunt and Masterman. They can travel with you."

"I agree," said Elgin, glancing at her again.

"I'd say that's very sound advice," barked Captain Maling.

She swept Matilda into her arms and hugged her. Bruce and little Mary rushed forward and clung to her dress, tugging at it, whimpering. In a conscience-stricken voice, she said to Dr. Scott,

"You will make certain that they get to Scotland safely?"

"I give you my solemn word," mumbled Scott. "The children will remain under my constant watch."

Elgin looked directly into her eyes for the first time in weeks. "I dare say it's an excellent suggestion. We certainly looked forward to this trip . . . and I know how eager you have been to visit Florence and the charming little towns of northern Italy."

Her eyes began to fill when Calitza gently took little Matilda from her arms. Young Mary instantly started to cry, and Bruce tightened his lips when Duff took hold of his hand and led him to the accommodation ladder of *La Diane*. Calitza and Dr. Scott followed quickly behind with the other children. Captain Maling was the last to climb on board.

Duff leaned over the rail and shouted, "I shall write to Your Ladyship in care of Ambassador Whitworth in Paris."

The children were waving to her, pulling at her heart.

Abruptly, Elgin swung away and began running down the dock. After exchanging words with the Italian authorities, he scrambled up the ladder. Her heart sank when he handed something to Duff. All the while, she thought he had changed his mind and had gone after the children.

He was out of breath when he returned. "I had a devil of a time retrieving that letter from those Italians. Now Duff can deliver it by hand to my mother."

As soon as Hunt hired a carriage, they started to pull away. Mary was determined not to look back, but at the last moment she turned her head and looked quickly toward *La Diane*. Beside her, Hunt had his nose pressed against the window of the carriage. "Look, my lady . . . Mount Vesuvius!"

She was on the verge of tears.

Elgin touched her on the arm. "Poll, you may never again have this chance. Vesuvius will soon be lost from view."

She lifted her eyes slowly and gazed at the lofty peak. Little Matilda's body still pulsated in her arms as the carriage struggled

up a high hill. Looking down, she saw Naples still white and gleaming against the darkening sea.

She dreaded the thought of darkness.

"Only ten years ago," Hunt murmured, "there was a terrible eruption of Vesuvius, which devastated the town of Torre del Greco. A greater tragedy occurred shortly after the death of Christ, when Herculaneum and Pompeii were completely buried." He closed his eyes for a moment and sat back. "It's hard to believe that those volcanic slopes were once clothed with the world's best vineyards."

She held her breath for a long time, then sighed. "How tragic . . . how tragic that even the most beautiful things must perish."

Hunt had a great longing to remain in Rome, to tour the city and view its ancient shrines. However, Elgin decided against it.

"But why, my lord?"

"Mr. Hunt, we've tarried long enough. We must leave for Florence immediately. It's a two-day journey. Why do you think I purchased this superb English post chaise?"

"You purchased it?" she asked with astonishment.

"Yes, here in Rome. It's a Leader, the best ever made. Indeed, I plan to take it back to England." He threw her a wide grin. "Poll, I got it for half the English price."

The coachman and his guard were already seated behind the carriage horses. Curious, she examined it, walking all around it, looking at its sturdy wheels, the doors, the large metal basket attached to the rear, laden with all their luggage. She studied the four black horses straining at their reins, snorting clouds of steam into the brisk morning air.

As soon as she stepped inside, she heard Hunt say to Elgin in a resigned voice, "But, my lord, I am certain that Florence is a full three-day journey from here."

"We shall make it in two days," snapped Elgin.

In a final effort to catch a glimpse of Rome's ancient splendor, Hunt attempted to have the coachman turn left into the street of Saint Gregory, but Elgin ordered the man to continue northward, into the Via Cassia. It was gutted with holes, causing the post chaise to pitch and bounce, tossing Mary against Elgin one moment, then throwing her forward, almost into the lap of Masterman. Nevertheless, they made swift time, passing Lake Bracciano just before noon and Lake Vico a few hours later. They stopped at San Lorenzo Nuovo for the night.

Satisfied at their covering such a long distance in one day, Elgin reluctantly admitted to Hunt that he had miscalculated the distance to Florence. "Indeed, three full days are required," he said. Turning to Mary, he asked, "How do you feel?"

"A little better." Her voice trembled with self-reproach. "I keep thinking about the children. Eggy, I miss them dearly."

"I miss them too, Poll, very much. But I'm sure we did the right thing. I wish you would stop worrying about it."

"I can't help feeling that perhaps we acted too hastily."

He whispered, "Please put your mind on something else. Imagine that this is our honeymoon carriage and that we are setting off for our palatial estate in Florence."

"My lord," said Hunt suddenly, "what about the horses? Should I arrange to have them replaced in the morning?"

"No, I don't want to part with them. They're unusually strong. After some oats and water and a good night's rest, I feel certain, they'll be in fit condition."

"Indeed, they are a hearty breed."

Shortly after dawn, the carriage was pounding its way toward Siena. The Tuscan countryside entranced her with its limpid light on the graceful hills, its umbrella pines, the serenity of the vineyards, the vibrant color of the forests and plains. Hunt started telling them about the ancient Etruscans, how they had come from the east and landed on the shores of Tuscany, spreading

out beyond the lakes and hills until they reached the Adriatic. "Theirs was the first great civilization of Western Europe. They nourished a sincere love of luxury and the good things of life, and their cities rivaled each other, not only in wealth and power, but in culture and the arts as well. They gave no thought to war. And then the invaders came, cruel Rome conquering and burning one Etruscan city after the other until nothing remained."

Through the assistance of a young priest, with whom Hunt conversed in Latin, they found clean lodgings at a small hotel just off the main square of Siena. Above the front door hung a bronze emblem bearing the coat of arms of Senus and Aschius, the sons of Remus. It was still a few hours before dusk, and the light of the day was playing upon the stones of the Piazza del Campo.

They walked for a while, proceeding down the Via di San Petro until they arrived at the great cathedral perched on top of a high hill, dominating earth and sky. Hunt called it "the Sleepless Sentinel for the City of the Virgin." He added, "A superb temple to Athena once stood on this very hill."

"It appears to be quite aged," observed Masterman.

"Its construction began in the eleventh century and was not completed until the fourteenth. The restored façade is the work of Giovanni Pisano, son of the famous Nicola Pisano, the creator of the extraordinary Pisa Pulpit."

"Aren't we going inside?" asked Masterman.

"Of course," said Elgin.

The interior was of astounding size — powerful Romanesque pillars of black and white marble, a cornice frieze with the busts of the popes in terra cotta above the main arches, the paving resplendent in mosaics depicting scenes from the Old and New Testaments, the Allegories, the Virtues, even the Sages Socrates and Dante, and finally the pulpit, an elaborate creation of sculptured marble.

Elgin kept chuckling over the mosaic of Socrates in the pav-

ing, and when they stepped outside he nudged Mary with his elbow. "The Italians are quite willing to sanctify anyone, even a pagan philosopher who lived five hundred years before Christ."

In the morning, after a substantial breakfast of sausages and eggs, they spent another hour visiting the rest of Siena — the Palazzo Pubblico, a sober yet graceful Gothic structure, with its spacious inner courtyard and enormous brick tower; the Baptistery of San Giovanni, which braced part of the cathedral's chancel; the Via di Cittá; the Via Banchi di Sopra . . . charming little streets with flagstones reaching to the walls of the many remarkable palaces that lined them.

Fortunately, the road out of Siena was well paved, and the carriage sped past Colle di Val d'Elsa into Certaldo, an earth-red town like Siena. They stopped here only briefly to stretch their aching limbs. With his keen sense of exploration, Hunt discovered an old house with a historical marker on its front door: *On this site, Boccaccio, friend of Petrarch, grew old and died.*

Seated in the carriage again, she leaned against Elgin and fell asleep. A roll of thunder awakened her. Ominous clouds blanketed the sky, and a heavy rain started to fall. Against the noise of the rattling carriage, the echoes of thunder, the hard rain splattering on the roof, she heard Masterman humming.

"What is that?" Mary asked.

"Just a silly old tune, my lady."

"I didn't know that you liked to sing, Masterman."

"I'm humming, not singing."

"May I hear the words?"

"I don't know them."

"Nor do you know the key," jabbed Elgin.

Masterman clamped her lips together and fell silent.

Mary closed her eyes once again and sank into a soft memory, recalling a song her father sang to her every night before putting her to bed:

Had we never loved so kindly,
Had we never loved so blindly;
Never met or never parted,
We had ne'er been broken-hearted.

Masterman's voice startled everyone. "My lady, I know that tune."

"Of course," said Hunt, lifting his voice stiffly. "Robert Burns wrote it." They all looked at him and broke into laughter.

Elgin's eyes turned to the amber hills and the drenched Tuscan countryside as she continued with the song:

A highland lad my love was born,
The lowland laws he held in scorn;
But he still was faithful to his clan,
My gallant braw, John Highlandman.

Suddenly Elgin swung around and joined her in the chorus:

Sing hey, my braw, John Highlandman,
Sing ho, my braw, John Highlandman;
There's not a lad in a' the lan'
Was match for my John Highlandman.

The rain stopped just when the carriage had climbed to the top of a high hill. Mary had never seen a more tranquil countryside — the blue Arno flowing through gentle green valleys, the rising hills where the metallic-gray olive trees brushed against the solemn green cypresses, and in the distance, reaching out to her, the glorious city of Florence, with its red-tile roofs, bluish-gray stones, delicate pastel houses, regal church towers.

Moving along the southern bank of the river, they skirted past Lungarno Cellini, Serristori, Torrigiani, then crossed over Ponte alla Carraia, the only wagon bridge into the city. Farther down the river was another bridge. "Ponte Vecchio," said Hunt, pointing. "It's the oldest bridge in Florence. Look, it has walls and a roof, and those are shops clinging to its sides."

"Shops, on a bridge?" Masterman giggled.

"They were originally rented to butchers until the sixteenth century, but now they are assigned to goldsmiths and silversmiths. Florence abounds with craftsmen."

Masterman tossed an admiring glance toward Hunt. "Mr. Hunt, how do you know all these things . . . bridges, cathedrals, butchers and craftsmen?"

"Through books."

Mary stirred. "Ah, but books are a mere substitute for what the eye can see."

"I agree." Hunt smiled. "But we must admit that they open one's mind to preliminary knowledge, which stimulates a deep desire to investigate with the eye. How else would one know that Florence attracted so many men of genius — Machiavelli, Dante, Petrarch, Michelangelo, Leonardo da Vinci . . . ?"

Elgin glinted mischievously at Masterman. "Surely you must be familiar with these names?"

"How could I be, my lord? They're all foreigners."

They had no problem finding lodgings. The fat squinty-eyed proprietor of the hotel nervously explained that most travelers came to Florence in late summer to avoid the torrential rains of spring that flooded the city, making everything damp and uncomfortable. Elgin suspected that there was another reason. "But we are already well into summer, my dear fellow. Perhaps there are no travelers staying in your hotel because it is crawling with lice."

Mary wished he wouldn't act this way. It wasn't the fear of lice that really concerned him. He was playing money games again, never accepting the first offer, always bickering.

Their rooms were attractively decorated and indeed quite clean. Standing on the balcony with Hunt, she saw crowds milling about the Piazza della Signoria. They had a direct view of the Palazzo Vecchio, so impressive and austere, its slender tower thrown straight up from the façade, lending a particular elegance to the whole building.

Her bath was ready.

After she took it, she felt refreshed, but she was still haunted by the thoughts of her children. Masterman's voice startled her. Even though long shadows were stretching into the bedchamber, she determined that they still had time to tour some of the city, and asked Masterman to summon the others.

"What time is it, my lady?"

"Near eight. Please hurry. We still can visit several places before we lose the light."

Vespers had just ended, and the church bells were silent. Mary suggested that they go immediately to the Cathedral of Santa Maria del Fiore, and as they rounded the fountain of the piazza, with its awkward gigantesque statue of Neptune, she grinned. "The Florentines never liked this work. It's called the *Biancone,* and was sculptured by Ammanati." With a flourish, she flung her arms toward the sky, " 'Oh, Ammanato, Ammanato,' they would moan, 'what lovely white marble you have ruined!' "

They burst into laughter.

In the Loggia della Signoria, Elgin stood entranced before Michelangelo's *David.* Masterman, on the other hand, was horrified by *Perseus,* sword in one hand, the severed head of Medusa in the other.

Priests were kneeling at the white altar when they entered the cathedral. It reminded Mary of Hagia Sophia, particularly the high dome, the vast space, the marble floor encircling the tall pillars. Hunt left them and went to talk with one of the young priests at the altar. A few minutes later, he came bustling back. "Come!" he exclaimed. "We have permission to climb to the top of the dome."

Mary's heart instantly sank when she saw Masterman turn pale. "It's all right, Masterman," she said in a comforting voice; "you and I will wait here while Lord Elgin and Mr. Hunt climb to the dome."

Hunt gave Masterman a reproachful look. "But there is no

reason to be afraid. A parapet walk, protected by a strong iron fence, circles the entire dome."

Masterman shrank away from him.

In desperation, Hunt turned to Mary. "My lady, I wish you would reconsider. The view from the dome should be most spectacular, one that Your Ladyship shall never forget."

"Mr. Hunt, you more than anyone else should know that I most certainly want to go, but I don't think Masterman should be left alone on this crowded street."

While they were gone, Mary longingly gazed at the dome and imagined herself looking down at the vast and beautiful panorama, the sprawling red carpet of Florence. Her mind kept going back to the dome, absorbed by the knowledge that it had required fourteen years to construct, that its builder, Filippo Brunelleschi, achieved such an architectural masterpiece, it had inspired Michelangelo to create the dome of Saint Peter's in Rome. It was hard to believe that Florence still retained all these superb treasures. No other city in Europe had suffered so much — one war after another, internal strifes and bickerings, floods, earthquakes.

Masterman began puffing at the strands of hair on her cheek. "My lady, must we limit our visit to churches?"

"Of course not. The Uffizi Galleria is nearby. But look," said Mary excitedly, "here's Giotto's Bell Tower, and just opposite stands the Baptistery, which Dante called 'my lovely San Giovanni.' "

It was almost dusk when Elgin and Hunt came down from the dome. They were both in raptures. Grabbing Elgin by the arm, she declared, "Eggy, I can't believe that we're in Florence. I truly can't believe it! I wish we could see all these places right now. Why does it have to be so dark?"

He squeezed her hand tenderly. "We'll have more time tomorrow."

They were dismayed to find the doors of the Uffizi closed, but they managed to enter the courtyard through a gate that had

been left unlocked. Fleetingly, she caught glimpses of several imposing statues encircled by beds of flowers. Just then, an attendant appeared and asked them to leave.

Before returning to the hotel, they stopped once again in the Piazza della Signoria. The crowds had thinned out, and the lamps in front of the loggia and at the Palazzo Vecchio were being lighted, but surprisingly, a door of the Vecchio was open. She took Elgin's hand and started running, pulling him and laughing happily. They entered quickly and proceeded into the courtyard. Although it wasn't entirely dark yet, lamps burned between each column. Mary instantly spied the Vasari frescoes lining the walls, depicting scenes of Austrian cities painted in honor of Joan of Austria on her marriage to Francesco de' Medici. Elgin pulled away from her and went to the center of the courtyard, his eyes fastened on the bronze statue of a cherubic boy with wings holding a fish in his arms. At that moment, the pale light from the lamps fell gently on Elgin, mercifully obscuring his face. She ran to him and linked her arm in his.

The next day she arose early, waking the others and asking them to hurry, because she was eager to return to the square in front of the cathedral, to study more carefully the bronze doors of the Baptistery, Giotto's Bell Tower, the interior of Santa Maria del Fiore. Yesterday had left her frustrated. Now, she wanted to absorb everything, see everything, touch everything.

Her heart trembled when she left the Bell Tower and stood in front of the Baptistery. She marveled at the Ghiberti masterpieces on the bronze doors, particularly those of Adam and Eve's expulsion from Paradise, and the Reception of King Solomon by the Queen of Sheba. She suddenly remembered that Dante had been baptized here. She lost all thought of Elgin and the others. This was one place where she wanted to be by herself, to study each of the ten panels, beginning once again with Adam and

Eve, their figures so perfectly portrayed as the most beautiful images of the Creator.

She stepped back and examined the Baptistery from a different aspect, observing its octagonal design, its colored marbles, dome, and pilasters. But again her heart was pulled back to the bronze doors.

She rushed inside now, stopping immediately before Donatello's statue of Mary Magdalene in old age, taking in every detail of the emaciated, repentent saint, staying there for a long time, losing herself in thought. Finally, she let out a deep breath and walked around the rest of the interior.

The others were waiting impatiently for her when she stepped outside. In a hurry to get to the Uffizi Galleria, she reached out for Elgin's hand and he accepted hers with warmth and a fond glance.

Inside the Uffizi, she went first to the works of Botticelli, then to the paintings of Leonardo da Vinci, Cimabue, Giotto, Duccio, Fra Angelico, Filippo Lippi, Ghirlandaio, Titian, Tintoretto, Andrea del Sarto . . . it was endless. Beside her, she heard Elgin gasp. "How could so much excellence and creative mastery be housed under one roof!"

Masterman looked worn out when at last they walked out of the galleria. Everyone was starving. They hadn't eaten anything all day.

They found a small inn just off the Piazza della Signoria, and as they ravenously dined on lamb stew and hot bread, Hunt talked about Savonarola, the monk from Florence who had tried to bring reform to the Catholic Church by denouncing the abuses and corruptions of the clergy. Hunt paused a moment and in a bleak voice added, "He was burned at the stake, along with two of his followers, but not before he had persuaded the people of Florence to make a bonfire of their vanities, including books, musical instruments, and even paintings by Botticelli. It was a terrible price to pay for religious fanaticism."

As soon as they left the inn, Elgin reached for her hand and said, "If we hurry, we can still see a few things before it gets dark."

Masterman cast an imploring look toward her. "My lady, perhaps we should continue tomorrow, after we're all rested."

"We shall be on our way to Livorno tomorrow," said Elgin.

Mary stopped walking. "Eggy, must we leave Florence so soon?"

His reply was gentle. "Poll, we're not on a grand tour. We have a long journey before us, an exceedingly long journey."

For the rest of the afternoon, he was an indefatigable guide, leading them from one place to the other, complying with every request Mary made — the Palazzo Strozzi, Palazzo Pitti, Palazzo Medici — then on to the Bargello Museum and the Monastery of San Marco, which was decorated almost throughout with the pure and delicate frescoes of Fra Angelico. Mary had to tear herself away from the artist's great masterpiece *The Annunciation,* which faced the monks' cells on the first floor. Becoming aware of Masterman, she suggested that they rest on a bench in the cloisters for a few moments. Several monks passed by, reading from their breviaries, never lifting their heads. She envied them — a life given to silence and contemplation, not one thought about the morrow, no burdens from the past.

Masterman prepared a hot bath for her when they returned to the hotel, but after taking it, she was unable to sleep. Her brain kept spinning back to the children. She could see them waving from the rail of *La Diane,* hear their clutching voices.

Slowly, she got up from her bed and walked across the floor to Elgin's bed. Pulling back the covers, she crept in beside him. He stirred.

"Eggy . . ."

"What is it?"

"I just want to say how happy I am. I'm so glad we came to Florence."

"No regrets about leaving the children on board *La Diane?*"

"I can't say that. I only wish they were with us."

"Try not to think about it. We shall be in France in a few days, and after that, good old bonnie Scotland."

She felt his manhood become erect against her thigh. Slowly, he started pulling up her nightgown. She helped him. Not another word passed between them, not even a gasp or a sigh. Everything happened so swiftly and with ease, she found herself sinking into a velvet sleep.

Eight

ON THE MORNING of May fifteenth, they sailed out of Livorno on a large Genoese merchant vessel. The ship did not take a direct course across the Ligurian Sea, but instead proceeded northward, hugging the hospitable Italian coast, making calls at La Spezia, Genova, Savona, San Remo. At every port, there was a flurry of turmoil and confusion among the Italian dockworkers, often culminating in wild gestures and contrived tears. With each stop, Elgin went below to inspect the post chaise and make certain it wasn't damaged.

At Nice, a new world suddenly emerged — pastel hues mingling with vibrant streaks of color, a pure marriage of sky and earth, a sublime aura of peace that became even more pronounced to Mary at Cannes, at Saint-Tropez, and at Toulon. She hated to see these charming towns dying in the horizon behind her, lost forever from her sight, never again to be savored.

The ancient harbor of Marseille, shaped like a horseshoe, had ships of all sizes anchored to its docks, their flags flying from the masts, their sailors and crewmen waving to them as they drifted by. Throughout the entire passage from Livorno, the sea had not bothered her.

Elgin too appeared in good spirits. "I think it would be best if we travel by barge up the Rhône and into Lyon."

"But my lord," said Hunt, "the Rhône lies farther to the west."

"I know. We can take the barge at Saint-Louis-au-Rhône. It's not too far from here."

"Does Your Lordship intend to go there now?"

"Of course. We still have time before it gets dark."

"I thought perhaps we might stay in Marseille a day or so."

"For what?"

"My lord, Marseille abounds with ancient sites, most of them only a short distance from the Vieux Port."

Elgin was too engrossed to pay attention to him. He had his mind on the dockworkers who were unloading the post chaise. After the luggage was latched securely to the back, everyone got in.

They traveled in silence for several minutes before Masterman asked, "My lady, are we getting close to Scotland?"

She laughed. "Masterman, this is southern France. We're hundreds of miles from Scotland."

Masterman tugged at her fingers. "I wish we had never left *La Diane*. We would have been in Scotland by now." Slowly, she looked up. "I just hope the children are in good health. There's something about that Greek nurse that bothers me."

"What is it?"

"I don't think she can be entrusted with the children."

"Why not?"

"She is a foreigner, after all."

"Masterman, I don't like to hear you talk like this. We're all children of one Father."

"One Father indeed, but many mothers."

Mary fell into a fit of laughter. "Masterman, you're impossible. In heaven's name, what shall I do with you?"

They were greeted with puzzling behavior by the captain of the barge at Port Saint-Louis-au-Rhône. Turning his eyes away

from Elgin, he said in a stiff voice, "Englishmen are not accepted on my barge."

"But our countries are not at war now."

"Monsieur, my uncle was killed in the Battle of the Nile. I would dishonor him if I permitted an Englishman to set foot on my barge."

"I shall pay you handsomely."

"It is not the money, Monsieur. I am a Frenchman."

Mary interceded. "Captain, you have no other passengers, and it is urgent that we get to Lyon. We have been separated from our children and are desperate to get home. I beg you, have pity on us."

The captain hunched his shoulders. "Very well, Madame, but I will not permit you to talk to any of my crewmen during the trip. If you have anything to say, speak only to me."

"Yes, of course."

"Gather your luggage and climb aboard. We shall be leaving in a short while."

"Will you please ask your crewmen to lift the post chaise into the barge?" asked Elgin.

"What?"

"The post chaise. I am taking it with us."

"I am sorry, Monsieur, but you must leave it behind. There is no room in my barge for such a large carriage."

"I will pay you a hundred francs."

The captain took off his cap and scratched his head.

"Two hundred," said Elgin.

The five crewmen had little difficulty hoisting the carriage into the barge. They tied it securely at a space near the stern and then prepared to set off, grasping their long poles and awaiting the captain's command.

As the barge moved slowly away from the dock, Elgin sighed deeply. "Well, we're off to Lyon. And after that, Paris."

Several wooden benches were attached to one side of the rail,

their rough edges jabbing into Mary every time she turned or changed position. Hunt was undaunted by the discomfort and kept rambling on about Marseille.

Moving away from him, Elgin whispered to her, "Now, if Mr. Hunt had wanted to pay a call on one of the many brothels at Marseille, I might have obliged him."

The barge fought its way upriver, past multicolored fishing shacks and fleets of small boats. As they approached a sleepy little village that lay sprawled on the right bank, a sudden current swept them into the deepest artery of the river. The crewmen pushed feverishly on their long poles, and sent the barge into Arles hours before their scheduled arrival.

After securing the barge to the dock, the captain informed Elgin that he never traveled at night. Furthermore, he intended to stay with relatives in Arles until noon of the next day. Elgin was disturbed over this unexpected delay. Nevertheless, he acceded to Hunt's wishes, and they embarked at once on an exploration of Arles. Two imposing structures dominated the Place de la République: the town hall, built in 1675, and the Museum of Pagan Art, formerly a church. Crowds of people were congregated around the square. A parade was passing through — toreadors in brilliant costumes, young people in masquerade, bands of musicians competing with one another, monkeys hopping around, everyone in festive dress and gay mood. Elgin suggested that they follow the parade to the Roman amphitheater, where a bullfight was about to take place, but both Mary and Masterman had no desire to witness such an appalling event.

Before it grew dark, they walked along a lovely tree-lined avenue, then dined at a small inn nestled between two handsome linden trees. The waiter who attended their table was cool in his manner but efficient, and Elgin rewarded him with ten francs.

The festival was still going on when they stepped outside. Groups of revelers pushed their way through the streets, singing and shouting greetings to people in the doorways and on the

balconies. A little boy stopped in front of Mary and handed her a lighted taper. Before she could thank him, he ran off.

They spent the next afternoon entirely on the river, fighting contrary currents all the way to Tarascon, and arriving at Avignon just before dusk. For the second time, Elgin showed his vexation with the captain. "In God's name, I wish you would change your mind and travel at night."

"That is impossible, Monsieur."

"But this way, it will take us ages to reach Lyon."

"Three days, Monsieur, not ages."

Hunt helped her out of the barge. She could see people strolling along the lamp-lit street. The night air was mild.

"Avignon is a large and busy town, Monsieur," said the captain, following Elgin as far as the dock. "You should have no trouble finding suitable lodgings here. But remember, we leave precisely at seven in the morning. Be on time."

"We shall be here," Elgin retorted. "And you had better keep a sharp eye on my post chaise. If anything happens to it, I shall hold you accountable."

It was an easy matter to find lodgings. The inn was very clean and within a few hundred yards of the river. "Think of it, my lord and lady!" exclaimed Hunt. "We are in Avignon!"

"Mr. Hunt," asked Masterman, with a playful toss of the head, "could you tell us the chief points of interest in Avignon?"

He looked at her in disbelief. "Indeed I can. The first place to visit is the Palace of the Popes."

"But I thought that was in Rome."

Elgin laughed.

"The popes lived here in Avignon many years ago," Hunt replied sternly. "In fact, there were two popes at the same time — one in Rome, the other in Avignon."

"Which of the two was infallible?" Elgin gibed.

They dined in the small restaurant adjacent to the inn — succulent lamb, its juices running pink and clear, wines of Château-

neuf-du-Pape, coffee in cups of fragile porcelain, almond-scented brandy.

The night air was still very warm, and they decided to stroll along the river bank. A full moon had already climbed over the rooftops of Avignon, glazing them in a coat of silver. Approaching the large bridge, they caught an alluring sound of music drifting toward them, and Mary increased her steps. People were dancing on a wide platform that floated between two arches of the bridge. The reflection of many lamps rippled and skipped gaily over the surface of the dark water.

"What is that they are singing?" asked Masterman, drawing up beside her.

"Something about a bridge," Mary replied.

Hunt raced to the water's edge and listened to catch the words. "Of course," he observed elatedly, "they're singing 'Sur le Pont d'Avignon,' one of the oldest songs of southern France."

"They certainly are enjoying themselves."

"It seems that way, my lady."

"I think we should join them."

"You are being ridiculous," snapped Elgin.

She put her hand on his wrist. "Eggy, we haven't danced together since Constantinople."

"I've no desire to mingle with inebriated French peasants."

Anchored in silence, they walked back to the inn.

At dawn, she awoke feeling tired and ill at ease, assaulted by thoughts of the children. The others ate heartily at breakfast, but she took only a cup of tea and a biscuit. The captain and his crew were waiting for them on the barge. Elgin went first to the post chaise and inspected it carefully while Hunt and Masterman looked after the luggage. Hardly any words were spoken between captain and crew. Everyone bent to his task, and before long, ropes were untied, poles brought out, and the barge was heading upstream toward Port Saint-Joseph.

Mary remained quietly by herself most of the day, absorbing

the quiet beauty of the river, the towns and hamlets, the reverberating echoes of children at play on the shore. That night, they lodged in Valence, dining on pigeon truffé in a crowded little restaurant on the right arm of the Rhône. Elgin was in excellent spirits and, in a rare and extravagant mood, ordered the most expensive wine.

In their bedchamber, he playfully restrained her from putting on her nightgown. As she perfumed her body and combed her hair, she was aware of his probing eyes. Turning, she saw him stretched out on the bed, hands clasped behind his head, penis erect, waiting. Perhaps it was the wine, the seductive knowledge that they were alone inside a remote room whose walls could not see, could not speak or hear . . .

Blocking out every intrusive thought from her mind in the same instant that she snuffed out the small lamp on the bureau, she made her way to the bed.

The following afternoon, they were in Vienne, stopping only long enough to draw a supply of fresh water from a spring. The town looked appealing to Hunt, and he wanted to investigate it, but the captain was determined to dock at Lyon before the sun went down. Masterman placed a pillow on the bench and asked Mary to sit on it. When the barge finally set off, Hunt joined them and, in vivid detail, started telling them about Lyon, its numerous bridges that straddled both the Rhône and Saône rivers, its massive stone houses, Roman theater, museums, Cathedral of Saint-Jean, and especially about the wonderful silk manufactured there. Mary's curiosity was stirred when he described the old quarter of Lyon, with its grand Renaissance houses, its galleries and shops.

The sun was about to touch the horizon when they came into view of the city. For the first time during the voyage, the captain began issuing harsh commands to the crew. The river's current

was pulling the barge away from the docks, and he yelled at them to work harder on the poles. Elgin observed them with annoyance, more concerned about the post chaise than about any impending danger.

After the barge was secured to the dock, Mary followed the others down the straining plank. Lyon looked gray and lifeless under a mass of low-flying clouds. Very few people were on the streets. Looking back, she noticed that Elgin was still with the captain, negotiating over the price, instructing the crewmen to be careful with the post chaise. He didn't pay the captain until the carriage was safely on the dock and rolled into the street.

They were about to put the luggage in the rear basket, when a detachment of horsemen, led by a young lieutenant, came racing toward them.

She heard Elgin mutter under his breath, "Another silly reception."

The officer slid off his horse and saluted smartly. "You are Lord Elgin?"

"I am."

"Who else is with you?"

"My wife, her maid, and Mr. Philip Hunt."

"Where are the other members of your embassy?"

"They continued on to England by ship."

Hunt looked at the lieutenant quizzically. "How did you know that we were arriving at Lyon?"

The lieutenant glared at him. "I will ask the questions, *citoyen.*"

"Why are you so mysterious?" said Elgin. "Who told you about our arrival?"

The lieutenant reached into his coat pocket and withdrew a folded document. "*Citoyen,* I have direct orders from the First Consul to place you and your party under immediate arrest."

"What?"

"We are at war again, *citoyen* . . . your country and ours."

"But a treaty was signed at Amiens!" Elgin exploded.

"The First Consul has abrogated the treaty and has already issued an ultimatum to your country. England must abandon not only Malta, but Egypt and Gibraltar as well."

"He is an idiot."

"I warn you to guard your tongue."

"But you have no right to arrest me. I am a diplomat, not a soldier."

The lieutenant's eyes wandered to Mary's bosom for a moment before he read from the document: "All soldiers of the French Republic are hereby instructed to be on the alert for the British Ambassador, Lord Elgin, who was observed entering France at Marseille. He and his party are to be arrested and brought at once to Paris, where they will be confined as prisoners of war. Each soldier of the Republic is charged with the execution of this decree under penalty of death."

"But you cannot do this," objected Mary. "My husband is an ambassador, the official representative of His Britannic Majesty to the Sublime Porte of Selim the Third, Sultan of Turkey."

"This is France, *citoyenne,* not Turkey."

"But we must return to our children in Scotland. You cannot detain us without just cause."

Hunt intervened. "My dear lieutenant, it is a convention of all wars that only soldiers participate. Civilians are exempt and cannot be made prisoners."

The lieutenant signaled to one of his men, spoke to him, then sent him scurrying down the street. Moments later, a heavy carriage, led by four powerful horses, came thundering over the cobbled street and pulled up before them. The lieutenant opened the door of the carriage and commanded them to climb in.

"What about our luggage?" asked Hunt.

"The soldiers will attend to it."

"I demand to know where you are taking us!" exclaimed Elgin.

"You heard the edict. We are to convey you to Paris as prisoners."

"You have no right to do this."

"Citoyen, if you provoke us in any way, we shall have to use force. Now then, get into the carriage. We have a long journey before us."

"Why must we rush off this way?" complained Hunt.

"It is imperative that we reach Tournus before nightfall."

Elgin pointed a trembling finger at the post chaise. "That carriage belongs to me. I intend to take it to Scotland."

"That is impossible."

"I paid a great deal of money for it."

"I am sorry, but you cannot take it with you."

"Then you must allow me time to sell it. Someone in Lyon will want to purchase it."

The lieutenant shook his head. "I have explicit orders to confiscate everything in your possession, with the exception of your clothing. The carriage is now the property of the Republic."

"Why are your soldiers conducting a search of the barge?" asked Hunt.

"We have been informed that you are carrying treasures from Greece."

"You are wasting your time," Elgin retorted. "Everything has already been sent to England."

"In that case, we must search your luggage."

"Why?" asked Masterman angrily.

"For jewels and other valuable possessions."

"You will find nothing in our luggage but clothing."

"Nevertheless, we must conduct the search."

One of the soldiers had already opened the valises and was pawing through the neatly folded clothes. Masterman wrung her hands and sobbed. After inspecting all the luggage, the soldier clamped the valises shut and strapped them to the rear of the carriage. Once again the lieutenant asked them to climb in. Everyone obeyed except Elgin.

The lieutenant drew his sword. "I order you to get into the carriage at once."

"I take my orders only from my King."

Mary spoke to him softly. "Eggy, please do as he says. It is pointless to argue."

Elgin squared his shoulders and climbed into the carriage. "This matter is not closed," he shouted back at the lieutenant. "I intend to bring it to Lord Whitworth's immediate attention as soon as we arrive in Paris."

"If you are referring to the British Ambassador, he and his embassy fled from France before the outbreak of war."

"How long are we to be held prisoners?" said Hunt.

"That is entirely up to Monsieur de Talleyrand, our Minister of Foreign Affairs." The lieutenant closed the door of the carriage and mounted his horse. He issued a command to half a dozen horsemen. They swung sharply around and took their positions in front of the carriage. "Remember the decree," the lieutenant warned them. "We are charged with these prisoners under the penalty of death."

Through the oval window of the carriage, Mary extended her gaze beyond the lieutenant to the horsemen mounted awkwardly on their steeds, their faces unshaved, mud caked over their boots and breeches, their uniforms filthy. She would never forgive herself for setting foot from *La Diane* at Naples.

Masterman stopped sobbing. "My lady, I watched the soldier closely. I don't think he looked between the petticoats, where I hid the jewels."

Elgin filled the carriage with his curses.

They spent a torturous five days, stopping late each night at wayside inns, getting up early in the morning, riding past an endless string of towns — Tournus, Chagny, Vézelay, Sens. Her body ached, and she felt feverish and exhausted. She worried

about Elgin. He looked terribly weak and depressed. In Vézelay, his catarrh flared up once again, and he coughed the whole night, depriving everyone of sleep. She requested a cup of camomile tea, but when the innkeeper brought it in, steaming hot and fragrant, Elgin refused it, burying his head under the covers.

They arrived in Paris on a damp gray afternoon, crossing a bridge called Pont Neuf, and riding down a wide avenue that brought them before a tall structure whose stone façade was cracked and discolored with age. Two thick cypresses guarded the front entrance; iron balconies hung over the street. Above the oak door, in black letters chipped and uneven, a sign read, Hôtel de Richelieu.

Two of the horsemen carried the luggage inside, over red carpeting that extended from the hallway up the circular staircase. Mary took hold of Masterman's hand as they passed by a number of closed doors. Behind her, Elgin was arguing with the lieutenant again. "I demand to see the Foreign Minister straightaway."

The lieutenant kept walking. When they reached the last door, he stopped and addressed them in a severe voice. "You will be free to move about the hotel grounds. There are gardens here and also many excellent walks. Upon arising each morning, and before retiring at night, each of you must register his or her name with the soldier standing guard in the front hallway. Is this clear?"

Masterman opened the door and quickly stepped inside. Blowing the strands of hair away from her face, she surveyed the room, the windows, rug, sofa, chairs, and table. It comforted Mary to discover that the bedchambers were freshly decorated with colorful wallpaper. The wooden floors had been swept clean, but the windows were streaked with grime and dust. An enormous bay window dominated the drawing room. She went to it and peered at the street below, her thoughts mired in anguish and despair.

Hunt came beside her and pointed over the distant trees. "We

can't see it, my lady, but just beyond that area lies the Jardin de Tuileries. It was designed by Le Nôtre, the brilliant and famous gardener of Louis the Fourteenth. But long before that, as far back as the fifteenth century, tiles were manufactured from the rich soil that abounded there."

Struggling to free herself from her thoughts, she followed his pointing finger as it traveled along the gray horizon. "The Palais-Royal is somewhere in the vicinity also. It's difficult to imagine that grand structure taken over by the Revolutionaries. It was built for Cardinal Richelieu, and for almost two hundred years it was the favorite haunt of Parisians, complete with a theater, eight courtyards, rows of arches, shops and restaurants, and avenues lined with statues."

His droning voice was beginning to bother her. Easing away from him, she walked toward Elgin, who was seated at the table, face buried in his hands.

"Eggy, aren't you feeling well?"

He made no reply.

Masterman busily began rearranging some of the furniture, dragging chairs across the floor, turning the sofa around to face the bay window. The suite had no kitchen or pantry, which sorely distressed her.

After a few minutes, Hunt went downstairs to inquire about dinner. He came back exuberant. "My lord and lady, we are to dine in the hotel's dining room, and from what I have gathered, there are many others detained here."

"Are they English?" asked Masterman.

"Indeed they are."

Elgin walked to the small table near the window and sat down to write. Mary asked him if he was writing to his mother, and he answered sharply, "No."

"To whom then?"

"Talleyrand," he barked, slamming his fist on the table. "He has no right to do this to me, no right at all!"

She decided it was best to leave him alone. In the bedchamber,

Masterman said to her, "My lady, which dress do you prefer to wear to dinner?"

"It's not important."

"The pale pink one?"

"It will do."

Suddenly Masterman began weeping.

"What is it?" Mary asked, touching her gently on the wrist.

"My lady, I'm expected in Scotland."

"We are all expected, Masterman."

The maid dabbed her eyes with a handkerchief. "Before we left Constantinople, I wrote a letter to my father and told him we should be arriving in Scotland within a month. Oh, my lady, I can see him pacing around our kitchen floor, wondering what has happened to me. And what will Mr. Nichols think?"

Mary squeezed Masterman's trembling hand. "You can send another letter to your father and explain that we have been detained. You need not tell him that we are prisoners. As for Mr. Nichols, I'm sure he will understand."

"But I was to return to Scotland in two years. This is what Your Ladyship promised. I remember the words exactly: 'His Lordship's embassy in Constantinople will be closed down in two years.' "

"I know, Masterman, but circumstances extended our stay. Dry your tears. If it will make you feel better, I'll write to your father."

"Would you, my lady?"

"Yes, I'll do it tonight, after dinner."

"It will be official, a letter from Your Ladyship. I'll be forever grateful."

"Now then, what about my dress?"

"I shall fetch it right away, my lady."

"You won't forget the white silk scarf?"

"Now how could I do that, my lady? If Your Ladyship recalls, it was I who insisted they be worn together."

Mary forced a laugh.

Hunt was lighting the lamps in the drawing room while Elgin still sat at the table writing under the candle flame.

"Are you almost finished?" she asked him.

He pressed heavily on the quill.

"Eggy, may I read what you wrote to Talleyrand?"

"I have already sealed that letter."

"To whom are you sending this one?"

"Lusieri."

She took a chair and sat down beside him. "Eggy, the work in Athens is completed. Since you released the other artists, don't you think Signor Lusieri should be released, too? The man worked hard for you and deserves to go home."

Elgin kept his head down, writing furiously. Suddenly he started coughing, his face turning scarlet, then white. She took hold of his wrist and asked if he wanted a glass of water, but he shook his head and slumped over the table, staying in that position until the seizure finally passed. Straightening his shoulders, he picked up the quill and continued writing.

She rose to her feet in anger. "Eggy, you must come to your senses before it's too late. This obsession over the Parthenon marbles has already eaten into your fortune and health. If you go on with this, it shall destroy all of us. I beg you, tell Lusieri that you have no further need of him. Tell him he is free to go home."

He was not listening to her.

Hunt went downstairs again, and when he returned, he joyfully exclaimed, "My lord and lady, this hotel is overflowing with English prisoners!"

There was a long silence.

"I dare say," Hunt rambled on, "there should be one good whist player in the lot."

The next morning, they registered their names with the soldier in the front hallway before going for a walk in the gardens. The day was sunny and mild; birds chirped in the magnolia trees. They were soon joined by some half-dozen people, the same guests that had sat with them the previous evening at dinner: Mrs. Keith Stuart, Mrs. Fitzgerald, Mr. and Mrs. Cockburn, Mr. Sterling, Colonel Crawford. Among all of them, Mary preferred the company of Mr. Cockburn. He was warm and sensitive, and displayed a sincere interest in everyone. He and his wife were in their early sixties. Mrs. Keith Stuart and Mrs. Fitzgerald were elderly widows who continually complained about their detention and the unforgivable departure of Lord Whitworth. Colonel Crawford walked with a cane, supporting the limp in his left leg. A compulsive talker, he kept sputtering ahead, even when no one was listening to him. Mr. Sterling, a master at a school near London, had a somber and studious look on his face, reminding her a great deal of Hunt. They were both about the same age.

Before returning to the hotel, Mr. Cockburn bounded toward her spryly and said, "We are entertaining all our friends at dinner tonight. I hope Your Ladyship and Lordship can join us."

"You have cooking facilities in your suite, Mr. Cockburn?"

He smiled. "Hardly. The hotel restaurant will prepare everything, at our expense of course."

Colonel Crawford hobbled closer to Mr. Cockburn. "And what about the guard in the front hallway? Will he permit all of us to come to your suite?"

"It has already been arranged, Colonel Crawford."

Colonel Crawford moved away, mumbling, "Soon they'll be asking us to sign our names every time we pick our noses or pass wind."

Mrs. Keith Stuart joined them. "Mr. Cockburn, I do hope that you invited that handsome devil from Scotland."

"Mr. Fergusson? I did indeed."

Elgin stopped walking. "Which Fergusson is that?"

"Robert Fergusson, my lord."

"Is he from Raith?"

"Yes, I distinctly remember that name."

"Then I know him. His father's estate is not too far from Broomhall. What an unexpected coincidence! I haven't seen Robert in years. Tell me, is he married?"

"Good heavens, no!" exclaimed Mrs. Keith Stuart, grinning. "As I recall, Robert was always a dapper young man. Every wee lass in Fife was after him."

Colonel Crawford caught up to them again. "Mr. Fergusson is also quite wealthy. He would be a fool to commit himself to marriage."

"Why do you say this?" asked Mary.

"My lady, I'm eight and sixty, and I pride myself for escaping those shackles."

"But surely you must have been in love?"

"Many times, when I was very young."

"And you never once gave thought to marriage?"

Colonel Crawford's eyes twinkled. "My dear Lady Elgin, in every relationship between a man and a woman, only the encounter matters. A woman's virtue lies neither in beauty nor in charm."

"In what, then?" asked Mary, raising her eyebrows.

"In novelty, my lady. Only in novelty."

Mrs. Keith Stuart gasped, but before she could respond, Colonel Crawford had spun away and was limping up the stairs.

Mrs. Cockburn patted Mary affectionately on the wrist. "You mustn't pay attention to Colonel Crawford. He really doesn't mean what he says."

"I find him quite amusing."

"What caused his limp?" asked Elgin.

Mr. Cockburn laughed. "Colonel Crawford claims it resulted from a wound suffered in the Far East."

"You don't believe him?"

"I say he has the gout."

At the top of the stairs, Mr. Cockburn reminded them once again to sign their names before coming to dinner.

Mary awoke from a brief nap at five o'clock and asked Masterman to open the imperial valise. She couldn't make up her mind about what to wear at the dinner, but after some deliberation, her preference fell on the white silk gown with the embroidered bodice. She looked feverishly for her pearls but was unable to find them. "I thought you hid them between the petticoats." She glared at Masterman.

"But I did, my lady."

"Where are they? I've searched everywhere."

"The soldier must have taken them." Her voice quivered. "He did it so quickly, I didn't see him."

Elgin came into the bedchamber. "What's the problem?" he asked.

"Eggy, that dreadful soldier in Lyon stole my string of pearls."

"Is that all?"

"But they were my best pearls, my very best."

He coughed. "I can buy you another set when we get to London."

Forgetting her indignation, she attached her gaze to his white uniform, freshly laundered and pressed. What with all the hardship and humiliation that he had endured, he still stood erect and proud. Clasping her hand, he led her to the bay window, then released her and drew away a few paces. She stood there for a long time, looking at the trees below, the gray buildings in the distance.

"Why are you so quiet?" he asked, taking hold of her hand again.

"I was thinking about the children."

"I wish you wouldn't. It's hard enough as it is, being confined here."

"Eggy, how long will they detain us?"

"I don't know. It depends on Talleyrand."

Once again, she plunged into silence.

The Cockburns' suite was larger than theirs. Everyone was pleased to see them, even Mr. Sterling, who smiled for the first time. Mrs. Keith Stuart's greeting momentarily embarrassed Mary. "My lady, I didn't realize how lovely you are. And that exquisite dress . . ."

They were led to a long table in the middle of the drawing room, and as a young waiter from the hotel served them cheese and wine, she heard Colonel Crawford say with a snort, "Now this is what I call royal imprisonment. I dare say I could enjoy this for the rest of my life." He looked at her and chuckled. "Indeed, I am rapidly losing my desire to return to England."

"Where in England do you live?" asked Mary, smiling.

"Newhaven. It's just a few miles southeast of Brighton."

"Then you're on the coast?"

"Yes. My house is within sight of the Channel."

"It must be wonderful there this time of year."

"Yes, quite." Colonel Crawford's voice became soft and apologetic. "My lady, I hope you didn't take me seriously this morning."

She laughed. "Of course not, Colonel Crawford."

"There are many women to whom my remarks would apply, but certainly not to Your Ladyship."

There was a knock on the door. The young waiter stopped attending the table and went to answer it. He received a tall man with a blond mustache and thick blond hair. A black cloak was draped over his broad shoulders. Mrs. Keith Stuart rushed toward him with elation. "Mr. Fergusson, I'm overjoyed to see you again."

"Thank you, Mrs. Keith Stuart. It's a pleasure to see you

again." His voice bore the stamp of Scotland, and during the introductions his eyes danced around the room, then stopped to latch on Mary. Mrs. Cockburn took his cloak and gloves and brought him to Elgin, who was standing beside the table.

"Robert, what a wonderful surprise!" Elgin exclaimed, slapping Fergusson fondly on the shoulder. "It's been a number of years since I last saw you."

"Yes indeed, my lord, it has been a long time."

"How is your father?"

"In excellent health."

"He must be near eighty."

"Six and seventy, my lord."

"Tell me, what brought you to France?"

"I was invited by the French Institute several weeks ago."

"For what purpose?"

"To deliver a series of lectures."

"What is your field, Robert?"

"Biology. I also have an interest in archaeology and philosophy."

Mary tried to keep her voice from faltering. "Have you visited Greece, Mr. Fergusson?"

"Not as yet, my lady."

"But you should. It's a very beautiful country."

Mrs. Keith Stuart patted Fergusson fondly on the wrist. "Robert has recently been appointed to the Royal Academy."

"That's wonderful news," said Elgin. "But aren't you rather young for such an honor, Robert?"

"I'm six and twenty."

At dinner, Fergusson sat wedged between Mrs. Keith Stuart and Mrs. Cockburn. Several times he lifted his eyes toward Mary and she quickly looked the other way. After the dessert, Elgin and Colonel Crawford became involved in a discussion of military maneuvers, referring particularly to Lord Nelson and Napoleon Bonaparte. Mr. Sterling asked to be excused, thanking

Mr. and Mrs. Cockburn and confessing that it was his habit to retire early.

When Mary and Elgin got up to leave, Fergusson walked as far as the door, then took her hand and bowed. "I trust that we shall meet again."

She nodded uncomfortably.

Fergusson turned to Elgin. "My lord, would you object if I paid a visit some evening?"

"We'd be delighted to have you, Robert."

"Do you play whist?" she asked.

"Quite poorly, I'm afraid."

"No matter." Elgin laughed. "I'm sure we can find other ways to entertain ourselves."

Talleyrand's reply was delivered to Elgin the next morning:

My Lord Excellency,

It is indeed regrettable that you and your party must be detained in France, but since the order for your arrest was issued directly by the First Consul, there is little I can do except offer my sincere hope that your detention will be of short duration.

Please be assured of my interest in your behalf.

I have the honour to be,
Charles-Maurice de Talleyrand-Périgord,
Foreign Minister of the Republic

Elgin's behavior was unbearable in the days that followed, and to distress him further, his catarrh and rheumatism flared up once again. For some reason, it seemed to occur only when he was most upset.

One morning, after a quiet walk along the garden paths, Mary returned to the suite and said to him, "Mrs. Keith Stuart and the Cockburns inquired about you."

"Did they now?" he answered curtly.

"I did my best to convince them that you were not avoiding their company."

Elgin grunted.

"Mr. Fergusson also asked about you. He returned from Versailles last night, where he was asked to deliver a scientific talk there."

"Where did you see him?"

"In the gardens. He said that Count Sebastiani accompanied him on the carriage ride back to Paris."

"He knows Sebastiani?"

"Quite well. Mr. Fergusson feels that Count Sebastiani is in the best position to help us. Eggy, I think we should invite him here. After all, he was very friendly to us in Constantinople."

"Where is Sebastiani staying?"

"Mr. Fergusson suggested that you send a message to the Palais du Luxembourg. It will reach Count Sebastiani. Do it now, Eggy. Please."

"But how can I get the message to him?"

"The soldier on guard can't refuse you. He will see that it is delivered."

Elgin ate heartily that night, and later he accompanied her on a walk through the gardens. Everyone appeared happy to see him. Only Mr. Sterling was missing. "The poor dear caught a dreadful cold," explained Mrs. Keith Stuart. "I wish he would marry," she added with a loud sigh. "Only this morning I said to him, 'Mr. Sterling, what you need is a wife, someone to care for you and love you.' "

Colonel Crawford barked, "Why don't you leave the man alone? It's quite obvious that the life of a bachelor suits him."

Mrs. Keith Stuart shook her head emphatically. "My mother always said there was nothing sadder in all the world than an unmarried man."

"Would your mother have said the same thing about Mr. Fergusson?" asked Mrs. Cockburn with a smile.

Mrs. Keith Stuart was offended for a moment but made no reply.

Two days later, a handwritten message was delivered to Elgin by an adjutant from the Palais du Luxembourg:

My dear Lord and Lady Elgin,

I shall be honoured to visit with you at three o'clock this afternoon.

Count Horace Sebastiani,
Personal Agent to Napoleon Bonaparte

Mary was elated and quickly asked Masterman to tidy up the suite and put fresh flowers in all the vases. Elgin sent Hunt downstairs to purchase a bottle of brandy from the hotel restaurant.

Sebastiani arrived at five minutes to three. Attired in a heavily decorated uniform, he bent to kiss her hand, then laughingly said to Elgin, "My lord, I can't understand why you are turning the world upside down to get out of our lovely country."

Elgin did not find this amusing. "Count Sebastiani, this entire affair is utterly preposterous. I demand that we be released immediately."

"But surely you have been accorded the best treatment, with kindness and courtesy?"

"Bonaparte has no right to hold us. We are civilians, not soldiers."

Sebastiani dabbed his silk handkerchief over his face, then took a seat on the sofa. "My dear Lord Elgin, our countries are at war."

"That is no reason to imprison us."

"But this is hardly imprisonment." Sebastiani politely laughed.

Mary waited until Masterman poured the brandy into the glasses; taking a seat beside Sebastiani, she said, "From the day of our arrival in Paris, we haven't been permitted to leave the confines of this hotel. Every move we make is closely scruti-

nized. We can't endure this much longer, Count Sebastiani. We haven't seen our children in many weeks. They are very young and they need us."

"My lady, I am willing to do anything in my power to help you."

"Then get us out of France right away," snapped Elgin.

"That is impossible . . . at least for a while."

"We've been humiliated long enough." Elgin fumed.

Sebastiani took a sip of brandy and leaned back against the sofa. "The First Consul has a keen memory. He will never forgive you for taking away the best sculptures on the Acropolis Hill, treasures that he himself wanted for the Louvre."

"Is this why he's holding us prisoner?" Mary gasped.

"That is one reason. Another is the war."

Elgin put down his glass. "Count Sebastiani, I repeat that we are not soldiers. Civilians are never held prisoner."

"My lord, as a student of military science, you should know that war is not governed by gentlemanly rules. Aside from this, let me remind you that your country has detained hundreds of French civilians."

Elgin's face turned scarlet; his body and hands started trembling. Fearing that he might do something extreme, she rose to her feet and addressed Sebastiani, smiling. "With your permission, I should like to sing something in your honor."

Sebastiani placed both hands on his knees and leaned forward.

"Of course, you must understand that I have no musicians to accompany me."

"What are you going to sing, my lady?"

"A French song."

"I'm delighted. Please begin."

As Elgin paced around the drawing room, still fuming, she hummed inwardly until she found the appropriate pitch. At first, her voice sounded strange to her. She had not sung at all since their last evening in Constantinople.

Allons enfants de la Patrie,
Le jour de gloire est arrivé . . .

Sebastiani stared at her in disbelief. "My lady, that is the anthem of the French Republic. You are singing 'La Marseillaise'!"

Mugir ces féroces soldats.
Ils viennent jusque dans nos bras . . .

Sebastiani leaped to his feet and stood rigidly in front of her, tears trickling down his face, his head upright, joining her in the chorus:

Aux armes, citoyens.
Formez vos bataillons.
Marchons! Marchons! . . .

At the end of the song, he seized her hand and kissed it. "That was excellent. Excellent." He put on his white gloves and walked to the door. Before stepping outside, he turned to Elgin and said, "My lord, you have my word as a French gentleman. I intend to call on the First Consul tomorrow morning and shall make a strong plea for your immediate release."

Count Sebastiani paid them a visit early the next afternoon, his face beaming with excitement. "My dear Lord and Lady Elgin, forgive me for coming here unannounced, but I have wonderful news for you."

A gnawing weakness racked her body. "Did you obtain our release, Count Sebastiani?"

Sebastiani did not remove his white gloves. Hands clasped behind his back, he walked to the bay window. "The First Consul refused to grant the request . . ."

"Is this what you consider to be wonderful news?" Elgin shouted.

Sebastiani took off his gloves and dabbed his forehead with a handkerchief. "The First Consul is about to issue an order for the transfer of all English prisoners. They are to be taken from Paris and sent into the country."

"Is this what he intends to do with us?" she asked bitterly.

Sebastiani shook his head and turned to face her. "I persuaded the First Consul to make an exception in His Lordship's case because of his poor health. The First Consul agreed, but with some reluctance, and thus the four of you have been assigned to Barèges, an excellent resort high in the Pyrenees and not too far from the Spanish border. It is famous for its hot springs and should prove beneficial for His Lordship's rheumatism and catarrh."

Tears began to well in her eyes. "Count Sebastiani, we can't endure this long separation from our children."

"It will be for only a short while."

Elgin fell into a fit of rage. "No, we have suffered enough. We refuse to go to Barèges."

"Then you will have to go into the country, like the others."

"I am an ambassador of His Britannic Majesty!"

Sebastiani put on his gloves and walked to the door. "My lord, please think about this seriously. Your health has been greatly impaired since you left Constantinople. A few weeks in Barèges will be of great therapeutic value. The war cannot last forever. If you must, look upon it as a holiday."

She followed him to the door. "When must we decide?"

"I shall have to know immediately. Otherwise, you will be taken into the country tomorrow morning. These were the First Consul's last words."

"Then we are left with no alternative, Count Sebastiani. We shall go to Barèges, but I respectfully request your word of honor that you will continue to do your utmost to obtain our eventual release."

"You have my most solemn word."

"How shall we travel to Barèges?"

"By carriage. Take whatever luggage you wish. Please be assured that you will be accorded proper treatment throughout the journey and during your entire stay at Barèges."

Elgin charged into the bedchamber, slamming the door behind him. She waited a moment and then asked, "Count Sebastiani, before you leave I have an additional favor to ask of you."

"I am your humble servant, my lady."

"I should like you to make the necessary arrangements for the release of my maid."

"That is impossible."

"But she is to be married in Scotland. Her wedding is long overdue."

"My lady, she has my deepest sympathy, but there is absolutely nothing I can do. She must accompany you to Barèges."

"What about our English friends in the hotel?"

"They have already been taken to a village about thirty miles east of here."

"All of them?"

"Except for the scientist."

"Mr. Fergusson?"

Sebastiani nodded. "The First Consul nurtures a strong respect for science. Mr. Fergusson is to be quartered here at the Richelieu and will be free to travel about as he pleases." He clicked his heels, opened the door, and bowed. "I wish you a safe and comfortable journey. *Adieu.*"

Nine

Barèges,
July 30th, 1803

My dearest mother,

At first glimpse, Barèges appears to be the most dreary place in the world — it has immense mountains but no trees. Mr. Hunt says this whole region was originally pine-forested, even to heights above six thousand feet, but continued cutting and subsequent erosion have left the place quite barren.

The real charm of Barèges lies behind these mountains. There is a carriage road which we take every morning that continues down a long and winding hill until it enters the Valley of Ossau, where most of the hot springs are located. Tourists come here from thousands of miles, seeking cures for their many ills, and I am thoroughly convinced that these hot springs have saved Elgin's life. I have never seen him in better health. He gets up at six o'clock each morning and goes shooting for partridge and duck with the Duke of Newcastle, who is also detained here with his wife. At one o'clock, he goes climbing with me, and one day soon we hope to scale the heights of Pic Long, although Mr. Hunt seeks to dissuade us, saying the mountain is at least ten thousand feet high and quite treacherous.

Elgin says the ancient Romans loved these mountains, the hundreds of therapeutic springs, the sublime climate. Only in Athens does the sun shine more brightly. The remains of Roman baths, temples, bridges, and amphitheatres still can be seen here. Grottoes are everywhere, but those of Bétharram are the most inviting. We visit them often, and each time I feel as though I am entering a glittering world of silver and gold, a mysterious planet sparkling with a million stalactites.

I am delighted that little Mary has won your heart. I knew that she would. Please give a little wine to all of them after dinner. We always made a practise of this at Constantinople, and I truly believe it is beneficial to their health. Pray tell the Greek *paramana* that I want her always to talk Greek to Bruce, not English.

In a house adjacent to ours lives la Duchess de Montmorency Chatillon. We have become good friends. I find her pleasant and extremely spirited. My father would be quite captivated indeed; she has large black eyes that pretend not to see a yard beyond a *petit nez retroussé,* a tall fine figure with good solid stumps, and is aged twenty-eight *ans!* Such is *ma très chère amie.* Her husband has been *mort* these past four years, and I recommended her taking unto herself another, but I suspect she is too wise to fall into that error a second time.

The Duchess of Newcastle is another dear friend. I cannot tell you how kind and obliging she is to me.

We play at whist almost every night, and who do you think *fait mon parti?* Why, no others than le Duc de Laval and le Comte de Marcoff, two of the best whist players in Europe. With more practise, I know not what I may come to, as they flatter me constantly and say that I play very well. But, alas, I have paid dear for my tuition, having lost eight rubbers running. My partner is a Madame Hulot, who keeps after me to play for higher stakes, but I tell her I never play above guinea whist. They want to play every day, including Sunday, but I tell them that I resisted this temptation at Constantinople and could not think of submitting to it at Barèges.

I wish my days were as occupied as the evenings. Elgin and

Hunt leave early every morning, sending me into the pits of despair and melancholy. But perhaps it is good for one to be miserable. It is one way to appreciate happiness.

I kiss my dear father's right hand and say I love him dearly. Kiss each of the bairns for me, dearest mother, and pray God that we embrace one another soon.

Your Poll

On the second day of August, the soldier on guard came to their house and informed them that the Comte de Choiseul-Gouffier would call on them at five o'clock. Mary remembered that he had served as the French Ambassador to the Porte for several years before he was recalled, and that he was one of the foremost collectors of antiquities in Europe.

"What do you suppose he wants?" she asked Elgin.

"I have no idea."

Choiseul-Gouffier made his appearance shortly after five o'clock, a pleasant-looking man neatly attired in a tight-fitting black suit and white silk shirt, his white wig heavily powdered. He carried a slender ebony cane. Elgin greeted him cordially, then invited him to sit in a chair by the window.

"It was because of my allegiance to the King that the First Consul treated me so unkindly," Choiseul-Gouffier recounted, "but after I returned from exile he forgave me and granted me a small villa outside Paris. I entreated him to return my titles and possessions, but he refused, and now I am penniless."

"My dear Comte," said Elgin, "how did you know that we were confined in Barèges?"

"Charles-Maurice told me. It was he who sent me here."

"Who?"

"Talleyrand. We have been the closest of friends from the time we were students at the Collège d'Harcourt. His parents neglected him terribly and hardly ever came to visit him. He had no one else but me. Yes, our friendship has endured all these years."

Elgin walked to the window. "Tell me, why did you travel such a great distance to see me?"

Choiseul-Gouffier touched his eyes with a silk handkerchief, then tucked it back into the sleeve of his coat. "My Lord Excellency, I came here to seek your help."

Elgin laughed sourly. "How can I possibly help you? I am a prisoner here."

The Frenchman's eyes became wet again. "My Lord Excellency, I refer particularly to one of my prize acquisitions . . ."

"I know all about it," Elgin interrupted sharply. "You were the first to take down a complete metope from the Parthenon, a whole section of the frieze."

Choiseul-Gouffier stared down at the floor. "Yes, my agent and his workers hauled it to the Piraeus, where it was brought on board the French frigate *L'Arabe*. The ship was out of port only one day when war broke out, and *L'Arabe* was captured by the British warship *Maidstone*. As Your Lordship knows, it is the law of the prize that the value of any enemy property captured must be divided equally among the officers and crew of the ship. *L'Arabe* was sold at auction in Malta, but my frieze was not included in the prize."

"What happened to it?"

"Lord Nelson sent it to England."

Elgin's eyes narrowed. "Are you saying that this frieze is now in England?"

"Yes. It is being held at the Customs House in London. This is the purpose of my visit — to appeal for your assistance."

"My assistance?"

"It is a known fact that you exert a great deal of influence with Lord Keith, Commander of the Mediterranean Fleet."

"So?"

"As Lord Nelson's superior, Admiral Lord Keith can issue an order to have my frieze returned."

"My dear Comte, you are asking the impossible. How can I

get in touch with Lord Keith from here? Barèges is the most remote place in the world."

"Your Lordship can write a letter to Lord Keith, tell him the frieze rightfully belongs to me . . . that Lord Nelson should never have confiscated it."

Elgin looked out the window, his eyes drawn to the distant mountains.

"Your Lordship can tell Lord Keith that I shall be willing to pay for the frieze," Choiseul-Gouffier pleaded.

Mary gave him a sympathetic look. "But you just told us that you are penniless."

"The money will be found. I will do anything to get my frieze."

Elgin turned away from the window and drew near the Frenchman, his hand extended. "You need not worry about this matter any longer."

Choiseul-Gouffier jumped to his feet and embraced him. "You will do it? You will help me?"

Elgin wrestled free from the Frenchman's grasp. Straightening out the sleeves of his coat, he said, "I shall write to Lord Keith today and ask him to make every effort to have the frieze returned to you."

Choiseul-Gouffier's eyes were flooded with tears as they escorted him to the door. He kissed Mary's hand and bowed many times, slowly moving away from them, never turning his back until he was lost behind the trees in the yard.

As soon as Elgin closed the door, she said, "Why did you lie to that poor man?"

Elgin's face twisted into a cynical smile.

"Eggy, you made a solemn promise to him."

He started pacing around the drawing room floor, hands clasped behind his back.

"You know perfectly well that you have no intention of carrying it out."

Elgin unhooked his musket from the wall. "That damned Frenchman, wasting all my time with his petty problems. Now it's too late to go duck-shooting with Newcastle."

The next day, Elgin left early for his visit to the hot baths, and for the rest of the afternoon Mary's thoughts fled to Archerfield. She wondered what her children were doing at that exact moment, what they were wearing, how Calitza was managing in a foreign country. She envisioned Bruce scampering through the tall summer grass, chasing after Boxer.

Unlike their rooms at the Richelieu, their cottage in Barèges had a stove and all the necessary cooking utensils. The pantry was stocked with food, and because of Elgin's fine marksmanship, they dined on roast duck or partridge at least once a week. Masterman was becoming quite proficient in preparing dinner every evening, using herbs and spices and even adding wine to various dishes. One of the soldiers regularly brought them supplies of rice, flour, sugar, and tea. A loaf of freshly baked bread was delivered quietly to their door every morning.

Two days after the visit of Choiseul-Gouffier, Elgin received a letter posted from Edinburgh. It was from Captain Maling, and after reading it hastily, he tossed it on the floor.

"What does Captain Maling say?" Mary asked.

"Only that he delivered the children safely to Archerfield."

She picked up the letter and read it.

"The damned fool." Elgin growled. "He was specifically instructed to take a complete inventory of the Parthenon marbles at Park Lane before going on to Scotland. I stressed its importance at least a dozen times."

She placed the letter on the table. "I wish you showed the same concern over the children."

"You read the letter. They are safely in Scotland with your parents."

"You care more about those marbles . . . you always have."

She had no desire to go for a walk that afternoon. As soon as Elgin left the cottage with Hunt, she retired to her bedchamber and escaped once again to Archerfield, to that glorious shrine rising from the mist surrounding Aberlady, her father's house reaching out to her, the tall oaks in the north meadow, the heather swaying in the gentle breeze, her children streaking toward her, gleefully shouting in Greek, "Mother! Mother!"

They were transferred from Barèges on the last day of August, moving into a large winter house in the neighboring town of Pau, where the cold winds were less furious and life still bloomed in the deep, rich valleys. Elgin did not welcome the change, and every day he moaned the loss of his hunting companion, the Duke of Newcastle, who was sent to Lourdes, together with his wife. In only two weeks, Mary noticed the marked change. Deprived of his hot baths, Elgin began to complain about his stiff joints. She suggested that this could very well have been brought about by his inactivity, and urged him to go hunting by himself, but he preferred to wallow in his misery. In the afternoons, he refused to take walks with her through the quaint and narrow streets of Pau, and sulking in his chair in the sitting room, he grew so irritable and ill-tempered, everyone kept away from him.

The tension was relieved by the unexpected visit of Count Sebastiani, who appeared at their threshold on the morning of September fifteenth. He looked more debonair than ever in his white uniform and red sash drawn across the chest, and after greeting them warmly, he turned to her and said, "My lady, I am pleased to inform you that the First Consul relented and has now agreed to grant safe passage to England for your maid."

Masterman's face became pale, and she asked to be excused. After she left the room, Elgin turned to Sebastiani. "What about us?"

"The First Consul has decided to keep you in France in an unofficial capacity."

"I don't understand."

"Since Lord Whitworth abandoned his embassy, Your Lordship has been chosen to act as the British Ambassador to the Republic."

Elgin ignited. "You can tell the First Consul that I accept my appointments only from the King of England."

Mary struggled to ward off her dejection. "Count Sebastiani, you promised to bring us good news after the summer."

"But I have brought you good news. Your maid can now return to Scotland and marry."

"But we too want to return to Scotland. We can't bear this interminable separation from our children."

"My lady, you must believe me. I have done my utmost. The First Consul is the only one who can effect your release. You shall have to be patient and take one step at a time. Meanwhile, Pau is a pleasant town. There are many ways to occupy yourselves in the winter, and above all, the climate will be beneficial to His Lordship's health."

"I want the truth," ranted Elgin. "Is Bonaparte ever to release us?"

"That depends on the war situation. Once peace is restored, everyone will be released."

She had heard all this before. It was pointless to go on. "When is my maid permitted to leave France?"

"Any time she pleases. Her papers are in order and waiting for her at Talleyrand's office in the Palais du Luxembourg."

"How long do you plan to remain in Pau, Count Sebastiani?"

"Only for a few days."

Masterman returned to the sitting room, looking infinitely better. "My lady, shall I prepare a bit of lunch?"

Mary glanced toward Sebastiani. "Will you join us?"

"I shall be honored."

Hunt went to the pantry and brought back two bottles of Bordeaux wine. During the meal, Sebastiani drank freely. Declining the dessert, he tilted his chair back and twittered, "My lord, perhaps you would like to hear what the people of the Republic think about you."

"They don't even know me," said Elgin.

"That is not true. They are well aware of your activities in Constantinople, how you attempted to deceive the French command at El-Arish."

"Preposterous. I'm the only one who came out of that muddle with any sense of honor."

Sebastiani filled his glass again. "The French people choose to believe otherwise. They say that you deliberately ill-treated French prisoners in Turkey and that you caused a French diplomat named Beauchamp to be put to death."

Elgin leaned forward on his elbows, face scarlet. "That is an abominable lie! I intervened favorably with the Porte to relieve the sufferings of those prisoners, and, in fact, I paid several visits to the Seven Towers to make certain that my request was carried out. As for Beauchamp, it was Sir Sydney Smith who wanted him beheaded. Not only did I rescue Beauchamp, but I gave him money and a passport to France."

She was bewildered by Sebastiani's attitude. He was purposely goading Elgin, contriving in every way to upset him.

"My lord, you spent a great deal of time in Barèges. During your stay there, did any Frenchmen converse with you."

"I did not care to have them converse with me."

"Surely you must have thought this strange, the way they shunned your company?"

She pushed back her chair and stood up. "Count Sebastiani, I think we should put an end to this conversation."

"Please sit down," said Elgin. "I want him to go on."

"The fact is, my lord, they dreaded to come near you," continued Sebastiani, helping himself to more wine.

"Why?"

"They were afraid you would contaminate them."

"With what?"

"The pox."

Elgin leaped from his chair and seized Sebastiani by the neck with both hands. With Hunt's help, Mary attempted to pull him away, but they could not deal with his strength. Suddenly, he released his right hand and sent a swift blow to Sebastiani's face, knocking him to the floor. She was horrified. Taking her napkin, she started to wipe away the blood from Sebastiani's mouth, but he shook his head and rose to his feet. There were bloodstains on his uniform.

All this time, Elgin stood by the table, shaking horribly, a confounded look frozen on his face.

At dusk, a contingent of French soldiers burst into the house, pulled Elgin out of his chair in the sitting room, ordered him to dress, then took him under guard to a waiting carriage. Mary demanded to know where they were taking him, but the soldiers instructed her to return to the house. As the horses bolted off, she felt a hand on her arm. It was the young soldier who kept guard outside their house. "*Citoyenne,* I know where they are taking your husband. He is to be confined inside the prison at Lourdes. It is a grave offense to strike a high official of the Republic. It could mean the death penalty."

Hunt and Masterman were waiting for her on the porch. In a choking voice, she said, "Mr. Hunt, Count Sebastiani is still in Pau. Please go to him right away and tell him that I am terribly sorry for what happened. Explain to him that His Lordship has been in ill health."

"Yes, my lady."

"The soldier on guard will understand. Ask him where Count Sebastiani is staying."

"Yes, my lady."

"Hurry, Mr. Hunt. You must speak to Count Sebastiani before he leaves for Paris."

After Hunt left the house, Masterman brewed a pot of tea and encouraged her to take a cup. They sat together at the round table in the kitchen, the small lamp sputtering under their faces, neither of them saying a word.

Hunt did not return until ten o'clock. He had a grave look on his face. "My lady, Count Sebastiani was reluctant to see me, but I was persistent."

"Tell me, what did he say?"

"He is still extremely upset, my lady. Nevertheless, he was attentive when I reminded him of His Lordship's ill health."

"What else?"

"He will recommend that the death penalty not be invoked."

"Did he say how long His Lordship will remain confined at Lourdes?"

"For an indefinite period, I'm afraid."

She stood up. "Mr. Hunt, I want you to make immediate preparations for a journey."

"A journey?"

"We're leaving for Paris tomorrow morning."

"But why does Your Ladyship want to travel to Paris?"

"It is urgent that I see Monsieur Talleyrand. He is the only one who can help us."

Hunt nodded nervously. "That's an excellent thought, my lady, and if I may offer a further suggestion, we could also collect Masterman's papers from Monsieur Talleyrand."

"Yes."

"How much luggage should we take?"

"We must travel as lightly as possible, Mr. Hunt."

"What about the soldier on guard?"

"He will grant us permission. Should he object, tell him that I will sign a document assuring him of our return."

"But what if he asks for a warranty?"

"Mr. Hunt, I would never leave this country without my husband. There is no better warranty than that."

Masterman's voice sounded troubled. "Shall I be taking all my belongings, my lady?"

"Only what's necessary. We shall send everything else later."

"I think that Your Ladyship should reconsider before taking such a long journey. After all, you're with child."

"Masterman, we're wasting valuable time. Start packing. We must be ready to leave first thing in the morning."

They entered Rabastens late the next afternoon. After a fitful sleep, Mary awoke early and was eager to move on, but Masterman insisted that they have a substantial breakfast, and she refused to leave until everyone finished eating. The moment they set off, it started to rain, a hard drenching downpour lashed by fierce winds. Nevertheless, the horses made excellent time, never letting up as they splashed over the gutted roads and deep puddles. Several times Hunt picked out certain points of interest and attempted to elaborate on them, but Mary was in no mood to listen.

She slept hardly at all that night, and at breakfast, she had no appetite for food. In the carriage, she leaned her head back and managed to sleep for a brief time, but the rattling of the wheels jounced her awake. The rain was coming down much harder now, and the driver had to pull back on the reins because of the flooded road and poor visibility. At noon, the storm clouds became perforated with patches of blue, and soon the sun began pouring its warmth over the land. Quite surprisingly, the road dried off within an hour, and the horses regained most of the time lost, speeding them into Limoges, where they found lodgings in a badly maintained inn that reeked of rancid cooking odors. Her bed was abominably uncomfortable, and she had to

abandon it in the middle of the night, moving to the lumpy sofa at the other end of the room.

Not a soul was in sight when they prepared to leave in the morning. Hunt, very much irritated over their poor treatment, wanted to depart without paying, but she firmly instructed him to leave ten francs on one of the beds.

After they stopped at the small village of Ambazac for tea and cakes, Hunt arranged for a fresh set of horses — two snorting white beasts who put up a hard contest before they were attached to the carriage. The owner of the ramshackle stable balked at Hunt's offer for the exchange, claiming the tired horses were old and had seen their best day, but Hunt adamantly refused to pay him the fifteen francs he demanded. The old proprietor was just as stubborn, holding his ground and insisting that Hunt at least pay him an additional two francs for the oats consumed by the fresh horses. They finally agreed on one franc for the oats and ten francs for the exchange.

Straining and tugging at the reins, the fresh horses brought the carriage into Orléans much sooner than expected. This time, Hunt was determined to be more assiduous in his quest for lodgings, and the guest house that he eventually located proved to be quite comfortable and clean.

Mary slept soundly that night, and awoke in better spirits. They breakfasted on croissants with sweet creamery butter, some jam, and ass's milk. The proprietor of the inn was a plump and kindly woman who preferred to be called Lily, with the accent on the *y*. Hunt was unable to restrain himself when they climbed into the carriage. "Can you imagine that Gibraltar of a woman carrying on so vainly? Lil*y*, indeed!"

They arrived at Chartres in the middle of the day. Everyone felt hungry. High atop the hill that was crowned by the medieval cathedral, they found an old restaurant whose rear windows overlooked the River Eure. Hunt selected a dish for all of them, then, in a hushed, awe-filled voice, said to her, "My lady, that is

one of the most admired Gothic churches in Christendom."

"How old is it?" asked Masterman.

"It was built in the eleventh century, on the very site of an earlier church that was destroyed by fire."

Masterman's attention flitted to one of the young waiters at the adjacent table, a handsome lad with wavy blond hair and an infectious smile.

Hunt's voice droned on. "Another conflagration laid waste the new structure even before it was completed, but clergy and congregation set themselves to work, and it was at last finished in the year 1240."

The fish was superbly prepared, the vegetable casserole cooked to perfection. Glancing through the window, Mary was entranced by the verdant plains sprawled along both banks of the river.

"Those are the farmlands of Beauce," observed Hunt. "The Eure divides into three branches not too far from here. Travelers can cross into the plains by several bridges, many of which were constructed by the ancient Romans."

She was fascinated by the way the Eure cut through the steep and narrow streets of the town, mirroring the graceful willows and multicolored houses.

"Chartres was sacked by the Normans soon after the cathedral was erected," Hunt droned on, "and subsequently the town was conquered by the British, attacked by the Protestants, and finally taken by Henry the Fourth."

Masterman pulled her eyes away from the young waiter and looked down at her plate. "What kind of fish is this, Mr. Hunt?"

"Fresh brook trout."

Masterman put down her fork. "My lady, I think I should go back to the carriage and look after the luggage."

"But you didn't finish eating."

"I'm not very hungry."

"You do look a bit tired, Masterman. Perhaps you should try

to take a little nap in the carriage while you're waiting for us."

"Yes, my lady."

After the maid left the table, Hunt remarked, "Masterman seems very ill at ease of late."

She smiled. "Every bride is nervous when her wedding day approaches."

Hunt became lost in thought.

"Mr. Hunt, what do you know about Talleyrand?"

Hunt put down his fork and knife. "My lady, I can only say that Talleyrand is one of the greatest statesmen the world has ever known. The First Consul was most eager to have him serve as his Foreign Minister, but before accepting the post, Talleyrand weighed the offer carefully, because he had to be certain about the aims and ideals of the Republic."

"What do you suppose his annual stipend might be?"

Hunt brought up his eyes in disbelief. "My lady, Talleyrand is undeniably a most dedicated and honest man. Bribery is out of the question."

She pushed back her chair and stood up. "Please forgive me, Mr. Hunt. It was foolish of me to infer this. It's just that I so desperately want to find a way to reach Talleyrand."

"But you already possess a way."

"What's that?"

"Your unmatched beauty, my lady."

She was granted an audience with Talleyrand on the third day after their arrival in Paris. His rooms were on the second story of the Palais du Luxembourg, a place of hectic activity, with men scurrying over the marble floor, officers everywhere, soldiers climbing up and down the spotless marble staircase. She had to wait almost an hour before the young adjutant escorted her into Talleyrand's study. He was sitting at an enormous desk, writing on a sheet of paper, but when the adjutant tapped him

on the shoulder, he straightened up immediately. He had some difficulty getting to his feet and had to rely on a sturdy walnut cane to limp toward her. The shoe on his bad leg was rounded, and a metal brace ran up the leg as far as the knee. Nevertheless, he made a most charming appearance in his brown velvet suit with its upturned collar. Bowing before her, he kissed her hand and said, "Madame, I am honored."

The adjutant placed a chair next to the desk and invited her to sit. He started to assist Talleyrand back to his chair, but the Foreign Minister impatiently waved him off. As soon as they were alone, he said, "Tell me, why did you undertake this long journey?"

"Your Excellency, I came here to seek your help in having my husband released from prison."

"Indeed, you must love your husband dearly." Talleyrand shifted forward in his chair and looked at her closely. "We are not barbarians, but on the other hand, we cannot easily brush aside the fact that Lord Elgin assaulted a high official of the Republic, and for this, punishment is necessary. However, I reviewed the matter carefully and found the death penalty too severe."

"Your Excellency, he is a sick man. He cannot endure confinement in a prison."

"He will be released in due time. As you know, this rests entirely with the First Consul. I need not remind you that he still finds it difficult to forgive Lord Elgin for taking away the Parthenon marbles."

"But he has been in ill health for many months. The First Consul should consider this."

Talleyrand brought up his hands, smiling broadly. "We know all about His Lordship's ailments. He has deluged us with his long and frequent letters. It was for this reason that we permitted him to go to Barèges. Indeed, he should be grateful."

"We have been separated from our children a long time."

"I understand, and you have my heartfelt sympathy, but as I just informed you, this case is entirely in the First Consul's hands." Suddenly his eyes glinted. "Of course, if the British Government and His Lordship would consider, there are two options that could help effect his release. The first relates to General Boyer, who is imprisoned in London. If the British Government would agree, we could grant you freedom for the exchange of General Boyer."

Her spirits were lifted. "I shall write to Lord Hawksbury today and request the exchange. What is the other option?"

Talleyrand lowered his eyes. "If Lord Elgin is willing to cede the Parthenon marbles . . ."

"I'm afraid he would never do that," she replied, getting up from the chair. Talleyrand opened one of the drawers of his desk and pulled out a folded document. "I have here the necessary paper that will assure your maid's safe conduct out of France."

"Thank you, Your Excellency." She took the document and put it into her reticule.

Talleyrand stood up. "You have my solemn word that His Lordship will be accorded kind treatment at the prison in Lourdes." Hobbling to the door, he opened it for her. "*Au revoir,* my lady. I hope you do not think unkindly of us. We are not savages. Indeed, we are not savages."

When Mary awoke the next morning, she found Masterman standing at the bay window, her eyes fastened on the street below. Birds chirped in the magnolia trees; the day was clear and warm.

"Are you packed and ready to leave, Masterman?"

"Yes."

"Did you have breakfast?"

"I'm not hungry."

"But you should eat something. You have a long journey before you."

"I wish Mr. Hunt would arrive with the carriage."

"He will be here soon. Stop fretting."

"Does Your Ladyship want me to prepare breakfast?"

"I'll eat later, Masterman, after you leave. Please come here by the sofa and sit with me. We have only a short time left, and I'd like to talk with you."

"What about?"

"We've been together for such a long time, Masterman, I don't know how I shall be able to manage without you."

"Mr. Hunt has already procured the services of another maid. He's told me everything about her. She comes highly recommended."

"Yes, of course."

"Mr. Hunt will be bringing her here with the carriage. She is to assume her duties the moment I leave."

"Do you have your letter of safe-conduct?"

"Indeed I do. It's here, in my purse."

"And the money?"

"That too."

She reached out and took hold of Masterman's hand. "We shall all have a grand reunion in Scotland, Masterman."

"Yes, my lady."

"Masterman, I should like to ask a favor of you."

"I am Your Ladyship's humble servant."

"Could you stop by Archerfield at some time and pay a brief visit with the children?"

"I should be delighted."

"And would you write to me after you see them, tell me how they are, what they look like?"

"But Your Ladyship's mother insists they are all in good health."

"I want your opinion also, Masterman."

"Of course."

"Masterman . . ."

"Yes, my lady?"

Mary released her hand, then looked at her intently. "All this time we have been together, and I never once thought about asking you what your first name was."

"It's Hortense, my lady."

Mary embraced her. "You will always be Masterman to me."

"I prefer that too. I hate Hortense. It was my grandmother's name. She was the black sheep of the family . . . ran off with an English sailor after giving birth to my mother."

Mary smiled. "Why did your mother christen you with that name?"

"It was the custom. She was bound to it and had no other choice."

Mary stood up. "I think I hear the carriage outside."

Masterman hurried to the window. "Yes, the carriage is here. I can see Mr. Hunt. Look, he's waving. And there is Félicité, Your Ladyship's new maid. I must say, she's quite comely."

Mary picked up one of the valises and headed for the door. Masterman was horrified. "My lady, I beg you . . . put that valise down."

"It's not heavy."

"I can carry both of them. In the name of God, what would Félicité think of me, treating Your Ladyship like that?"

Outside, Mary spoke softly to the new maid while Hunt carried the two valises to the carriage. "Your name is Félicité?"

"Yes, my lady. It is a great honor for me to be here."

"Where did you learn to speak English?"

Masterman whispered, "Félicité was for six years employed in the household of the former Ambassador to France."

"Lord Whitworth?"

"Yes, my lady."

Mary turned to Félicité once again. She was a demure young

woman, with raven hair cut scandalously short. "Félicité, I have a few questions to ask you."

"Yes, my lady."

"But first, I should like to introduce you to my former maid and dearest friend, Masterman."

"I am pleased to make her acquaintance."

"And I likewise," said Masterman, nodding politely. Hunt was having trouble with the luggage, and the driver had to come down to help him.

"What did Your Ladyship wish to ask me?" said Félicité.

"Are you promised to anyone?"

"I do not understand."

"Are you engaged to be married?"

"No, my lady."

"What about children; do you like them?"

"Very much."

Masterman walked to the carriage and impatiently waited while Hunt and the driver worked with the luggage.

"Am I accepted, my lady?" asked Félicité.

"What did you say?"

"Does Your Ladyship accept me as the new maid?"

"Yes, of course. Please take your valise inside and wait for me in the front hallway."

Mary watched her climb up the front steps of the Richelieu. Her blue gingham dress fitted so snugly, it accentuated every contour of her body. Glancing toward the carriage, she noticed that the driver had stopped working, his eyes following every step Félicité took.

In time, the luggage was securely attached to the rear of the carriage, and the driver climbed to his seat. Hunt bade Masterman good-by, and as they both fumbled for words, Mary rushed forward and blurted, "Masterman, I shall never forget you . . . never."

Masterman slumped into Mary's arms, and Mary kissed her

on both cheeks. "You won't forget to visit the children at Archerfield?"

"No, my lady," moaned Masterman. Tears were streaming down her face.

"Good-by, Masterman. God be with you."

"I shall pray for His Lordship's quick release from prison, my lady . . ."

Mary waited until she climbed into the carriage, then extended both hands to her. Masterman clasped them and kissed them tearfully; then with a loud command, the driver lashed out his whip, and the horses reared back. Another lash and they vaulted forward, speeding down the cobbled street, tails flying. At the corner of the Palais-Royal, the carriage slowed down to make the turn, but before it disappeared from view, Mary caught sight of Masterman's thin arm waving from the window.

Ten

SHE WOULD never forget that terribly cold winter day when Elgin was finally released from prison and brought to the house at Pau, his body gaunt and hunched, his face deathly white except for the blotchy remains of his nose. His first words were "Who gave you leave to go to Paris without my approval?"

"Eggy, I wrote and told you about it. We went there in your behalf. I wanted to speak privately with Talleyrand."

"And we also obtained Masterman's letter of safe-conduct," added Hunt.

Elgin glared at her. "What did Talleyrand say to you?"

She was afraid to look at him. "He offered us two options for freedom. One involved the British Government, and depended upon their willingness to agree to an exchange between you and a French general named Boyer, who is imprisoned in London. I wrote to Lord Hawksbury and requested him to accept the exchange."

"What was his reply?"

Slowly, she walked to the writing desk and pulled out Hawksbury's letter from the top drawer. "I considered sending this to you while you were in prison . . ."

"What did Hawksbury say? Read it."

Her hands shook as she brought the letter close to the window and read:

Downing Street,
24 November, 1803

Madam,

Please forgive the long delay in answering Your Ladyship's letter, which, owing to the press of Government matters, I was unable to lay before His Majesty until recently.

It would have given His Majesty the most sincere satisfaction to contribute to the release of Lord Elgin by allowing his exchange for General Boyer, who is confined here in London, but a sense of duty renders it impossible for Him in any way to admit or sanction the principle of exchanging persons made prisoners according to the laws of war, against any of His own subjects who have been detained in France in violation of the law of nations and of the pledged faith of the French Government.

I can assure Your Ladyship that it is with the deepest regret that I find myself unable to render you the assistance you desire. I should have felt the greatest pleasure in contributing by any practicable means to Lord Elgin's release, and to the deliverance of Your Ladyship and His Lordship from the very unpleasant situation in which you have been placed by arbitrary proceedings of the French Government.

I have the honour to be,
Hawksbury

There was a deep silence.

"What was Talleyrand's second option?" Elgin snapped.

"Eggy, I don't think that you want to hear it."

"In God's name, must I beg you?"

"Talleyrand said that we could obtain our immediate freedom . . . if you agreed to cede the Parthenon marbles to Napoleon Bonaparte."

He gave her a sour look.

She moved closer to the window and peered at the snow-capped mountains in the distance. "Eggy, I wish you would consider it seriously. Surely you don't value those marbles more than our freedom?"

He ignited. "For the last time, I don't want you meddling in my business. I've sacrificed everything to get those marbles. They will never leave my possession." Suddenly his gaze fell on Félicité. "Who is she?"

"My lord," volunteered Hunt, "she is Her Ladyship's new maid. Her name is Félicité."

"Where is Masterman?"

Mary swung sharply around. "Eggy, I've already told you. She departed for Scotland."

Elgin took several steps toward Félicité. She made no motion to turn her face away. Bowing, she said, "It is a great honor to be employed in this household."

Elgin straightened his shoulders.

After dinner, he asked Mary abruptly, "Where did you stay in Paris?"

"At the Richelieu."

He said nothing further.

Little William opened his eyes on the fourth day of March, 1804. It was snowing heavily. Mary had never experienced a more dreadful winter — those long cold nights without her children, without Masterman. Félicité was unstinting in her efforts to attend to her, but she was not Masterman. Hunt too lost much of his zeal, becoming morose and sullen, speaking only when asked a direct question.

Late in the spring, they left Pau and returned to the same cottage they had occupied at Barèges. The weather there was un-

seasonably hot, and Mary cautioned Félicité to dress little William in the lightest of clothing and to be very watchful in protecting his skin from the burning rays of the sun. Within a short time, Elgin regained some of his lost flesh, and eventually he started making daily visits to the baths.

One evening after dinner, he went abruptly to the writing table in the front room. His feverish movements worried her. Crumpling sheet after sheet of paper in his fist, he growled, "I can't understand why my mother hasn't responded to my letters. Three times, I wrote to her, detailing exactly what she has to do to get Choiseul-Gouffier's frieze out of the London Customs House. Doesn't she realize that it keeps accumulating heavy duty charges every day?"

The next morning, Hunt returned from the village with the announcement that their Paris friends had been reassigned to Barèges. Elgin asked, "Are all of them here?"

"Except for Mrs. Fitzgerald. She passed away two weeks after Yule Day."

"Oh, I'm sorry to hear that," said Mary.

"What about Robert Fergusson?" inquired Elgin.

"Mr. Fergusson is not here either. He is still in Paris. My lady, I would like to suggest that we invite them for dinner this evening."

"That's very thoughtful of you, Mr. Hunt."

"Your Ladyship is agreeable then?"

"Of course. I'm most eager to see them."

At dinner, after several toasts from their friends, Elgin spoke for the first time about his long confinement in the prison at Lourdes. "No sooner was I thrown into my cell than I was told by the commandant that I had to pay for my own bed and linens. Then, on the afternoon of the next day, a sergeant-of-the-guard came to my cell and handed me a letter that was purportedly from another prisoner. It said that if I wished to talk to this prisoner, I could do so from the window of my cell that was adjacent to his. I called back the sergeant and warned that if he

or anyone else dared bring me another unofficial letter, I would notify the commandant at once. The following afternoon, someone tossed a packet of letters into my cell from the window. They were from the same prisoner. One letter attested that he had been caught in an attempt to set fire to the French fleet at Brest. He begged me to forward all the letters to the Comte d'Artois, who is the leader of the anti-Bonapartist movement in England."

"What did Your Lordship do about this?" asked Mr. Sterling, leaning forward with his elbows on the table.

"Absolutely nothing," replied Elgin hoarsely. "I saw through the treacherous scheme."

"I don't understand."

"Bonaparte was baiting me. It was all a ruse, an attempt to get me involved in a crime of treason against the Republic."

"Thank God, Your Lordship did not succumb to it," said Mrs. Keith Stuart, shuddering.

Elgin poured more wine into the glasses. "I understand that Robert Fergusson is still in Paris."

"Indeed he is."

"Is he staying at the Richelieu?"

"Yes."

Mrs. Cockburn fondly touched Mary on the wrist. "In all the bustle, we neglected to ask about Your Ladyship's baby."

"He's in excellent health, Mrs. Cockburn."

"What is his name?"

"William."

"Is he sleeping now?"

"Yes. I could ask Félicité to bring him out here, but he had some difficulty sleeping last night, and I think I should not disturb him."

"I understand. We can see him tomorrow or the next day."

"Did the other children reach Scotland safely?" asked Mrs. Keith Stuart.

"Yes, they are with my parents at Archerfield."

Mrs. Keith Stuart scraped her chair closer and whispered, "His Lordship looks fit, considering his harrowing experience."

"Yes, he suffered a great deal during his confinement, Mrs. Keith Stuart."

"I think it's unpardonable, throwing a man of His Lordship's station in prison."

"Are you to remain in Barèges through the summer season?"

"We hope to."

Colonel Crawford put his hand to his mouth and coughed. "I wonder if you are aware of the talk in London about His Lordship's activities in Athens."

"What kind of talk?" she asked.

"It has been published in all the newspapers. The presence of the Parthenon marbles has touched off a furor of debate. His Lordship is being castigated everywhere, and particularly by Richard Payne Knight."

"Who is he?"

Elgin slammed his glass on the table. "He is an idiot . . . a damned idiot!"

Colonel Crawford stared at him for a moment, then cleared his throat once more and went on, "Knight is perhaps England's foremost patron of the arts. His reputation and influence are felt throughout every art circle in Europe. Not too long ago, he wrote a diary of a journey to Sicily that so impressed Goethe, he arranged to have it published in Germany. His newest book has already received wide acclaim. It is called *An Analytic Inquiry into the Principles of Taste*."

"And what conclusions does he draw, Colonel Crawford?" asked Mary.

"He claims that ideal beauty rarely exists."

"That is a strange statement for a patron of the arts."

Colonel Crawford flashed her a smile. "Knight does concede that there are certain standards of excellence, such as the precious remains of Greek sculpture, which afford an essence of grace and elegance that can never be questioned."

"I didn't know that you were interested in Greek sculpture," snapped Elgin.

"Very much so."

"I dare say," Mrs. Keith Stuart bubbled, "Colonel Crawford has an avid devotion to art."

Colonel Crawford kept his eyes on Mary. "Not long after the arrival of Lord Elgin's collection of marbles, Knight personally went to the museum at Park Lane to inspect them."

"What was his reaction?"

"He concluded that they were not Greek, but Roman . . . of the time of Hadrian."

Elgin stormed into the bedchamber, cursing. Suddenly Mary felt faint. She heard Mrs. Keith Stuart asking, "My lady, you look pale. Are you ill?"

She shook her head, dazed.

Mrs. Keith Stuart reached over and handed her a glass of brandy. She brought it to her lips but managed only one sip. Rising unsteadily from the table, she invited everyone into the sitting room for tea.

The next morning, Elgin summoned a young physician from Pau, who examined Mary and diagnosed the condition as acute fatigue brought on by the birth of little William. He sternly advised against another pregnancy and, before leaving, suggested that she avoid excessive physical activity for at least a month and that she take one full glass of wine before each meal. During the recuperation, Félicité took admirably to her duties and was especially attentive to little William, spending most of the day with him, changing and dressing him, feeding him, putting him in the carriage, and sitting with him under the shade of the linden trees in the yard.

On the seventh day of July, Mary received a packet of letters from her mother. Mrs. Nisbet now spoke fondly of Calitza, and

even went so far as to say there were no English nurses to compare with her. It pleased Mary to hear that Bruce, in particular, was keeping diligently to his study of Greek. Her heart skipped when she recalled the lad's first salutation every morning in Constantinople — "Good morning, mother. I love you." Such impeccable Greek. And little Mary trying her best to emulate him, her lips moving with each syllable, stumbling but not giving up.

Three days later, Elgin received an unexpected letter from Professor Carlyle's sister in London:

June 14th, 1804

My dear Lord Elgin,

Please be informed that my brother, Joseph Dacre Carlyle, passed away last month. I need not tell you that his death was a great loss and disappointment. Soon after he returned to England, he resumed the quiet life of a scholar, his chief concern being the preparation of a new edition of the New Testament, aided by the manuscripts he had brought back from Constantinople and the Princes Isles. It was his further intention to publish a book of verses and journals from the many notes he compiled while serving in Your Lordship's embassy.

At his own expense, he gathered numerous scholars and theologians and set them to work on this huge task of collation and editing, assisting them by having printed a memorandum that he entitled "Hints and Observations which Mr. Carlyle takes the Liberty of suggesting to the Consideration of the Gentlemen who have kindly promised their Assistance in Collating the Greek Mss. of the New Testament."

Five of the manuscripts were marked *S* as coming from Syria. Four were marked *C* for Constantinople, and eighteen *I* for Princes Isles. My brother mentioned in his "Hints and Observations" that some manuscripts belonged to the Patriarch of Jerusalem, but he did not make clear precisely which ones.

A few weeks after the work of collation began, my brother fell gravely ill and died. As his sister and lone survivor, I find

it my duty to bring to Your Lordship's attention the following matters:

Joseph's journey to the East made severe inroads into his fortune, and all he had to show for this were these manuscripts. As executrix of his estate, I arranged to have published a posthumous edition of his poems, with a public subscription that included the great names of England. The book has enjoyed a modest sale, but hardly enough to defray the burden of Joseph's enormous debts. For this reason, I decided to sell his manuscripts. The Syrian collection was sold to the East India Company and is now deposited in their library. The others went to the Archbishop of Canterbury, who has deposited them in his library at Lambeth.

I could not have fixed upon a more agreeable person than the Archbishop. Although it gave me great pain to separate what cost my brother so dearly to collect, circumstances entitled me to accept the Archbishop's generous compensation. I was fortified in this action by my brother's dying words, stated clearly and emphatically, that his unfortunate journey to the East had been attended with a great pecuniary loss to his family and that I must derive whatever I can from the sale of the manuscripts.

Believe me to be,
Sarah S. Carlyle

Elgin read the letter once more, then flew into a rage. "That silly fool, she had no right to sell those manuscripts. They belong to me. My name was affixed to the promissory note."

"The note that assured their safe return," Mary added caustically.

He was not listening to her. "That irresponsible, desiccated woman!"

She was worried about little William. Although the child had a wonderful disposition, he ate like a sparrow and was constantly

plagued by a looseness of bowels. Elgin showed concern, but at the same time assured her the problem was not serious, stating that it was not uncommon for infants to suffer from such ailments.

However, when little William's symptoms persisted, she asked Félicité to bundle him up in the carriage, and together they traveled to Pau for a consultation with the young physician. The child was pronounced fit, but Mary was told to take him on periodic visits to the baths to ensure his having a sound constitution. As for the looseness of bowels, the doctor prescribed a diet of boiled rice three times a day for one whole week.

On the last day of August, they were told by the sergeant-of-the-guard that they were to be reassigned to Paris in two days. Their English friends received the same notice.

Their last evening in Barèges was spent at the Cockburns' cottage. Everyone was in good humor, including Mr. Sterling, and after the dessert, Colonel Crawford entertained them with a humorous account of his experiences in Egypt and the Far East.

When they returned to their cottage, they found an envelope wedged under the door. Elgin pulled it free and brought it inside. He lighted a taper, then went to his desk and tore open the envelope. Mary drew closer and leaned over his shoulder. It was a page from *The Times* containing a large cartoon — poor and starving people crowded around an English gentleman who was proudly pointing to a large collection of crippled and maimed figures carved in marble. It bore the title "The Elgin Marbles: or, John Bull collecting stones at the time his numerous family want bread!"

Elgin tore the thing to shreds.

They left Barèges at daybreak, passing swiftly through the sleeping village, heading toward the northeast. Hunt was

puzzled. "My lord, why are we taking this road?"

Elgin responded curtly, "The Toulouse road is more direct to Paris, and far more scenic."

Mary was not concerned about the road they were taking. She was happy that they were returning to Paris, leaving the desolate Pyrenees and the tight confinement of Barèges.

Within three hours they had passed Montréjeau and were approaching Saint-Gaudens. After freeing themselves from the high mountains, they found warmth in the green countryside. Everything looked clean and peaceful — the little churches, the farmhouses, the trees and brooks. Elgin looked more relaxed, and at one point reached out and clutched her hand.

Mary's eyes kept flitting to little William. "Let me hold him," she said to Félicité. "Perhaps I can get him to fall asleep. His eyes are so red."

Little William wiggled and squirmed in her arms. She kissed his cheek. It was hot. Keeping her lips on his face, she softly began singing:

> Oh, hush thee, my baby,
>   Thy sire is a Knight;
> Thy mother a Lady,
>   Both lovely and bright.
>
> The woods and the glens
>   From the towers we see;
> They all are belonging,
>   Dear baby, to thee.
>
> Oh, hush thee, my baby,
>   Thy sire is a Knight . . .
> Oh, hush thee, my baby,
>   So bonnie, so bright.

Toulouse slipped past them almost before they realized it — sturdy farmhouses of pink stucco, a huge Romanesque cathedral, dozens of Renaissance buildings and churches. In the late

afternoon sun, everything in the town was coated in soft red hues. Hunt ecstatically called it "La Ville Rosée." "My lord and lady, the Basilica of Saint-Sernin contains the richest collection of relics in France, including the remains of no less than one hundred saints, six of the apostles, and a thorn from the Crown of Thorns."

When little William finally fell asleep, Mary felt tired. "I think we should look for lodgings. It will be dark soon."

"It was that damned Colonel Crawford!" Elgin suddenly exclaimed. "I'm certain of it."

"Certain of what?" she asked.

"It was he who put that envelope under the door of our cottage."

"Eggy, it's getting quite dark, and I'm worried about little William. I think we should look for lodgings."

He shook his head. "We must proceed."

Hunt questioned him. "But the next town, Cahors, is a full day's journey from here."

There were lights in the distance. After a few minutes, they entered a small village, and Elgin tapped the roof of the carriage. The driver pulled to a halt and informed them that the name of the village was Grisolles. They found lodgings at an inn that was only a stone's throw from the town hall in the center of the village, and after the driver attended to the horses, Elgin stopped him at the front door and sharply instructed him to seek lodgings elsewhere in the village.

"But Eggy," Mary intervened, "the man is tired and hungry. He can't find other lodgings at this late hour."

Elgin coughed. "I'm paying him enough. He can provide for his own lodgings."

"My lord, I'm willing to share my room with him," said Hunt.

"Do as you wish," Elgin barked.

They retired immediately after dinner. Mary tossed for an hour before closing her eyes, then suddenly Elgin's low hoarse voice stirred her. "Poll, make room. I want to lie beside you."

"Eggy, not now."

He pulled away the covers and slid into her bed. He was naked.

"Eggy, you heard what that young physician from Pau said. I mustn't get pregnant again."

"There's nothing to fear."

"What do you mean?"

"I'm wearing something."

"But you're naked."

"It's something that will prevent you from getting pregnant."

"Eggy, what on earth are you talking about?"

"Before leaving London, I stopped off at the Green Canister on Half-Moon Street in the Strand."

"For what reason?"

"The proprietor had sent me a handbill at Broomhall shortly after I was given the post at Constantinople. It stated that ambassadors, travelers, and captains of ships going abroad could be supplied from Mrs. Phillips' Warehouse with any quantity of the best goods, on the shortest notice and at the lowest price."

"What kind of goods?"

"Cundums. Here, feel. It wraps over the penis like this."

She withdrew her hand quickly. "You actually went to this place on Half-Moon Street and bought these . . . these things?"

He squirmed. "I saw many gentlemen there. One of them told me that the great lover Casanova relied very much on 'the English riding coats.' "

"How many did you buy?"

"Several dozen. They were quite reasonable and of the best quality."

She bit her lip. "Did you use them with Madame Ferchenbeck?"

"Who?"

"You heard what I said. Madame Ferchenbeck."

"How do you know about her?" he exclaimed, sliding his body away.

"The wife of the German Ambassador in Constantinople told me all about the lavish parties you conducted while you were Minister Plenipotentiary to the Court of Prussia, how your house in Berlin was open to everyone until midnight, but after that, only to 'your fair favorite, Madame Ferchenback.' "

Elgin slowly rolled off the bed.

"You didn't answer my question. I want to know if you used those things with her."

"Of course not."

"Have you used them with anyone else?"

"No."

"Then why did you buy them?"

His silence poisoned her.

He crawled into the bed again, edging close to her, his hand stroking her thigh.

"Get away from me!" she cried.

"Poll . . ."

"Go to your prostitutes, if you must. I never want you to touch me again!"

She was awakened by Félicité's trembling voice. "My lady, come quickly. The child is very ill."

"What ails him?"

"He just vomited, and his face is burning with fever."

Elgin jumped up from bed and followed them into the adjacent room. Hunt was standing at the threshold, wringing his hands, his eyes closed as though in prayer.

"Summon the innkeeper," Elgin ordered. "Ask him if there is a physician in Grisolles."

Hunt returned in a few minutes, shaking his head. "My lord, the nearest physician lives in Montauban, almost ten miles to the north."

"We must bring him here. Wake up the driver. Tell him to hitch the horses to the carriage. I'll get dressed."

"Shall I be going to Montauban with Your Lordship?"

"Of course. Hurry."

Mary bathed little William's face and wrists with vinegar, then quickly bundled him up in a soft blanket. His body was on fire. "Please go to bed," she said to Félicité. "I'll stay with the child until His Lordship returns with the physician."

A few moments after Félicité left the room, little William was plagued by convulsions. She bathed him in vinegar again, then clamped her arms around him to keep him still. It seemed as if hours had passed before Elgin and Hunt finally returned. A spry gray-bearded old man in a tight-fitting black suit was with them. He went immediately to little William and put his ear over the child's heart. Shaking his head, he reached into his black leather bag and pulled out a razor.

"What are you going to do?" cried Mary.

The old doctor brought up his hand. "There is nothing to fear, Madame. A few quick strokes across the child's buttocks, a firm squeeze, and all the impure blood will leave the child's body. After that, the fever will subside."

She couldn't bear to watch.

One hour after the physician left, little William looked much better. His fever had gone down, and he was able to take some broth that the innkeeper's wife prepared. Elgin sighed with relief, then dcclared that they should continue their journey as soon as they had a little breakfast.

"I think we should wait another day," she said. "William is not fit for travel."

Hunt agreed. "My lord, we have swift horses and a capable driver. One more day will not delay us that much."

The innkeeper kept a paternal vigil outside their door, periodically asking if she needed anything. "My wife and I are at your humble service, Madame."

"Thank you," said Mary. "Tell me, what is your name?"

"Daudet. Pierre Daudet."

"And your wife's name?"

"Therèse."

She clasped his hand. "My husband and I are very grateful for the help you are giving us."

"Je vous en prie, Madame."

Limoges.

A city of porcelain factories, shops displaying exquisite china and matchless ceramics, men and women in native costumes walking along the wide boulevards, happy children dancing. Hunt was ecstatic. "My grandfather visited here many years ago and brought back a gift for my grandmother — two porcelain dishes, so delicate and translucent, I kept asking her to take them out of the cabinet so that I could run my fingers over them."

"You're fortunate to have known your grandparents, Mr. Hunt. I never saw mine."

"I shall never forget the joy those treasures afforded me, my lady. Indeed, the porcelain of Limoges cannot be equaled."

"Why is that?"

"It's because of the unique white clay that was discovered just south of here, in Saint-Yrieix."

Félicité cast an admiring glance toward Hunt. "You seem to know more about my country than I do, Mr. Hunt."

Elgin bristled. "That's because he's had his nose buried in books all his life. I wish he would divert one ounce of that energy to more fruitful pursuits."

Hunt drew back, a hurt look in his eyes. "I have no regrets about the way I have been living."

"You call it living?" Elgin snorted. "Take a close look at yourself, Mr. Hunt. You're crawling through life like an old man — alone, without wife and children, basking in a falsely intellectual world, throwing away the best years of your life on empty dreams."

"That is most unkind of you, my lord. The Apostle Paul says . . ."

"I don't give a damn what the Apostle Paul says."

". . . He that is unmarried careth for the things that belong to the Lord, how he may please the Lord; but he that is married careth for the things that are of the world, how he may please his wife."

Little William started crying. His face looked flushed again. Mary held out her arms, and Félicité passed the child to her. She kissed him. His face was burning. Alarmed, she turned to Elgin. "We must find a physician. Little William is very ill."

Elgin placed his hand on the child's brow. "Yes, he has a high fever." He pounded on the roof of the carriage with his cane until the horses were pulled to a halt. "Look for a physician right away," he shouted to the driver.

As the heavy wheels of the carriage rattled over the street, she tightened her arms around little William. The porcelain world of Limoges looked frozen, and already the sun had dropped behind the rooftops, cloaking the city in a gray mantle.

Eleven

Paris,
18th September, 1804

Pray for me, dearest mother:

Take me into your arms. My adored William is gone. From the moment of his birth to that fatal hour when it pleased God to call him, I doted upon him. And now my happiness is destroyed forever.

Pray for me, dearest mother. Bless your miserable daughter . . .

After Elgin took the letter and sealed it, Félicité asked if she needed anything.

"I just want to be left alone," she replied.

Elgin handed the letter to Hunt. "See that it is dispatched right away."

Returning to the sofa, he sat down beside her and put his arm around her shoulder. "I received permission from Talleyrand's adjutant yesterday. I'm taking you on that long-delayed tour of Paris today."

"I'm not up to it," she muttered. "Some other time."

"But I insist. You can't go on like this. The child has been dead for eleven days. You must try to compose yourself."

She clamped her eyes shut.

"I think little William should be buried. This is why you keep thinking about him, tormenting yourself while he is lying in that tin tank, his little body bloated with embalming fluid."

"My child will be buried in Scotland, not in France."

"But what if Talleyrand refuses to grant us permission to leave?"

"We shall wait until we get permission. I don't care how long it takes. Little William will be buried in Scotland."

He pulled her up from the sofa. "Come, get dressed. We have many things to see in Paris."

"Not today. Please."

He was insistent. "It's the only way you can free your mind from William. Once we step outside, you'll feel better. It's a lovely day."

"I'm really not up to it."

"We're going today and that's final. We may never have another opportunity like this. Besides, there's something I very much want you to see."

"What?"

"I can't tell you now. Please put on your dress. We're losing valuable time."

Reluctantly, she took off her robe, and Félicité selected the blue muslin dress and blue hat. She dressed slowly, then walked into the drawing room. Elgin cast an admiring glance at her, but she repressed every feeling in her body. As soon as they stepped outside, he took her by the hand and led her across the Rue de Richelieu, into a wide boulevard bordered by gigantic chestnut trees. Soon they found themselves inside a spacious garden of graveled terraces, flower beds, white sculptures, and marble arches. The delicate colors dazzled her — pastel greens and yellows catching the streaking rays of the sun between low-hanging

branches. Children played around an octagonal pond, pushing their paper boats with long sticks while their nurses kept a vigilant watch from the benches. It was a fairyland of gossamer beauty, and she wanted to linger here, but Elgin pulled her gently away, pointing his finger toward the farthest end of the garden. "There they are!" he exclaimed.

They continued at a swifter pace until they reached a high iron fence. The gate was closed; two soldiers on horseback guarded the entrance. Through the iron fence she saw another large garden leading toward a stately palace. There were lamps running along the front of the fence, and four stone piers were spaced about twenty yards apart from each other, two on each side of the gate. They were at least ten feet in height. Each supported a huge horse, front foot up high, head thrust back, tail flounced, snorting defiantly at the Paris sky. The bronzed hides bore traces of gilt.

Elgin walked up to one of the piers and stretched his arm high, trying to touch the leg of the horse. "It's incredible!" he exclaimed. "Incredible!"

Hands trembling, tears streaking down his face, he said chokingly, "These superb sculptures date back to the time of Alexander the Great. They were once attached to a gilded chariot, but no one knows what happened to it. It was either lost or stolen. In God's name, we're looking at one of the finest masterpieces ever produced."

Again he stretched his arm high in a vain attempt to touch one of the legs; then, darting from one pier to the other, he studied each horse closely. His voice became somber. "Bonaparte took down these magnificent sculptures from the Cathedral of San Marco in Venice. It was a sad populace that witnessed the humiliating sight of the horses' departure. And now they are stationed here as gate piers for Bonaparte's residence."

"Bonaparte lives here?"

"Yes, in that building, the Palais des Tuileries. You can't

imagine how much I longed for this day, to stand in front of these splendid horses."

"How did you know they were here?"

He coughed. "I read it somewhere — I think it was in *The Times.* It would interest you to know that they were originally placed near the entrance to the Hippodrome in Constantinople, but in the year 1204, when the city was sacked during the Fourth Crusade, the Knights of Venice stole everything they saw. The Hippodrome was not at all the way we viewed it — fallen chunks of stone and stray columns tilted by the winds from the Bosphorus. It was one of the showplaces of the Eastern world, a political and cultural center as well as a sports arena. Great columns and obelisks rose from the central barrier that divided the racecourse. Many beautiful sculptures lined the structure — busts of emperors, pagan divinities — but the greatest spectacle of all was these four golden horses."

Her gaze wandered to the enclosed palace. She could see soldiers standing guard all around it. Perhaps Bonaparte would come out at any moment. She wondered what he looked like, how he was dressed, how he walked.

"Each one of these horses weighs a ton," Elgin murmured. "It was a remarkable feat, pulling them down from the cathedral and transporting them all the way to Paris."

She moved away from the fence and walked slowly toward the garden. The thought obsessed her: tender beauty and the ravages of war at arm's length from each other. It was insanity. They were living in a mad world, evil devouring everything good, death devouring life.

"Are you thinking about little William again?" Elgin asked.

Before she had time to reply, he clasped her hand in his and said, "Come, there are many more things for us to see. I've everything planned. First, we're going to the Cathedral of Notre-Dame. The Revolutionaries stole many of the treasures and even destroyed some of the best sculptures, but there is still much to

admire. After that, we shall take a leisurely stroll along the Seine, visit the shops, and dine in the very best restaurant."

Her eyes welled with tears.

Early the next morning, Elgin left for the Palais du Luxembourg and an audience with Talleyrand on the matter of obtaining their release so that little William could be buried in Scotland. He returned shortly after midday, his face flushed.

"What did Talleyrand say?" she asked.

"You must dismiss your maid right away."

She was elated. "Then he granted us permission? Oh, dear God, we can go home now with little William."

He started pacing around the drawing room. "Only you and Hunt will be going home."

"But what about you?"

"Bonaparte refused to consider my release. I must remain in France until the war ends — if it ever ends."

"Then I too shall stay. I'm not leaving without you."

He scowled. "If you want your child to be buried in Scotland, you must go. Tell the maid to pack all your belongings before you dismiss her. Take everything you can. Use the two trunks."

"But this is not the way I wanted it . . ."

"You're leaving from Le Havre the day after tomorrow on H.M.S. *Defiance*. Stop whimpering. You know how much it bothers me."

Hunt was silent all this time.

Elgin charged toward him. "I thought you'd be overjoyed."

"I am, my lord."

"Then speak. Say something."

"What can I say, my lord?"

"You could thank me. It was no easy matter convincing Talleyrand."

"Indeed, I'm most grateful to Your Lordship."

He spun around and came back to her. "Before I forget, someone else will be traveling on the same ship."

"Who?" she asked.

He hesitated, his eyes studying her intently. "Robert Fergusson."

The Channel crossing was perilous. Stormy winds ensnared the *Defiance* not more than an hour after they sailed away from Le Havre, and all the passengers confined themselves to their cabins, including Hunt, who was usually a good sailor. But Mary could not endure the close quarters for more than a few minutes. Taking a woolen blanket, she went on deck and sat at the stern, the blanket wrapped over her head and shoulders, her eyes fixed at a point where the demented sky lashed at the swirling waves. She still found it hard to believe that she was finally going home, that her precious little William would be buried on Scottish soil, that she would be embracing her children soon, her mother and father, Archerfield.

The storm blew off in the middle of the night, and at the first rays of dawn, the Dover cliffs came into view. The stiff wind sent the *Defiance* past Margate, then swiftly toward the mouth of the Thames.

At noon, Hunt joined her on deck, still looking very much under the weather. His face seemed to get even more pale when he told her they were invited to dine at the captain's table. Fergusson was already seated when they walked into the spacious cabin. Quickly, he came toward her and bowed. "I'm sorry that His Lordship has to remain in France. You have my heartfelt sympathies, my lady."

"Thank you, Mr. Fergusson."

"I was also sorry to hear about the death of your infant son."

"How did you know?"

"Mrs. Keith Stuart brought it to my attention."

The sight of food tormented her. She took only a glass of wine, sipping it slowly.

After the meal, Fergusson walked on deck with her while Hunt went below to look after the luggage. Leaning against the rail, she gazed at the rooftops of London. "Mr. Fergusson, where exactly is Raith?"

"It's but a short distance from Broomhall. Why do you ask?"

"I was only curious."

"Will you be going directly to Broomhall from London?" he inquired.

"That's my intention."

"If I'm permitted to say, my lady, you look very weary. It's a long journey, and it might be advisable for you to stay in London for a while to rest."

"Mr. Fergusson, I must attend to the burial of my son."

He looked at her with compassion. "I would be honored to make the necessary arrangements for your son's burial. I could accompany the bier to Broomhall and make final preparations with the rector of the church at Dunfermline if you wish."

"I couldn't ask you to do that, Mr. Fergusson. What would Lord Elgin's mother think if I were not present at my own child's burial?"

"She has known my family for years. I'm sure she would understand if I explained everything to her."

"You're most kind, Mr. Fergusson, but it's too much of an imposition."

"Believe me, it will be a great honor. With His Lordship being confined in France, it's the least I can do for an esteemed friend of the family."

She closed her eyes for a moment. "Throughout the Channel crossing, I dreaded the thought of the burial, and kept worrying how I could do it, how I could go through with it without Lord Elgin."

He touched her on the arm tenderly. "Then it's settled. I shall

accompany the child's bier to Scotland and attend to his burial at Broomhall."

"My parents have a winter house in Portman Square," she said thoughtfully. "I could go there to rest, but I should have to notify the servants. Until then, I could stay at Bramwell House."

"Where is that?"

"It's a hotel not too far from our town house. We use it whenever the house is being refurbished." Slowly, her voice drifted off. "Bramwell House is quite close to Park Lane."

"Is it true that His Lordship has constructed a museum there?"

"Yes. He asked me to visit it as soon as possible and take a complete inventory."

"Of the Parthenon marbles?"

"Yes."

They walked across the deck.

"My lady, no doubt you are aware of the ill feeling being stirred in London against His Lordship by Richard Payne Knight?"

"I am."

"There are scores of others also — John Spencer Smith, Lord Aberdeen, Edward Dodwell. They regard the whole affair as deplorable and keep demanding that His Lordship return the marbles to Greece at once."

She made no reply.

"Did you hear about the prize-fighters?"

"Prize-fighters?"

"A very famous pugilist named Gregson was paid to stand nude in His Lordship's museum, posing for several hours in various attitudes so that his anatomy could be compared with the sculptured figures. A large number of gentlemen paid as much as a guinea to witness the exhibition, and shortly after this, an actual boxing match took place between Gregson and another English pugilist."

Hunt stepped on deck and came puffing toward her. "I've gathered together all the luggage. Is there anything else Your Ladyship wishes me to do?"

"No, thank you, Mr. Hunt."

Hunt looked troubled. "Begging Mr. Fergusson's forgiveness, I'd like to speak privately with Your Ladyship."

Fergusson bowed, then excused himself. She could see that Hunt was struggling with himself, not knowing how to begin. "My lady, I must admit that it will be very painful . . ."

"Yes, Mr. Hunt?"

". . . never seeing each other again."

"Why do you say that? I'm sure we shall meet in the future."

Hunt walked to the rail and peered down at the water.

"You must be looking forward to joining Lord Upper Ossory again." She smiled.

"In a way."

"We shall all miss you, Mr. Hunt."

"My lady," he blurted, "as I mentioned once before, I had the sincere hope of attaining an independent income when I entered into His Lordship's service — nothing large, just enough for subsistence and my pursuit of scholarship."

"Of course, Mr. Hunt. You must seek that which pleases you most."

"Unfortunately, I can't do that."

"Why not?"

"I have no money."

"I don't understand."

"His Lordship hasn't paid me one farthing from the day we left Portsmouth."

"Mr. Hunt, I find this difficult to believe."

"Nevertheless, it's true. Your Ladyship must recall His Lordship's unusual behavior on the voyage out. He made it quite clear that no one would be paid until the embassy at Constantinople was shut down. Never did he volunteer to pay any of our expenses. The very subject of money often sent him into severe coughing fits. Surely Your Ladyship must remember all this?"

She forced a smile. "His Lordship is a bit parsimonious at times, but certainly he intends to reimburse you, Mr. Hunt."

"I doubt that very much. I'm now inclined to believe that I shall never be reimbursed." He looked at her sadly. "I never expected His Lordship to go against his word at the end. I was a good and faithful servant, and more than once I performed services that exceeded the terms of my contract."

"Mr. Hunt, I'm sure His Lordship will oblige you. You mustn't forget that he has been under great strain. Once he obtains his release and returns to Scotland, he will make full payment for the services you rendered."

"Do you honestly believe this?"

"Yes."

"Would it be too much of an imposition if I asked Your Ladyship to remind His Lordship about this matter?"

"I'd be most happy to do so."

"I shall be forever grateful to Your Ladyship."

"Is there anything else, Mr. Hunt?"

Hunt's eyes moistened before he spoke. "No. I had better attend to the trunks now. We shall be docking soon."

"Mr. Hunt . . ."

"Yes, my lady?"

"It was you who put that article from *The Times* under the door of our house in Barèges . . . the article with the cartoon?"

Hunt wrestled with his fingers. "I suspected that Your Ladyship knew."

"But I don't understand. Why did you do it?"

"I think it was because I wanted to strike back at His Lordship for not reimbursing me."

"You could have discussed this matter with him. Why did you have to resort to something so cruel and deceitful?"

"I felt wretched after I did it. I wanted to apologize to His Lordship."

"It's not too late, Mr. Hunt."

Hunt nodded. "Before I leave London, I shall write to His Lordship and beg his forgiveness. Farewell, my lady. Please kiss the children for me . . . and give Bruce a special hug."

"Good-by, Mr. Hunt. You hold a dear place in our hearts, and I shall never forget the wonderful times we shared together."

She was despondent after he left. How could Elgin have been so insensitive and dishonest, making promises that he never intended to keep? And what about the others — Professor Carlyle, Dr. Scott, Dr. McLean, Duff, Hamilton, Morier, Stratton, Félicité, Calitza, Masterman, Lusieri and all the artists in Athens . . .

Fergusson escorted her on the short carriage drive to Bramwell House. The sky was overcast, yet the streets were filled with people. She should have been happy to breathe English air once again, but the sadness and anger still clogged her lungs. As the carriage swung into Portman Square, she drew her eyes away from the window. "Mr. Fergusson, what about the bier? Have you made the arrangements to convey it to Scotland?"

"Yes, I shall be taking it by carriage tomorrow morning."

"Where is it now?"

"Under the care of a reputable embalmer, here in Portman Square."

The carriage halted before Bramwell House. The place hadn't changed — the same gray stone building with its ornamental grilles over the windows that faced the street. The driver carried her valise inside while Fergusson spoke with the proprietor about lodgings. She was assigned to Rooms Six and Seven on the second story; he took Room Eight. Two servants carried their luggage.

Stopping before the door of her suite, Fergusson said, "Would you object if we dined together this evening?"

"Thank you, Mr. Fergusson, but I'm very tired."

He bowed. "Should you change your mind, I shall be only a door away."

The servant with her valise unlocked the door and entered. He

brought the valise to an adjacent door, opened it, and left it inside. She thanked him, then turned to Fergusson, who was still standing at the threshold. "Are you sure you would not care to dine with me? I don't enjoy eating alone."

She smiled and started to close the door. "Perhaps some other time, Mr. Fergusson."

Fifteen minutes later, there was a knock on the door. She opened it and saw Fergusson smiling once again and holding a newspaper in his hand. There was something about the way his eyes crinkled at the corners that reminded her of her father. "You're quite a persistent man, Mr. Fergusson, but I'm afraid I must decline your invitation once more."

He laughed. "That's not why I came back. There is an article here on the front page of *The Times* about His Lordship."

"Please come inside, Mr. Fergusson." She took the newspaper and brought it to the waning light at the window.

> One of Napoleon Bonaparte's confidential ministers disclosed recently that any high intercession from kings or emperors relating to Lord Elgin's captivity in France might very well prolong His Lordship's imprisonment.
>
> However, it was suggested by this source that consideration might be given for Lord Elgin's release if a formal application were submitted from a learned society in England, stressing that His Lordship is an enlightened and liberal patron of the arts.

She walked back and handed him the newspaper. He tucked it into his coat pocket and said, "Well, what do you think about this?"

"I don't know."

"I dare say it's worth a try."

"Who would write the application?"

"I'd be very willing to do it. I'm a Fellow of the Academy of Science, and it could bear some influence."

"I shall be obliged to you, Mr. Fergusson, if you would do this for His Lordship."

He opened the door slowly. "Would it be too bold if I asked you to call me Robert?" She quietly closed the door.

After bidding farewell to Fergusson the next morning, she reached up and touched one corner of the bier, which was strapped to the rear of the carriage. "Good-by, my adorable little William," she murmured softly. "Don't be afraid. My heart will be with you always."

She remained in the middle of the street until the carriage was lost from her view; then slowly she headed toward Park Lane. Why did Elgin have to insist that she go there? The last thing she wanted was to look at the Parthenon marbles again. Bracing herself, she hastened her steps, armed with the assurance that after today it would be all over. Not another word about those marbles, not another thought.

She had no trouble finding the museum. It was a one-story wooden structure just off Portman Square. She tried the door. It was open. She trembled when she saw the marbles — metopes and sculptures leaning against the walls, the exquisite Caryatid from the Erechtheum still gloriously beautiful among the strewn figures from the east and west pediments.

A raspy voice startled her. "Madam, have you been issued a pass to visit this museum?"

"I'm Lady Elgin," she replied tersely. The man was old and bent, his face grooved with lines. "Are you the curator of the museum?"

His laugh irritated her. "Curator, did you say? His Lordship's mother merely asked me to stand guard over the marbles and to make certain no one enters without a pass."

"What is your name?"

"Hastings, my lady. Thomas Hastings."

"I've been instructed by His Lordship to take a full inventory of the museum."

"That won't be necessary. I've already compiled an accurate list of everything here. I keep it in that small desk by the door. Each item is described in detail, along with its placement and condition. Here, let me give it to you."

She thanked him for the list, and after scanning it briefly, she folded it to put into her reticule and walked toward the first sculpture — the beautiful torso of Iris that for centuries had adorned the west pediment of the Parthenon. She went next to Dionysos, then proceeded to Persephone, Demeter, the Three Fates, Selene, the Ilissos, the head of Helios rising from the sea. She lingered for a brief moment before Aphrodite, who was lying on her mother's lap, the rhythmic grace of her garment clinging to her exquisite form.

Her eyes now traveled to the continuous frieze that depicted the great festival of the Panathenaea — ships manned by priests and priestesses wearing crowns and garlands of flowers, Athenian warriors donning their sandals or bridling their horses, stately maidens carrying urns on their shoulders, musicians followed by austere elders, chariots, and bearers of sacrificial offerings.

Elgin's hoarse cries still rang in her ears.

There was no end — Centaurs fighting with Lapiths at the marriage feast of Pirithous, warriors on horseback, giants grappling in a battle of death. She had never fully realized the extent of Elgin's pillage, and was stunned even more by the huge collection of vases, ancient coins, jewelry, and treasures of gold and silver that were kept in glass cabinets.

She almost stumbled over a young man who was kneeling on the floor, sketching one of the sculptured figures. As she backed away, Hastings drew up to her and whispered, "That is Benjamin Robert Haydon. He comes here every day and paints continuously until nightfall. I often have to ask him to leave, because he loses all sense of time. He records everything he does here in a journal. Would you care to see it?"

"Yes."

Hastings again walked to the small desk near the door and pulled out a black notebook. She took it from him and read one of the pages.

> Eight April — drew at Lord Elgin's museum from ten in the morning 'till one quarter past two in the afternoon, and from there 'till six in the evening. I then walked about and observed these matchless productions before me. I consider it truly the greatest blessing that ever happened to this country, their being brought here by His Lordship.

She handed the notebook back to Hastings and started for the door. The old man hastened to open it for her. "Does it disturb Your Ladyship to hear that the populace of London has reacted sharply against the presence of the Parthenon marbles in His Lordship's museum?"

She did not reply.

"Mr. Haydon and myself were discussing it only last evening. The people of England should be grateful. His Lordship has done a remarkable thing for the improvement of the fine arts in this country."

"Good day, Mr. Hastings."

"Does Your Ladyship plan to come here again?"

"I think not."

"Did I give Your Ladyship the inventory list?"

"Yes, Mr. Hastings, and I thank you very much."

"I hope that His Lordship is liberated soon from his detainment in France. Perhaps when Your Ladyship next writes to him, she can say that I have dedicated myself to guarding this fine collection."

"I shall do that, Mr. Hastings."

The next morning, she received a message from Mrs. Gosling, the housekeeper at the Portman Square residence, informing her that the town house was now ready for occupancy. Mary asked the messenger to wait while she scribbled a brief note of reply.

My dear Mrs. Gosling,

The loss of my infant child has left me with a desperate need for rest and peace of soul. I am sorry that I put you to the unnecessary labour of preparing the house for me, but after giving the matter much thought, I have decided that it would be intolerable for me to live there, as it would harbour too many memories of my family and make me dreadfully homesick. Thus, I have chosen to seek a temporary abode somewhere else. Please ask Mr. Duff to find a suitable house nearby, and as soon as it becomes available, I should like to have you and the other servants there at my arrival.

Without realizing it, she had signed the note "Mary Nisbet."

After the messenger left, she went to the bay window and looked down at London. In the few years since she had last been here, the city had undergone rapid and haphazard change. The houses were more cramped than ever in streets so narrow and tight that carriages jostled the pedestrians. Only a fool would think of walking in the middle of the street, and those who chose to walk on the pavement either hugged the walls or had to give way. Even in broad daylight, brawls resulted from people being pushed into the gutter. *The peaceable and the quarrelsome.*

As a child, it was the noise that had bothered her most. She had to block her ears from the grating sound of ironshod wheels, the clatter of hoofs from the stagecoaches and wagons that entered the city in the middle of the night — all this coupled with the steady drones from the taverns, coffee houses, and shops at the riverside, the secondhand clothesmen, knife-grinders, coalmen, chimney sweeps, chair-menders, gingerbread men, milkmaids, oystermongers, sellers of watercress, of cat's and dog's meat, slippers and doormats.

But somehow, the noise didn't offend her now. Indeed, it inspired her to do something she had always wanted — investigate the entire city by herself, go anywhere she pleased without answering to anyone. Through the proprietor of Bramwell House, she arranged for the hire of a carriage, and at noon she set off.

Hyde Park was emblazoned in beauty, the scent of flowers, trees, and shrubs saturating the air. Speeding past the reservoir at the eastern edge of the park, the carriage reached Rotten Row, and instantly her father's words filtered into her memory: "That's a vile neighborhood, lassie . . . notorious for duels and footpads."

They approached Piccadilly, its modest town houses with their colorful Venetian windows uniformly stretching along the street. The road was not crowded, and the carriage was able to move rapidly northward, past the Strand at Charing Cross, then down the left bank of the River Thames, to the Tower. Shouting down to her, the driver asked where she preferred to go next, and she instructed him to continue down the river road.

Soon they were in the midst of the butchers' stalls — busy men in bloodied white aprons tossing guts and other refuse into the street, creating such a deplorable stench, she had to cover her nose with a handkerchief.

On the way back, the driver prepared to make the turn at the Strand and proceed once more into Piccadilly, but she stopped him in time and directed him to maintain the same course. When they reached the Palace of Westminster, she tapped the roof of the carriage, and the horses were pulled to a halt. Stepping out of the carriage, she said to the driver, "Please wait here for me."

Elgin had served in the House of Lords as an elected peer, but he had always nourished the hope of being granted automatic peerage, which would save him the trouble of seeking election. Mary had visited Westminster several times as a child. Her father loved to come here. But this was to be a special visit. Tonight she would write to Elgin and tell him that she had seen with her own eyes the bench reserved for him in the House of Lords.

She entered through the Robing Room, casting her eyes on the walls and ceiling ornamented with the sovereigns' badges and frescoes depicting the legend of King Arthur. A uniformed attendant conducted her through the Royal Gallery, past the

frescoes and gilded bronze statues of monarchs, the portraits of sovereigns and their escorts.

She suddenly realized that the Lords were sitting in session — wigs, robes, speeches, loud laughter, raillery. With reservation, she edged her way into the White Hall, her eyes darting everywhere, marveling at the superb workmanship of the red-buttoned leather benches, the sovereign's throne beneath the niched Gothic canopy, the ribs of gold on the ceiling, the entire chamber encrusted in gold and scarlet . . . and catching the light from the medieval windows, the bronze statues of the barons who witnessed King John's assent to the Magna Carta.

Her eyes stopped at one of the benches, and she envisioned Elgin seated there in his wig and robe, his chest inflated with pride.

The thought brought tears to her eyes.

Two days later, she received a message from Mrs. Gosling. Duff had located a suitable residence at Sixty Baker Street, a short distance from Portman Square. The message closed with the assurance that the house would be ready for occupancy within three days.

Fergusson returned from Scotland on the day before she was to leave for the Baker Street house. He was very quiet and chary of conversation, but after some probing he finally told her about little William's interment in the family vault at Broomhall, recounting all the details, even naming the people who were in attendance — Lord Elgin's aged mother, the rector of the church at Dunfermline, certain relatives and friends.

His gaze fell on the valise near the door. "Are you leaving for Scotland?" he asked.

"No, I've decided to remain in London a while longer."

"You're leaving Bramwell House?"

"Yes, Mr. Duff rented a house on Baker Street. He will be here with the carriage at noon tomorrow."

Fergusson reached into his coat pocket and withdrew a folded

document. "This is a copy of the application for Lord Elgin's release which the President of the Royal Academy sent to the French Institute. I copied it myself and would like you to keep it."

Slowly, she unfolded it.

To the Fellows of the French Institute:

The rage of war ought not interrupt the intercourse between men of science. Being always willing on our part to lend assistance to your scientific men who visit our country, we beg leave to represent the following case for your consideration:

A British nobleman, an ambassador imbued with the love of the arts, at a great personal expense remitted to England a very large collection of ancient Greek art. As yet, and to the great disappointment of artists and men of science throughout the learned world, notice of this nobleman's achievement has not been properly published, nor has his collection been appropriately exhibited, because he is not here to supervise this grand project.

The world of science suffers as a result.

It is our sincere hope that the members of the French Institute will intercede in Lord Elgin's behalf and that an official request be made to the highest authority for his safe return to England.

Fergusson walked to the door.

"Thank you very much," she said. "I shall be forever grateful to you. It was merciful and kind of you to help me in my hour of need."

He opened the door. "How long do you plan to stay at the Baker Street house?"

"I really can't say at this time; several weeks, perhaps. All I know is that I can't return to Scotland yet."

"Would you object if I paid you a visit at Baker Street?"

She didn't answer.

"What is the address there?"

She hesitated for a long time. "Number Sixty."

Twelve

GRIEF-RIDDEN days and nights, weeks of self-condemnation and reproach, hating herself one minute, then trying to justify everything the next. Duff was a blessing, her savior and compassionate friend, daily assuring her that she was indeed right in delaying her departure for Scotland, that she certainly couldn't return to her children and parents feeling this way; and both Mrs. Gosling and the young maid, Mary Ruper, doing their utmost to care for her and attend to all her needs, cooking the choicest and most nourishing foods, standing beside her at the table until she finished everything on her plate, imploring her to take a cup of camomile tea before retiring each night, sitting at her bedside and comforting her with long passages from Holy Writ. In the afternoons, she walked with Mrs. Gosling's little black dog, Prancer, watching him skip over the green at Portman Square, his tiny tail wagging furiously, reminding her so much of her own dog, Boxer.

It seemed that everyone in the household had concurred on an unsparing plan to oversee every move she made, never allowing her to be alone for one minute. The instant she opened her eyes each morning, Mary Ruper waited devotedly beside her bed, her

adorably plump face smiling down at her, asking, "And what would Her Ladyship like for breakfast this morning?"

Her footman, Thomas Willey, also solicitous, volunteered daily to take her on carriage drives through the park. The smell of alcohol was constantly on his breath, and she had to admonish him many times, but she could never stay angry with him for more than a few minutes. His booming theatrical voice, accompanied by the most amusing gesture of bowing lower than necessary, sweeping his hat over the ground and grinning, always melted away her anger.

One day, just past noon, Mrs. Gosling stepped into the drawing room to announce that a gentleman was at the front door.

"Did he give his name?" asked Mary.

"Mr. Robert Fergusson, my lady."

"Please ask him to come in."

When Fergusson took her hand to kiss it, she noticed for the first time how long and slender his fingers were. "My lady, it's such a lovely day, I wondered if you would like to join me in a stroll through Hyde Park."

She waited for Mrs. Gosling to leave the room.

"The fresh air will be very beneficial."

"I didn't realize that you were still in London, Mr. Fergusson." She took his hat and placed it on the table.

"I've been rather busy," he replied, seating himself on the sofa.

She smiled. "I can understand, Mr. Fergusson. Could it be a young lady who has kept you here all this time?"

He leaned forward uneasily. "Hardly. It was my work."

"Just exactly what is your work, Mr. Fergusson?"

"The physical sciences, but my real love is philosophy."

"Philosophy?"

"Yes, Greek philosophy."

"Really?"

"But of course."

"Do you know the Greek language?"

"Indeed I do."

"Who is your favorite philosopher?"

"Aristotle."

"Mine is Plato."

Fergusson's eyes widened. "What did you say?"

"My favorite philosopher is Plato," she answered, smiling.

"Your Ladyship has an interest in philosophy?"

"It's far more than an interest, Mr. Fergusson. I have a burning love of it."

"This is quite unusual."

She stared at him. "Are you implying that only men have the capacity for studying philosophy?"

"It's not that at all. What I'm trying to say is that women generally pursue other interests. It's quite rare, and very delightful, I must say, to find one who loves philosophy."

She went to the closet and put on her black and white straw bonnet. "I think I shall go for a stroll with you after all, Mr. Fergusson."

He jumped to his feet. "That's wonderful."

Mrs. Gosling gave them a long look as they passed through the hallway. Handing Mary her parasol, she said, "Your Ladyship will be needing this. It's quite warm under the sun."

At the end of Baker Street, they turned into Bayswater and continued until they reached the northernmost end of Hyde Park. The place was entirely surrounded by a high wall, but she remembered that there was an opening in the wall just a short distance from the reservoir. As soon as they passed through it, they were greeted by the melodic songs of many birds. Some fluttered from tree to tree, chirping gaily; others strutted unafraid in the grass, pecking at the ground and flapping their wings. Fergusson kept a steady eye on them, following their spasmodic movements, listening to their endless calls. "The species of birds here are quite numerous," he remarked. "I try to come to the park every time I visit London. Did you know that this place over the years was used for military maneuvers and encampments . . ."

". . . and that Henry the Eighth enclosed it completely before stocking it with deer for the royal chase."

They both burst into laughter.

The open parasol kept striking the low-hanging branches, and she decided to close it. Fergusson took it from her hand and used it to clear a path through the high grass. Suddenly she was aware that he had stopped and was looking at her.

"What is it, Mr. Fergusson?"

"My lady, I'm highly pleased that you share my love for philosophy, but tell me, why is Plato your favorite?"

"I find him more human than the other philosophers, particularly Aristotle."

"What makes you say this?"

"With Aristotle, the process of reasoning seems to hold precedence over everything else."

"And with Plato?"

"He's more concerned with ideas and feelings, Mr. Fergusson — and I agree. Philosophy must be a living experience, not an abstract speculation. It should speak to the heart."

"But the heart can't think."

"Praise God for that, Mr. Fergusson."

He walked around a tree and came back, an intent look on his face. "It seems that we are moving about in circles."

She laughed. "You, Mr. Fergusson, not I."

"But Aristotle had a sincere concern for living things. He was always asking the question 'What is the function of man?' To him, life was more than food and drink, wealth and earthly pleasures. Indeed, he was deeply interested in the activity of the soul."

Her voice changed. "Just what is the soul, Mr. Fergusson?"

"Aristotle says it is the life principle, that which sustains life."

"What happens to it after death?"

He shook his head and laughed. "Where did you learn to argue in such a scientific manner?"

"My manner is philosophical, not scientific."

"Is there any difference?" He grinned. "My lady, I just want

to say that this is the first time that I've ever engaged in such a stimulating discussion with a woman."

"There you go again, Mr. Fergusson."

"I beg your forgiveness. I meant to say that this is the most extraordinary event in my life, one that I shall never forget."

She too would not forget it. She couldn't believe that this was happening. Happily, she recalled those wonderful long nights in Constantinople, sitting with Hunt in the drawing room while all the others were asleep, filling her heart with new thoughts and ideas, opening her eyes to a world of golden beauty. But it wasn't at all like this. Hunt did all of the talking.

Fergusson stopped before a dying linden tree. Although the trunk was split open, a few leaves sprouted from one of the gnarled branches. "Does this tree have a soul?" he asked.

She laughed. "Aristotle would have us believe there is a soul in everything."

He reached up and touched one of the leaves. "But look, this leaf still clings to it, drawing life. Surely, it must have a soul."

She pointed to another linden tree. "Plato would say that even this tree, which looks so stately and superb, is but an imperfect copy of what a tree really should be."

"Indeed?"

"In fact, Plato wouldn't call it a tree at all."

"What would he call it?"

"A blurred vision."

"Then everything we behold is but an imperfect idea?"

She placed her hand on the dying trunk. "How do you explain it, Mr. Fergusson? This tree is about to fall, but that one just behind us stands upright and strong."

"I can't explain it."

"Is there a hidden law that determines what will fall, when it will fall?"

"Only God determines that."

She looked down at the ground. "It's hardly scientific, running to God when we can't find the answer."

"But He's the creator. Every law in the universe was made by Him. If what you say about blurred visions is correct, then God must be responsible for this imperfection in us."

Carefully, she peeled away a dry strip of bark.

"I can't believe that God is the creator of imperfections," insisted Fergusson.

"Perhaps He permits them as a means to attaining a greater end — the vision of the real world."

"Is everything around us unreal . . . the trees, the birds, the sky?"

"Yes, according to Plato."

"You and I?"

Again she looked down at the ground. "We're all living in bondage, a bondage that prevents us from seeing things as they truly are. It's impossible for us to comprehend reality, because our vision is fallible and imperfect."

A hurt look swept across his face. "Shall I ever see a real tree, a real sky . . . a real you?"

She started to walk away. "It's a desperate and horrible thought, Mr. Fergusson."

"What?"

"That only death can make us free."

She invited him to remain for dinner that evening. They talked far into the night on every subject conceivable, and although she wanted to examine more of Plato, he preferred to skip and bounce, settling finally on the Ionian physicists. "Miletus was the most prosperous of the many Greek colonies along the coast of Asia Minor. It was a great tableland, a plateau chiefly given up to sheep-farming. The wool was sent down the two great river valleys that penetrated the interior; then, dyed with the same murex coloring that was discovered by the Phoenicians, it was exported to all parts of the Mediterranean world."

"What has this to do with philosophy, Mr. Fergusson?"

He smiled. "Miletus stood at the mouth of these two great rivers and consequently enjoyed much wealth and prosperity. Her position was enhanced by still another factor: she had earlier entered into a strong alliance with Alyattes, the King of Lydia, and this treaty was renewed with Croesus. It released the citizens of Miletus from political and military fear, and thus they were able to indulge in the leisure of philosophical discourse. Thales emerged from this ideal environment. It was his belief that the quest for wisdom should be confined only to what we know, and since there is nothing more basic than water, he maintained that water indeed was the primary cause of all things. His pupils proceeded even further, claiming that fire and air brought about the creation of the world. But the greatest pupil of Thales, Anaximander, found all this difficult to accept. Insisting that it was impossible for matter to create itself, he staunchly believed that there had to be something over and above matter that was the cause of all things. Therefore, he concluded that it was indeterminate, infinite. Creation arose from this infinite cause and would one day return to it."

Fergusson paused a moment to look at her. "Perhaps this next Miletian may prove more to your liking. The entire philosophy of Heraclitus centered around three words, *ta panta rei.*"

"I know what that means," she said. "Everything undergoes continual change."

"Exactly. Heraclitus contends that waking is sleeping, day is night, youth is old age, life is death. He once remarked that a man couldn't step twice into the same river, because it would be a different river when he made his second step."

"And in the time it took him to walk from the bank to the water, he too would be different," she observed elatedly.

"That's quite true."

She was ecstatic. "Think of it, Mr. Fergusson, just think what this could do to the whole structure of our lives, to our education, customs, religions and laws . . ."

"And to the institute of marriage," he broke in. "Vast changes

occur, both physical and emotional, prior to and after marriage."

She sank into silence.

"I was certain that you would like Heraclitus."

"There is a bit of Plato in him," she murmured softly.

"Really?"

"The other Miletians seem to concern themselves primarily with the material cause of things; yet, if I understand you correctly, Heraclitus stresses the importance of the idea as it pertains to the process of change. Yes, if this is what you mean, then indeed I like Heraclitus very much."

Mrs. Gosling appeared at the drawing room door.

"What is it?" Mary asked her.

"It's near midnight. Your Ladyship should think about retiring."

Fergusson rose to his feet. "Forgive me. I never dreamed it was so late."

She escorted him to the front door. "Doesn't it fill you with awe and wonder, that with each blink of the eye, each heartbeat, everything changes?"

"It does indeed."

After opening the door, he turned to face her. His lips lingered on her hand. "I should like very much to continue our war of words."

She smiled.

"May I call on you tomorrow evening?"

"Yes, Mr. Fergusson."

"But before plunging into battle" — he laughed — "perhaps we can dine at Bramwell House."

"Yes," she said, quietly closing the door.

In the days that followed, Fergusson called almost every evening at the house on Baker Street. For hours, they argued over

the subjects of evil, of justice, the existence of God, the transmigration of souls. On several occasions, Fergusson invited her to the opera and to the theater, but as soon as they got back to Baker Street, the logomachy resumed. It was a duel from which no real victor emerged, but neither of them cared about winning or losing. It was joy enough to savor the stimulating deductions and syllogisms.

Late one balmy afternoon she returned from a stroll around Portman Square with Mrs. Gosling's dog, Prancer, and found Fergusson waiting for her at the front door of the house. His eyes flashed teasingly. "I never thought I'd be jealous of a dog."

She unhooked the leather leash from Prancer's collar, slapped him fondly on the rump, then watched him scurry off toward the back of the house.

"I've been waiting here for an hour," he said.

"Indeed?"

"I had this terrible thought that you had left for Scotland . . ."

She wished he hadn't said that. She was still not ready to think about Scotland. "What brings you here so early in the day, Robert?"

"I wondered if we could go for a walk through Hyde Park, but you must be tired now."

"I'd enjoy that very much."

"I don't want you to overexert yourself. Are you sure you're up to it?"

"Of course. Please wait here a moment while I let Mrs. Gosling know about it. How long shall we be?"

"Just an hour or so."

"Perhaps you would like to stay for dinner."

"I shouldn't."

"Why?"

"I think Mrs. Gosling doesn't approve of seeing me here so often."

"Nonsense. Mrs. Gosling isn't that way at all. She's a kind and hospitable person. It would please her exceedingly to set another place for dinner."

When they entered the park, it saddened her to discover that the leaves had lost much of their color. Fergusson led the way under the trees, his long strides broken only as he stopped to hold back some of the lower branches. Suddenly, he took hold of her hand and said, "Come, let's run."

Streaking over the grass, head flung back, laughing, she pulled off her hat and allowed the wind to seize her hair. At one point, they raced so swiftly, she would have fallen if Fergusson hadn't taken a firm grip on her hand.

Finally they stopped under a group of trees at the extreme end of the meadow, both of them out of breath. He released her hand, then slowly removed his suit coat and spread it over the limp grass. "Shall we rest here for a while?"

She folded her dress under her legs and sat. "What shall we discuss today?"

He remained standing, his eyes never leaving her face. "I don't know how to put this . . ." He walked away a few strides, then came back. "Believe me, I've tried to prevent it. You can't imagine how hard I've tried. But it's impossible. I can't keep it inside me any longer . . . I've . . . I've fallen in love with you . . ."

"No!" she exclaimed.

"I think about you every minute of the day . . ."

"Please, I don't want to hear this." She looked frantically away from him.

He dropped to his knees beside her and clasped her hands. She tried to pull away, but he cupped her face in his hands and softly kissed her.

"No," she murmured. "Please, I beg you."

As his lips went quickly to her mouth again, to her face and neck, a poison began gushing through her veins. Her arms around

him now, she accepted the full weight of his body, the hardness of his manhood against her thighs, his hands pulling gently at the hem of her dress, touching her skin and secret hair. In the next instant, the hardness was inside her, entering slowly and with tenderness, unselfishly waiting for her response, pressing deeper, unlocking feelings she never dreamed she possessed.

At last she opened her eyes.

The sight of grass made her tremble. This was the grass on the plains of Troy, the same grass upon which she and Elgin had lain, arms and bodies entwined. Elgin, strikingly handsome, his face entirely whole.

Running.

She was running again, fleeing over the stained grass, scratching her face against the low branches, dashing blindly, wildly, not knowing where she was, who she was, never once looking back.

Thirteen

IT WAS RAINING when Thomas Willey walked her to the waiting carriage the next morning. Even so early in the day, the footman's breath reeked of alcohol. While Mrs. Gosling and Mary Ruper remained outside the front door, oilskins over their heads, waving to her and shouting good-by, Prancer chased after the carriage, barking and wagging his tail furiously until he couldn't keep up with it any longer. She lost sight of him when they turned into Bayswater.

Duff was very quiet.

"I'm very grateful to you, Mr. Duff," she said.

"Why so, my lady?"

"This is a terrible imposition, taking you away from your family."

"My wife understood the situation perfectly. Surely we couldn't let Your Ladyship travel all the way to Scotland alone."

She peered through the window. "Why does it rain so many times when I travel?"

"It's just a passing shower. It should clear before noon. I must say, I'm quite eager to see the children again. Bruce must be a big lad now."

"Yes."

"I'm sorry about little William."

"I want to thank you, Mr. Duff, for attending the burial. Did Lord Elgin's mother say anything about my absence?"

"Not a word, my lady. Mr. Fergusson . . ."

She cut him off. "When we reach Edinburgh, I'd like to have you proceed to Archerfield with the luggage."

"Without Your Ladyship?"

"I shall take the coach to Dunfermline. I want to visit little William's grave."

Within an hour London was lost from view. She leaned back and tried to close her eyes. She felt like a lost meteor, burning itself out, spinning dizzily around in a foreign sky.

The wind's velocity increased at Waltham Abbey, sending slashes of rain against the window, and even though the driver had to slow down the horses to avoid the deep puddles in the road, they managed to reach Cambridge before it got dark.

During dinner, her mind was in turmoil, manacled to little William inside that cold vault at Broomhall, suffocating, his tender skin decaying. Turning her head toward the rain-streaked windows, she thought about the marbles at Park Lane, once so alive as they basked under the Attic sky, now lying in cold death. She could see them clearly, weaving and flickering in the gray shafts of rain.

There was a full-length mirror attached to the door of her room. After bidding Duff good night, she closed it and looked at herself. Slowly, she started to undress. Her brain was still pounding as she studied her naked shoulders, her breasts. It was a relief to discover that the skin over her abdomen was smooth once again. She ran her fingers over it, then brought them down and combed the fine hair with gentle lingering strokes.

It was still raining when the carriage pulled away from the inn the next morning. The road took them past King's Lynn, hugging the coast along the Wash all the way into Wainfleet, where

Duff made an exchange of horses before they retired for the night.

They awoke to a clear sky in the morning, the sun already pouring warmth over the countryside. The road along the bank of the River Witham was narrow but in excellent condition, and they passed through York late in the afternoon before moving rapidly into Richmond.

Although the room at the inn was comfortable and clean, she slept very little and had no appetite for breakfast in the morning. Throughout the day, Duff kept urging her to try to sleep. In Darlington, they stopped at a place called Durham Inn, and again he begged her to eat something, but she could manage only half a biscuit and a little tea. The River Tees flowed behind the inn. On the opposite bank lay Stockton, its countless chimneys pouring columns of dense smoke into the cloudless sky.

They crossed the old wooden bridge into Stockton, then continued at a steady pace until they arrived at Newcastle. Her appetite improved slightly, and she managed to eat most of her dinner and even drink a glass of wine.

Two fresh horses were attached to the carriage in the morning, and they sped off, past Bedlington, Morpeth, Ainwick, Belford. It gladdened her heart to see heather again, wide sweeping fields of it swaying in the wind.

For the first time in days, she slept soundly through the night, knowing that Archerfield and her children were less than twenty miles to the east.

She took leave of Duff in Edinburgh, on the eastern end of Queen Street, just below Calton Hill. "A daily coach leaves here at noon for Dunfermline," she told him.

"Will you be coming to Archerfield directly after Broomhall, my lady?"

"If it's not too late. Otherwise, I shall have to stay at Fortune and Blackwell's."

"What's that?"

"A hotel on Princes Street."

"What time does the coach return to Edinburgh from Dunfermline?"

"Seven o'clock, but it's usually late."

"I wish I could remain at Archerfield, but I must return to London as soon as possible."

"I understand, Mr. Duff."

"I bid Your Ladyship farewell."

"Good-by, Mr. Duff. I shall always be grateful to you."

"Please kiss little William's gravestone for me."

"I shall."

The coach was just about to set off, but all the places had been reserved. In an anguished moment, she begged the driver to allow her to sit with him on top.

"But that's not for a lady," he blurted.

"I must get to Dunfermline today. I have to visit my child's grave."

The driver put on his hat again and bowed. "M'lady, if ye don't mind the smell o' the horses and the rough ride, it's a pleasure to have ye."

It was awkward at first, sitting on the hard seat, the two horses swishing their tails in front of her, brushing her coat, people staring at her from the street. She gripped the rail so tight, the veins of her hand swelled. Beside her, the coach driver was inflated with pride, glancing repeatedly at her, then down at the gaping eyes on Queen Street. He was no more than thirty, a bull of a man with bulging muscles on the arms and neck. Tugging at the reins, he grinned. "I should have told ye about me own smell, m'lady."

She smiled.

The coach ground its way past the General Register House and headed west down Princes Street. After the horses had established a steady gait, the driver tipped his hat spryly and said, "M'name is Daniel, m'lady. Daniel Stuart."

"I'm pleased to make your acquaintance, Mr. Stuart."

"I ne'er allow anybody to sit wi' me, let alone a lady like yourself."

"I'm honored, Mr. Stuart."

"Nay, 'tis ye that honor the likes o' me."

Edinburgh was behind them now. Without losing stride, one of the horses defecated in front of Mary's rigid feet, and she had to clamp her hand over her nose. Daniel laughed. His high-pitched voice was vibrant with emotion as he pointed out various places to her. "Ah, there we have the Craig flower grounds, m'lady. A bonnie place at one time, but now there's nothing there but kind o' auld bits o' gravestones. 'Twas formerly a kirkyard, y'see."

She fastened her eyes on the grass-grown mounds, the tilting gray headstones.

"The resting places o' dead shipmasters and saltmakers, artisans and mediciners, m'lady," Daniel went on. "Some stones bear the insignia o' their craft — here a quadrant, there a hammer."

The church stood in ivy-clad ruins, roofless.

" 'Twas once populated by the monks of Culross, m'lady," added Daniel. He pointed to the south side, where a line of tall yews ran. "Ghostly sentinels o' the past, m'lady."

There was a spectacular view of the firth, and of both shores. She was enchanted by the still beauty of deserted harbors, little stone landing piers, lean white houses crouched against the sea.

"That village once had forty sail o' seagoing craft, m'lady. A hundred and sixty ship carpenters worked here. But nobody goes there any longer 'cept the remains o' the auld Burial Society — and little they've left to do but bury one another."

The carriage swerved sharply into the heart of Dunfermline, a town of hills and braes. On the crest of one hill lay the remains of a church tower, and Daniel was quick to inform her that the Bruce was buried there.

"Yes, I know," she said.

"His name is set in conspicuous stone letters: 'King Robert the Bruce,' it says. From the top o' the tower, m'lady, all fourteen counties that he saved were once clearly visible."

It saddened her to look at the fallen ruins of a once-magnificent abbey. "The Westminster of Scotland," her father called it. Not too distant from there lay Saint Margaret's Cave, tucked in a glen just off Chalmers Street. She didn't need Daniel to tell her about Queen Margaret, a name she had revered since childhood. Daughter of King Henry the Third and sister of King John, wed so young to little Alexander the Third, she wept so much because she was homesick throughout her reign. She was buried finally in the abbey, along with her husband and the two sons that died before their father. Nor did Daniel have to tell her that Dunfermline was the oldest town in Scotland, a place where kings loved to dwell. Looking at it now, its proud hills swollen into ugly tumors, reeking with the smell of death, she felt a heaviness of heart and had to close her eyes.

Her father once again infiltrated her thoughts. There was no prouder Scot than William Nisbet. When she was a child, he often took her on his knee and spoke to her about Scotland, how the Picts and Scots were united in the year A.D. 800, and always at this point he'd throw his head back and laugh. "Actually, lass, there was no union at all, because by this time we Scots had put the last of the Picts to rest; but the peace was short-lived, and once again we had our hands full with the Norse invaders. The true history of Scotland, lass, begins with the eleventh century — with the reign of Malcolm the Second . . ."

Her body shuddered at the first glimpse of Broomhall. Elgin's touch was everywhere — on each red stone, each turret and window, door, chimney, spire, on the long iron railing that separated the slate roof from the third story. He had always referred to it as a country house, but it was more a castle, with patterned brick walls, battlements, and pointed arches.

Daniel pulled the horses to a halt before the front door. "I shall be returning to Edinburgh around six this evening, m'lady. I can stop by if ye wish."

"Yes, please."

"Would it be too much if I asked m'lady to kiss the child's stone for me?"

She nodded. "You've been most kind, Mr. Stuart."

His face cracked into a wide grin. "Perhaps m'lady would care to sit wi' me again on the return journey to Edinburgh."

"Thank you, Mr. Stuart. I shall be pleased to sit with you."

He assisted her from the seat.

"I hope I didn't take you too far out of your way, Mr. Stuart."

"Hardly, m'lady. I'll be disposing the passengers at Bruce Street in the center o' town, and after that, I'll be enjoying some o' that famous 'Dunfermline Nut-Broon Ale.' "

A footman, dressed in splendid livery and holding a long staff in his hand, emerged from the carriage house and, bowing before her, asked her name.

Her voice sounded hollow to her own ears. "I am Lady Elgin."

He looked at her closely, then bowed again. "I shall inform Her Ladyship. Please follow me."

She stopped him at the front door. "Before we go inside, I should like you to direct me to the family burial ground."

"Of course, my lady, but it's a bit of a walk. There, just behind the chapel in the far meadow. Come, I'll take you to it."

The headstones in the burial ground were tilting in the wind, jabbed into the soft earth like broken spears in a wounded animal. She walked quietly past them, then placed her hand on the young footman's arm and leaned on his strength.

He became alarmed. "Are you ill, my lady?"

"No," she murmured.

Stopping before a mound of earth, the footman pointed to the

headstone. "There it is, my lady. The child's grave. 'William Bruce,' it says; 'age six months and three days . . .' "

Elgin's mother sent instructions that the steward of the kitchen prepare some broth for her while the butler fetched the brandy. Mary's head was still spinning. She tried to sit up, but Elgin's mother eased her back against the pillows of the sofa. "Mary, you frightened us." She stiffened for a moment. "You've gone through so much . . . William dying at such a tender age, Thomas still imprisoned in France."

The brandy burned her throat.

"Thomas should never have accepted that post in Constantinople. I warned him against it, but he refused to listen. It was a terrible decision. Terrible."

Slowly, Mary's eyes focused on the drawing room. Everything here reminded her of Elgin — the splendid paintings, the rugs, the priceless collections of antique furniture, vases, sculptures, ancient armor and weapons. A mighty sword hung from the wall above the high arch leading to another grand room, which was lined with bookshelves and more paintings.

Elgin's mother kept an attentive eye on her. Moving away from the sofa, the Countess walked to the arch, stood beneath the two-handed sword for a moment, then came back. She moved with grace and poise, exactly like Elgin. She even had his inflection of voice. "Mary, that sword belonged to Robert the Bruce, first King of Scotland."

"I know."

"He carried it in the Battle of Bannockburn. Scotland gained her independence from his great victory there."

The steward of the kitchen came as far as the drawing room door and nodded his head. The broth was ready to be served in the dining room. The Countess asked if she needed assistance,

but Mary shook her head. "I feel much better now. I think the brandy helped."

Elgin's mother smiled. "But you scarcely touched it, Mary." She took Mary's hand and walked with her into the dining room. "Tell me, did you have time to stop off at the museum in Park Lane?"

"Yes."

"What were your impressions?"

Mary didn't reply.

"It was I who arranged the placing of the entire collection. Mr. Hastings is a trusted employee and keeps a sharp watch on things."

"Yes, he seems quite dedicated," said Mary.

The broth was piping hot.

"I can't wait for Thomas to be released from his imprisonment. Under the circumstances, I did my best. It wasn't an easy matter, getting those workmen to comply with my instructions."

Mary toyed with her spoon. "I sent Elgin the complete inventory. Mr. Hastings had everything written down."

In time, she finished the broth; then, pushing back her chair, she rose to her feet and walked back to the drawing room for her reticule. Quickly, she put on her coat and hat.

"Mary, what are you doing?"

"It's almost six o'clock. The coach to Edinburgh will be stopping here at any moment."

"But you can't leave like this. We've many things to discuss. The chambermaid has already prepared your bed."

"I'm sorry, but I must go. Another time, perhaps."

The pained expression was slow to leave the Countess' face. "I understand. You're impatient to see your children."

"Yes."

"Will you bring them here soon?"

"I shall."

In the marble hallway, as the footman stood by the open front door, the Countess embraced her warmly and kissed her on both cheeks. Daniel Stuart was waiting beside the coach, a broad smile on his face.

"Is m'lady certain about sitting with me again?"

"Of course."

He helped her up to the seat, his breath heavy with ale. "Did m'lady kiss the child's stone for me?"

She clamped one hand on her hat and the other on the rail. "I did, Mr. Stuart. I most certainly did."

Archerfield.

Nothing had changed. It was as though she had never gone away — the same tall oaks in the north meadow, Scotland's birds frolicking in the juniper bushes, the stone walls and green fields where she played as a child, the glorious heather. Everything was the same. And when she saw her mother and father rushing toward the carriage, Bruce trying to outrace them, with Mary and Matilda faltering behind, she was unable to hold back the tears. She couldn't stop kissing them, embracing them with her love. They all fought gleefully to wedge themselves into her arms. Everyone wept.

And Boxer.

He wasn't a pup any longer. Full-grown and strong, he darted away from her at first, then came forward and sniffed her shoes, her clothes. He barked when he recognized her. She bent down and ruffled his coat, kissed his wet nose.

Calitza looked more beautiful than ever, a Caryatid with shiny raven hair parted in the middle and swept back in a low loose bun at the back of her head. Her first words sent tremors of joy to her heart: "Welcome, my lady. Welcome to Scotland."

They embraced, kissed, and wept. Greece was still carved on her face.

Mary walked toward the line of servants standing obediently in the driveway. She greeted them all: Miss Lucy Vane, Mr. Molvitz, steward of the household, Nelly Bell, Robert Oliver, William Hammerton, Mrs. Hall, and finally Andrew Davidson. Archerfield had never known another carriage master. Andrew, more like a member of their family, was still spry, though his hands trembled and he had lost considerable flesh.

The children huddled around her, grabbing hold of her arms, her dress. She didn't know which one to hug first. Her mother pulled her gently away and led her into the family library. "Mary, you have several letters. I've kept them here in the desk."

She took the letters and riffled through them. None bore the familiar scrawl of Elgin's hand. The first was from Masterman. She had given birth to a seven-pound girl and had named it Mary. Mary closed her eyes and reflected for a moment: Masterman. Such wonderful days they spent together. Such happy memories. Mary could still see her standing fretfully in the cabin of the *Phaeton,* clutching that bottle of vinegar in her hand.

Another letter bore a London address: Mrs. Keith Stuart announcing that she had arrived safely from France, and inviting her to visit with her in London.

There was a letter addressed to Elgin from Lusieri in Athens.

"Perhaps you should take a nap," her mother suggested. "Calitza will look after the children. She takes them walking every afternoon."

"Where do they go?"

"Mostly to the north meadow. They play hide-and-seek around the oak trees. Indeed, they have a grand time."

She unbuckled her shoes the moment she entered her bedchamber. Here too, nothing had changed. The coverlet on the bed still conveyed her mother's painstaking love, the long winter hours with needles and yarn. Her clothes hung in the wardrobe exactly as she had left them; her bonnets lay in perfect array on the top shelf, her petticoats neatly folded and tucked inside the drawers of the mahogany chest.

Lying back on the pillows, she stared at Lusieri's letter for a long time before she finally decided to read it:

My dear Lord,

Soon after your departure from Greece, I set forth plans for further removals and excavations throughout Athens, as Your Lordship requested. It was tedious work, but in time we amassed a remarkable collection of marbles and vases, and succeeded in transporting everything to the Piraeus for shipment. This was accomplished at a time when Count Sebastiani was in Turkey, persuading the Turks to break their alliance with Russia in favour of the French. When the British heard of it, they sent their fleet to the aid of Russia, but as the British ships passed through the Dardanelles to make a show of force, the Turks fired at them from the forts in the straits, inflicting heavy losses.

As British relations with Turkey were strained once again, the Voivode of Athens prevented us from putting the marbles on board the waiting vessels. His animosity was so intense that I was compelled to flee Athens and leave all these treasures at the mercy of the French, who were now on friendly terms with the Turks. I later learned that the cases containing most of the vases were broken into and then sent overland to Epirus, whence they were forwarded to France and Bonaparte's Louvre Museum.

The real prize, Your Lordship's collection of marbles, presented a more difficult problem for Bonaparte because of their excessive weight. His agents pleaded with the muleteers of Ioannina, but they refused to haul them over the treacherous mountain passes of Epirus. In desperation, the agents called upon the French Admiralty for assistance, but it was to Your Lordship's advantage that not one ship could be spared from the French fleet.

After many tribulations, I managed to reach Sicily, and at Palermo I negotiated with an agent of the Levant Company to act as Your Lordship's representative. Considerable bickering over money ensued, but we at last arrived at a plan to save the marbles. It involved, not only the persuasion of Admiral Lord

Keith to despatch a war vessel to the Piraeus, but also the more daring scheme of seizing the French agent, Fauvel, by force of arms and holding him hostage until the marbles were safely brought back to the Piraeus.

I equipped Your Lordship's representative with large sums of money, which I had to borrow from several sources in Sicily and Malta, and I will send Your Lordship an itemized list of these loans so that these bankers can be reimbursed as soon as possible. I remind Your Lordship that much of this money went towards the purchase of silver pistols and English watches in anticipation of the bribery that we expected from the Turkish Voivode. Admiral Lord Keith issued further instructions to have Lord Nelson's warship accompanied by a transport vessel carrying horses, tackle, ropes, and carts.

Your Lordship's representative traveled at once to Constantinople and obtained a firman that would allow me to return to Athens. Shortly after I came back, I presented the firman to the Voivode and then took possession of my house once again. I found the doors and windows broken, and a ladder was attached against the garden wall, enabling anyone to enter at will. Everything of value had been stolen — vases, scaffoldings, ropes, all my paper and supplies.

However, my more immediate concern was the collection of marbles now back on the Piraeus docks. To my astonishment, they were unharmed. Working swiftly, I obtained permission from the Voivode to embark the collection on a chartered vessel from the Isle of Hydra. Nelson's ships had yet to arrive for transport, and there was no time to lose.

The marbles were carried on board the chartered vessel in haste, but as soon as she was to set sail, an order reached the Voivode from Constantinople demanding that all the marbles be unloaded at once. Fauvel had successfully thwarted us and was standing arrogantly on the dock, cane in hand, gloating.

Nelson's warship and transport vessel arrived at the Piraeus the next morning. I called upon the Voivode once more and showered him with gifts, but he adamantly refused to permit us to load the marbles into Nelson's ships.

Typical of their nature, the Turks, as Your Lordship can

readily understand, soon became disenchanted with the French, and within a very short time they veered once again towards an alliance with Britain. Your Lordship's representative in Constantinople wrote to me within a fortnight and reported that he had now obtained an order directly from the Sultan that would permit the immediate embarkation of Your Lordship's collection from the Piraeus.

This firman reached Athens two weeks later, but by this time Nelson's ships had sailed away, leaving the marbles on the docks. Just when everything seemed hopeless, Admiral Lord Keith came to Your Lordship's assistance by despatching H.M.S. *Pylades* to the Piraeus in haste. Meanwhile, the chartered Hydriote vessel still lay at anchor in the harbour.

Even to the last hour, Bonaparte tried his utmost to block our plans, largely through Fauvel's bribery and intrigue, but the Sultan's firman was sovereign, and the collection was at last hauled on board the *Pylades* and the Hydriote ship, and both ships set sail for England.

My Lord, I have been a good and faithful servant, and have endured many hardships these past years while in your employ. My work here in Athens is completed, and I now ask you to release me from the bonds of our contract. I sorely yearn to return to my home in Sicily; to die there and be buried with my ancestors.

At this time, I find it necessary to remind Your Lordship that a full and complete accounting must be made between us, subject to the terms of our contract. Please remember that I have yet to receive any of the salary promised me.

Your obedient servant,
Giovanni Battista Lusieri,
Painter to the King of Naples

She was awakened by the touch of her mother's hand, the intimate voice telling her that dinner was ready. Even with the familiar aromas of Mrs. Hall's cooking, her parents' loving glances, she still had difficulty eating. She kept staring at the children,

reassuring herself that it was not a dream — seeing them at the table, listening to their voices — but in time, the turmoil within her abated, and she was able to finish her dinner.

After the dessert, she went for a walk with the children. Boxer followed closely at their heels most of the way, then, in a flash, scampered off to flush out a bird from the tall grass in the north meadow. The sky was cold and cloudless; the earth shivered. In an effort to free herself from the sudden memory of Hyde Park, she started running through the heather. The children chased after her, flying, shouting gleefully, clutching at her coat and hands. Soon Bruce was running ahead of her, coaxing her with excited gestures, challenging her to catch him. He raced like a whippet. It was a brief but joyous moment, one for which she had waited such a long time.

Aberlady Bay called out to her.

A strong wind gusted in from the sea when they reached the top of a sandy slope. Bruce begged to be allowed to slide down a smooth path of sand that led to the water's edge, but she forbade him. All four stood on the slope and looked down at the rolling waves.

Bruce broke the silence. "Mother, when is Father coming home?"

"I don't know," she replied softly.

"Why does he want to stay in France so long?"

"He doesn't want to stay there, Bruce. He's a prisoner."

"Mother, look how much I've grown," exclaimed little Mary, cuddling into her arms.

"Indeed, you have. I hardly recognize you."

"I shall be getting married soon."

"To whom?"

"Bruce."

She laughed. "But you can't marry him. He's your brother."

Matilda started to shiver. Her lips were turning color.

She stood up. "It's time to go back. It will be dark soon."

They locked hands and ran all the way to the meadow. Bruce tugged his hand away, once more challenging her to chase after him. She did. Little Matilda and Mary joined in, both of them shrieking and stumbling over the grass.

She encountered stout resistance from them when it came time for bed, but after much hugging and kissing, they finally went off with Calitza. Matilda's eyes were already half-closed.

Her heart was slow in healing. Scotland did her utmost to anoint it, skipping and dancing before her eyes, flooding her days with song, soothing her unrest and disquietude. But Scotland could do nothing for her at night. Desperately, she tried to ward off her anguish by writing long letters to Elgin, scribbling furiously far into the night, but it was fruitless. He never answered.

She kept hounding Andrew and her father every morning, asking them if the post had arrived yet, bringing a letter from Elgin. William Nisbet finally lost his patience. "Lass, why don't you pay a visit to Broomhall? Elgin may have corresponded with his mother."

"That's an excellent thought, Father. I'll have Andrew drive me there tomorrow. I'll take my sweet darlings. Elgin's mother is most eager to see them."

Andrew Davidson drove her father into Dirleton early the next morning for the London newspapers. She and the children were dressed and ready to depart for Broomhall when the carriage pulled into the driveway. Her father flung open the door and ran toward her, holding high a newspaper. "Elgin is in London!" he shouted. "Look, it's here on the front page!"

Her hand trembled as she reached for the newspaper. The notice was brief and blocked off in the center of the page.

> Thomas Bruce, Earl of Elgin, has this day arrived in London after a long imprisonment in France.

"Lass, say something. Why are you so quiet?"

She couldn't speak.

"In God's name, your husband is coming home."

Hurrying back to the children, she said, "We shan't be going to Broomhall." She couldn't control the tremors in her heart.

Bruce was crestfallen. "Why not, Mother?"

She knelt down and gathered them into her arms. "I have wonderful news . . . your father has been released from his imprisonment."

"Will he be here soon?" asked Bruce, overjoyed.

"Yes."

"I hope I can recognize him, Mother," said little Mary.

"What do you mean?"

"Perhaps he's wearing a new nose. I didn't like the old one."

After dinner that evening, her father walked to the pianoforte and beckoned her to sing something, and although her heart wasn't in it, she obliged him:

My bonnie lass, I work in brass,
  A tinkler is my station;
I've travel'd round all Christian ground,
  In this my occupation.

I've ta'en the gold, I've been enroll'd
  In many a noble squadron;
But vain they search'd, when off I march'd
  To go and clout the caudron.

Awakened from an unsettled sleep by the first rays of the sun streaking through her bedchamber window, she was about to pull down the blind when she heard a soft knock on the door. It was the maid, Nelly Bell.

"What is it?" Mary asked.

"I have a message for you, my lady."

"Can't it wait?"

"The man who delivered it said it was very important."

"From where did he come?"

"Edinburgh, my lady."

"Who sent it?"

"A Mr. Robert Fergusson."

She reached for her robe. "Is the man still here?"

"Yes, he's waiting in the hallway. He refuses to leave until Your Ladyship reads the message."

"Please give it back to him."

"But he said it was most important, my lady."

"Very well."

"What shall I do with the message, my lady?"

"Put it on the table in the hallway. Tell the man I'll read it later."

"But, my lady . . . ."

"Please do as I say."

"Yes, my lady."

She waited until the maid walked out of the room, but before closing the door, she was startled by the sight of her father standing outside the door of his bedchamber, his nightcap perched on the side of his head. "Who was that at the front door?" he asked.

"Just a messenger."

"What did he want?"

"He delivered a letter."

"From where?"

"Edinburgh."

"Well, speak up, lass. Who sent the letter?"

"Mr. Fergusson."

"Who is he?"

"He was at the Richelieu when we were detained in France. Elgin knows his family quite well."

"What do you suppose he wants?"

"I don't know."

"You didn't read the letter?"

"I'll read it later."

"I don't understand you, lass. The man went out of his way to dispatch a messenger here at this hour of the day. Surely it must be important. Where is the letter?"

"There, on the table near the door."

"Well, read it."

"But Father . . ."

"If you don't read it, I shall."

She walked down the stairs to the small table and picked up the letter. It was still dark in the hallway. She opened the front door to let the light in, then looked at the envelope. It wasn't sealed.

"What does it say?" her father called out from the stairs.

Her eyes scanned over the words hurriedly. "It's very brief, Father. Nothing important at all. Mr. Fergusson wishes to visit with us this afternoon."

"For what reason?"

"He doesn't say."

When she reached the top of the stairs, her father pounced on her again. "Lass, who is this man? Where does he live?"

"In Raith. It's not too far from Broomhall."

"Is he married?"

"No."

William Nisbet gave her a long look, then sighed. "Go back to bed, lass. You seem very tired. I'll ask Mrs. Hall to bring you a cup of warm milk. It'll put you to sleep quickly."

Fergusson arrived at Archerfield shortly after two o'clock. She had to look away when his eyes touched hers. Mrs. Nisbet hurriedly stepped into the kitchen to consult with Mrs. Hall about serving tea, while Fergusson was escorted into the drawing room by William Nisbet. Mary tarried several steps behind.

Fergusson remained standing even after her father invited him

to sit on the sofa. Flitting his eyes toward her again, he reached into his coat pocket and brought out a folded sheet of newspaper. His voice quivered. "No doubt, you must know that Lord Elgin was liberated from his detainment in France and is now in London?"

"Yes, we're quite aware of it, Mr. Fergusson," said her father, shifting himself in his chair. "Did you come here all the way from Edinburgh to tell us this?"

Fergusson held out the newspaper. "Sir, there is an article here in *The Times* that perhaps you may not have seen. It explains how His Lordship's release was effected. With your permission, I should like to read it."

"Please do, Mr. Fergusson."

The combination of his voice and the words swirled around her head:

> His Lordship's freedom was brought about in large measure by the intervention of the Royal Academy of Sciences, whose strong letter to the French Institute elicited the appropriate response from Napoleon Bonaparte.
>
> It is common knowledge that Lord Elgin accumulated an enormous expense in bringing his collection of marbles to England. To settle with his many creditors, and help defray the staggering drain on his resources, His Lordship has offered the entire collection to the British Museum, and is currently negotiating with Parliament on the price of the sale.

After tea, Fergusson rose from his chair in the dining room and said, "Begging your forgiveness, sir, I should like to speak privately with Lady Elgin."

She looked up from her cup and quickly put it down.

Fergusson waited until her mother and father walked out of the room; then, moving behind his chair, he murmured, "Why did you leave London without saying a word?"

"I don't care to discuss this, Mr. Fergusson. If you have nothing further to say, I must ask you to leave."

There was silence.

"I can't understand why Lord Elgin would want to do such a thing. It will be disastrous, the scandal and humiliation."

"Mr. Fergusson, what are you trying to say?"

"Lord Elgin is suing me. The very day he arrived in London, he filed charges against me."

"He filed charges?"

Fergusson's eyes darted away from her.

"What are the charges, Mr. Fergusson?"

"Adultery . . ."

Everything inside her was torn asunder.

She avoided her parents for the rest of the day. How could she face them? How could she look into her children's eyes? What madness could drive Elgin to do this, to drag his noble name into the gutter, to pull her along with him? What did he hope to gain?

She couldn't finish her dinner. Her father followed her up the stairs and stopped her at the threshold. "Lass, what's the trouble?"

She shook her head.

"Surely you can tell your own father?"

"Please, Father . . . I need to be alone."

"What did Mr. Fergusson tell you? I want to know."

She couldn't hold it back any longer. The tears were choking her. "Elgin is suing Mr. Fergusson . . ."

Through broken sobs, she told her father everything. He remained frozen at the threshold for what seemed an eternity; then slowly he moved toward her, reached out, and took her into his arms. "There now, lass, no more tears. Do you want your mother to see you this way?"

"Father, what shall I do? I've disgraced you."

William Nisbet straightened his shoulders. "This could very well be a scheme on Elgin's part. The whole world knows that

he is desperate for money. Fergusson must be a wealthy man."

She grasped his hand. "Father, many times I wanted to disclose in my letters that I could see a horrible change taking place in Elgin, almost from the very day he started to tear down the marbles from the Parthenon. He's not the same person I married. I've been reluctant to say anything, but I believe he may be . . . insane."

The tears began flowing again.

"Father, you won't tell Mother about all this?"

"Of course not, lass. Now then, lie down and try to get some sleep. I'll ask Calitza to put the bairns to bed."

She was awakened by Calitza's trembling voice. "My lady, come quickly. Bruce is very ill!"

Her father and mother were already in Bruce's bedchamber, standing over him as he lay on the floor, writhing, the corners of his mouth coated with saliva. Mary took the bottle of vinegar from Calitza and began to dab some on Bruce's forehead and wrists, but he let out a piercing scream and shoved her away. Calitza could do nothing to restrain him. In a somber voice, William Nisbet instructed Calitza to send Andrew after a physician.

Almost an hour went by before the physician arrived. Fighting to remain calm, Mary waited until he had listened to Bruce's heart. "What ails my son?" she exclaimed.

"I think that it's not serious, my lady. Tell me, is he an excitable lad?"

"Yes, very much so."

"Then I suspect that the seizure was brought about by an extreme fantasy of mind."

"What can you do for him?"

He withdrew a brown bottle from his leather bag and handed it to her. "Give him two full spoons of this four times a day."

"What is it?"

"A mixture the apothecary at Dirleton compounds for me. It's a nerve tonic derived from sage and valerian. I also recommend that the lad be put on a diet of stewed prunes and water for several days. Please be assured, my lady, that it's only a minor ailment. The lad should be fit within a day or two."

She plunged into a tormented sleep and didn't awake until three o'clock in the afternoon. Just before dinner, there was a knock on the front door. Nelly Bell answered it.

"Constable Gordon wishes to speak to you, my lady," she whispered to Mary.

"What does he want?"

"He didn't say, my lady."

The constable had his hat off and was rolling it in his hands. He was an enormous man — thick-necked and with powerful shoulders, ruddy face pockmarked with beads of perspiration. He reached into his coat pocket and pulled out two folded documents. "My lady, I have a court order here that says . . ."

"A court order?"

". . . the three children residing here must be brought to Lord Elgin's home in Dunfermline no later than five o'clock tomorrow afternoon."

"Why?"

Constable Gordon handed her the documents. "My lady, you are hereby summonsed to appear at the main courtroom in Edinburgh precisely at ten o'clock one week from today."

Feeling faint, she made no effort to take the documents from him.

Her father's voice. "Give me those papers, constable."

"But I was instructed to hand them to Her Ladyship personally."

"Who instructed you?"

"Lord Elgin's barrister, Mr. Garrow."

"Give me the papers, constable. I shall be responsible."

"Thank you, Mr. Nisbet. Thank you very much indeed."

As soon as the constable was gone, she fell into her father's

arms. He closed the door quietly and walked outside with her. The sun was just about to drop behind the oak trees in the north meadow.

"Father, you must help me. I don't want Elgin to take my bairns away."

"Now, now, lass, I'm sure that it will be only for a short while. Once the trial is over, we shall bring them back to Archerfield."

"Why is Elgin doing this?"

"God only knows."

She was panic-stricken. "I'll take them away from here, away from Scotland. He'll never find us."

"I'm afraid the law is on his side, lass. He's mad enough to track you down, no matter where you go. We must comply with the summons. Don't worry about your mother. I'll tell her that the bairns are going to visit their grandmother at Broomhall."

"But what about Bruce? He's ill."

"He'll be well by tomorrow."

"Father, I shall die if my bairns are taken away from me."

William Nisbet glanced back at the house. "They'll be wondering about us. Come, let's go inside. Here, take hold of my hand. There's nothing to fear. We must have faith in the Almighty."

In the morning, she stood beside her father in the driveway, holding back the tears until Andrew Davidson gave rein to the horses. When the carriage swung toward the Dirleton road, she caught a last glimpse of Bruce's arm waving from the window.

Two days later, she went with her father to Edinburgh. William Nisbet's solicitor, Mr. Kincaid, had persuaded one of Scotland's leading barristers to undertake the case, and Mary was to have an interview with him in his chambers. His name was Edward Topping, a very short man with sharp beady eyes and a head

completely bald. His chambers were in the heart of Princes Street. A member of Gray's Inn, and holding the high rank of King's Counsel, Topping politely asked William Nisbet to leave while he talked privately with Mary in chambers.

"I'm sorry to put you through this, my lady, but I have several questions to ask that pertain to your case."

"I understand, Mr. Topping."

He waited until she sat, then started pacing around the room. "I must first tell you that Lord Elgin has prepared himself well for this trial. He has Mr. Garrow for his barrister, London's best; and he intends to call upon many witnesses."

"Mr. Topping, I do not want to lose my children."

"I shall do my utmost to prevent this, my lady, but in order to do so, we too must have witnesses. Can Your Ladyship think of a few that I can call upon who will attest to your good character and sound qualities as a mother and as a wife . . . those perhaps you knew before your marriage, or during the time you spent in Constantinople, Athens, and France?"

"But the trial begins in five days, Mr. Topping. It would be too difficult to locate them. Some are in various parts of Scotland; others, in England."

"It would benefit our case a great deal, my lady, if you could ask them to appear at the trial." Topping rubbed his hands in agitation and turned to face the window. "My lady, are you guilty of this charge?"

"What charge?"

Topping spun around. "Adultery."

She withdrew into silence.

Topping studied her for a long time; then, going behind her chair, he waited until she rose to her feet. "We shall meet again at the trial, my lady. One final word: I do not want you to discuss this case with anyone. Is that clear?"

Andrew Davidson had the carriage waiting outside the front door on the day of the trial. The sky was heavy with clouds, but toward the east a thin shaft of light was emerging, and her father took this as a good omen. After stepping into the carriage, she asked her father, "What did you tell Mother?"

"She believes that we're going to Dunfermline to visit Elgin's mother."

"But what if the trial should last more than one day?"

"Stop fretting, lass. I'll think of something else to tell her."

It was Andrew who had first put her on a horse. She was only five and very much afraid, but somehow he had found a way to quiet her terror, stepping boldly toward the horse and shouting into its ear, "Jock, eno' o' that. Stop your huffin' 'n puffin'. Show a bit o' respect for this beautiful lassie, else I shall have to cuff ye behind the ear!" It was an endearing portrait, one that she would never forget. Faithful Andrew; nothing but skin and bones and wasting old age.

Princes Street was already wide awake — crowds flooding the pavements and street, carriages everywhere, and high above them, the gravestones of Calton Hill pointing at the bleak sky.

Andrew pulled the horses to a halt in front of Parliament House, where a large throng had assembled on the steps and along both sides of the street. Pushing his way through them, William Nisbet led her to the gigantic oak door. His solicitor, Mr. Kincaid, was waiting for them in the marble hallway. "Mr. Nisbet," he whispered, "as I already told you, I presented every detail of this case to Mr. Topping. He seemed unwilling to undertake it at first, but I stressed it to him that Lady Elgin's future and good name are in jeopardy."

"Thank you, Mr. Kincaid."

Kincaid had a youthful face, but he was exceedingly corpulent, and his cheeks jounced with each word. "I was pleased to learn that Her Ladyship had a talk with Mr. Topping in

chambers. He has agreed to represent Mr. Fergusson also. Now, on the matter of witnesses, my lady . . ."

"I decided against the witnesses, Mr. Kincaid."

"But, my lady . . ."

"The last thing I want is to involve my friends in this unpleasant matter."

Kincaid said nothing further.

They followed him across the great hall, Mary's mind trailing back to a time when she was ten years old, when Mr. Gibbon, the schoolmaster of Dirleton, conducted his class on a tour of the building. Nothing had changed — the same high oak-timbered ceiling, the stained-glass windows, the barristers in their silly wigs, the young pages scurrying from room to room, the rigid statues in the marble rotunda, the busts of all the court's Lord Presidents dating back to the year 1685. Mr. Gibbon's voice clearly echoed in her ears: "This great building houses every book published in Great Britain from the time of Charles the Second . . ."

A constable was stationed at the door of the main courtroom, his eyes riveted on her bosom. Suddenly she wanted to flee. What was she doing here? Where was she? Who was she? There was still time. She could dash down the stairs and lose herself in the street, never see anyone again, never touch anyone, never let anyone touch her.

She felt her father's firm grip on her arm, and together they entered the courtroom. The young constable led them to a bench in the first row, then returned to his post at the door. She couldn't raise her eyes. Someone banged a gavel, and slowly she looked up. The Lord President walked briskly into the courtroom, his slight frame sagging under wig and robe. Behind him came the four Lord Judges, moving in solemn dignity. Everyone in the courtroom stood up.

Lifting a document from his desk, the clerk unfolded it and began to read.

Fourteen

"THE TRIAL OF Robert J. Fergusson, Esquire, for adultery with the Countess of Elgin, wife of the seventh Earl of Elgin and the eleventh of Kincardine, in the Court of Sessions at Edinburgh, Scotland. The defendant, Mr. Fergusson, having suffered a previous judgment to go by default in London, a jury is this day called for the purpose of assessing the quantum of damages.' "

The Lord President instructed the clerk to call in the jury. When the twenty-one men filed into the courtroom and took their places on the right hand of the Lord Judges, the Lord President lifted his eyes. "Who pleads for the plaintiff?"

She glanced quickly across the courtroom and saw a tall man in black wig and robe rise to his feet. Something made her turn her eyes farther back, to a figure sitting alone at the opposite end of the barrister's table. She gasped at the sight of him. It was Elgin, looking dreadfully pale and emaciated, his shoulders stooped and hunched over like an old man's. He didn't see her.

His barrister was addressing the court. "My Lord President and Lord Judges, gentlemen of the jury, my name is Thomas Garrow and I reside in London. I have the honor of attending

you on behalf of my noble client and plaintiff, Lord Elgin, for the purposes of ascertaining the damages allowed him in the misconduct of the defendant, who permitted a previous judgment in London to go by default.

"Of the many melancholy cases with which my practice for twenty years in the courts of Westminster has led me to become acquainted, this exceeds them all. I bring to your attention that the noble plaintiff is the representative of one of the most respected families in Scotland, a direct descendant of Robert the Bruce, first King of this land. My noble plaintiff was solemnly joined in marriage to Mary Nisbet, who was also of an esteemed and opulent family. At the time of the marriage, she was nineteen years of age and possessed every accomplishment of mind and person which made her the object of the warmest attachment. His Lordship was thirteen years her senior, but there was no disparity as could make the match in the slightest degree unequal.

"A short time before the marriage, Lord Elgin had been appointed Ambassador to the Sublime Porte at Constantinople, and such was the ardor of his attachment to his bride that he proposed to abandon all those splendid prospects which his appointment held out for him, and to retire to scenes of domestic happiness and endearment, if such a course should be more agreeable to her. However, she consented to accompany him in his embassy to Constantinople.

"My Lord President and Lord Judges, I intend to prove that throughout this whole period Lord and Lady Elgin exhibited the strongest mutual affection and regard, and afforded a true picture of perfect conjugal harmony. Their well-regulated family revealed a pattern of the best English manners, as well as a devoted attention to domestic and religious duties. Lady Elgin resisted the batteries of ridicule and never gave card parties on a Sunday nor indulged in the fashionable follies of dissipation. Quite to the contrary, she adhered in a strict manner to the prac-

tice of those virtues in which she had been educated by her respectable parents. During the interval in Constantinople, three children were born, one son and two daughters.

"After closing down the embassy in Constantinople, Lord Elgin visited Greece with his family and some of his staff, then continued to Italy. At Naples, the children were sent to Scotland by ship while Lord and Lady Elgin remained, visiting Rome and Florence before arriving in France. We all recollect that breach of diplomatic courtesy which took place at that time, when English citizens were seized and held as prisoners of war. Among those detained with Lord and Lady Elgin was Mr. Fergusson. Lord Elgin recognized a friend and neighbor of his family, and thus His Lordship's relationship with Mr. Fergusson was fixed upon terms of the greatest respect and honor.

"Because of a recurring indisposition, Lord Elgin was granted permission to seek the baths at Barèges for the recovery of his health. From here, they removed to Pau, where a fourth child was born, a male. A few months after this, Lady Elgin traveled to Paris and was unceasing in her efforts to procure Lord Elgin's liberation from the prison at Lourdes.

"Upon the untimely death of her infant son, Lady Elgin was permitted to return to England while Lord Elgin remained confined in France. Instead of coming directly to Scotland, she preferred to stay, not at her parents' winter home, but at Number Sixty Baker Street in Portman Square . . . and there, my lords and gentlemen of the jury, the peace of a noble family was ruined, bringing about that injury for which this jury is assembled. Since judgment was previously allowed to go by default, it is now my duty to submit proof of this criminal correspondence between Mr. Fergusson and Lady Elgin. I hope not to dwell long on this unpleasant subject, because I wish to smooth the feelings of my noble client, and also because I do not mean to bring more pain upon the heart of that lady whom Lord Elgin revered."

She turned around to look at her father, but he had his head down. The portly gentleman at his side had his eyes fixed on her. There was a deathly silence in the courtroom.

"My lords and gentlemen of the jury, before calling upon my noble plaintiff's witnesses, permit me to bring certain facts to your knowledge. First, in order to prove adultery, it is necessary to establish that a valid marriage existed between the two spouses, and that there was sexual intercourse between the defendant and the guilty spouse. Second, adultery may be proved by a preponderance of evidence, but the proof must be sufficiently definite, showing the approximate time, the place of the offense, the circumstances under which it was committed, and that the libelee was a party to the illicit act. Here I must remind you that it is a fundamental law of English jurisprudence that it is not necessary to prove the direct act of adultery, because there could not be one case in a hundred in which such proof might be attainable. Indeed, it is quite rare that the parties are surprised in the direct act. Thus, in almost every case, the fact is inferred from circumstances that lead to it. Otherwise, no protection could be given to marital rights. Finally, a completion of sexual intercourse is not required, nor is the birth of a child essential. The only important element of adultery is a guilty intent. Intercourse must be voluntary. An act accomplished by force or fraud is not sufficient ground for divorce. I must add that an adulterous disposition is one of gradual development, and even if it can be proved with negligible circumstantial evidence, this should be adequate to justify an inference that adultery took place.

"My lords and gentlemen of the jury, I will now proceed to furnish you with such proof. I submit that the defendant, Mr. Fergusson, indeed seduced by degrees, and in such a way as to especially suit the character of Lady Elgin. The behavior, the views, and the objects of Lord Elgin were all to be misrepresented. His public and private conduct were to be attacked. He was to be brought down from being the object of Lady Elgin's love and adoration and be made instead a victim of scorn and

disgrace. Amidst all such exhortations, the defendant was considered to be a friend of the family, but in truth his one object was to prevail upon Lady Elgin to despise her husband and alienate him by the coolness of her conduct. For this reason did the defendant volunteer to convey the bier of their dead child to Scotland." Garrow clasped his hand over his brow. "Unhappy woman! How little did she foresee her fate, that her own husband's friend should be the means of making her children orphans . . ."

Topping rose to his feet. At first, she did not recognize him. He was almost totally transformed, in his wavy gray wig. "My lords, such histrionics may be appropriate in the courts of Westminster, but surely not here in Edinburgh."

"Sustained," agreed the Lord President, giving Garrow a hard look. "I think it is time that we hear from your first witness, Mr. Garrow."

Garrow went back to his bench and looked through some notes. "On behalf of my noble client," he declared, "I call Mr. William Richard Hamilton to the witness cage."

She stirred with uneasiness at the sight of Hamilton. His limp seemed more pronounced than ever as he hobbled to the witness cage.

"Your name is William Richard Hamilton?" asked Garrow, clearing his throat.

"It is."

"I understand that you held a situation under Lord Elgin?"

"I did."

"What exactly was that situation?"

"I acted as private secretary to His Lordship."

"And did you sail with him on his embassy?"

"I did."

"How long did you continue with him?"

"For a brief period on the Isle of Sicily, and then for several years at Constantinople."

"Was Lady Elgin with him during all this time?"

"She was."

"Did you observe the demeanor of Lord Elgin and Lady Elgin as husband and wife?"

"I did."

"During your residence at Constantinople, were you always at their table?"

"I was."

"And during the whole time of your being in their company, how did they conduct themselves as husband and wife?"

"Lord Elgin was an affectionate and tender husband."

"And Lady Elgin?"

"A most dutiful wife."

"Tender and affectionate also?"

"Yes."

"Mr. Hamilton, in what manner was the household conducted in the matter of religion?"

"With great propriety. There was a chaplain attached to the embassy, Mr. Philip Hunt, and his prayers were attended by the whole family with the greatest regularity."

"What was the service?"

"That of the Church of England."

"Would you say that Lady Elgin's affections toward His Lordship were evident in their public as well as private concerns?"

"I would."

"Were any children born while you were with them?"

"A son, the name of Bruce."

"Did you observe Her Ladyship's conduct toward this child?"

"I did. She conducted herself like a tender mother."

"Mr. Hamilton, can you tell the court about His Lordship's frequent indispositions?"

"Lord Elgin suffered from rheumatism and catarrh."

"What was Her Ladyship's reaction to these indispositions?"

"At first, she was quite patient and attentive."

"And later?"

"She seemed withdrawn. I suspect it was because . . ."

Topping stood up. "My lords, must we subject ourselves to Mr. Hamilton's suspicions?"

The Lord President nodded his head. "Please answer only the questions that are put to you, Mr. Hamilton."

Garrow moved away from the witness cage and planted himself in front of the jury. "Mr. Hamilton, regarding this withdrawal on the part of Lady Elgin, would you say it was due to a definite reason?"

"I would. Shortly after arriving at Constantinople, His Lordship contracted a severe ague, which consequently resulted in the loss of his nose."

Another commotion drifted through the courtroom. Garrow used every moment of it, then asked, "Would you conclude that Her Ladyship's love for Lord Elgin began to wane at this point?"

The Lord President reproached him. "Mr. Garrow, the court concludes, not your witness."

Garrow kept his eyes on the jury. "I beg the court's forgiveness. I shall rephrase the question. Mr. Hamilton, would you say that Her Ladyship's affection for her husband diminished with the gradual loss of his nose?"

"I would."

"And did you notice any manifestations of Her Ladyship's waning love?"

"Only after His Lordship brought the matter to my attention."

"What exactly did he say to you?"

Hamilton hesitated.

"You must answer the question," said the Lord President.

"His Lordship told me that because of her tender age, Her Ladyship had a marked weakness for men."

Again the courtroom stirred.

"Mr. Hamilton, were you able to substantiate this statement of Lord Elgin?"

"I was. One day, while in Her Ladyship's presence, I heard her remark of Signor Lusieri, 'Now that is a handsome man!' "

"Who is Signor Lusieri?"

"A painter who was assigned by His Lordship to supervise the work in Athens."

"Was he, in fact, handsome?"

"I would say so."

"Were there any other men to your knowledge for whom Her Ladyship felt the same way?"

"Count Sebastiani."

"And who is he?"

"The personal agent of Bonaparte. He made a visit to the embassy in Constantinople one day, and I distinctly heard Her Ladyship say to her maid, 'What a smart French *beau,* so *parfaitment à la mode,* and so extraordinarily good-looking!' "

"She was speaking of Count Sebastiani?"

"She was."

"I ask you now to press upon your memory, Mr. Hamilton, and tell us if you ever saw Mr. Fergusson and Lady Elgin together?"

"I did."

"Were they alone?"

"They were indeed."

"Where exactly did you observe them?"

"At Bramwell House, in London."

She was overwhelmed by gushes of heat on her body.

"Is that a hotel, Mr. Hamilton?"

"It is."

"Did you come upon them by chance?"

"Certainly not. I was instructed to observe them."

"By whom?"

"His Lordship."

"For what reason, Mr. Hamilton?"

"His Lordship knew beforehand that Mr. Fergusson would be departing from France on the same ship as Lady Elgin."

"Do you recall the name of this ship?"

"It was the brig *Defiance.*"

"But you did not sail on this ship yourself?"

"No."

"Then how did you know that you were to keep them under surveillance?"

"His Lordship entrusted a letter to the captain of the vessel, and upon the ship's arrival in England, the message was delivered to my residence."

"How did you know that Lady Elgin and Mr. Fergusson were at Bramwell House?"

"One of the midshipmen followed them there."

"And after that, you assumed the watch?"

"I did."

"You were never detected?"

"No," said Hamilton, nervously clearing his throat.

Garrow walked to his bench and took a cup of water. "Mr. Hamilton, please tell the court how long Her Ladyship and Mr. Fergusson remained at Bramwell House."

"Mr. Fergusson stayed there overnight."

"Where did he sleep?"

"In an adjacent room to Her Ladyship's, on the second story."

"I want you to think carefully before answering this question, Mr. Hamilton: Did Mr. Fergusson spend the night in Her Ladyship's room?"

"I can't say exactly, but he may have."

"My lords!" shouted Topping.

The Lord President leaned forward on his elbows and admonished Hamilton. "Kindly tell the court only what you saw, nothing else."

"After Mr. Fergusson was shown to his room, he returned to Her Ladyship's room and spoke with her for quite a while at the threshold."

"Did he enter the room at all?" asked Garrow.

"He did."

"How long did he remain inside?"

"I don't know exactly. It was quite late, and I was feeling very tired. I had to leave."

"Did you go directly to your house, Mr. Hamilton?"

"I did."

"And you resumed the watch at Bramwell House the next morning?"

"Yes."

"What were your observations on that day?"

"Mr. Fergusson left Bramwell House early in the day for Scotland."

"And Lady Elgin remained at the hotel?"

"Yes."

"For how long a period, Mr. Hamilton?"

"Five days."

"Did Her Ladyship then go to her parents' winter residence at Portman Square?"

"No, she rented a house at Number Sixty Baker Street. It's not too far from Portman Square."

"How long did Her Ladyship reside there?"

"Several weeks."

"Did she receive visitors?"

"Mostly Mr. Fergusson."

"But you told us that he had set off for Scotland."

"He returned to London shortly after that."

"Mr. Hamilton, how often did Mr. Fergusson call at Number Sixty Baker Street?"

"Almost every evening."

"Did he ever leave the house with Lady Elgin?"

"Many times."

"Where did they go?"

"Occasionally to the theater or the opera; at other times, they went walking in Hyde Park."

The words pounded in Mary's ears.

"And this relationship between Mr. Fergusson and Lady Elgin continued during all this time?"

"Yes."

"What happened after that?"

"Her Ladyship left London with Mr. Duff."

"Where did they go?"

"To Scotland."

"Did Her Ladyship go directly to her parents' home in Dirleton?"

"No, she took the coach to Dunfermline. Mr. Duff proceeded to Dirleton with the luggage."

"Why did Her Ladyship go to Dunfermline, Mr. Hamilton?"

"I can't say."

"You didn't follow her there?"

"No."

"Then you returned to London after this?"

"Yes."

"Mr. Hamilton, do you swear again that the testimony you have given here is true?"

"Entirely true."

Garrow let out a deep sigh. "My lords, I have finished with this witness."

The Lord President motioned to Topping, who slowly left his bench and approached the witness cage. "Mr. Hamilton, you said that you sailed with Lord Elgin on his embassy to Constantinople?"

"I did."

"And that you remained with him in Constantinople for several years?"

"Yes."

"What was your employment after this?"

"I worked as a secretary in the service of the government."

"In London?"

"Yes."

"Are you currently so employed?"

"Yes."

"Now then, Mr. Hamilton, when you were making these clandestine observations of Lady Elgin and Mr. Fergusson, was anybody else in your presence?"

"No."

"You strike me as an honest man, Mr. Hamilton. You have sworn here under oath that Lady Elgin was a dutiful wife."

"She was."

"And that she took an avid interest in His Lordship's affairs, whether private or public."

"She did."

"Mr. Hamilton, if Lord Elgin hadn't forewarned you, would you have been aware of Lady Elgin's alleged weakness for handsome men?"

Hamilton looked at Garrow, then at Mary.

"You must answer the question," demanded one of the Lord Judges.

"I don't think that I would have been aware of it."

"Then it was upon His Lordship's instigation that you first entertained these suspicions?"

"Yes," Hamilton responded, his face now devoid of color.

"Bearing this in mind, can you honestly say that Lady Elgin was involved in an affair with Mr. Fergusson?"

"Throughout Her Ladyship's stay in London, they were constantly together, even into the late hours of night."

"Mr. Hamilton, if Lady Elgin wanted to have an affair with Mr. Fergusson, don't you think that she would have been more secretive about it? One can hardly have an affair while surrounded by servants and housekeepers."

Garrow jumped to his feet. "My lords, in my opening remarks, I described at great length the full extent of the law regarding criminal conversation."

"That's entirely correct," agreed the Lord President. "I sug-

gest that Mr. Topping desist from that course of interrogation."

Topping heaved back his shoulders. "My lords and gentlemen of the jury, I submit that Mr. Hamilton's testimony be weighed carefully. His clandestine surveillance of two individuals whose honor and good names are beyond reproach proves indeed that his employer, Lord Elgin, issued these contemptible instructions out of insane jealousy. How cruel and un-Christian to use such abominable measures for the perpetration of his demoniacal schemes!"

"Have you finished with the witness?" said the Lord President.

"I have," replied Topping hotly.

Garrow waited until Topping seated himself at his bench. "My lords, I call Mr. John Morier to the witness cage."

She was still shaking from Hamilton's testimony. She wanted to reach out for her father but didn't dare lift her eyes. And now Morier was being sworn as a witness against her.

"Mr. Morier, did you also accompany Lord Elgin on his embassy to Constantinople?"

"Yes."

"In what capacity were you employed?"

"I was His Lordship's private secretary."

"Did you reside in the same house as Lord and Lady Elgin?"

"Yes."

"And did you have the opportunity of observing their conduct as husband and wife?"

"Lord Elgin was a tender and affectionate husband."

"Answer the question," admonished the Lord President.

"I had many opportunities to observe their conduct."

"Would you say that Lord Elgin was indeed a tender and affectionate husband?"

"My lords, Mr. Garrow is leading the witness," Topping interjected.

"Sustained."

"Mr. Morier, what were your observations regarding Lord Elgin's conduct with Lady Elgin?"

"He was a tender and affectionate husband."

The courtroom erupted with laughter.

"What were your observations of Lady Elgin's conduct toward her husband?" asked Garrow.

"At first, she was a most dutiful wife."

"Did her conduct change?"

"Yes."

"When?"

"As His Lordship's affliction became progressively worse."

"Are you referring to Lord Elgin's rheumatism and catarrh?"

"No, the illness of his nose."

"Did you detect any outward signs of Her Ladyship's change in conduct?"

"Yes. She became more abrupt in His Lordship's company."

"What else, Mr. Morier?"

"She left the house quite often."

"For what reason?"

"To attend afternoon teas and socials. Her Ladyship had a fond admiration for parties."

"What about the evenings?"

"She retired early."

"Mr. Morier, would you say that Lady Elgin, in fact, had a weakness for handsome men?"

"Her Ladyship is a very beautiful woman. Men are quite attracted to her."

"You did not answer my question, Mr. Morier."

Morier thought for a moment. "Her Ladyship was always drawn to handsome men."

"Can you recall an actual incident?"

Morier shifted his feet uneasily. "Many times I observed a certain look in Her Ladyship's eyes whenever a man, particularly a handsome man, visited the embassy."

"Can you describe this look?"

"It was a look of admiration."

"Nothing more?"

"Of attraction too."

"Sexual attraction?"

"My lords!" protested Topping.

The Lord President bellowed at Garrow, "Let me remind you that you are still on direct examination. This court will not permit another leading question. Is that clear, Mr. Garrow?"

Garrow nodded his head, then turned again to Morier. "Will you please give the court a more lucid explanation of what you meant about Her Ladyship's look?"

"It was a flirtatious look."

"Are you certain about this, Mr. Morier?"

"Quite certain."

Garrow strode back to his bench. "I have no further questions to ask of this witness, my lords."

Topping did not choose to interrogate Morier.

Garrow addressed the court. "My lords, I call Mr. Richard Sterling to the witness cage."

She was aghast. What was this odious shadow doing here? Where did Elgin unearth him? What could he possibly say against her? He hardly knew her.

Under Garrow's guidance, Sterling testified that he had met the Elgins when they were all detained at the Hôtel de Richelieu, that Lady Elgin and Lord Elgin were seldom seen together, and that Lady Elgin was usually in the company of the Cockburns, Mrs. Keith Stuart, Colonel Crawford, and Robert Fergusson. Toward the end of his testimony, Sterling stated that he had seen Fergusson walking alone with Lady Elgin in the gardens.

"Mr. Sterling, would you say that Lady Elgin was particularly interested in Mr. Fergusson?" Garrow asked.

"Yes, she always inquired about him."

"How exactly would you describe this interest in Mr. Fergusson?"

"It went beyond mere curiosity."

"Please be more explicit, Mr. Sterling."

"I would venture to say that Lady Elgin was infatuated with him."

"What about Mr. Fergusson's reactions?"

"He was quite enamored of her from the moment they first met. It was at a dinner given by the Cockburns. I studied them very closely. His eyes were constantly on her throughout the evening."

At this point, Garrow finished with Sterling, and Topping slowly stepped forward.

"Mr. Sterling, I have only one question to ask: under oath, you just testified that you saw Mr. Fergusson walking alone with Lady Elgin in the gardens of the Hôtel de Richelieu. Is this correct?"

"Yes."

"You are absolutely certain that they were alone?"

"Yes."

"That no one else was walking in the gardens at this time?"

Sterling did not answer.

"Mr. Sterling, I asked you a question."

"Our English friends were also in the gardens . . ."

"Were they close by?"

"I can't say exactly."

"Come now, Mr. Sterling, you certainly can remember this."

"I . . . I imagine they were close by."

"Then Mr. Fergusson and Lady Elgin were not actually alone?"

"They had pulled away from the others and were talking by themselves."

"But always in sight of the others?"

Sterling's response was hardly audible. "Yes."

"Mr. Sterling, you owe this court an apology."

"Why?"

"You lied under oath."

"I did not mean to say that they were entirely alone . . ."

"Nevertheless, you left this court with that impression."

"I ask the court's forgiveness."

"You admit, then, that Mr. Fergusson and Lady Elgin were not alone when they were walking through the gardens?"

Sterling nodded.

"Say it, Mr. Sterling."

"They were not alone."

Topping walked back to his bench. "I have no further questions to ask this witness."

Garrow was slow in rising to his feet. "My lords, I call Mr. Charles Duff to the witness cage."

The sight of Duff let loose an avalanche of memories. Poor Duff; it was only yesterday that he had gone ashore to Palermo to secure lodgings for them — so terrified of Captain Maling's wrath, so dedicated and affectionate to the children.

"Mr. Duff, where is your residence?"

"In London, at Number One Weymouth Street, Portland Place."

"Did you accompany Lord Elgin to Constantinople?"

"Yes."

"And did you remain with the embassy there until it closed?"

"Yes."

"What was your impression as to the relationship between Lord Elgin and Lady Elgin?"

"I never saw a happier couple."

Tears flooded her eyes.

"Mr. Duff, was it Lady Elgin's decision to send her children back to Scotland by ship?"

"Both Lady Elgin and Lord Elgin arrived at this decision."

"Mr. Duff, were the children a burden to Lady Elgin?"

"At times, perhaps. Bruce, especially, is a spitfire of a lad."

"To your knowledge, Mr. Duff, did Lady Elgin subsequently travel alone to Paris?"

"Yes."

"How do you know this?"

"Before returning to London from Archerfield, I was instructed by His Lordship . . ."

"But wasn't he confined in prison at this time?"

"His Lordship sent a letter to me in London, requesting that I stop off at Broomhall."

"For what reason?"

"To call on His Lordship's mother and inquire about Mr. Choiseul-Gouffier's frieze that was still being held at the London Customs House. During the brief span of my visit with the Countess, she spoke about how troubled she was over a letter she had received from His Lordship, which he dispatched from the prison at Lourdes."

"Did you read this letter, Mr. Duff?"

Duff clamped his hand over his mouth. "Heavens, no."

"Did Lord Elgin's mother disclose the contents of the letter to you?"

"She did."

"Could you please tell the court what was in this letter?"

Topping objected vehemently. "My lords!"

The Lord President silenced him. "Mr. Duff has every right to tell the court what Lord Elgin's mother said to him regarding this letter."

"Please continue, Mr. Duff," said Garrow.

"His Lordship complained about Lady Elgin's trip to Paris."

"Did she go alone?"

"As I understand it, Her Ladyship was accompanied by Mr. Hunt and Masterman."

"Who is Masterman?"

"Her Ladyship's maid."

"Surely, Her Ladyship consulted with her husband before undertaking this journey?"

"Indeed not. His Lordship was imprisoned at Lourdes."

"What was His Lordship's reaction when he learned that his wife had traveled to Paris without telling him?"

"He did not believe Her Ladyship when she informed him that she had gone to Paris to personally call on Monsieur Talleyrand. He suspected that Her Ladyship went to Paris for another reason."

"Another reason, Mr. Duff?"

"Yes . . . to see Mr. Fergusson."

A droning wave rolled over the courtroom.

"Now then, Mr. Duff, did you receive any instructions from Lady Elgin after she arrived in England from France?"

"Her Ladyship sent a messenger to Mrs. Gosling, the housekeeper at the Nisbet winter home in Portman Square, requesting that I locate a temporary residence for her."

"Did you yourself have any conversation with Lady Elgin during this time?"

"Yes."

"When exactly?"

"I assisted Her Ladyship in packing up, prior to our journey to Scotland. She was much distraught, and I tried to soothe her by recounting some pleasant incidents that occurred during our long stay in Constantinople."

"She considered you to be a trusted friend, Mr. Duff?"

"Yes."

In cross-examination, Topping's voice was soft and sympathetic. "Mr. Duff, what were your personal feelings toward Lady Elgin?"

"I greatly admired Her Ladyship, and still do. I feel exactly the same toward Lord Elgin. This is why I'm very uncomfortable testifying this way."

"I understand and appreciate your feelings, Mr. Duff. To resume, we are led to believe that you spent considerable time in the company of Lord and Lady Elgin?"

"That's true."

"What were your observations of Lady Elgin's conduct toward His Lordship?"

"Most commendable."

"And toward her children?"

"Equally so."

"Was Her Ladyship that type of woman who would abandon the needs of her children for selfish pursuits?"

"Decidedly not."

"Are you absolutely certain of this, Mr. Duff?"

"Her Ladyship was a devoted mother and wife."

"That will be all, Mr. Duff. Thank you. You may step down from the witness cage."

The Lord President leaned over to talk with one of the Lord Judges. They both nodded several times, and the Lord President rose to his feet. "This court will stand adjourned until nine o'clock tomorrow morning."

She waited until the crowd left the courtroom, then slowly walked out and looked for her father in the hallway, but he was nowhere in sight. She felt a hand on her arm. Without looking up, she said, "Mr. Fergusson, I do not care to talk with you."

"But I want to tell you how I feel about all this."

"Please release my arm."

"Mary, I love you very much. When this terrible ordeal is over, I want to marry you . . . to take care of you and love you the rest of my life . . ."

She tugged her arm free and dashed down the stairs. Andrew was standing beside the carriage in the street. She peered inside, but her father wasn't there.

"Mr. Nisbet is at home, lassie," said Andrew.

"Home?"

"I took him back to Archerfield more than an hour ago. He didn't seem well at all."

"What ails him?"

"I don't know, lassie."

It was a dreary ride back to Archerfield. She was worried about her father. It was not like him to go off like that, without saying

a word. He should have told her that he wasn't feeling well. They could have left the courtroom together.

As soon as the carriage pulled into the driveway, the front door opened, and Mrs. Hall came rushing toward them, wringing her hands and muttering words that Mary couldn't piece together.

"Mrs. Hall, what is it?" she asked in alarm.

"Mr. Nisbet is very ill, lassie."

"How serious is it?"

"Young Dr. Campbell was just here from Dirleton."

"But he seemed quite well to me this morning."

"You know your father, lassie. He never complains. He suffered the attack a few minutes after Andrew brought him back from Edinburgh."

"Is he upstairs?"

"Yes, your mother is with him."

She raced up the stairs, Mrs. Hall puffing behind her. Her mother was leaning over the bed, applying a damp cloth to her father's forehead. She looked confused and frightened. Tears were streaming down her cheeks. Mary pulled her gently away from the bed and embraced her. She couldn't find one word to say. Dropping to her knees, she placed her trembling hand on her father's brow. It was warm. She could hardly bear to look at him. His eyes were closed, and one side of his mouth was twisted grotesquely. She leaned closer and kissed the unresponsive lips as Mrs. Hall muttered behind her, "Dr. Campbell said he would be here again tonight, lassie."

"Is my father going to die?"

Mrs. Hall took hold of her hand. "It's too early to tell."

"He looks so still, so different. Can't something be done for him?"

Her mother spoke for the first time. "Dr. Campbell is hopeful that the trauma isn't too severe."

"But father always had a strong heart."

"It's not his heart, Mary. Your father has suffered a paralytic stroke. We shall have to wait several days before Dr. Campbell can determine how serious it is. Until then, he's in the hands of the Almighty."

She hadn't noticed that Calitza had entered the room until the nurse embraced her. Neither of them spoke. A long moment passed; then she took hold of the nurse's hand and moved out of the room. "I just had a terrible thought, Calitza."

"What is it, my lady?"

"I remembered what you said the night before we left Constantinople for Greece . . ."

"I don't recall what I said."

"It was about the goddess Nemesis, how vengeful she could be."

Calitza instantly fell silent.

The words drifted away from her. "Her vengeance has fallen upon us, Calitza. I'm certain of it. First, the affliction of Lord Elgin's nose, then little William's death, Bruce's terrible hallucinations, this deplorable trial in Edinburgh, my children taken away from me, and now my father . . ." The tears were streaming down her face.

Mrs. Hall came out of the bedroom and touched her softly on the arm. "Perhaps we should try to give Mr. Nisbet a bit of tea, lassie."

"But we tried to do this a while ago," said Mrs. Nisbet. "He couldn't accept it, and it spilled down his chin."

Mrs. Hall turned her attention again to Mary. "You look exhausted, lassie — and you must be starving. I'll cook you some ramekins for dinner."

The thought of eggs and cheese made her stomach churn.

"But first, you should take a wee nap, lassie. I'll call you when everything is ready."

Dr. Campbell's visit was brief. Before leaving, he offered Mary a word of encouragement. "Praise God, your father's heart is exceptionally strong, my lady. That's a good sign."

"Is he going to die, Dr. Campbell?"

"I'm more hopeful of his recovery now, but we still must pray."

"What about his face?"

"Some of the paralysis has left him, but his right arm and right leg are still without feeling."

"Will he walk again?"

"That's difficult to say."

Holding a lighted taper in her hand, she led the way down the stairs. At the front door, Dr. Campbell asked, "My lady, how long will this trial in Edinburgh go on?"

"I've no idea."

"Your father's condition is at a very critical stage. He needs constant care. If I may say so, it would be more advisable if you were at his side. Mrs. Hall told me that you have always been very close to your father. It would mean a great deal toward his recovery if you were to devote as much time as possible to him."

She opened the front door. "When will you be coming back, Dr. Campbell?"

"Early in the morning. Until then, try to get some sleep. We've a long vigil before us."

It was impossible for her to close her eyes. The children kept flitting into her thoughts. How could she ever endure without them? She didn't want to think about the trial.

A soft rain was falling when Dr. Campbell called just after sunrise. Nothing had changed. The diagnosis was the same. Before leaving, he told her to persist in giving her father a few spoonfuls of brandy, but to do it carefully and make certain it did not choke him. She walked with him as far as his carriage, unmindful of the rain. "Dr. Campbell, I'm afraid . . . terribly afraid."

"My lady, the longer your father bears up to this, the stronger he'll get. It's important that he not suffer a relapse. This is why someone must be close to his side at all times. Good day, my lady. I'll look in on him later this afternoon."

Mrs. Hall had prepared a light breakfast, and, though the very thought of food made Mary ill, Mrs. Hall refused to let her go until she ate. She hated to leave her father, especially after what Dr. Campbell had said. Why did she have to go to that abominable trial, listen to more witnesses, feel all those condemning eyes on her?

The moment she closed the front door, Boxer came running across the driveway toward her and followed her all the way to the carriage. Andrew Davidson tried to wave off the dog, but she opened the door of the carriage and beckoned him to climb in. He jumped up and nestled in her lap. By the time they reached Dirleton, he was asleep. As easy as that. She envied him.

The rain stopped just as the carriage pulled up in front of the courthouse. Topping was pacing back and forth in the hallway. "Your Ladyship is late. The Lord Judges have already entered the courtroom."

"My father is very ill," she said.

"I'm sorry to know that," he replied, taking her quickly by the arm.

"Did you hear what I said, Mr. Topping? My father is very ill, and all because of this dreadful trial."

His voice softened. "We have no choice, my lady. We must go through with it."

She stopped him outside the main courtroom door. "Mr. Topping, I want your solemn word that you will not call me to the witness cage."

"What?"

"I won't go into this courtroom unless you give me your word," she persisted.

"But it will shatter our case completely."

"Mr. Topping . . ."

"My lady, if you remain silent, the jury will assume that you're guilty."

"You must do as I ask, Mr. Topping."

Topping glared at her. "Then you cannot hold me responsible if the verdict goes against us."

He pulled the door open and she followed him inside, past the gaping faces, to the bench in the first row. Garrow waited until they sat. "My lords and gentlemen of the jury, I call Mr. Hay Donaldson to the witness cage."

An old man, bald and appallingly thin, stepped forward. He was hard of hearing, and the clerk had to repeat each word of the oath. Garrow lifted his voice even louder. "What is your occupation, Mr. Donaldson?"

"I am a writer to the signet."

"Do you practice here in Edinburgh?"

"Yes."

"Mr. Donaldson, have you any information regarding the estate of the defendant's father in Raith?"

"I have."

"Upon whom is the estate entailed?"

"It is entailed upon Mr. Robert Fergusson after the death of his father, without division."

"Is Mr. Fergusson the only son?"

"No, but he is the eldest."

"In your professional opinion, is it a substantial estate?"

"Most assuredly."

"Have you ascertained its real value?"

"Yes. It is quite large, between one hundred and fifty and two hundred thousand pounds."

"Thank you, Mr. Donaldson. I have no further questions."

Topping came briskly toward the witness cage. "Mr. Donaldson, during your examination of the estate at Raith, did you find any prohibiting clauses?"

"I did."

"Did these clauses burden the estate with certain obligations?"

"Yes."

"Then the estate is not entirely free of encumbrances, as Mr. Garrow would like this court to believe?"

"It is not."

"Mr. Donaldson, when did you last see the defendant's father?"

"A few days ago."

"Did he appear to be at death's door?"

"Hardly."

"In fact, would you not say that he is a hale and stout man, exceptionally strong for his years?"

"I would," admitted Donaldson.

Topping returned to his bench. "You may step down, Mr. Donaldson."

Peering into his notes, Garrow straightened his shoulders, rose pensively to his feet, and announced, "My lords, I should now like to present further evidence in this case. I have in my hand a deposition signed by Mrs. Sarah Gosling, servant to Lady Elgin at the Baker Street house in London."

"Why a deposition?" asked one of the Lord Judges. "The other witnesses came all the way from London. Why isn't Mrs. Gosling here?"

Garrow gave him a tight smile. "I am afraid that would have been impossible. Mrs. Gosling died shortly after making the deposition."

Topping voiced his objection. "My lords, certainly we cannot accept the deposition of a dying woman. Whatever she had to say might be irrational and without logic."

"Mrs. Gosling's mind was quite stable, my lords," retorted Garrow. "May I add that she was expected to be our key witness until she fell ill. The commissaries agreed to grant the deposition request to the Chief Commissioner, who examined Mrs. Gosling in the presence of the Clerk of the Court."

"Where was this deposition made?" asked the Lord President.

"At Knightsbridge, my Lord President. It is a suburb of London."

"How many pages does it include?"

"Quite a few," said Garrow.

"Very well," said the Lord President. "The court will permit you to read this deposition, but first, I must examine it."

Garrow waited impatiently as the Lord President scanned the pages. He passed them to the Lord Judges; then Garrow took the deposition, walked back to his bench, and started reading. Each word dug sharply into Mary's brain.

> APPEARED Sarah Gosling, now residing at Knightsbridge, in the County of Middlesex, married, age thirty-eight, and being solemnly sworn according to the form directed by the Commission, and the usual questions of a preliminary nature being put to her, hereby swears that she holds no malice or ill will toward either of the parties in this case; that she has neither received nor been promised any money or good deed for being a witness; that Mr. Bichnell, Lord Elgin's solicitor of London, now present, did apply to her and inquire what she knew concerning the conduct of the Countess of Elgin, to which the deponent answered. Mr. Bichnell then told her that he was acting for Lord Elgin, asking her several questions with regard to an intercourse between Lady Elgin and Mr. Fergusson; that the deponent answered these questions to the best of her knowledge and conscience.
>
> DEPONES that she was one of Lady Elgin's servants during Her Ladyship's residence at Number Sixty Baker Street in London.
>
> DEPONES that she knows Robert Fergusson, Esquire, of Raith, and that he frequently visited Lady Elgin in her house at Baker Street during the time of Lord Elgin's imprisonment in France; that Mr. Fergusson called many times in the daytime and also in the evening; that Lady Elgin was in the habit of going out with Mr. Fergusson even after dinner and not returning until well past midnight.

DEPONES that she saw Lady Elgin admit the visits of Mr. Fergusson on these evenings, and that there was no person with Lady Elgin except Mr. Fergusson.

DEPONES that Mr. Fergusson, when leaving the house after these visits, was sometimes let out by the deponent and sometimes by Mary Ruper, Lady Elgin's maid, but not by the footman, Mr. Willey, and that at different times the deponent and other servants had gone to bed when Mr. Fergusson was still in the house.

DEPONES that she had known Mr. Fergusson to continue with Lady Elgin until one o'clock in the morning; that there were no other persons in the house on these occasions except Mr. Fergusson and Lady Elgin; that it was Lady Elgin's general custom to direct the curtain of the window that was behind the sofa in the drawing room to be let down and that the deponent made many observations on the state of the sofa after Mr. Fergusson had been with Lady Elgin and found impressions of two persons on it.

All this is truth, as the deponent shall answer to God.

[Signed] Sarah Gosling
James Chalmer, Commissioner
William Moncur, Clerk

What is written on the five preceding pages is the report of the Act and Commission mentioned in the first page, and returned to the Court sealed up as directed.

[Signed] James Chalmer, Commissioner
William Moncur, Clerk

Next, Mary Ruper was summoned by Garrow: servant at Number Sixty Baker Street, aged two and twenty, unmarried. She confirmed the deposition of Sarah Gosling, and added, "I walked into Her Ladyship's drawing room one day to tidy up things, and I was shocked to find that Mrs. Gosling's little dog had dirtied the sofa."

"What did Mrs. Gosling say to this?"

"She wrung her hands and cried, ' 'Twasn't the dog who dirtied the sofa, but that rogue, Mr. Fergusson.' "

"Miss Ruper, did you and the other servants of the house at Baker Street form any opinion of this situation?"

"We did indeed, m'lord. We all agreed that there was an improper connection between Mr. Fergusson and Her Ladyship."

Garrow's last witness was Thomas Willey: aged one and forty, unmarried. "I was well acquainted with Mr. Fergusson of Raith," stated Willey, in a loud booming voice. "Mr. Fergusson was frequently in the practice of calling on Her Ladyship, both throughout the day and during the evening. I dare say Lady Elgin was always at home to Mr. Fergusson. Mr. Fergusson was shown more attention by Lady Elgin than any other visitor, and she seemed most happy when in Mr. Fergusson's company. Every time they greeted each other, they held hands for a long while and showed great familiarity."

"Can you recall a particular incident of their intimate relationship, Mr. Willey?"

"Yes, I can. I opened the drawing room door one day without knocking, and . . ."

"Mr. Willey, you entered Her Ladyship's drawing room without knocking?"

"It was always my custom to knock, m'lord, but on this occasion I was in a hurry to deliver an important message to Her Ladyship from one of her friends."

"Go on, Mr. Willey."

"The first thing I saw was Lady Elgin stretched full length on the sofa. Upon my coming in, Mr. Fergusson was in the act of placing a shawl over Her Ladyship's legs."

"Were Lady Elgin's petticoats up?" asked Garrow.

"I could not positively say, m'lord. A small writing table stood in front of the sofa, and I was prevented from seeing whether Her Ladyship's legs were uncovered before the shawl was thrown over them, but from the shocked expression on Mr. Fergusson's face, I'd imagine that Her Ladyship's petticoats indeed were up."

"My lords!" cried Topping.

"Sustained," replied the Lord President, glaring down at Willey. "We want facts, not your imagination."

"Mr. Willey, what did Mr. Fergusson do after this?"

"His face was much flushed, and he walked toward the fireplace, keeping his back toward me, pretending he was interested in something on the mantel."

"Were Mr. Fergusson's breeches unbuttoned?"

The courtroom stirred once again. Had it all come to this — those days of marble, of Attic skies and azure seas, glorious Constantinople and her Golden Horn, sun-splattered Athens, Palermo, Rome, Florence, Marseille, Lyon, Paris, London? Was this how everything would end, in shame and degradation, indelible scandal and disgrace?

"He turned his back so quickly, m'lord, I didn't have time to observe."

Glancing at Mary, Topping didn't question Thomas Willey.

The wagging tongues behind her didn't stop until the Lord President pounded his gavel on the desk. "This court will be in recess until two o'clock this afternoon."

Topping waited for the courtroom to empty before speaking to her. "There's a little inn not too far from here that serves the most delicious bowl of chacklowrie."

She shook her head. From the corner of her eye, she could see Fergusson lingering just outside the door.

"My lady, I insist that you join me. I have something very important to discuss with you."

"Mr. Topping, it's much too upsetting for me to discuss this trial. I'm very concerned about my father."

A wry look flashed across his face. "I think Your Ladyship will be interested to hear what I have to say."

The inn was but a stone's throw from the courthouse. A waiter led them to a table at the farthest corner. The smells from

the kitchen were unsettling to her stomach, and she asked Topping to order some brandy for her.

"Of course." He signaled the waiter and ordered the brandy and a bowl of chacklowrie.

After a few sips of the brandy, she felt much better, and when Topping's bowl of cabbage in barley broth was placed on the table, piping hot, its aroma rising from the gusts of steam, she smiled. "The last time I had chacklowrie was two days before we set sail for Constantinople."

"Are you sure you won't have some now?"

Her smile broadened. "Perhaps a small bowl."

She finished the chacklowrie and the dessert of bread pudding and raisins. Looking up from his cup of tea, Topping said, "My lady, I must say that I envy you."

"Why, Mr. Topping?"

"I can't think of anyone your age who has gone to so many foreign lands, seen so many places. The farthest I've traveled is to London, and that was more than ten years ago."

She studied the pattern of the tablecloth.

"I wish you'd reconsider about testifying."

"That's out of the question, Mr. Topping."

Topping raised his voice. "How can I be expected to defend you and Mr. Fergusson if I get no cooperation? In God's name, we have no witnesses!"

She kept her eyes on the tablecloth.

"Another thing; why don't you want me to interrogate your husband?"

"He has suffered enough, Mr. Topping. We all have suffered enough."

Topping asked the waiter for more tea. "This trial could be very costly to you and to Mr. Fergusson. As your barrister, I intend to do everything in my power to win, and I won't be dissuaded. Since you refuse to testify, then you must give me more information."

"About what?"

"I want to know every detail about your husband, his likes and dislikes, how he spent his days and nights, who his friends were, his enemies, how he treated you and the children . . . and, most important, if he had relationships with other women."

She remained silent.

"My lady, how long has your husband suffered from the disfigurement of his face?"

"I don't know exactly. I think it became manifest shortly after we arrived in Constantinople."

"Was there a physician on the embassy staff?"

"We had two physicians, Dr. McLean and Dr. Scott."

"Did they examine your husband's affliction?"

"Yes."

"What was their diagnosis?"

"Each believed that it resulted from an ague and that it was not contagious. Dr. Scott was especially certain of this."

"Did your husband examine the credentials of these physicians before employing them?"

"Of course. McLean and Scott were highly qualified medical authorities. Dr. Scott was an expert in infectious diseases."

"Each was certain that this disease was not the plague?"

"Most certain."

"Or leprosy?"

"Decidedly not."

"My lady, do you know what an ague is?"

"Mr. Topping, everyone knows what an ague is."

"I want to hear your definition of it."

"It's a fever characterized by successive attacks of cold and hot fits. It's usually accompanied by much sweating and shaking chills, as well as pains in the muscles and joints."

"If this was the diagnosis of the embassy physicians, how then did they explain the catastrophic effects to your husband's nose?"

"Neither one could offer an explanation."

"Nor cure?"

"They tried, but the illness progressed so rapidly, there was no hope for cure."

Topping reached down and brought up his black leather case. Opening it quickly, he pulled out a thick book and began leafing through its pages. "My lady, I'd like to read something from this book that may shed a bit of light upon your husband's affliction." He brought the book close to his eyes and began reading. "The characteristic forms of this particular infection are deposits called *gummata.* They are of tenacious appearance, ulcerous and oozing with discharge. Soon after their initial attack, molecular death results, and, in time, the entire organ disappears, leaving only scarred tissues.' " He looked at her intently over his spectacles before continuing. " 'These gummata usually infect one organ of the body, *the nose.'* "

"From what book are you reading, Mr. Topping?"

Topping didn't answer her. "I consulted this book many times after Mr. Kincaid presented all the facts of this case, and then I had three prominent physicians here in Edinburgh examine the book further in reference to Lord Elgin's disease. They all concurred that his symptoms constitute the tertiary manifestations of the pox — a disease that results from impure sexual intercourse."

She scraped back her chair and stood up. "Mr. Topping, why are you telling me these things?"

Topping slowly closed the book. "Quite simply, I intend to call your husband to the witness cage and confront him with this matter."

"No, you mustn't. I forbid you!"

"We are left with no other choice. If I don't call him, we shall lose this case."

"Mr. Topping, if you do this, I swear that I shall leave the courtroom."

Topping said nothing further.

As soon as the Lord Judges took their places in the courtroom, the Lord President peered down at Topping and said, "Your witnesses, Mr. Topping."

There was a throbbing silence.

"Mr. Topping, it's time to bring forth your witnesses."

"My lords, I have no witnesses."

The Lord President was stunned. "Then move on, Mr. Topping."

Topping was slow to rise from his bench. "My lords and gentlemen, much has been said here these past two days against the defendants — yet no real evidence has been offered, other than the circumstantial testimonies of certain witnesses brought here at a great expense to Lord Elgin. My learned opponent, Mr. Garrow, remarked yesterday that it is your duty to scourge the defendants with criminal punishment, but I find it necessary to remind you that it is not within the province of this jury to scourge. If there is an injury here, it is a civil injury, and the compensation, if any, must be a requital by a civil remuneration.

"Finally, with respect to the financial situation of Mr. Fergusson, I am free to say that in fact he exists upon the bounty of his father. He is not an only child, but the eldest son of the family, and, as such, is recipient of only a small independent income. Yes, he will inherit a large portion of his father's estate, but his father may live many additional years — and until then Mr. Fergusson does not command a guinea of it. We all know that the laws of Scotland entail every estate. At best, Mr. Fergusson is but a life-tenant, without the power of raising twenty shillings. The estate is also burdened with provisions for relatives, which could preclude the possibility of his ever paying heavy damages, should they be imposed upon him today. I am convinced that this case is now in honorable and sympathetic hands. Furthermore, I entertain no doubt but that you will deal with it mercifully. My lords and gentlemen, I thank you."

Before the Lord President could stop him, Garrow inserted,

"My lords and gentlemen of the jury, I repeat to you that Mr. Fergusson's father is a very wealthy man. Mr. Topping's claim of Mr. Fergusson's poverty is nothing but a courtroom maneuver, and I feel certain that it will not influence or sway the jury. I thank you."

The Lord President rose to his feet. "The jury will now retire to its private chambers. If a verdict is not reached by five o'clock this evening, its deliberations will resume at nine o'clock tomorrow morning. Before you retire to your chambers, I deem it necessary to call your attention to the importance of this case. It involves the greatest injury that one man can inflict upon another. In all actions of this nature, it is the task of the plaintiff to make out his title to a claim and to show if this claim is well-founded. You must act with caution, deliberately considering if there is an offense here, and, if so, its appropriate retribution. I trust that your verdict will afford public gratification, as well. Retire then to your chambers. This case is left altogether in your hands."

Fifteen

TOPPING dashed after her just as she was about to climb into the carriage. Gasping for breath, he said, "My lady, where are you going?"

"Home," she said coldly.

"But the jury may reach its verdict soon. You must stay here."

"Why?"

"If we lose the case, the divorce decree will follow."

"Divorce?"

"A decree always comes after a trial of this nature. I thought you understood it, my lady. This is why Lord Elgin took the children even before the trial began. The court can grant him full custody if he wins the case."

She was too upset to speak. Her head spinning, she opened the door of the carriage. It was a balm for her nerves to see Boxer, to run her fingers over his fine coat, pat his head, feel his moist nose on her wrist. He leaped into her lap the moment she sat down. Closing the door, Andrew said, "Shall we be going home now, lassie?"

"No, Andrew . . . not yet."

He put his cap on. "I'm sorry, lassie. I'm sorry about what

they're doing to ye inside that courtroom, a fine lady like yourself."

She stared through the window. Suddenly she saw Elgin coming down the steps of the courthouse. He was alone. She opened the carriage door and hurried toward him, but just then the door behind him opened and Garrow came out. He took Elgin by the arm, and they went back inside, heads close together.

Almost in the same moment, Topping came rushing toward the carriage, panting. "My lady, the jury is returning to the courtroom. The members have reached a verdict."

There were still many spectators in the courtroom. The Lord Judges had already seated themselves. In a tired voice, the Lord President asked, "Gentlemen of the jury, have you arrived at a verdict?"

A gruff-looking man with peasant hands grabbed the rail and stood up. "We have, my Lord President."

"What is it?"

"We have found for the noble plaintiff."

"And the damages?"

"Ten thousand pounds sterling, my Lord President."

Fergusson's face was the color of wax. Elgin began pumping Garrow's hand elatedly, a wild, gloating look in his eyes. Raising his hands, the Lord President turned to the jury. "The court is grateful to you. You are now free to return to your homes."

The constable escorted the spectators from the courtroom as soon as the four Lord Judges retired into another room.

Numb and confused, she still couldn't understand what she was doing here, sitting opposite Elgin, the Lord President looming over her with his fierce countenance, Garrow and Topping busily studying their notes, the clerk's hollow words reverberating in her ears:

" 'At Edinburgh, anent the action and cause for divorce, raised, intended, and pursued before this court at the instance of the Right Honorable Thomas Bruce, Earl of Elgin and Kincardine,

against Mary, Countess of Elgin and Kincardine, by virtue of the said court, its libeled summons raised there, which maketh mention that where the said Thomas, pursuer, and where the said Mary, defendant, were regularly married and cohabited together as husband and wife, owned and acknowledged each other as such, and were holden, treated, and reputed married persons by their friends and neighbors, of which marriage four children were procreated, and of whom three are alive today.

" 'And although Mary, Countess of Elgin and Kincardine, stood bound and obliged to preserve the marriage bed inviolate, yet true it is that she, regardless of her marriage vows and of the whole attachment which ought to subsist between married persons, and of her duty as wife and mother, has for some time past had carnal intercourse and has been guilty of acts of adultery with Robert Fergusson, Esquire, of Raith.

" 'Therefore concluding that in all law, equity, and justice, the said court, finding and declaring that the said defendant has been guilty of the crime of adultery, divorcing and separating her from the noble pursuer's society, fellowship, and company in all time coming.

" 'Finding and declaring that the pursuer is free of the marriage contracted, solemnized and completed between him and the said defendant, and that the said pursuer may now marry when and whom he pleases in the same manner as if the said defendant were naturally dead.' "

She reeled from the clerk's final words. " 'It ought further to be found and declared that the said pursuer has a just right and title to the provisions made in his favor, which shall include the care and upbringing of the surviving children.' "

The Lord President patted down his wig with both hands and rose to his feet. His eyes touched hers for an instant before he left the courtroom. The clerk tarried a while, gathering documents and other notes from the desks of the Lord Judges. Garrow and Topping shook hands, then walked together out of the courtroom, leaving her alone with Elgin.

They both rose to their feet, their eyes locked. She wanted him to say something, anything, but he remained silent. His lips twitched when her words finally came blurting out: "I hope you won't speak ill of me in front of the children."

"You needn't worry."

"Eggy . . ."

"Stop calling me that!"

She struggled to hold back the tears. "Shall I ever see you again?"

He stared at the floor.

"May I come and visit our children some time?"

His eyes returned to her, softened for a moment. "You heard the clerk."

"He said that you were to treat me as though I were dead . . ."

He stepped back, then turned away from her and headed for the door.

She rushed after him. "May I at least send Caltiza to Broomhall? She'll take good care of the children. They adore her."

He nodded, his back still toward her.

"Do they ask about me?"

His voice was muffled. "Yes."

"What do you tell them?"

He swung around and looked at her. "That you've gone away on a very long journey."

Her hand went to her mouth. Reaching out, she touched him lightly on the arm. "Watch over them . . . and please guard your health."

He was gone, his long strides obscured by the railing of the staircase, his last words burning in her ears.

Garrow and Topping were conversing on the pavement. When Garrow saw her, he immediately left Topping and came toward her. "My lady, did you have a talk with Lord Elgin?"

"Yes."

"Then he told you about Bruce."

"Bruce?"

"The lad is seriously ill."

"No!"

"He suffered a violent convulsion soon after he was brought to Broomhall. His Lordship summoned the best physicians in Edinburgh, but it grieves me to say that they pronounced Bruce a hopeless epileptic and that nothing can be done for him."

Boxer climbed into her lap again, and as the carriage drove off, the tears began to flow down her face. Looking up at her, Boxer started whining softly and didn't stop until she patted him tenderly on the head.

The next morning, after attending to her father's breakfast, she came downstairs to find her mother sitting alone in the drawing room, looking blankly into space. Mary touched her lightly on the shoulder but got no response. Her eyes moved toward her mother's portrait on the wall. She stood before it and gazed at it for a long time, then returned to her mother's side. Kneeling in front of her, she put her head on her lap, and slowly her mother's fingers came alive, stroking her hair, her face and shoulders.

"Mother," she murmured, "all the time that I was away, I kept thinking about coming home and rushing into your arms, holding you forever. I can't tell you how frustrating it was to be so many hundreds of miles away from you . . . and now that I've finally come back, it's not at all the way I thought it would be. Everything has changed so much. It terrifies me. I don't know what to do."

Her mother looked down, then gently placed her hand on Mary's chin and lifted it up. "Mary, I wish you had confided in me about the trial in Edinburgh. I didn't believe that you had gone to Broomhall. You poor dear, there was no need to suffer alone like this."

Mary threw her arms around her. "Mother, will you ever forgive me?"

"Of course — but you should have told me from the very beginning."

"I was too ashamed. I still am."

Her mother kept patting her with tenderness. "I never really wanted you to marry that man. I consented only because of your father. He felt so proud to have his only child marry a nobleman."

"What shall I do, Mother? I can't live without my children."

"We shall find a way to get them back."

"But how?"

"We can go to the courts and prove that Elgin is not a fit father, that he's insane. We will think of something."

"You truly believe that we can do this?"

"Yes."

"You're not saying this just to console me?"

"I mean every word, and after you gain custody of the children, we will move away from this provincial place."

"Leave Archerfield?"

"I begged your father not to take me away from London, but he insisted that I would love it here. If we had stayed in London, this deplorable thing would never have happened. You would have married someone else, someone who would have cared for you and loved you. But it was my fault. I should never have allowed you to marry that man. Never!"

Seasons dying, endless nights and dreary days spinning ominously over Archerfield. Another Yule without her children, without their happy voices and the warmth of their embrace. Her father still trying to re-enter the world, speaking in an incomprehensible slur, scuttling over the drawing room floor like a crab in a foreign sea.

March showed its face, cold and unforgiving.

One morning, after Mary put on her coat and started for the door, her mother asked, "Where are you going?"

"Just for a walk as far as the bay."

"Don't stay too long. Wrap yourself well. It's damp and cold outside."

Mary stopped at the threshold, then ran back and kissed her. "Mother, I love you with all my heart."

When she returned from her walk an hour later, she was handed a letter by her mother. "It was delivered here just after you left, Mary. It's posted from London."

Instantly recognizing Fergusson's hand, she took off her coat and started walking up the stairs. Boxer followed her and spun two or three times around the rug in her bedchamber before lying down. She sat on the edge of the bed for a long time before opening the letter.

My dear Mary,

Please know that I have been sitting in Parliament as a member of the Whig Party. I have taken a house here in London and am quite involved in the political life. My only regret is not having you here beside me.

I first must inform you that the ten thousand pounds awarded to Elgin could not cover one tenth of his indebtedness. He owes money everywhere and is hounded by creditors from every corner of the world. On the verge of bankruptcy, he was left with no other choice but to offer for sale his entire collection of the Parthenon marbles. As a prominent Tory, he himself presented a petition to the House of Commons, requesting them to proceed at once on this matter and appoint a Select Committee. Eighteen members of Parliament were asked to assess the monetary value of the collection; all had opposing opinions.

I was present when Elgin rose to the floor and recounted in impassioned words how the idea of seeking the post at Constantinople was first suggested to him by his architect, Thomas Harrison; how he went ahead at his own expense to obtain the

service of artists and draughtsmen, architects and *formatori* — all for the purpose of embellishing the arts of Great Britain.

I need not tell you that Elgin did not hesitate to say that he never thought of cost when it came to the question of the marbles. He produced authentic accounts to the Select Committee, showing every penny spent from the first day to the last. His many gifts to the authorities at Constantinople and Athens amounted to more than seven thousand pounds. The interest alone on the large sums borrowed from bankers at Malta came to seventeen and three-quarters percent. Then there were the artists, the *formatori* and draughtsmen, the costs of transporting the marbles to the Piraeus, the price of three ships, payment to all the sailors, the loss of the *Mentor,* and, finally, the staggering expense of building his own museum at Park Lane, not to mention the heavy duty charges at the London Customs House.

Elgin has summoned the most eminent names of art to testify in his behalf — Nollekens, Flaxman, Westmacott, Sir Thomas Lawrence, Benjamin West. They all agree upon the great worth of the marbles, and that their acquisition will bring a much needed embellishment to the arts in Great Britain. But unfortunately for Elgin, these authorities cannot place a true monetary figure on the value of the collection, and thus the committee has called upon Richard Payne Knight. Being pushed to arrive at an arbitrary figure that the committee could put against the collection, Knight has suggested the grand total of twenty-five thousand pounds. Elgin, of course, thinks this preposterous, and argues that he has spent more than twice that amount.

The hearings should reach an end soon, and when the committee's report is prepared and made public, I have been led to believe that it will recommend an unyielding price of thirty-five thousand pounds. Elgin is hard-pressed for money and he should accept it.

I write all this, knowing how great a source of agitation for you the sculptures from Greece have been. Please be assured that they will soon be out of Elgin's hands entirely. An Act of

Parliament shall then be voted upon, making them the sole property of the British Government, and confining them to the permanent collection of the British Museum.

Most of Elgin's assets, including his country estate at Broomhall, have already been put into trust, and he has dismissed all of his servants, with the exception of the Greek nurse, Calitza. It grieves me to say that the man doesn't have a penny to his name.

Ironically, Elgin has been released from one debt. His artist in Athens suffered a most horrifying death, a breaking of the blood vessel. A full account was written in *The Times* recently. It seems that the unfortunate man bore the full brunt of the animosity aroused by Elgin's taking down of the Parthenon marbles, and he barricaded himself inside his house for fear of losing his life. One day, the neighbours reported his strange behaviour to the British Consul, and help was summoned, but after breaking open the front door, they found the artist extended on the floor, a pool of blood about him, a black cat seated on his chest. Scattered about the place were a half-dozen drawings, all of them unfinished. Poor devil, after all these years of servitude to Elgin, he never completed one drawing. He was buried on the grounds of the Capuchin monastery in Athens, and I understand that Elgin plans to erect a monument there in his memory.

My dear Mary, I felt that you should know these things. They are over and done with now, and you must put them out of your mind forever.

I hope to be visiting Raith in the very near future, and yearn very much to see and talk with you.

Robert

On the first day of May, Andrew Davidson drove into Edinburgh for the London newspapers and periodicals. Ever since Mary could remember, he did this once each month for her father, but now William Nisbet did not read them. He took one of the periodicals from Andrew, ran his fingers over the print, gazed at

the words with that distant expression, then stared down at the floor. She could not bear to look. Taking it from his trembling hands, she heard Andrew remark, "There's something ye may want to read, lassie. It's there, on page three."

She spread it on the table. The entire page spoke of Elgin. Another adversary had risen against him, a young poet named Lord Byron. The account revealed that he had recently traveled to Greece and was so appalled by the sight of the ruined Parthenon that he composed a terse article castigating Elgin:

> It is to be lamented that a war more than civil is raging on the subject of Lord Elgin's robberies in Greece. We can feel or imagine the regret with which the ruins of cities, once the capitals of empires, are beheld. But never did the smallness of man, nor the vanity of his very best virtues, appear more conspicuous than in the record of what Athens was, and what she is now.
>
> This theatre of contention between mighty factions — of the struggles of great orators, the exaltation and deposition of tyrants, the triumph and punishment of generals — has been a scene of petty intrigue and personal disturbance between the bickering agents of Lord Elgin and Bonaparte. The wild foxes, the owls and serpents in the ruins of Babylon, were surely less degrading than such as these.
>
> The Turks have the excuse of conquest for their tyranny; and the Greeks have suffered the fortune of war with valour and bravery . . . but how the mighty have fallen when two lascivious men contest the privilege of plundering the Parthenon, each triumphing in turn according to the tenor of succeeding firmans!
>
> Sulla could not punish, Philip subdue, and Xerxes burn. It remained for one paltry Scotch nobleman, and his despicable agents, to render Athens contemptible as themselves.

There was a short verse on the page, but she felt too ill to continue. She was about to put the newspaper down when the last lines caught her eye.

First on the head of him who did this deed,
My curse shall light, on him and all his seed;
Without one spark of intellectual fire,
Be all the sons as senseless as the sire!

The newspaper slipped out of her hands and dropped to the floor. Dashing from the room into the hallway, she flung open the front door and ran outside. Boxer spotted her from the carriage house, where he had been sniffing around the wheels of the open-sided cart. She didn't want him to follow her, but when she kept running toward the meadow, he took it as an invitation to play, and came barking after her. On the sandy slope overlooking the bay, he caught the scent of a young tern scampering through the sea grass and gave chase to it. She called out to him, but he had disappeared. Suddenly not one bird was in sight. Nothing moved. Even the sea had fallen asleep against Scotland's ribs.

The silence paralyzed her.

A Last Word

LORD ELGIN married again. His second wife was Elizabeth Oswald of Dunnikeir, daughter of a neighboring landowner in Fife. Hounded incessantly by his army of creditors, Elgin eventually had to escape to France with his wife, leaving the care of the children to the dowager Countess of Elgin and the Greek nurse. It is ironic that he sought refuge in the country where he was formerly imprisoned. He died in abject poverty in Paris on November 4, 1841, and his enormous debts were not fully paid off by his family until seventy-five years later.

In time, Mary Nisbet was quietly married to Robert Fergusson, and lived for a while with him at Raith, Fergusson's family estate; but his political position demanded a permanent stay in London, and they soon took residence in the Nisbet town house at Portman Square. After Fergusson's untimely death, Mary returned to Scotland, to her beloved Archerfield. She died in 1855, still an object of scorn and disgrace. It was not until 1916 that her name was finally inscribed on her neglected tomb.